Uncorrected 1

Danger is closer than you think...

Single Mum Kate Wilde has escaped an abusive marriage and hasn't had a holiday in years, so when she wins a five-day trip to Paris to learn about perfume - in a competition she can't remember entering – it's a dream come true. Or is it?

Almost as soon as she arrives, Kate's ex texts with evidence that he's in Paris too. Kate can feel she's being watched, and she's sure someone has been in her apartment. Then she discovers that there's a killer in the city focusing on red headed women like her. And his kill count is rising.

Who should she fear the most?

All Kate's senses are on alert. But can her instincts keep her safe?

Also by Sam Blake

Little Bones

In Deep Water

No Turning Back

Keep Your Eyes on Me

The Dark Room

High Pressure

Remember My Name

The Mystery of Four

Three Little Birds

For young adults:
Something Terrible Happened Last Night
Something's About to Blow Up

THE KILLING SENSE

SAM BLAKE

> A note to reviewers: please note that this text is uncorrected and changes may be made before the book is printed. The appearance and contents may not resemble the finished book. You have received this proof on the understanding that neither the proof nor any of its contents may be reproduced before publication of the finished book without the publishers consent. This proof may not be sold.

First published in Great Britain in 2024 by Corvus, an imprint of Atlantic Books Ltd.

Copyright © Sam Blake, 2024

The moral right of Sam Blake to be identified as the author of this work has been asserted by her in accordance with the Copyright, Designs and Patents Act of 1988.

All rights reserved. No part of this publication may be reproduced, stored in a retrieval system, or transmitted in any form or by any means, electronic, mechanical, photocopying, recording, or otherwise, without the prior permission of both the copyright owner and the above publisher of this book.

No part of this book may be used in any manner in the learning, training or development of generative artificial intelligence technologies (including but not limited to machine learning models and large language models (LLMs)), whether by data scraping, data mining or use in any way to create or form a part of data sets or in any other way.

This novel is entirely a work of fiction. The names, characters and incidents portrayed in it are the work of the author's imagination. Any resemblance to actual persons, living or dead, events or localities, is entirely coincidental.

10 9 8 7 6 5 4 3 2 1

A CIP catalogue record for this book is available from the British Library.

Trade Paperback ISBN: 978 1 80546 015 2
E-book ISBN: 978 1 80546 016 9

Printed in Great Britain

Corvus
An imprint of Atlantic Books Ltd
Ormond House
26–27 Boswell Street
London
WC1N 3JZ

www.atlantic-books.co.uk

To you, my reader, with huge and heartfelt thanks for making it possible for me to tell stories and call it my job.

Prologue

AT FIRST HE thought it was a ball. A football, or maybe a basketball. Trapped at the curved junction between narrow underground tunnels, it had created an island of debris coated in the foul brown-grey sewer slime that coated the walls, his waders, and thick rubber gloves.

It was only as Jean-Claude got closer, one foot placed carefully in front of the other, steadying himself with both hands on ancient brick walls that arched just above his head, that he began to realise it wasn't.

Directly behind him, his colleague Robert grumbled about Jean-Claude's walking pace, at the rats that scurried beside them, at the fact he had to bend slightly in these tributaries, that they seemed to get narrower as he aged. Jean-Claude wanted to stop him with a reminder that the rats were their friends. If the rats ran, it was a sign that they should, too: that there was a gas escape or some other threat, like the crocodile that had once been found living down here. But he was too busy grumbling to listen.

And when Jean-Claude stopped sharply to take in what was ahead of him, Robert collided with him, and swore.

When he'd started work for the Wastewater Treatment Department, aged seventeen, Jean-Claude had constantly gagged at the smell of raw sewage down in the tunnels. He'd been sure, then, that he would become accustomed to it. Now forty-odd years later, with only a few more days left until retirement, his stomach still turned as he trekked through the warren of passageways that wove beneath the city, each one mirroring the boulevard above, each marked with a cheery blue enamel sign.

Right from the first breath of the day – thankfully, it was February; it was always worse in the summer – when he lifted the heavy manhole cover and the escaping stink of the sewers blended raucously with the morning alert of freshly baked bread, Jean-Claude felt his stomach react. Sometimes he felt as if it was taunting him, the smell. This city was all about scent. It billowed from the doorways of boutiques, snatched your attention as a woman passed in the street, grabbed you by the throat as you turned a corner: the astringent tang of tobacco;

the earthy perfection of garlic; the sunshine of oranges; the beckon of coffee. Paris was a city of scent.

And now, in a tunnel below a narrow lane off Rue de Rivoli, the unmistakable shock of rotting flesh met Jean-Claude at the exact moment that the light from his head-torch cut through the darkness, falling on the brackish water swirling around what he'd thought was a football, and now realised was coated with thick, matted, red hair.

Chapter 1

KATE WILDE FELT her phone vibrate in her hand as she headed down the wide Eurostar carriage, looking at the numbers below the luggage rack for her seat. Glancing at the phone screen, she saw it was Hanna texting her again.

When will you be home mummy?

Pausing, she felt a dark hole opening in her stomach. In all of Hanna's almost ten years, this was the first time they had ever been apart; she wasn't sure who was more anxious. And leaving her for the whole of the February half-term week, when they were both at home, just made Kate feel even more as if she was the world's worst mother. She'd had no idea when she'd trained as a geography teacher how vital her job would become to managing as a single parent, but the guilt was still there.

As she found her seat, battling the sick feeling, Kate tried to channel her sister Orna's words: 'You haven't had a holiday in years, except for going home – and Galway isn't exactly Marbella. You've never won *anything* before. Not like this. It's a gift, Kate. You *have* to go.'

Orna got things right – she always had done. She had to be right about this, too. And she'd offered to take her niece. She'd never wanted children, but she'd approached the prospect of entertaining a nine-year-old as if it were a competitive sport. Hanna was going to have a fabulous fun-filled week that she'd remember forever.

Spotting her seat number, Kate pushed back a stray strand of red hair and lifted Orna's hard cabin case into the overhead luggage rack. She sank into her seat, divided from the one opposite by a table, and looked at her phone screen. Anxiety curled inside her like wisps of smoke around paper as her fingers flew over the keyboard.

Just 5 nights. Be good for Auntie Orna. I love you sweet pea xx

Kate unhooked her handbag from her shoulder, checking again that her passport was safe and her train ticket was tucked inside it. She looked at it quickly: arrival at Gare du Nord was 15.47. She checked her phone again. It was 12.25. In six minutes she'd be on her way to Paris.

Her best friend Trisha's laughing face flashed into her mind, glowing after a cross-country run, her school gym kit splattered with mud. Kate felt tears prick at her eyes; she wished again that she could reach out and touch her, to hug her and tell her everything would be OK. After all these years, she was finally on her way to the city they'd both dreamed of.

At thoughts of Trisha, Kate could feel her emotions surging with memories of being sixteen, guilt threatening to engulf her. She knew what separation felt like, and the thought not seeing Hanna for a week had brought it all back. She tried to focus on the carriage and the people getting on the train around her. Since she'd started planning this trip, in the back of her mind the prospect of being away from her daughter had felt as if someone was slowly tearing a piece of paper in two. Not any paper, but the page of a diary inscribed in Trisha's sloping teenage hand, with wishes and hopes and dreams of true love.

And today was Valentine's Day, of all days ...

But this wasn't like before. Kate would come home, and she and Hanna would turn over to a fresh page and write their own list, and all those dreams would come true.

It was only for five days ...

Trying to still her thoughts, Kate looked out of the carriage window at the platform beside her. Although she couldn't see it from here, at the end of the station the iconic clock ticked on, Tracey Emin's neon pink I Want My Time With You scrawled below it as if it had been spray-painted above the station's red-brick Gothic arches. Above her, the monumental glass roof of St Pancras station curved like a force field. It might only be the start of spring, but it was a beautiful morning, crisp and cold.

The moment Kate had been called with the news that she'd won a prize, in a competition on Facebook that she couldn't even remember entering, and that it was an expenses-paid week in Paris, Orna had been even more excited than she was.

Paris.

It had jarred Kate for a moment, the lid she'd kept tight on her memories of Trisha suddenly thrown open, her sadness and failure like a wound that had never healed.

It had to be a sign, though – a sign that her life was changing, that things were getting better. If this had happened at any stage in the past, she couldn't have even considered it, but now she could. Now she needed to go to Paris. This trip was a chance to fulfil her promise and finally lay her ghosts to rest.

And Orna was right: what were the chances of it falling during the February half-term?

Kate had been so sure that it had to be some sort of scam that she initially hadn't taken it seriously at all. But Orna had checked everything out and it was all real. And the company running the promotion had sent the Eurostar booking details through straight away. Orna had even checked to see if the seat they'd booked was taken, just to be sure that Kate didn't get to the station to discover it was all some sort of hoax.

So here she was.

Chapter 2

AGATHE DELEVINGNE LEANED her elbows on the black counter top at Café Rodolphe and looked out of the window at the briefly empty pavement running along Rue des Corbeaux. It was grey outside, the sort of all-pervading grey that only February could bring, the stone of the narrow cobbled street almost the same colour as the ancient walls of Le Marais and the narrow shops that crowded like customers at a market stall along its length.

They'd been flat out since they'd opened up, but there was a brief lull now before the next wave of lunch goers arrived. Oumar was out the back, clearing tables and chatting to the old woman with the plaits. They invented stories about her past when things were quiet: everyone had a story, Oumar said. Sometimes he sounded like her Uncle Gabriel. He was always looking for a story. But right now there was only one story that Agathe wanted to hear, and that was what had happened to her flatmate Sandrine to make her go so silent. It was as if she'd fallen off the face of the earth.

Agathe closed her eyes for a second, her empty stomach turning over again. She couldn't eat when she was this worried. Whichever way she looked at it, something had to be wrong. It wasn't as if she was Sandrine's keeper – they only shared an apartment – but she'd never vanished like this before. She'd been chatty and excited when Agathe had last seen her the previous Wednesday morning, but now it was Tuesday. She hadn't been home over the weekend, and she wasn't answering her phone.

By Sunday night, Agathe had started looking at Sandrine's Instagram and following her friends, so she could ask if they'd seen her. She'd been up half the night, but the response had always been the same: *Pas d'ici; Haven't seen her.* And a few: *Who is this?*

Agathe bit her lip. They were right to ask. Was she being irrational? Sandrine was twenty-six, and had a proper job for a high-end property sales company. She didn't have to report her movements to Agathe, or to their other flatmate, Roland. They had different friends; Agathe didn't even know where Sandrine's parents lived.

Her father and brother worked in Toulouse, for Airbus, but Agathe had no idea how to reach them in such a huge company.

It was bright and cheery inside the narrow café, its mirrored wall reflecting back the display of pastries and the colourful teapots on the shelf behind her. But looking out of the door, Agathe felt the gloom of the day seeping in under the threshold like a bad smell.

The day before – Monday – the girl she'd spoken to at Sandrine's office had confirmed that Sandrine had had a viewing appointment in their diary for a penthouse the previous Friday. On Friday evening, Sandrine had emailed to say there would be a follow-up viewing on Monday, and asked them to take the property off the website. That had struck Agathe as a bit strange. Sandrine was always telling her that a deal wasn't done until the ink was dry, so why remove it from sale after a first viewing?

Agathe pushed her fringe out of her eyes as she went over the conversation she'd had with the receptionist. Sandrine hadn't come back in, had kept the keys for the next meeting with the prospective buyer, so the girls in the office hadn't actually seen her since Friday morning, when she'd collected the keys before her appointment.

In the reflection on the wall opposite her, Agathe looked critically at her highlighted blonde hair, messily piled on top of her head, the roots black. It needed a wash, and she'd gone too heavy with her black eyeliner this morning, trying to distract attention from the plum-coloured circles that came with a lack of sleep. *A bit late to notice that now.* She ran her finger under her long lashes, softening the kohl, the row of earrings running up her ear catching the light.

Agathe heard the dishwasher below the counter gurgle as it began its final cycle. She tapped her phone screen, looking to see if Sandrine had replied to any of her messages in the few minutes since she'd last checked.

Still nothing.

She texted Roland again, to see if he'd heard from her. He should be in university by now, if he wasn't asleep and skipping his lectures. The hours he needed to put in for economics didn't suit him at all. Both he and Sandrine were night owls, up until the early hours talking, or partying, or, in Roland's case, vanishing with his spray paints to create street art down narrow lanes or beside the Seine. It was a miracle he hadn't been caught, but Paris wasn't like other big cities where there were surveillance cameras everywhere. In Paris there were hundreds of hidden corners. Nobody wanted to be watched going about their business – there had been an outcry about improving CCTV on the streets in advance of the Olympics next year.

Worry gnawed at Agathe. Had Sandrine gone out on Friday night and met someone? But surely she'd have come home on Sunday, if only to change, especially if she had that follow-up client viewing on Monday.

Where on earth could she be?

The coffee was scalding hot, black, the aroma awakening all the memories as he cradled the cup in the palm of his hand.

Her voice high and piercing, screaming at him, making him freeze, the trickle of urine running down his leg. Then the pain of her cigarette on his arm, the smell of burning flesh. The heat of the coffee on his young skin as he fell backwards, crashing onto the tiled floor.

'Your fault, you made me trip.'

He'd been hypnotised, he knew now – hypnotised by the pain and the fear and the need for her attention.

And then her red hair, falling over her painted face, her perfume thick and strong like a drug as the guilt overcame her and she picked him up, clutching him tightly, as if only he could save her. He closed his eyes, breathing in the memories.

Her red hair, her scent.

He needed it again. That release. The moment when all the pent-up tension flooded out of him as she held him to her breast.

That special moment.

The one this weekend had been a disappointment. That's what came of spontaneity. What had looked too good to be true, was. But he supposed the practice was always good.

This one would be different. He glanced again at the photograph, the image clear on his phone. She was laughing, her hair tumbling around her like a waterfall, the child beside her unmistakably her daughter. As if they were poster girls for the Redhead Convention.

Her red hair.

He breathed in slowly, imagining her earthy scent, like ambergris. And then the mist as he sprayed her with the perfume: flowery layers of summer – bergamot, lily of the valley and jasmine. Each tone altered by her pale skin into a scent that was unique to a redhead. The thought of it made him dizzy with desire – the scent of her skin ...

It was all set up. She'd be here soon.

Chapter 3

GLANCING AROUND HER as the Eurostar carriage filled, Kate could hardly believe it: *she was finally going to Paris.* She'd got this far, had got her life back on track, and now it was time to make good on her promise to her best friend. She could almost hear Trisha's laughter, bright like the sunshine lighting the platform beyond the train.

They had been so close, but then Kate had let her down. Her grief and guilt was like a stone in her shoe, constantly rubbing.

The time they'd sneaked off to the cinema in Galway to see *Amélie* had been the start of it. The same day that their ephemeral, vaporous teenage dreams had condensed into something magical and real on the huge screen had been the day Trisha had had her first headache. Kate could still see the rich colours of every scene, feel their joy as they'd left, arm in arm, mesmerised by thoughts of working in a café in Paris, of puzzles and photo albums, of artists and finding true love. Of a future.

But nothing had quite gone as they'd expected. Trisha hadn't realised anything was really wrong for another six months. Six months in which their plans formed and they'd mapped out a year abroad between school and university; six months in which her cancer had become terminal.

Kate's phone pinged again.

Hanna had sent her a photo, her strawberry blonde hair gleaming in Orna's kitchen lights. Despite having so many golden tones in her straight hair, a complete contrast to Kate's own Titian curls, they were unmistakably mother and daughter.

Hanna had Kate's blue eyes and button nose, the dimple beside her full mouth, and – thankfully – very little of her father. Part of Kate's heart shrank at the thought of Erik, echoes of the storm whistling in through the cracks if she let them.

When she looked back, Kate felt as if she'd been trying to get away from him from the day they'd met. She'd been twenty-six, still finding her feet living in London, in a new job – they'd only been dating for a year when she'd discovered she was pregnant, and foolishly she'd been sure he would change. They were both from Catholic families; marriage was the next logical step despite the feeling, deep down, that she was making a terrible mistake.

But Erik had charmed everyone – her parents, her friends. Only Orna had seen through him. Kate didn't think she'd ever forget the pressure of Orna's hand on her arm as she'd turned to walk into the church. 'You don't have to do this …'

Kate hadn't wanted to listen then. Orna had everything and Kate had wanted part of that. Orna was the lucky one; she was the one who'd refused to go to university, instead leaving home to find her fortune in London, getting a job in Selfridges that had taken her to womenswear buyer, and now her own shop. With marriage to the wonderful Declan, investment banker, thrown in.

The only things thrown into Kate's marriage had been suspicion, constant fear and too many trips to A & E.

It had taken her the next six years, but Kate had finally got away from him. She'd found herself a job, and left the women's refuge for a room in a shared house. Eventually she'd found a fantastic landlord and a tiny attic flat. Last summer, the day they'd moved downstairs, gaining a bedroom and those huge windows – so much light after the darkness of the attic – had felt like a turning point, a new start.

And now she was going to Paris to fulfil her long overdue promise to Trisha. *Things were changing, everything was going to be OK.*

Kate's phone pinged again. This time the message was from an international number.

Tell Hanna I miss her, I want to see her.

Kate froze, old fears ripping through her insides. She stared at the message for a few moments, part of her mentally picking up her child and running as fast as she could.

Erik.

It had to be.

How had he got her number? He was working away, his access to Hanna scheduled, and he knew he could only contact them through her solicitor.

Why was he texting her now?

Chapter 4

AS AGATHE LET the café door fall closed behind her and stepped out into the narrow street, she pulled her phone out of her backpack. Oumar had seen how distracted she was and, insisting that he'd be able to manage the rest of the lunch crowd, had let her finish her shift early. University, and her afternoon lecture, were across the river, but first she wanted to call her uncle Gabriel.

The bad feeling Agathe had about Sandrine's absence had grown exponentially. Was she being over-anxious? If Agathe had suddenly got the opportunity of a holiday, would she think to let Roland and Sandrine know? They shared an apartment but they led different lives.

She needed to talk to someone – someone who knew about missing people, and who knew her well enough to be honest with her. Calling the police seemed like a massive overreaction. *Sandrine probably wasn't even missing.*

Her uncle, Gabriel Beaudin, would know whether she should be worried or not. He'd always been straight with her, and he was editor of *Paris Heure*, the morning tabloid that everyone read on their way to work. He always knew what was happening ahead of everyone else, so if there was bad news – Agathe didn't even want to think about that – he'd be the most likely to know, and more importantly, to tell her.

Her uncle picked up after one ring. 'How's my favourite niece? Steeped in the history and architecture of our beautiful city, I hope. How long before you come to work for me properly and put those research skills to the test?'

Agathe almost rolled her eyes. He said this every time she called.

'You know I'm not a journalist—'

Her uncle interrupted. 'I know, I know, you want to work in some dusty archive, preserving the past.' Agathe could tell he was smiling. 'How can I help? You need money?'

'No, I ...'

'Every student needs money. I keep telling you, there's a job waiting for you here that will pay double what that café pays. I was going to call you today, actually.'

Agathe had worked in the *Paris Heure* office for him over the summer, juggling her hours at Café Rodolphe with a few days each week in the newsroom. Even at night it hummed with conversation: discussion on what they would print, what they could print, and when. In her mind's eye Agathe could see him sitting at his huge, untidy antique desk, his silver hair slicked back, craggy face creased in a frown. His office was on the second floor in the corner of the building, its windows overlooking the Seine where it snaked through the city.

He was going to call her? What about? A sick feeling of worry filled her stomach.

'I'm good for money, it isn't that.' Agathe took a breath, conscious her tone was sharper than she'd intended. He must have picked up on it. At the other end she heard a rustling sound, the squeak of the unoiled wheel on his chair rolling back, and then the gentle closing of his office door.

'Go on, what's the problem?'

'It's my flatmate, Sandrine. She didn't come home over the weekend. I haven't heard from her since last week and no one has seen her. I'm probably getting anxious over nothing, but I wondered if you'd heard anything, about … anything.'

She couldn't say it.

Glancing up at the graphite sky, clouds clotted with rain about to fall, Agathe began walking quickly along the pavement, her phone to her ear. She bit her lip. *She was being silly. He was going to tell her not to worry and it would all be fine.*

But there was silence at the other end. Not good.

Like the giant clocks on the Musée d'Orsay, their glass faces overlooking what felt like the whole city, you could almost hear the cogs clunking around as Gabriel Beaudin ruminated on an issue.

She was pretty sure the silence was him working out what to say.

A moment later, as if the hands on the clocks had come together, he started to speak, his voice low.

'This goes no further. I have heard something, but Carlier wants us to keep a lid on it for now. He's worried about scaremongering, creating a panic.'

Her uncle had been at school with Pierre Carlier, who, as Prefect of Paris, was one of the most powerful government representatives in the country. They'd always been close, and had stayed in touch as their careers progressed, developing a symbiotic relationship that benefited them both. Carlier understood the power of the press.

'What?' Agathe's voice was little more than a whisper.

'This isn't Sandrine, OK – definitely not. But some workers found something in the sewers. A body part, shall we say.'

'What body part?' Agathe could have screamed at him. *What body part, and why were they not saying anything? It was his job to report ...*

'They don't know how long it's been there ... not that long, anyway. But I don't think it's Sandrine.'

'But it's female?'

'Yes, it's female. And we know she didn't die from natural causes. The criminal investigation division are trying to identify her before anyone is alerted to the find.'

Agathe couldn't answer, her thoughts racing. She felt physically sick. *How could he know it wasn't Sandrine? What part had they found?*

'The thing is, there are some similarities to a previous case, from 2012.' He sighed. 'It's ... Well ... I have Maxim checking the archives for missing persons.' He cleared his throat. 'For missing heads, specifically.'

'Heads? But what ...?'

'We don't know. That's the point, but there could be other cases – similar ... Well, it's hard to know, but these two we do know about were young females with red hair. And they were both found in the sewers.' He sighed. 'Carlier is worried that, even – what ... eleven years apart? – it might not be a coincidence. Only a tiny percentage of the population has red hair. It's very rare. And ... Well, the sewers.'

'More than two? A serial killer?' Agathe couldn't believe she was saying it. She let out a sharp breath that she hadn't realised she was holding, and at the same time stopped walking abruptly. She turned to look into the candle shop she'd halted beside, the window display filled with Valentine's roses and pink paper hearts, multiple flames flickering at the top of a huge cream candle. Leaning on the dove-grey wooden surround, she could suddenly see her own reflection like a ghost above the flame. She was pale, her foundation barely concealing the shadow of acne, her grey eyes made larger by the heavy black eyeliner. She looked down at her chunky Chelsea boots and pulled her coat around herself as he continued.

'Perhaps. But there seems to be this big gap between killings, which is why I'm telling you. That's what I was going to call you about. Maxim doesn't have your research skills – or patience, come to that. I have him out now talking to his sources, but I was thinking you could go through the archives, here and at the university. We'll pay you, obviously. Your library archives include material from the local and regional papers, stuff my people can't access easily. We may need to go back a good few years, but ...' He lowered his voice. 'Listen, I'm sure Sandrine is quite safe.'

Agathe closed her eyes. 'I don't know if I should call the police – or her parents. Assuming I can find them. I don't know what to do.'

'Call the police and report it. I'm sure Sandrine is fine. She's very sensible, from what you've told me. And she doesn't have red hair.'

Chapter 5

'SORRY, MAY I?'

Her focus on her phone, Kate looked up abruptly, surprised by the male voice suddenly beside her in the carriage. Only half concentrating, she smiled, and its owner hoisted a leather holdall onto the luggage rack above her head. Slipping off a dark cashmere overcoat, he rolled it carelessly and thrust it in after the bag.

As Kate's thoughts tumbled, the train began to roll smoothly out of the station. She quickly typed out a message to Orna.

Erik's back, he wants to see Hanna.

She hit *send*, gripping the phone as the man sat down opposite her.

Would Erik try and take Hanna again?

The last time, he'd sworn to the judge that Kate had been mistaken, that he'd only wanted to show his daughter the sea. That his proximity to the ferry port was a coincidence.

They were moving, it was too late to get off.

The man who had just arrived in the carriage was a few years older than her – around forty, perhaps, his blond hair cropped with military precision. His face was weathered, a cleft lip and pale blue eyes giving him a worn look that seemed at odds with his crisp navy suit and oxblood tie, a matching silk square protruding from the top pocket of his jacket. He hooked the handle of a walking stick onto the table between them.

Kate tapped her phone nervously on the table. How long would it take her sister to respond?

Sitting across from her, the man reached inside his jacket pocket to retrieve his own phone. Catching her eye, he smiled, nodding a greeting as he dipped into his jacket again for a sleek black spectacle box. He was wearing a heavy watch, the steel bracelet laced with gold links, a rotating bezel marked with the compass points in gold. It looked old, and incredibly expensive, and as if it tracked every possible permutation of time.

Time. Why did Kate always feel as if there was a clock ticking somewhere, that she had to run and keep running to beat it?

She had felt that she was getting on top of things, more in control. But now ... At her worst, her classroom had been the only place where she'd had any sense of herself, any faith in her abilities to function. Teaching had been the only part of her life that Erik hadn't infected. 'Coercive control' the counsellor had called it. And it had crept in so slowly, she hadn't noticed until the first time he'd hit her.

Suddenly desperate to talk to someone – anyone – to stop her racing thoughts, Kate looked across the table and smiled. 'Have you caught this train before?'

If he was surprised she was starting a conversation, the man opposite didn't show it.

'Fairly often. I'm in Paris on business every few months. However, this trip is a mission for my aunt. Great-aunt, I should say, although she hates that.'

Kate immediately had an impression of a very elegant older woman, taking tea from a china cup in Fortnum's.

He paused. 'It's a beautiful city, but ...' He grinned ruefully. 'The Parisians can be a little impatient – and not just with visitors.'

'Really? Well, I'm not just sightseeing. I'm going to do a course – on making perfume.'

Was that too much information? She just needed to

keep the conversation going or she knew her mind would begin to spiral.

He raised an eyebrow. 'That sounds interesting. Parisians might not be the friendliest people, but there's lots to see. Are you staying somewhere central?'

She went for the least detailed answer she could. 'Somewhere near Le Marais.' It was a big area. *Near* wasn't *in*.

As if he hadn't noticed her deliberate vagueness, he continued. 'That's a beautiful part of the city – medieval, tiny twisting streets.' He paused. 'There's a cheesecake shop there. It's quite an experience.' His mouth twitched in a smile. 'My aunt is more worried about the impact of a visit to Paris on her waistline than on mine.'

Kate nodded, her mind darting to her phone again. The train was picking up speed, sidings rushing past. Concrete and steel, rubble, graffiti. *She should have got off.* But it felt as if Erik had timed his text deliberately so she couldn't have done. He couldn't know she was going away, could he? The thought made her stomach churn.

Kate's phone suddenly buzzed, vibrating on the table between them.

All OK, will keep her safe. Promise. Relax and enjoy your week. Don't let him spoil this too.

Kate felt less shaky as the next text arrived.

Enjoy Paris. DO NOT WORRY XXX

Thank God for her sensible big sister.

Orna was right – she'd look after Hanna. Erik couldn't know where she was; his text arriving now had to be a coincidence.

'Something important?' The man's voice cut through her thoughts. What had he just said? His job, his aunt.

'It's fine.' Kate laid her phone down on the table. *Orna knew about Erik; it would be OK.* Kate forced herself to relax. Erik had sworn he'd kill her after the last incident, but he couldn't find her in Paris. 'And your mission for her – your aunt?'

'I have to go to Christie's to inspect something ... a perfume bottle, actually. She doesn't trust photographs. She wants to be sure it's genuine, and undamaged.'

'You're going all the way to Paris to look at a perfume bottle?' Kate's tone betrayed her incredulity.

He flushed slightly. 'I know. It sounds mad. She was all set to come herself, but her doctor told her that she can't travel at the moment – apparently. I'm starting to think that she was intending for me to come all along.' He rolled his eyes. 'It's a wedding present for my niece. My aunt was given the same one when she was married in 1939 – it was the only thing that survived when their house was bombed during the Blitz. She's convinced it will be a lucky charm.'

He didn't look convinced himself. 'Honestly, I'm not sure it will be, but my aunt's a hundred and three and very insistent.'

'I see.' Kate paused, trying desperately to focus on this moment, in this carriage. She needed to distract herself, to keep thoughts of Erik, the flashbacks, firmly at bay. *Who would go all the way to Paris to buy a perfume bottle?*

'Goodness …'

'Indeed.' He cleared his throat, turning his watch bracelet as if it was a habit. 'I suppose there's a romanticism to her finding one for sale in Paris. It's a city of scent. And indeed, the perfect place for a course on perfume.' He smiled warmly.

Kate let out a breath, releasing some of the tension in her chest. 'I hope it will be. I won it in a competition that I can't even remember entering, something online. But my Instagram is always full of ads for hotels in Italy and mountain treks.'

'Our phones do seem to listen to us rather, don't they? My aunt says the same thing, but she's a lot more tech-savvy than I am.' He paused. 'Daniel … Daniel Langton.'

He held out his hand across the table.

Maybe Erik had found out about her trip through social media? The thought jumped suddenly into her head. She only used Facebook and Instagram, and she was very careful about what she posted, but was that why his text had come now, just as she'd got on the train?

Automatically Kate shook his hand, her mind only half on the carriage. 'Kate.'

'This prize sounds rather wonderful, a definite benefit to being online.'

Was it? Suddenly she wasn't so sure. 'I didn't believe it at first, but it all seems to be real. And the competition covers everything – an apartment for the week, all my travel …' She paused. 'They even booked my seat.'

Chapter 6

'GOOD AFTERNOON, MATEY, so what's this all about?' Lucien Arnaud let the imposing purple door of Le Loup Gris swing closed behind Maxim as he stepped inside the hallway. The air was chill – the building always felt hollow somehow when the nightclub was closed.

'Need somewhere discreet for a chat. This was the only place he'd agree to come to.' Maxim ran his hand into his highlighted fringe, ruffling his hair where it had been flattened by his motorcycle helmet, now slung over his arm. 'He can say he was making enquiries if anyone wonders what he's doing here.'

His boss, Gabriel Beaudin, had been insistent that Maxim follow up on the discovery in the sewers ASAP, but trying to organise a meeting at short notice always brought complications.

Inspector Raymond Travère of '*La Crim*', the criminal investigation division of the Préfecture de Police, couldn't afford to be spotted speaking to a tabloid journalist, and he was a man who liked his comforts. The idea of sitting in a car on a piece of freezing waste ground hadn't filled him with joy. It hadn't been high on Maxim's wish list either, especially as he didn't own a car, and persuading Gabriel Beaudin to lend him his ancient treasured Mercedes, and then ensuring it didn't get so much as a scratch on it, was more than his job was worth.

Then Maxim had thought of the club.

Lucien grinned and indicated Maxim should follow him down into the heart of his seven-floor empire. He was wearing pale tan suede brogues with narrow-legged chinos, his shoes silent as he ambled along the black and white tiled passageway, Maxim's steel-tipped cowboy boots, in contrast, clicking off the marble. Lucien glanced down at them and shook his head, his ongoing despair at the state of Maxim's wardrobe evident in his face. At least this time he didn't comment on it.

'This place is like a morgue until the staff come in at seven, so you've got the place to yourself. The chefs are here, but they're down in the kitchens. They won't disturb you. And I can buzz open the side door. Discretion is assured for all our clients.'

Maxim caught Lucien's grin. The underground entrance for celebrities and anyone who might be visiting them was a closely guarded secret, allowing guests to discreetly enter and leave Paris's hottest nightspot.

'Can we use your office?'

Lucien narrowed his eyes thoughtfully. 'Danger someone might walk in on you, and if they found the door was locked all hell would break loose. They'd think I was being held hostage. We have a small private dining room on the second floor, right beside the lift. I'll bring some foie gras. We've got a Côtes de Gascogne that goes beautifully with it.'

'Sounds great. And he'll like that – much appreciated.'

Lucien nodded as they reached the lift doors and punched the call button. 'I'll show you up.'

'He a friend of yours, this Lucien Arnaud?' Inspector Travère sat down in an elegantly upholstered dining chair and picked up the wine Lucien had left in the cooler. The table was oval, polished to a gleam, and filled the centre of the room. Travère didn't look any healthier than the last time Maxim had seen him, his jowls florid, belt straining under the weight of his stomach. He had to be nearing retirement.

Despite their differences, they'd developed a good relationship in the years Maxim had worked for *Paris Heure*. There were times when it suited Travère to let information out, and it was easily deniable when it appeared in a tabloid.

It was like a dance. A dance that, today, Maxim hoped, would be the quickstep.

Maxim nodded. 'We were in university together, same rowing club. We're tight.'

Travère made a humphing noise and poured himself a generous glass of wine, then leaned back and looked around the room. Huge, mildly erotic nudes hung on deep grey painted panels, the plaster ceiling dripping with gold.

'I remember this place when his mother owned it. She was something. Voice like velvet. She could hold the whole room when she went on stage. Never been another like her.' Maxim nodded obligingly. But he wasn't here to talk about Lucien's celebrity family background. Before he could say anything, Travère continued. 'Tragic, what happened. To go like that in the Métro, straight under a train. Horrible.' He paused as if he was expecting Maxim to comment, but then continued before he could say anything. 'I always wondered about it, you know ... An accident, too much ...' He tapped his glass and shrugged. 'Or perhaps she didn't intend for it to be so final. She was very dramatic, known for it, and her moods ...' He shrugged again. 'Artistic, I suppose. There was talk of a national day of mourning.'

Maxim cleared his throat. 'Awful, but Lucien has made a huge success of this place.' He picked up his empty glass and reached for the bottle. 'What can you tell me about the recent find? It's your investigation?'

Travère took a long sip, nodded, and screwed up his piggy eyes. 'Nasty one. Clean cut, though, someone who had practice.'

'Any idea who she was?'

'This is off the record?'

'Of course, strictly between us. If you can give me a direction, I can look elsewhere for the information – join the dots, so to speak.'

Travère nodded. 'It'll take a while to see if there's a DNA match on the system, but she had a tattoo behind her ear.' He picked up a knife and, helping himself to a round of bread, scooped a generous lump of the pate onto it. Maxim watched as he took a huge bite, and a moment later finished it. He picked up his napkin as he chewed and wiped his fingers, obviously savouring the contents of his mouth.

Maxim edged forward on his chair. He didn't have all day for this. He had things to do.

'A tattoo?' He looked at Travère, willing him to divulge a little more.

Travère finished preparing his next mouthful, and continued. 'Unusual – stars and the like, some symbol. We're searching the files to see if there's a match, obviously.' He paused significantly. 'Pathologist thinks the remains have been frozen.' Maxim's eyebrows shot up as Travère looked at him, nodding slowly. 'That's the problem. The one before, Bénédicte Écuyer, hairdresser, disappeared in 2008 and we found … Well, not much apart from her head, as it turned out, but her remains didn't turn up until 2012.'

Picking up his own glass to take a sip, Maxim looked across at Travère, part of him wondering how he could be so relaxed, talking about body parts and eating at the same time. But he knew the answer: Travère was a career policeman; he'd seen worse.

'There was evidence that her body had been frozen, too?'

Travère bit into his foie gras, speaking with his mouth full. 'Don't have her body to know about the rest, but definitely the head. And there was very little decomposition, so it hadn't been down there long when it was found. Of course, Carlier's going nuts. It's fairly obvious that these two must be connected, and the last thing he wants with the Olympics next year is a load of press about a crazed killer going on some rampage in Paris, sticking women in freezers and cutting off heads.'

'Women with red hair.'

'Exactly.' Travère looked at Maxim. 'Carlier wants the story buried for now, but … You know. If I was a young woman with red hair …' He shrugged.

'You'd want to know.'

Travère raised his eyebrows, nodding silently.

Chapter 7

WHEN AGATHE GOT home from the library, it was starting to spit freezing rain that hit the back of her neck like shotgun pellets. Hunched against the gathering dusk, she punched in the door access code, the lights in the stone hallway flicking on as she swung open the street door. It was only just after four, but she hadn't been able to concentrate, and now she had a ton of reading to do.

Her arms folded tightly, Agathe waited for the lift. Her uncle was right: *when she got up to their apartment, Sandrine would have the heating switched on and coffee on the stove and her magazines strewn across the living room table.*

Agathe had called the police the minute she'd got off the phone to her uncle, but the detective she'd spoken to had been less than helpful. He'd taken the details, told her to check with Sandrine's parents, and told her to call back in the morning if there was still no sign. He'd as much as said that Sandrine was an adult and could make her own decisions. 'People go missing for lots of reasons, all the time. Maybe she doesn't want to be found right now.'

Yeah, right.

But she could only check with Sandrine's family if she could track them down. Surely that was something the police could do?

On their landing, Agathe put the key into the deadlock, willing it to be on the latch and to turn easily.

It didn't.

She wrestled with it. It was sticky, despite her constant requests to Roland to fix it. It was his parents' apartment, so technically he was the landlord, but he was too busy being creative to actually worry about anything practical, like faulty taps or draughts. It usually fell to Agathe to sort things out. The front door was the one thing she kept forgetting.

Inside the narrow tiled hallway, Agathe could feel the silence in the apartment, heavy with disappointment. She switched on the light quickly, banishing the darkness as she paused for a moment to listen. But there were none of the sounds that Sandrine usually made. No humming from the bathroom, or the strains of classical music from the living room. Or even the guttural sounds of sex that sometimes slipped under her bedroom door when she thought they were all out.

She and Roland had a non-exclusive relationship, but there was open and there was open.

He'd crashed around the house for a week after the last time it had happened. And then had gone and covered a subway with a terrifying image of a vampire that Agathe was still trying to work out the message behind. His anger had made him sloppy, and the police had called the next evening. Agathe shook her head as she headed down the narrow passageway to the living room with its kitchenette corner. Sandrine had given Roland an alibi that night – it was as close as he'd ever come to arrest. But they were watching him, Agathe knew. With all the interest in his work that *Paris Heure* was generating, they wanted to make an example of him.

And they'd gone to her uncle's office to find out how the newspaper seemed to have a photographer who got to each mural location before the paint was even dry. The public were loving the cat-and-mouse hunt for the mysterious street artist, Requin. His identity was a secret, but his tag – an open-mouthed shark – was becoming one of the most recognisable in the city, much to the anger of the authorities. Street art was a huge part of the cultural scene in Paris. Loud, like a revolutionary voice, it came from below the surface – but only in the right places. Roland was still on the fringe, enjoying the danger, but the media coverage was helping build his career, and her uncle was enjoying being one step ahead of everyone. Win-win. As long as it stayed that way.

Agathe could see Roland's bike was leaning against the hallway wall, the Senegalese flag above it, assorted designer trainers scattered below.

No sign of Sandrine's leather boots.

Agathe flicked on the lights in the living room. The only sound was the methodical ticking of a clock Roland's parents had installed in the vague hope that their only son might join the rest of the human race and function during normal daylight hours.

From what she'd seen – and Agathe had only known him for a year or so – Roland was just as focused as his high-flying parents, but in a different way. He wanted to be Banksy – maybe Banksy was Black and French, too; no one knew – but he would do whatever it took to achieve that dream. Which basically meant spending a lot of time cycling around the city in the middle of the night, his spray cans hidden in a bright green Uber Eats insulated pannier that he'd acquired specifically for the purpose. The police might stop a cyclist, but they weren't likely to check to see if he was delivering curry or pizza – or in Roland's case, street art so stylised its tag was hardly needed.

Swinging her bag onto the counter, Agathe could see Roland's spray cans were scattered across the smooth glass table. And the sink was still full of washing-up.

Sandrine hadn't been home.

Chapter 8

ROLLING HER CASE across the worn granite slabs of a grand hallway, Kate followed the woman who had met her at the door of 32 Rue des Corbeaux to the foot of a magnificent curved stone staircase. A tiny, rather ancient elevator nestled beside it, looking like an ornate iron birdcage.

Her conversation on the train had calmed her a bit – hearing about Daniel Langton's world had put her own problems into perspective.

'Royal Engineers. Afghanistan and the like. Invalided out. Bit of a tangle with a landmine.'

'Oh …' Her eyes had flicked to the walking stick handle latched onto the table.

'Occupational hazard, as they say. Now I work in patents, mainly.' He'd grimaced. 'Patents aren't very interesting but, as my aunt says, it's very, very safe.'

Safe was what she needed. What everyone needed. *Safe* was what pressing charges against Erik had given her. She'd been terrified that he'd twist things, that nobody would believe her, but the judge had been unimpressed with his excuses. And his sentence had bought her the time she needed to get back on her feet.

Leaving Gare du Nord in a taxi, Kate had been slightly wowed that everywhere looked so … well, *French*. She didn't know why she was surprised. Perhaps it was because she'd taken the train: one minute in London and the next … here. As she looked out at shopfronts and ranks of motorbikes and bicycles lined up at the sides of the streets, electric scooters leaning dangerously into them, she felt as if she'd landed on a movie set. The streets had got narrower as they'd neared her destination, the buildings still elegant, ornate ironwork balconies running like ribbons around them.

And now she was in one of those haughty period buildings, climbing a polished stone staircase that swept up from the ground floor, an oak banister smoothed with time guiding her up.

The woman who met her at the door had introduced herself as Céline Arnaud. She lived downstairs. And Céline spoke English, so Kate's hasty excursion with Duolingo to polish her school French would have to wait to be tested.

'Here we are.' Arriving on a broad landing, Céline crossed to open the panelled apartment door, painted an elegant grey, locks clunking back as she turned a series of keys. She pushed the door open and gestured for Kate to go inside. 'As I said, if you need anything, just ask, but you should have everything. I'll show you around.'

In front of Kate, across the narrow parquet hall, a set of double doors stood open to an enormous living room with a white-painted dining table at one end. The sofas, a coffee table and the half-moon side tables between the windows all appeared to be slightly too small for its proportions.

'Goodness, it's huge.' Surprised, Kate glanced back at Céline, who was running what looked like a golden apple charm along her necklace, unashamedly assessing her.

Céline smiled by way of reply. 'Lucien always says we should move up here and let downstairs instead, but I'm a psychologist. My patients need access from the street.'

Her English was perfect – the slightest hint of an accent, as if she'd learned to speak it in America, or watched a lot of American films. But she looked very French, her raven hair long and straight, dark eyes watchful. She wore a silk scarf tied cleverly over a navy polo neck sweater, the gold necklace contrasting with the midnight cashmere. Tailored jeans were finished off with perfect navy ballerina pumps. She had to be in her mid-forties, but she had that indeterminate age and casual elegance Kate had always envied in European women.

Kate wasn't sure who Lucien was, but she guessed from Céline's tone that he must be her husband.

As if she suddenly remembered that she was showing Kate the apartment, Céline stopped studying her and moved to her left along the corridor, past several doors, opening one further down. 'This is the master bedroom, with an en suite bathroom inside. There are two more bedrooms and a master bathroom as well.' Continuing down the narrow corridor, Céline moved catlike, her soft-soled pumps silent on the wooden floor. 'And the kitchen is here.'

At Céline's invitation, Kate stuck her head inside the narrow galley. Everything was white; a window at the end was as wide as the room itself.

'There's everything you need. And the washing machine and dryer are in the laundry in the next room.' Céline stood back from the doorway as if she was expecting Kate to go inside and inspect and approve everything. The kitchen looked as if it had been designed by a chef.

'This is wonderful, thank you. Perfect.'

Pointing to another set of double doors opening opposite the kitchen, Céline threw open one half to show Kate the other end of the living room.

'The windows open onto the balcony, obviously, but I think it's too cold to be sitting out.' Céline held out the keys she'd been carrying with a jangle. 'Enjoy your week.'

'Oh, I will, thank you.' Kate paused, taking the proffered bunch. 'They open the street door, too?'

'No, there's a keypad for the front door. The code is in the notes in case you forget. But there's an electric key fob here. Just touch that off the receptor on the panel and the door will open. You'll only need the code if you leave the fob behind for some reason.' She waved vaguely into the living room, and Kate spotted a large file on a low coffee table between the two sofas. 'The code is different for each apartment. This one is 1789. My telephone number is in the file, too. Call me if you run into any problems. If I'm with a patient there might be a delay, but I'm at home most of the time.' Céline seemed to hover as if she was about to speak again.

'That's grand, thank you. I'm sure I won't need to bother you.'

'*C'est bien*. I'll leave you to it.'

Smiling her thanks, Kate couldn't get Céline out of the apartment fast enough.

Chapter 9

AGATHE LOOKED AT the clock on the microwave as she stood in the kitchenette. It was almost 4.30 now. Sandrine wasn't here at the apartment, but she *could* be at a friend's or shopping. Maybe.

She hadn't been into the office – Agathe had called again – and they were as mystified as she was. Sandrine hadn't returned the keys of the apartment she'd been showing, and they hadn't heard from her since her last email.

Leaning against the counter, Agathe closed her eyes and clasped her wrist with her hand, running her thumb over the butterfly tattoo on the inside of her wrist. She didn't know if she was praying or trying to hold herself together, but the pressure helped focus her mind away from the fear that was nipping at her like a small dog.

Releasing her wrist and turning, Agathe pulled open the fridge door, looking blindly inside, the black hole of worry in the centre of her stomach starting to spin again like an internet page loading symbol. That's what this felt like – as if there was a page missing, and she was waiting for it to download. The page with all Sandrine's news and movements on it, the page that would tell Agathe where the hell she was now.

Finally focusing on the inside of the fridge, Agathe realised someone had eaten the pasta she'd left last night and put the empty bowl back on the shelf. Much as she wanted it to be Sandrine, she knew it was Roland.

Letting the door swing closed, Agathe turned to her bag and pulled out the cream and bacon she'd bought to have with the pasta. Her scarf and a bottle of milk were shoved in with them on top of the pages she'd printed off – a wad of reports and half-completed reports. She'd known as soon as she'd got off the phone to her uncle that she wouldn't be able to concentrate on her lecture, so she'd taken herself off to the university library instead. There was no point in having a research degree if you didn't use it. And she needed to be useful today, needed to *do* something, to keep her mind occupied.

Pulling out the sheaf of papers, Agathe scanned them. Missing women. There had been more than she'd expected, with the vast majority light on the detail her uncle needed, which meant she'd need to cross-reference with other reports.

But worst of all, as she'd gone down the dark rabbit hole of misery, she'd quickly realised that whatever had happened to them, the locations these women had lived in directly correlated with the amount of media coverage given to them. Any hint that the women – girls, often – were involved in the night economy, homeless, or on the periphery of life, meant they got a mention on page 20. When a girl went missing from Agathe's university, or a middle-class neighbourhood, she was front-page news.

Deep in Agathe's bag, her phone pinged with a notification from BeReal. Putting the papers down on the dining table beside the empty spray cans, Agathe pulled it out and opened the app.

She quickly took a snap of the living room, and then a selfie, scrolling back to see what her friends were doing. BeReal was spontaneous, unlike Instagram, with its airbrushed influencers and perfectly composed shots. You got a couple of chances to retake the photo if it was really terrible, but BeReal wasn't about looking good; it was a snapshot of your life, a photo of what you were doing and where you were. Agathe loved that she could see what her friends were doing, whether they were in the library studying or at work, or skiing, or having a coffee somewhere.

The app sent you a reminder to post every day, but Sandrine hadn't posted today. Or yesterday.

Agathe frowned, closing her eyes and summoning images from her BeReal feed. She was sure Sandrine's last post had been from the hair salon. She'd been laughing into the mirror as the hairdresser had added another silver foil packet to the mass on her head.

Could Sandrine have said something to the hairdresser about her plans for the weekend? You always chatted in the salon – at least, Agathe did – and she had the details of the place Sandrine used pinned to the board in her bedroom. Agathe had mentioned needing to get her roots done, and Sandrine had said they had model nights when their own students practised, and did cuts and colour for free.

Perhaps they would remember if Sandrine had said something about meeting someone or going away? Suddenly not hungry any more, Agathe put her phone down on the counter and went to her room to find the card.

*

'Hello?' It had taken the salon ages to answer.

Leaning on the windowsill, Agathe ran her eye over the clothes she'd dumped on the bedroom floor and prayed the girl would remember if Sandrine had said anything about her plans for the weekend.

'Yes, hello. I'm a friend of Sandrine Durand's. She was with you on Wednesday evening, I think, getting her hair done.'

At the other end, Agathe could hear dryers going, pop music tinny.

'Yes, she was here at—'

Agathe interrupted her. 'Could I speak to whoever did her hair, please? It's important.'

'I'll see if she's free.' The receptionist sounded annoyed.

A moment later, another voice came on the line.

'Hello, how can I help?'

'I'm a friend of Sandrine's.' Agathe paused. 'The thing is, she's disappeared, and I just wondered if she might have said anything about going away, or … or …' Agathe ran out of words. She ran her free hand across her forehead, a pain beginning to form at her temple.

The hairdresser hesitated, as if she was trying to remember. 'No, she didn't say anything. Is there a problem with her hair? Does she not like the colour?' The woman sounded defensive, as if she hadn't listened to what Agathe had said.

'The colour? What colour?'

'She wanted to go red. I gave her a base colour and then highlights. I thought she liked it.'

Suddenly, Agathe realised she couldn't breathe. It took all her willpower to force the words out.

'Thank you, thank you. I'm sure she loved the colour.'

Sandrine had had her hair dyed red. Her uncle had said the woman they'd found … A wave of nausea engulfed her.

Chapter 10

KATE LEANED BACK against the front door of the apartment and breathed in. It smelled of beeswax and lavender. Even this late on a grey afternoon, the huge floor-to-ceiling windows in the lounge – Kate made a mental note to try and call it the *salon*, as Céline had – let in a soft light that reflected off the pale wooden floor. Across the narrow street, another identical building rose, the windows glowing. It looked close enough to touch.

Kate felt the need to pinch herself. This place was more than a little unreal. Heavy cream drapes hung at every window, and above the white marble fireplace, a huge antique gold-framed mirror reflected the room. On the coffee table was a round bowl filled with blowsy pale pink hydrangeas. It was perfect, as if an interior designer had chosen every last detail.

She held up her phone and quickly took some photographs, sending them to Orna.

Have arrived. Look how gorgeous. xxx

Almost immediately her phone pinged with an emoji, a smiley face with heart-shaped eyes followed by a heart.

Everything was OK. Perhaps she was overthinking. Perhaps Erik wasn't even in London, or even the UK. He spoke four languages – he was a chef, could be running a kitchen in a restaurant anywhere.

Kate sighed. *Had her anxiety about taking the holiday and being separated from Hanna made her overreact to his text? Orna would keep her safe. And she'd already promised to message regularly.*

Glancing around the room, Kate headed back to the bedroom. There was something she needed to find before she did anything else.

The bedroom was as tasteful as the *salon*, the furniture dark wood, making the cream bed linen brighter somehow. Unzipping her case, pulling back the first few layers of clothes, Kate found the battered brown envelope, soft with wear, nestled safely inside.

Trisha's diary.

They'd swapped the spare keys to the padlocks on their diaries every year, promising each other that if anything ever happened to them, the other would keep their secrets safe. At the end, Trisha had wrapped her diary up in this envelope and, without explaining what it was, had asked her mother to give it to Kate.

The Kate who had barely been able to visit as her best friend had become progressively more ill.

The Kate who hadn't known what to talk about, hadn't been able to deal with watching her friend dying.

The Kate who had done the worst thing possible, and buried her head, praying for a miracle.

Which hadn't come.

The diary had been delivered the day after Trisha had slipped away. Addressed in her weak handwriting, she must have put it in the envelope herself. Nobody but Kate knew that she'd kept a diary, but Kate was quite sure her grieving parents would have wanted to read it.

It had been years before she could look at it, to read the final entry.

It had butterflies printed on the cover, bright pink, soft green and gold, a pattern imprinted on her memory. Even before she'd had the courage to read it, she'd started seeing butterflies everywhere: in fabric prints; made of glass; dangling from a pair of earrings or on a necklace. Every time she saw one, it was as if Trisha was there, standing behind her, pulling at her elbow to find a quiet corner for a chat, just as she had in school.

They'd promised each other when they'd gone to see *Amélie* that when they got to Paris, they would put the locks from their diaries together on one of the bridges. A sign of their friendship, of their hopes for the future, a wish that their lives would flow as strongly as the river Seine itself. Trisha had become obsessed with the idea as soon as she'd read about the Pont des Arts, Love Lock Bridge, and the symbols attached to it. But Trisha was never one to run with the crowd – she'd wanted a more symbolic bridge, deciding on the pedestrian link across the Seine between the Louvre and the Musée d'Orsay. That would be their place.

Kate had kept the diary and the precious locks all these years, knowing she had to make good on her promise.

Folding back the flap of the envelope, she opened it, slipping out the small hardcovered book with its gilt-edged pages. As if she was finally releasing the butterflies, Kate could smell what had become Trisha's favourite scent, Coco Mademoiselle – amber with hints of orange.

After seeing *Amélie*, Trisha had absorbed everything French, even getting her dark hair cut short like the actress who played the lead. And Coco Mademoiselle had been released that same year.

Kate sighed. Trisha would have loved this apartment – the elegance, the view. She'd have loved the ironwork balcony, the scrolls and flourishes unfurling like a love story of their own. Kate could feel the sadness of loss welling up inside her.

When she tipped the envelope up on the bed, her own lock and the tiny keys fell out. Kate deftly unlocked Trisha's padlock, taking it off the diary and, clipping it onto her own lock, clicked it closed. Sliding the diary back inside, Kate folded the envelope again, keeping Trisha's secrets safe. She shut her eyes for a moment, seeing her friend's smiling face posing next to the movie poster for *Amélie*.

So much had happened since that day.

But being able to fulfil her pledge to Trisha made Kate feel that, at last, everything was finally going to work out.

The planning was as important as the moment itself – or moments. Many moments.

It was all about the detail. Making sure everything was right. And couldn't be traced back to him.

He grinned to himself. Finding somewhere to bring them made things so much easier. It meant that he could take his time, savour the whole process.

He couldn't take them too often, or connections could be made, but not often enough and he felt like he was going to die from the need, the ache.

After the first one – and that really had been a happy accident – he knew he'd have to do it again. How else could he get that thrill, that high?

That relief.

It brought it all back.

He should have planned the second one better: she had been more complicated, but it worked out better than he could possibly have imagined.

She'd definitely been worth all the risk – a natural beauty, unaware of her impact. And the scent on her skin had blown him away.

He'd bought her some for her birthday, had joked that

she'd better not tell anyone it was from him, that maybe it was too personal.

But Paris was a city of scent; she needed something to remember it by.

She'd worn it that night and it had tipped him over the edge. It had had to be then; he couldn't wait another minute.

But everything had gone smoothly. It always did when you had a plan, when you paid attention to the detail.

And it had set him on a path. Finding them, checking them out through social media, making sure that they were perfect for his needs.

From out of town. Tick.

New to Paris. Tick.

Estranged from their families. Tick, tick.

Invisible people – waitresses, baristas, night workers. Tick.

Red hair. Tick, tick, tick.

He took a sharp intake of breath and licked his lips, suddenly dry.

Red hair.

And the scent of the perfume on their skin.

He closed his eyes, reaching for the silk scarf, breathing in the fragrance still clinging to it. He could still smell her, despite the years. He breathed in again, the scent conjuring up the memories so strongly he could almost touch them.

He'd set himself rules. Tried his best to stick to them. There had been moments in the past when he'd slipped, when he couldn't help himself, when things had got messy, but everything had been OK.

He should have stuck to the rules this time. He breathed in the scent again, trying to calm himself, but he could feel the anger swirling inside him like smoke.

The last one had been stupid, not properly researched, but he hadn't been able to help himself. All the preparation, all the waiting, was killing him with anticipation, and then there she was, as if she'd walked right into his story.

She hadn't ticked all the boxes. He should have waited. When he stuck to the plan there were no mistakes.

But it would all be fine – he'd been careful.

The next one was so much more complicated, so much more exciting. He could barely stand the thought of her; the anticipation was intoxicating, painful. And he could keep this one again.

It had been so hard to let the other go, but it was the right thing to do. He needed to make space.

And that made the next one all the more worth it.

Chapter 11

'GOOD AFTERNOON, MR Langton, welcome back to Le Meurice. A pleasure to see you again so soon.'

Daniel rolled his eyes to the receptionist, who looked faintly amused. 'I know. I don't know why I went back to London, I should have just stayed.'

He picked up the proffered pen to sign. He always booked the same room, spacious and airy, exactly what he needed after the steel and glass of his office in Canary Wharf. Not that he'd spent a lot of time in his office in the past few weeks. When his aunt had rung with news of the auction, explaining that she needed him to view the bottles before the sale took place on Wednesday morning, he'd rubbed his hand over his eyes. It had been easier to agree than argue.

Daniel suddenly realised he hadn't caught whatever the receptionist had said. Seamlessly, he repeated himself.

'Your guest telephoned to say he would be a little delayed. He hopes to be here before six and will meet you in the bar.'

Daniel smiled in acknowledgement and laid down the pen, only half concentrating, his mind back on the woman on the train. Then, realising the receptionist was looking at him expectantly, he passed the form back across the counter.

'That's perfect. I've some work to do. Can you reserve my table?'

The receptionist inclined his head. 'Of course. We'll bring your bag up now.'

Daniel never ceased to be impressed by the staff here. He didn't often meet people when he was away, but at Le Meurice the staff made the effort to get to know their guests and their habits. It was why he favoured staying in the same place whenever possible. He'd had quite enough of travelling rough during his career. Life was short and he'd managed to survive – rather unexpectedly – this far. He intended to enjoy what was left of it.

Upstairs, as Daniel pushed open the door to his fourth-floor suite, he could already smell the fresh gardenias that he knew would be in the room. Somehow the valet had made it upstairs before him, and his leather bag was already beside the bed.

Daniel leaned his walking stick against the arm of the cream brocade armchair that faced the coffee table and, slipping off his coat, threw it over the back of the chair. Going straight to the coffee maker, he switched it on, giving it a moment to heat.

Glancing out of the French window, he could see clouds were gathering outside, the sky grey. He cracked open the door, tempted to step out onto the balcony, but instead breathed in the city, the distinct sounds of French sirens blending with birdsong, and – he smiled – the quack of a passing duck. The trees below in the elegantly formal Jardin des Tuileries were bare, their tops perfectly trimmed, the sandy paths between them busy with tourists and joggers. Always joggers – a way to keep fit he could never understand. To his left, the distinctive shape of the Louvre rose above the skyline; on his right, the Eiffel Tower.

Christie's was a twenty-five minute walk from here, and he'd made an appointment for first thing in the morning. The sale was at ten o'clock and the perfume bottles were early lots. With a bit of luck, he'd have everything settled by 10.30. Calling his aunt would probably take longer, but then he could get on with the rest of his business in Paris.

Closing the balcony door, he dropped a pod into the coffee machine, turning over the waiting porcelain cup and slipping it into position. Paris wasn't Paris without the rich aroma of hot coffee in the air.

As he waited for the machine, he thought again of the woman on the train: Kate Wilde, with the incredible red hair. He'd found her quite fascinating.

He'd put his guard up all those years ago and had never got close to anyone since. Somehow he'd felt that she was the same – guarded, the shutters closed. But by the time they'd got off the train, there had been a crack where the light was trying to struggle in. Had she felt the same? He didn't know; she was a puzzle.

Her very expensive silk dress hadn't been a fit at all with her much older coat. And the text she had received had rattled her badly, fear hovering behind her eyes like a shadow. She'd hidden it well, as if she was used to masking her emotions, chatting easily, her reaction manifest only in a slight tautness to her jaw, the tremble in her hand. She'd only told him her full name as they disembarked, and he'd shown her to the taxi rank outside the station.

Perhaps the text she'd received related to the indent on her left hand, which suggested that for some years she'd worn a wedding ring. He wasn't sure, but one thing he was sure of – the little finger on her right hand had obviously been broken at some point and not properly strapped. It had set slightly awkwardly, betraying the type of break that he'd only seen in quite different circumstances, and which he didn't associate with an accident.

But it hadn't been his place to pry. He'd learned early on in his career that everyone has something to hide. It had been his job to discover what that might be, first through covert military surveillance of insurgent groups, and later through diplomatic channels, mingling with ambassadors and academics, looking for weak links, gathering information in a myriad of ways. His curiosity hadn't done him much good in the end, but that didn't stop him wondering about Kate Wilde. She'd struck him as a woman who had secrets.

Chapter 12

SMILING TO HERSELF, Kate hung up the last of the beautiful clothes Orna had lent her in the wardrobe. Orna was an expert at packing; she'd managed to get five days' worth of clothes into a cabin case and still left Kate enough room for souvenirs.

Kate picked her washbag up from the bed and popped it into the bathroom, on the shelf behind the basin. Despite missing Hanna, this trip felt like a bookend, exactly the type that Trisha would have adored: an ornate antique one that held the last few stressful years of her life neatly back, allowing space for the new. Trisha had been all about new starts, about adventure and finding true love.

New experiences, new memories.

Kate knew she would be more than open to them, once she had fulfilled her promise. First she needed to get her bearings, find Trisha's bridge, and then she'd leave the locks. Carrying them with her until then would be like showing Trisha the city, discovering Paris with her.

And, as Orna had said, it would be good for Hanna to have a week with her aunt. She was almost ten now, would be wanting a mobile phone soon, needed space to be her own person. Now Erik was safely at a court order's length away, that could happen.

At least, Kate hoped he still was.

Erik had known exactly how that text would impact her. He didn't do anything without a plan, one that was designed to destabilise her, to make her doubt her own mind.

But Kate knew she was a different person now. Therapy and rigorous self-defence lessons had helped her get her life back on track. Erik had been a bend in the river, rapids she'd had to navigate, but she'd survived. And she wasn't going to let anything jeopardise things now.

Her phone let out a string of pings as she went back into the *salon*, marvelling again at its lofty moulded ceiling. Part of her still couldn't believe that all of this was real. Looking at her phone, she could see Orna had sent her pictures of Hanna pointing at the lions in Trafalgar Square, and part of her heart lifted at her daughter's huge grin. She was already having lots of fun.

The keys Céline had given her were on the dining table beside a brochure from Le Studio des Parfums, where the course was running. She wanted to look at it now, but her stomach was reminding her that she needed to think about dinner. Kate wasn't sure she was ready to go out and eat dinner on her own quite yet, but she'd seen a little supermarket from the taxi, where she could get some basics and something for this evening.

Outside the apartment building, she pulled up the collar of her coat. Le Rue des Corbeaux was a narrow cobbled street with a strange mix of boutiques and a tiny café with a grumpy-looking art nouveau black cat painted on the wall beside the door – perfect for breakfast.

In the supermarket, browsing the unfamiliar shelves packed full of exciting products, Kate found herself wishing Hanna was with her, and felt a tug at her heart. There was a whole display of Valentine's chocolates and boxes of pretty pink macaroons that Kate knew Hanna would love. She picked one up as she hurried to pay for her groceries. Walking briskly back to the apartment, Kate smiled to herself. Valentine's Day had lost its charm for her a long time ago, but the macaroons would be a lovely surprise and would fit easily into her case.

Inside her building, Kate put her bags down on the doorstep to find the keys. It took her a moment to get the hang of the locks, but as she pushed the door, she jumped back, her hand to her chest as a dark grey shape shot out and down the stairs.

A cat? Where had that come from? Surely she would have noticed it if it had been asleep somewhere inside – she thought she'd looked around the whole apartment.

Kate caught her breath and, picking up her bags, cautiously opened the door, glancing over her shoulder to the top of the stairs. *How on earth had she not noticed a cat?*

Pushing the door closed, Kate leaned back on it, pausing for a moment to let her heart slow. No matter how much therapy she had, anything sudden – like the cat appearing – still sent her flight or fight response into overdrive, all her senses on high alert.

She closed her eyes. *This was Paris. She was safe. It had just been a cat.*

As her heart settled back to normal, Kate realised she could smell something different: a waft of something new in the hallway. She opened her eyes, frowning. It was hazy, like a memory, sandalwood perhaps, something musky and masculine blending with the lavender she'd smelled before. *What on earth was that?*

Chapter 13

AGATHE PACED UP and down the hallway in the apartment as she tried to call her uncle again. She'd been doing circuits of the bedroom, coming out here to the front door and back again. *Why wasn't he answering?* He was going to see about fifty missed calls when he finally picked up his mobile. She'd tried the direct line to the *Paris Heure* reception, but they'd said he was in a meeting.

What could he be doing that was more important than this?

The hairdresser's words had been going around her head since Agathe had spoken to her, making her feel worse the more she thought about them.

This was all so surreal. On Wednesday morning they'd been talking about Agathe's essay on Charles Garnier, about the Opéra and its secret entrance. They'd talked about the new property Sandrine was trying to sell – a magnificent penthouse – and the commission she'd get if it moved.

Suddenly she heard her uncle's voice in her ear.

'Agathe, what's happened?' Agathe jumped as he continued. 'I'm sorry, I was talking to … people.'

Heading into their small living room, Agathe sat on the edge of the sofa, her legs suddenly weak.

'I called.' Her voice came out as a croak. She cleared her throat. 'I called Sandrine's hairdresser. I remembered that she went there on Wednesday evening, we'd talked about it, but … Anyway, she had her hair dyed. She had her hair dyed red.'

Agathe could barely get the words out. There was silence at the other end, then her uncle started speaking as if he was half talking to himself. It sounded as if he was pacing around his office.

'This could be unrelated. There could be a completely innocent explanation.'

'I know. But it … What do we do now? Who do we tell?' She pushed her hair out of her face, trying to keep as calm as she could. But her heart was beating like a train going over the tracks, the tension in her head and neck like a vice.

'I'm going to call Travère. Can you give me the reference number they gave you when you reported her missing?'

Agathe jumped up and, grabbing her bag off the easy chair, started to dig through it for her purse.

'I can't ... Just a minute.' The number the officer had given her was scribbled on a piece of paper that she'd stuck in with her credit cards. But searching with one hand ... She turned the bag upside down and tipped everything onto the seat of the chair. There was all sorts of rubbish in the bottom, but her purse landed on the top. Flipping open the popper, she found the number and reeled it off to him.

'Right, I'm calling Travère. I'll get him to escalate this right now. His people will call for a statement from you, but they'll go and talk to the people in her office and pull the CCTV from the area around that place she was showing.'

He sounded as if he was ticking off the list of things they should be doing.

'Won't they have done that already?'

He drew in a breath. 'I doubt it, not for a missing person. Like they said to you, she's an adult.' He paused. 'Let's hope they can find something.'

Agathe didn't know what to say. But it didn't stop him. 'I'm going to call Max, too, and fill him in. He'll need a photo of her. We need Travère to get his investigation in gear.' He paused for a moment. 'Did you talk to her parents?'

'Not yet, I don't have their details …'

'I'll get Travère to check.'

'What do I do?' Agathe's voice cracked as she spoke.

'Go to your lectures, do what you normally do. Sitting at home worrying isn't going to help her.'

'OK, OK, and you'll talk to *La Crim*?'

'Right now. And try to sleep, Ag. She'll need you to be strong for her.'

With that, he hung up. Agathe looked at the phone in her hand. *Whatever had happened to the other women couldn't have happened to Sandrine.* It couldn't. It was just a coincidence – *it had to be.*

Chapter 14

DANIEL CAME IN through the revolving door of Le Meurice into the mirrored hallway with its gleaming black, white and gold décor, and shook the rain from his shoulders. Before he could speak, the uniformed doorman met his eye, inclining his head in the direction of Restaurant Le Dalí, and beyond it, the bar.

'Your guest's just arrived, Monsieur Langton.'

'Great stuff, Gilles, thank you.' Even speaking fluent French, Daniel knew he sounded as English as the King.

Daniel handed Gilles his stick so he could unwrap his scarf and slip off his overcoat, the doorman reaching for each item automatically.

'I'll get these dried and sent up for you.'

Walking through the restaurant with its dramatic painted ceiling, Daniel could see that Bar 228 was relatively quiet. A grand piano was positioned between the two rooms, linking them, the pianist in the middle of something classical.

Maxim Verdier was at Daniel's preferred table at the back corner of the bar. He was slouching in one of the deep brown leather button-back chairs, a glass of Heineken already in front of him on the small round table, a silver stand holding bowls of olives and cashew nuts in the centre. It was the one table from which you could see the whole bar. A couple were in one corner, their heads close together; three women with similar dark bobbed haircuts, were drinking Martini cocktails at another table. Amused, Daniel noted the little folding stools beside the womens' chairs that the staff had provided for their handbags. The stools tickled him every time he saw them. But he supposed if you'd paid $50,000 for a Birkin bag, you'd be reluctant to put it on the floor, even one this plushly carpeted.

Bar 228 was dark and atmospheric after the brilliance of the hall and the café au lait shades of the restaurant. Table lamps threw soft light on to a huge classical mural of a landscape on one wall.

Maxim stood as he saw Daniel approach, pulling him into a bear hug. 'How are you, me old mucker?' His attempt at London slang was completely lost in his heavy accent. Daniel laughed, shaking his head.

'Let's stick to French, Max, your English hasn't got any better – or your haircut.'

Maxim looked as if he was wearing the same faded jeans and scuffed tan cowboy boots that he'd worn every day when they'd been in university; his heavy leather jacket was slung over the back of the chair. His hair was even longer, though, streaked with blond – a sort of 'surfer chic' look, not that Maxim had ever been surfing, as far as Daniel knew.

Maxim punched him on the shoulder. 'Why didn't you call me the last time you were here?'

Sitting down, Daniel shrugged. 'It was a flying visit. How are you doing? What are tomorrow's headlines?'

Maxim shrugged. 'Let's not talk about work.' Daniel raised an eyebrow, surprised. Maxim was usually full of whatever story he was working on.

Before Daniel could comment, a dark-suited waiter appeared with his Delamain XO.

Maxim rolled his eyes. 'I see you haven't changed.'

Daniel shook his head. 'I know what I like. Same vintage, same hotel. I'm never disappointed.'

'Same seat on the plane.' Maxim shook his head as he picked up his beer.

'And the train. The Eurostar is so much easier than flying.'

'You're hilarious.' His face lit by the flicker of a delicately scented candle, Maxim picked up an olive and tossed it in the air, catching it in his mouth.

The first time Daniel laid eyes on Maxim at a university social event at the Rowing-Club Paris, he'd been tossing olives. A keen rower, Daniel had been in Paris as an Erasmus student, spending a year abroad. Maxim, as natural an exhibitionist as he was an athlete, loved the idea of racing up the Seine. They were like two sides of a coin, Daniel quiet and studious, Maxim retaking his first year after failing every single one of his exams.

Now he chomped on the olive, spitting the stone into a folded napkin he pulled from a silver stand, as Daniel answered. 'I'm a creature of habit.'

'You were like an old man back then, too – so English, so predictable.' Maxim took a sip of his beer. 'How's the leg?'

'Best kept away from the British weather. I need more exercise. I'm thinking of getting back on the water.'

'Come down with me. We're rowing against Toulouse next week.'

'I was never a good spectator.'

Maxim chuckled. 'Too competitive. But you're nothing compared to Lucien. Remember when he lost it with that cox from Lyon?'

'Got him suspended, though, didn't it?' Daniel said it with satisfaction.

'Sorry, I shouldn't have brought him up.' Maxim paused. 'So I hear you're here for an auction? She messaged me, your aunt did, a couple of months ago.'

Daniel rolled his eyes. He scooped out a handful of cashew nuts with the spoon in the bowl. *What the hell had his aunt been up to? Now she had his niece's wedding in her sights, she must be moving on to meddle in his life.*

'Let me guess ... Facebook?' Daniel threw the nuts into his mouth, his watch catching the light from the candle.

Maxim nodded. 'She PM'd, wanted me to take you out on the town, I think.'

Daniel reached for his glass. 'My aunt's determined to fix my love life.'

Maxim looked at him. 'Did you ever hear anything from Meredith?'

Daniel swirled the amber liquid around his glass. 'No. Nothing at all, and I'm not sure I want to, in all honesty. Meredith's probably married now, with 2.4 children and a summer house in the Hamptons.' Daniel could feel the hurt beginning to swirl inside him. He placed his glass carefully on the table, deliberately focusing on the patina on its black leather-covered surface. *He couldn't let it overwhelm him, not now.*

Meredith McCarthy had been the love of his life, and he'd never been able to find another woman like her, never had that connection with anyone else.

Things could have been completely different if Lucien hadn't set his sights on her. But maybe Daniel was clutching at any idea that made her disappearance less about himself – looking to blame someone else.

Daniel cleared his throat. 'I've thought about getting in touch with her aunt and uncle in Phoenix again, but that text she sent them saying she'd decided to go travelling was very clear – she didn't want anyone in Paris to know where she was. Which fairly obviously meant me.'

Daniel swirled his cognac around his glass again as Maxim shook his head, his face indicating that he was looking for something consolatory to say. Daniel glanced across at him. He'd been so hurt back then that, despite their bond, he hadn't even been able to talk to Maxim about it. He'd pulled down the shutters instead and tried to focus on building a different life.

Daniel cleared his throat. 'I wrote her a letter when I got back to London – I don't think I told you that. I posted it to their address for when she came back, but I never heard anything.' He raised his eyebrows in resignation. He'd sent her a Christmas card, too, but Maxim didn't need to know that. He'd never understand why it had happened, but Meredith's silence had made it very clear that she'd moved on.

Chapter 15

STILL PUZZLED, KATE looked quickly into the *salon* before she took her groceries to the kitchen. *Where had the cat come from? And what was that masculine smell?* Something she'd missed earlier? But she'd noticed the lavender and beeswax ... why not that? Had someone – a man – been inside the apartment, or had the smell been here all along, and she was only noticing it now her senses were in overdrive?

Feeling a bit spooked, Kate went into the kitchen and unpacked her bags, opening the fridge to find a bottle of white wine chilling in the door, a tiny patisserie box wrapped with golden ribbon on the middle shelf. She pulled it out. Inside was a cheesecake, a beautiful creation in layers topped with a swirl of cream and raspberries.

Her hosts had thought of everything.

She opened the box and quickly took a photo for Hanna.

Trying to push the cat and the unexpected smells from her mind, Kate finished putting away her purchases. She filled the kettle and flipped it on as she took some more pictures – the kitchen and, swinging around, the *salon* through the open double doors. Kate quickly sent the photos to Orna along with the pictures she'd taken in the supermarket. *More to come.*

Her mind half on the kettle, she dipped into the bedroom to take her coat off, stopping in surprise as she draped it over the end of the bed.

The bathroom door was ajar.

Had someone been in there? Maybe the cat had been asleep on the towels and she hadn't seen it? Kate tentatively pushed the door of the bathroom wider open.

She looked inside. It was a sizable bathroom, a huge walk-in shower at the end of the bath.

There was a table against one wall, with towels and a bathrobe folded onto it, but there wasn't any sign of an indent from a sleeping cat. Turning, she glanced at the sink. At the back of the deep windowsill behind her washbag was a pair of what appeared to be very expensive glass bottles. She'd only slipped inside the bathroom earlier to put her washbag down, but she couldn't remember them being there then.

She picked one up. *Collection Belle de Nuit Savon Liquide* – liquid soap; was that a body wash? The other was body lotion: *Lait Sérum pour Corps, Mains et Décolleté.* Both smelled gorgeous. Had she missed them before? She must have done. *Belle de Nuit* – the beauty of the night. Even with her rudimentary French, she could translate that.

Her mind on the bottles in the bathroom, Kate went back to the kitchen and popped one of the herbal tea bags she'd brought with her into a mug, the aroma of lemon and ginger rising as she filled it with steaming water. Her tea in her hand, Kate went through to the *salon*, flicking a switch and turning on the soft glow of the lamps.

Still unsettled, for a moment she felt as if she had stepped back in time: could hear the laughter caught in the corners of the room, trapped behind the drapes.

Heading for the sofa, she looked at the coffee table and froze for a moment. She was sure the bowl of hydrangeas had been in the centre earlier. Now they seemed to be slightly to one end and … the brochure about the perfume course was next to them, on top of the file with the apartment information in it. That had been on the dining table, with the apartment keys. *Hadn't it?*

Her heart fluttering, Kate tried to find a rational explanation. *There must be a cleaner Céline hadn't mentioned.* Someone who had come in when she'd popped to the shops to make sure she had everything ... and the cat had followed them in and got trapped inside.

But the apartment hardly needed cleaning – it was spotless. *And how had they known she'd gone out?* Kate shivered. Perhaps she should say something to Céline, assure her that she didn't need housekeeping while she was here. Kate bit her lip and scanned the room again. Had anything else been moved?

It was getting late, the buildings opposite lit to the evening, hazy figures passing across the netted windows. The closeness of the buildings across the street suddenly made her feel very exposed. If she could see into those buildings so clearly, there was no question that someone could see straight into hers.

The sound of the heavy front door slamming made Kate jump. She went over to the window, catching sight of a man immediately below her, crossing the street. She couldn't see his face, but he was wearing a short dark wool coat, was winding a scarf around his neck as he strode down the road. Bad temper rose off him like vapour.

Chapter 16

AGATHE ARRIVED AT the café, breathless. The night before, when she'd got off the phone to her uncle, she'd stayed up until she couldn't stay awake any longer, hoping to catch Roland when he came home. She'd had to haul herself out of bed this morning, running late before she'd even left the apartment.

There was still no sign of Sandrine.

But then, there had been no sign of Roland either. She'd decided to leave a hurriedly scribbled note under his door. That had made her realise she hadn't actually seen him since Wednesday either, but she hadn't even questioned that he was safe and well. Roland was very different from Sandrine.

Her conversation with the hairdresser had kept coming back to her as she'd tossed and turned. And her conversation with her uncle.

It *had* to be a coincidence. Sandrine had only just had her hair done; how could she possibly have become the victim of a crazed serial killer in a few short hours? Maybe she'd told Roland she was going away, and everything was fine.

Maybe.

Grabbing one of the green electric scooters from the first stand she'd come to, Agathe had zipped along the broad empty pavement beside the Seine, the waters a dull grey green this morning. Crossing to the right bank beside Notre-Dame, encased in scaffolding so complex that it looked like lace, she focused on avoiding the pedestrians hurrying to work.

Café Rodolphe was in Le Marais, a thirty-minute walk from their apartment on the left bank of the Seine in Saint-Germain-des-Prés, and in totally the opposite direction to her university, the Sorbonne. Going into work was the best thing she could do right now. Her uncle was right – if she stayed at home, she knew she'd go mad.

Wiggling through the winding streets, Agathe had hopped off the scooter and leaned it against the wall of the café, trying to look calm and unstressed as she unlocked the door. Oumar would be in later – Wednesday was his late morning and her day to open up. As soon as he got here, she'd head into university and get back into the library. She needed to check over the reports she'd found in more detail. She needed to feel as if she was *doing* something.

Their regulars began to arrive as Agathe grabbed a sunny yellow apron from the pile under the counter, a black cat embroidered on its pocket. Flying through the queue, she barely had time to think. It was only when there was a break in the flow of customers that she leaned on the counter top and closed her eyes, centring herself.

'*Bonjour.*' Agathe's eyes flew open at a woman's voice. Straightening, she smiled.

'*Bonjour. Qu'est-ce que je vous sers?*'

'*Un chocolat chaud et un croissant, s'il vous plait.*' The woman said it slowly, tucking her red hair behind her ear nervously as she spoke. She was wearing a navy coat, belted firmly at the waist, and dark green leather gloves.

'*En porte?*'

'I'm sorry?'

Agathe grinned, switching to English 'To have here or take away?'

'Oh, I see, to have here please.'

'Sit down, I'll be with you in a second. Are you Irish?'

The woman looked surprised. 'Is it that obvious?'

Agathe hid a smile, spooning chocolate powder into a mug and then pouring milk into a stainless-steel jug, slipping it beneath the steam spout. 'My dad's Irish. He lives in New York now, but he's never lost his accent.'

'I've been living in London for years, and I've still got mine.' The woman paused, meeting Agathe's eye with a smile. 'At least you didn't think I was English.'

'There is that.' Agathe found herself warming to the woman. She looked as if she was in her mid-thirties, and her thick red hair seemed to be about twenty different shades, blending to one incredible colour. Right now, talking to someone new took her mind off panicking about Sandrine.

'Sit down and I'll bring this over.' Agathe poured the hot milk into the mug and slipped it onto a tray, picking up her tongs and reaching into the display for a croissant. Coming around the counter, she slid the tray onto the woman's table.

'Are you on holiday?'

The woman picked up the paper napkin from beside the hot chocolate and spread it over her knee. 'Sort of. I won a prize on Facebook – a perfume course and an apartment for the week.'

'Wow, nice.' Agathe leaned back on the counter and crossed her arms. 'I've always been intrigued by perfume

– you hear stories of secret recipes and marketing wars. Where's the course?' She watched as the woman took a sip of her hot chocolate.

'Goodness, that's so creamy. My daughter would love it.' The woman took another sip. 'Near here, I think. But it's in the afternoons, so I've got the mornings free to sightsee. The prize included tickets to the Louvre this morning and the Eiffel Tower tomorrow – but there seems to be a time on them.'

'They get so busy, it helps control the crowds, even in February.'

The woman glanced out the door at the encroaching grey. 'I think it's going to lash rain, so it looks like the Louvre is a good plan. I'm Kate.'

'Agathe.' She smiled. 'The Louvre is huge, there's loads to see.'

Kate looked at her curiously. 'Are you French – or Irish?'

'I'm French, technically, but I have both passports. My mum's French, she lives near Cannes. I learned English from my dad so I think I have a bit of an Irish accent.'

'You do, it's a lovely blend. What keeps you in Paris instead of Cannes or New York? They sound very glamourous.'

Agathe shifted against the counter. 'University. A master's in Architecture and Art History at the Sorbonne. I do a couple of mornings a week here, and a day at the weekend. Helps with the bills.'

Kate looked sympathetic, as if she understood the problems of being a poor student. 'Is it terribly expensive to live here?'

Agathe shrugged. 'Can be. I'm lucky, my friend's parents have an apartment. I share it with him and another girl.' Agathe faltered for a moment. She felt Kate looking at her expectantly. 'Her name's Sandrine but … she's disappeared.' She said it lightly but could feel herself getting emotional again. She cleared her throat. 'I'm really worried about her, actually.'

The building was unnaturally silent, the tang of bleach catching in his throat as he'd pushed open the door to the master bathroom. The penthouse was sprawled across the whole top floor, empty, pristine. Perfect. Or so he'd hoped.

Holding his breath, he'd glanced around. In the cold morning light it was easier to check that he'd cleaned up thoroughly. He'd been sure that he'd done a proper job, but he'd needed to check again, the thought that he might have missed even the smallest speck of blood or body fluid like an itch he needed to scratch. A compulsion.

But this one had been simpler than the others. For all the wrong reasons.

As soon as he'd realised that she was a fake, an imposter, everything had changed. The anticipation, the excitement had soured like old milk.

He'd known as soon as the perfume mist had enveloped her that he'd made a mistake. The fragrance was completely different on her skin – its ability to conjure the memories, lost. Like a pianist hitting a discordant note at the end of a symphony, he'd fallen back, shocked, confused.

And then it had slowly become clear what had happened. He hadn't followed the rules.

There was little point in the process, in his rituals, in taking his time to get to that moment of ecstasy.

He could feel the crashing feeling of disappointment again as he thought about it now – about the moment he'd realised. Like the sound of glass breaking. But it had been too late to change things by then; he was already committed.

It was a big bathroom by anyone's standards. The huge square shower head hung over a bath big enough to get three people in. Plenty of space to do what he needed. Gleaming white tiles on the walls and floor contrasted with a black ceramic sink, its sharp corners mirroring square taps.

He'd left the blind up, the glass in the slim window dappled. He looked around again. In his memory, he could see her lying in the bath, her skin as pale as the porcelain, her hair tangled around her, her mouth, red, hanging open in a silent scream.

He should have stuck to the rules. They'd never failed him. Perhaps he was getting too confident, taking bigger risks with each one.

His mouth was bitter at the memory. It was just as well it had been raining so hard. There had been no one about to see her enter the property. Or to leave it.

Now he just had to be sure that he'd removed every trace of her.

He was good at cleaning up; he had a system.

And he'd cleaned this one until nothing remained.

Chapter 17

'**PERHAPS YOUR FRIEND'S** just gone to visit friends, or her family?' Sitting in the café, Kate nursed her hot chocolate and tried to sound confident. But she could see Agathe was deeply worried.

Why did women always try and put a brave face on situations like this, when they all knew that it was so easy for something awful to have happened? Kate pushed the thought from her head; they had to be positive.

Kate could hear the echo of that same positivity in her words to Hanna, every time she'd had an argument with Erik.

It's fine, everything's fine. I got my finger caught in the drawer, how silly was that?

Daddy just got a bit cross, he didn't mean to shout.

I must have brought the wrong keys, let's call Daddy to let us in.

Agathe didn't respond immediately, and Kate could see a shadow crossing her face. Even though she didn't know this girl, Kate knew what loss felt like, and part of her wanted to reach out and hug her.

Agathe cleared her throat. 'I've checked with all her friends and no one's seen her.'

'Has she done anything like this before?'

Agathe shook her head, her arms still folded tight across the bib of her apron, the stylised black cat embroidered on its pocket regarding Kate with interest. She glanced at Kate as she replied.

'She loves a party, but she always turns up the next day. I keep thinking her phone could have run down, but you can charge a phone anywhere these days. She hasn't answered any of my messages.'

Agathe bit her lip and glanced out of the café door, as if she was hoping to see Sandrine nonchalantly heading down the street, a takeaway coffee in her hand. 'Oumar said she dropped in here on Thursday morning. She was on her way to work, he thinks. He can't remember, he had a queue, was in the middle of serving someone.'

Kate slowly tore off the end of her croissant, thinking before she spoke.

'Perhaps there's been an emergency, and she's gone home but hasn't had a chance to call?' She tried to sound hopeful, but she had a feeling Agathe wasn't telling her everything.

Agathe shrugged again and tucked a strand of bleached hair behind her ear.

'But your gut is telling you differently?'

Agathe nodded, sighing loudly.

Kate could see the fear on her face. 'She didn't mention that there was anyone in her life who might be ...' It took her a moment to find the word. 'Difficult?'

It didn't say what she meant, but Agathe seemed to understand. *Someone at work who made her uncomfortable; an abusive boyfriend; someone who couldn't take no for an answer.*

Did men have these issues to deal with as part of life? Kate doubted it. Often, the problem was admitting it. Not only to others, but to yourself. It had taken Kate far too long to come to terms with the fact that the man she'd loved, and had thought loved her, had actually loved the idea of controlling her more.

'And there isn't anyone in her life that you've had a funny feeling about?' Kate had learned – the hard way – that other women had an acute radar for trouble, a sixth sense that recognised danger. But sometimes they didn't feel that they could speak out. And even if they did, sometimes the women at risk couldn't hear them. Orna had tried to tell her about Erik, but Kate had been convinced she was wrong, jealous or ... Kate didn't even know what.

And admitting you were wrong was hard. Kate had only realised that Orna was right when Erik had hit her with the frying pan. Before, it had always been his fists – usually somewhere no one would see – but that Sunday morning, when she'd broken the yolk of his fried egg and the whole lot had gone across the kitchen, she'd realised she'd got it wrong.

Interrupting her thoughts, Agathe cleared her throat. 'Not that I know of. Sandrine's one of those people who is just ... well, happy. She hasn't had creepy boyfriends or anything as far as I know.'

Picking up her hot chocolate, Kate nursed the warm mug in her hands. She'd tried to bury the memories of that Sunday morning, but whenever they reoccurred, she always felt unmoored, everything rolling around inside her like a boat on stormy water. It took her a moment to come back to the café, to Agathe.

'Have you been to the police to see what they suggest?'

Before Agathe could answer, Kate's phone pinged with a text, but it seemed rude to look at it now.

Agathe uncrossed her arms and leaned back on the counter, some of her tension gone. 'Yes, my uncle said to call them, but they didn't seem to be very interested originally.' She paused, as if she was about to say something more but was stopping herself. 'I mean, people don't just disappear – she must be somewhere.' She took a ragged breath. 'But that's enough of my problems. You're here on holiday, to enjoy Paris. Is your daughter with you?'

Kate shook her head. 'She's staying with my sister.' She half laughed. 'It's the first time I've ever been away from her, and I'm finding it harder than I expected. She's having a fabulous time, though, my sister's spoiling her rotten. I'd say she's barely given me a thought.'

Agathe grinned. 'That's children for you.' Kate's phone pinged again. 'You'd better check that, it could be her.'

Reaching for her bag, Kate smiled as she unzipped it and pulled out the phone, waking it up.

It was a WhatsApp message.

But it wasn't from Orna.

The gasp slipped out before Kate realised she'd made a noise.

'What's happened? Is she OK, your daughter?' Agathe stepped forward, crossing the narrow passage between the counter and the bench seat, her hand going automatically to Kate's shoulder as if she'd known her for years. Kate realised she must have paled.

'I'm ... er ... It's ...' Gripping the phone in her hand, Kate closed her eyes, trying to find the words. *How did he do this to her? How did he send her spinning back to her old self – the self who had had to curl up and cover her head just to survive?*

Agathe sat down beside her, rubbing her arm. 'What's wrong? You look like you've seen a ghost.'

Kate took in a sharp breath, not sure even sure how she could begin to explain. She turned her phone to Agathe. The messages were photos. Two versions of the same picture – a man standing below the arch of the Arc de Triomphe.

'It's my ex. He's here, in Paris.' Kate fought to keep her voice level. 'There's ... He's quite ...' *What should she say? Dangerous? Violent? Utterly unpredictable?* 'We have a restraining order. He wants to see my daughter, he must think she's with me.' She paused. 'I don't even know how he knows I'm here.'

Chapter 18

AGATHE SLID ALONG the bench seat, closer to Kate, so she could see the image on her phone more clearly.

'Why wouldn't he just call?'

Kate drew in a shaky breath. 'He texted, but he knows he can only see Hanna on supervised visits. I'm guessing, but I think he's working up to asking to see her on his own.'

Agathe pursed her lips. 'Trying to intimidate you, you mean. That's not very logical, is it?'

When Kate had opened the message and looked at the picture, she had blanched, and now her hand was shaking.

'Honestly, nothing he does is logical. He only ever sees one way to do things, and it's often not the same as everyone else's. He gets an idea fixed in his head, his perfect version of a solution for whatever his problem is, and he can't get away from it. It's like he has tunnel vision.'

Agathe took another look at the photo. 'Perhaps he isn't here at all, but he just wants you to think he is. The sky is clear there. It hasn't been sunny in the last few days – a week, at least. Either it was taken a few days ago or he's photoshopped it or something.' Agathe paused. 'See if you can open the photo to see the location information or the date it was taken.'

Kate looked at the phone in her hand blankly. 'How do I do that? Can you?'

Taking the phone, Agathe opened the photo. 'No location. He must have it switched off. But it definitely wasn't taken today.' Agathe looked out of the door. It was starting to spit rain.

Kate nodded slowly. 'He used to work in Paris, years ago, but I didn't think he was here now. He travels a lot. I supposed … Oh God, why's he here? He texted yesterday to say he wants to see Hanna, but I didn't reply.'

'It looks like he's trying to frighten you. Sending this with no message, that's not normal. The best thing you can do is ignore him. You don't want to show him that he's rattled you. Can you let your lawyer know that he's been in touch like this?'

Kate glanced at her. 'I think the restraining order only applies in England. I doubt anyone can do anything about him being here.' She bit her lip. 'I'd better text my sister to let her know.'

As Kate spoke, her phone pipped again with another message and she jumped physically. She glanced quickly at Agathe and then back at the screen.

'It's my brother-in-law.' Kate trailed off, her face confused.

Agathe stood up. 'You'd better call back, something could have happened at home.' A shadow of what looked like fear crossed Kate's face. 'Go down to the back, it's more private there. I'll make you another hot chocolate, on the house.'

As Agathe went back behind the counter, Kate looked at her gratefully and, picking up her bag, headed to the stone arch at the back of the shop.

Switching the steam on, giving the machine a moment to heat, Agathe glanced down the café. She couldn't hear Kate from here – she must have gone deep into the back section, any sound absorbed by the raw limestone walls. At the very back of the café, steep steps led down to more rooms divided by arches, some of which had once connected with the other buildings on this side of the street, just like the attics above them.

One of the reasons Agathe had decided to study architecture here, and not in Dublin or New York, was her love of these Haussmann buildings. When she was seven, her dad had bought her a Lego set – he'd been Napoleon III and she'd been Georges-Eugène Haussmann, transforming the dark, winding medieval streets of the city into bright airy boulevards. They'd built the Eiffel Tower and the Palais-Royal, and when they'd walked to the park, her dad had told her stories about the buildings. She loved their order and uniformity, all with steeply sloped, four-sided roofs in distinctive pale grey slate and zinc. She'd outgrown the Lego, but not her love of architecture or history. In less than twenty years, Haussmann had built a water system, sewers and railway stations, creating one of the most beautiful cities in the world.

As Kate reappeared, her eyebrows knitted in a frown, Agathe turned to her, swinging the handle on the coffee machine and banging out the old grounds. 'Sit down. I won't be a second. You look like you need coffee this time.'

Seemingly dazed, Kate slipped back into her seat, putting her handbag down beside her.

'What did your brother-in-law say?' One eye on the coffee flow, Agathe glanced over her shoulder at Kate.

Pushing her red hair out of her face, Kate looked at her, not quite focusing, as if she was still trying to process the conversation. 'It was my sister – she's using his phone. She's lost hers, she thinks it might have been stolen in the park. My brother-in-law has another one for work.' She hesitated as she tried to explain. 'She said that after they went to the swings, Hanna told her a man was asking where her mum was. She thinks it could have been a friend of Erik's, and that maybe he took her phone. She's always losing it, though, so she didn't realise until she got home that it wasn't in her bag.' Agathe let Kate draw a breath; she looked shell-shocked as she continued. 'Hanna told this man that I was on holiday here.' Kate looked at Agathe directly, her eyes full of fear. 'I sent Orna photos of where I was staying when I first got here. They'll be on her phone still.'

Agathe picked up the coffee slowly, considering what Kate had said. Coming around the counter and slipping the mug onto the small round table, she pushed her hands into the pockets of her apron.

'Even if he had your exact address, it would be hard to track you down. The apartment buildings here have entry systems, assuming he can even work out which apartment you are in.'

'But what if someone let him in?'

Agathe thought for a moment. 'Parisians are very security conscious. They can be very hostile to strangers, so on balance I think you're probably safer here than anywhere else.' She frowned. 'And honestly, the chance of the man speaking to your daughter and the same person taking your sister's phone are slim, aren't they?'

Agathe didn't really believe it as she said it. It did seem incredibly suspicious, but perhaps Sandrine's disappearance was making her paranoid.

'Do you think so? I'm always worried I'm overreacting. I mean, like you said, this photo Erik sent wasn't taken recently, and certainly not today.' Kate ran her fingers into her hair. 'But maybe that means he's been here for longer. He has a cousin living in Paris somewhere, I think.' She screwed up her eyes. 'I can't remember, it wasn't important at the time.' *The only thing that had been important back then, was surviving.*

'It'll all be fine, really. Your daughter is safe with your sister. Focus on enjoying your time here. Don't let him spoil it.'

Chapter 19

FINISHING HER COFFEE, Kate felt calmer. Talking to Agathe had helped a lot. She picked up her bag and hooked the strap over her head decisively.

'You're right. There's not much I can do. And I can't let him ruin this trip.' Kate glanced out of the café door into the street. Despite her brave words, she still felt anxiety swirling.

But she'd regret it forever if she didn't see some of the city. And she had Trisha's lock in her bag, and a promise to fulfil. 'I'm going to walk down to the Louvre. That way, I can see the city and the river.'

'You should get there before it lashes – and you can always get the Métro back. It's a direct line from the Louvre or the Tuileries Garden to Saint-Paul, just a few stops. You should have plenty of time.'

Kate smiled genuinely. '"Lashes?" That sounds so

Irish. Thank you. And thank you for listening. I'm sorry to be so nervy—'

Agathe held up her hand to stop her apologising. 'We've all known difficult men. Enjoy the walk down beside the Seine, there's lots to see.'

Kate pulled her gloves on and moved towards the door, lifting her hand to push it open. 'I hope you find your friend.' She suddenly felt her own loss acutely. Agathe's friend's situation was different from Trisha's, but Kate knew how she must be feeling. When she'd lost Trisha, unable to accept the truth, Kate had shut everyone out who had tried to support her, but that had made it all so much worse. If Agathe was telling a total stranger about this, perhaps she didn't have anything like that support. And she'd been so lovely, Kate wanted to reciprocate. She made a quick decision. 'Will you still be working when I'm finished? I think the class runs until six.'

Agathe thought for a moment. 'I need to go to the library this afternoon, but I could meet you later? I'd love to hear about the course.'

Kate smiled warmly. Sometimes you just connected with people, as if they were on your wavelength. Part of her had always wondered whether perhaps these were people you'd been close to in a previous life. Agathe was lovely, and sensible, and although she was so much younger than Kate, she had a worldliness about her that Kate found refreshing. Before Erik, she had been outgoing, curious, and she wanted – needed – to get fully back to that.

And Agathe obviously needed someone to talk to about her friend.

Agathe went to pick up Kate's empty mug and plate. 'I can meet you here. About 6.30?' As she spoke, there was a roar that sounded like a plane landing and a low-slung, open-top sports car drew up outside the café.

'Oh, here we go.' Agathe rolled her eyes.

Kate looked out of the glazed café door as the driver checked his appearance in the rear-view mirror, running his hand through his already perfectly groomed dark hair. He was wearing Aviator sunglasses despite the gloom, and a sheepskin-lined leather flying jacket, the collar turned up. The car's paintwork was a gleaming red.

Kate looked back at Agathe, her eyebrows raised. 'He looks like he's expecting a camera crew.'

Agathe screwed up her nose. 'He probably is – he's sort of famous in Paris. He owns this incredibly hip nightclub. It's always in the press. He's got a bit of a reputation, but thankfully he's not interested in slightly bohemian – or what my mum prefers to call "scruffy" – students. I'm practically invisible.'

The man reached the door of the café as Kate put her hand on it. Graciously pulling it open for her, he bobbed his head.

'*Madame.*'

Kate glanced back at Agathe, smiling sympathetically. 'I'll see you later.' She turned back to him. '*Merci, monsieur.*'

Talking to Agathe had definitely helped, but as Kate walked towards the end of the road and the market square she'd seen on Google Maps, all she could think of were Erik's photographs. She knew she should be concentrating on her surroundings – absorbing the architecture in the elegant streets, looking at the shops – but the image of him standing beside the Arc de Triomphe was burned into her brain. Was 'triumph' supposed to be part of some sort of message?

Skirting the edge of the square, reaching the wide main road, she paused to check the map on her phone and make sure she was heading the right way. It was only a twenty-minute walk, and she had plenty of time.

The wide Rue de Rivoli in front of her was busy after the quiet side streets, the flow of traffic constant, buses and bikes on the other side of the road in their own lane, as well as several lanes of cars. According to the map on her phone, she needed to cross over and keep walking until she found the Seine.

Lost in her thoughts, Kate almost bumped into a woman with a pushchair who had stopped abruptly ahead of her. Her child had thrown a pink fluffy elephant onto the pavement. Without thinking, Kate bent to pick it up, handing it back to the mother. Smiling briefly, she hurried on, her mind going to Hanna.

Kate felt a pang of loss and loneliness as she pictured Hanna sleeping, curled up under her pink duvet, clutching her own comfort bear, her freckles picked out by the revolutions of her carousel night light, surrounded by her snow globes. The soft glow from the dancing horses bounced off the glass and created delicate rainbows on the walls of her tiny bedroom.

Would Hanna be OK with Orna? Were the messages Erik had sent a ruse to make Kate think he was here in Paris, so Orna's guard would be down and he could take Hanna? Or was he here somewhere, waiting to push her into the traffic, like he had once before, or into the Seine, so he could take custody of Hanna and have her all to himself? Kate knew it sounded dramatic, but his threat was always at the back of her mind. She glanced over her shoulder, scanning the broad pavement, looking across the road, the hairs rising on her neck as she suddenly felt as if she was being watched.

He knew following her was dangerous, but he couldn't resist.

So much planning had gone into getting her to Paris that he wanted to savour every moment.

To see her move.

To hear her voice.

To capture her on video, so he could relive these moments later.

She was more nervous than he'd expected – easily spooked. So he'd hung back so far, kept to the shadows. He was good at this, knew how to make himself invisible. Not quite as invisible as Jean-Baptiste Grenouille had been, but then, he wasn't a fictional character and he didn't need to murder virgins to make his own precious perfume. He smirked to himself; the thought always aroused him. Grenouille, the deformed grotesque Patrick Süskind had made famous in his book Perfume. *Süskind – or rather, Grenouille – had understood the allure of redheads, but of the twenty-four maidens he'd clubbed to death and shorn, only one had been flame-haired. He'd missed out there.*

He'd read the novel when he was a teenager, long before the first killing had happened, but then again afterwards.

They were different, he and Jean-Baptiste, by epoch, and birth, but there were parallels in their pursuit of a perfect scent. Perhaps he should write a book about the impact of perfume on the senses, and make his fortune.

But he didn't need money, or notoriety. He just needed that unique moment of ecstasy. To breathe in the scent on her skin.

Not long now.

Soon he'd be able to have her completely to himself.

Chapter 20

THE ARTS AND Humanities library was busy, the white strip lights reflecting off bright white shelving and desks as Agathe made her way towards a row of huge monitors. It was always busy here in the mornings, but there were a few seats free. Oumar had made her take a coffee and pastries with her when he'd arrived to take over. She knew he was worried that she wasn't eating, but she couldn't when she was worried. Agathe slipped into a seat at the end of a row, dropping her backpack to the floor, relieved to be actually doing something useful. She needed the distraction.

She logged on. The research that she'd been working on the previous day had been pulling her back since she'd woken up – her short shift in the café had been a distraction, but now she was itching to find out more. Yesterday she'd created a folder of clippings, finding and saving as many reports as she could, printing them so that she could go through them later. She'd been looking for missing women, now she could drill into their similarities – anything that they might have in common. She'd combed the local press, but then searched #missing #Paris on Instagram. The posts were more recent, and there were far more than she had expected.

Every one of the teenagers and twenty-somethings that stared back at her had a story, had people. As she'd scrolled through each one yesterday, despair had risen inside her like the tide. The only thing that was good, if that was the right word, was that there *didn't* seem to be many women with red hair. She'd only found five so far. Apparently unconnected, and all still missing.

As she'd uncovered article after article, she'd felt as if this work was important. Remembering them was important.

Now they might only be names in black and white, grainy photos underneath the headlines, but once they'd been real people with real lives, with hopes and fears and moments of joy and – this was what bothered Agathe most – moments of terror.

Had the women – those whose bodies had been found – known what was going to happen? Had their last moments been filled with darkness and fear? The thought gave Agathe a pain that stretched across her forehead. Every year, she knew, she unknowingly passed the date she was going to die – everyone did – with no idea when or how she would breathe her last. Didn't we all want to slip away in our sleep, just not wake up one day?

Beside her, an undergrad began to gather her belongings, her fine bleached braids falling over her shoulder as she bent to grab her backpack. She glanced at Agathe's screen as she shoved her notebook and iPad into the bag, looking with unveiled curiosity at the photograph of a girl in a glittery dress.

The girl glanced at her and smiled. Agathe pretended she was concentrating, at the same time feeling terrible. The girl probably just wanted to talk to someone. The first few months of university could be lonely, especially if you were the type, like Agathe, who didn't do groups, but preferred to hang out with just a few friends. Finding those friends was hard. But Agathe couldn't get into a conversation right now; she had too much on her mind.

The undergrad finished packing her belongings and Agathe softened enough to give her a grin as she pushed her chair under the desk.

Agathe clicked to the next search result and checked the date at the top of the scanned page.

16 February 2009.

Bénédicte Écuyer had been nineteen, a trainee hairdresser working at a boutique in the Passage du Havre shopping centre. She'd gone out to a club and never come home. Her friends had last seen her weaving her way towards a taxi rank.

Agathe scanned the rest of the article, reaching the description that had been issued with the appeal for sightings. And abruptly stopped reading. She bit her lip and drew in a long, shaky breath.

Red hair. Bénédicte was a redhead.

And she'd disappeared after a night out, heading for a taxi rank. Agathe stared at the screen for a moment. She'd found this article while searching for missing women. Now she searched for Bénédicte's name.

Her heart almost stopped as the search results appeared.

Bénédicte Écuyer's remains had been identified three years after she vanished, her head discovered by sewer workers in a tunnel under the city. She'd been the first one Agathe's uncle had mentioned. But now she wasn't just a statistic; she was a real person with a job and a life and …

Agathe felt vomit rising as she read back the report. Questions fought their way through her shock. *Why their heads? Was there some sort of link to the city's history? To the guillotine? Was this a punishment? Why the sewers?* Of all places. Was that what the killer thought of these women – that they were only fit for the sewers?

Agathe clicked back through the open tabs across the top of the screen – the other missing redheads – and hit the print button. She needed to read each of these reports properly, and look for more connections between these girls.

Chapter 21

AS KATE HEADED down towards the river, a chill wind was starting to play around her knees. Her arms folded tightly, as much against the cold as to keep her emotions strapped in, she paused as the tiny side road she'd been following opened up into another broad multi-lane road. On the other side, divided from the pavement by a wall, the Seine cut through the city like an open wound.

Following the indicator on her phone, as she moved away from the river, the buildings on both sides felt too grand to be in the centre of a city. But that seemed to be the essence of Paris, its history a bold presence at every turn.

She walked on until, looking up, Kate realised she had reached the entrance to the museum, huge gold letters etched into the stone above stern-looking black iron gates, topped with more gold. Three French flags fluttered above the words Musée du Louvre.

To each side of the double gates were pedestrian entrances, gates standing open, a constant flow of tourists coming in and out. Passing through, Kate found herself in a huge arched passageway, cathedral-like in its proportions, thronged with people. What looked like groups or tour parties were having their tickets checked in roped-off sections. Over their heads, between pillars as big as the trunks of ancient oaks, Kate could see brightly lit windows overlooking the museum itself and the classical white marble statues she'd been looking forward to seeing.

At the end of the passage, the famous glass pyramids of the Louvre rose, filling her view. Pausing at one side of the flagstoned arch, Kate pulled her ticket out of her bag. She had no idea which entrance she was supposed to use, or how she might find it.

She'd walked briskly, trying to shake the feeling that someone was following her and had arrived ahead of her allotted slot. But now, stepping out into the light, she could see that the main square, surrounded by majestic buildings, was heaving with people.

Despite the heavy skies, the courtyard felt bright after the darkness of the tunnel, the multifaceted surfaces of the pyramids reflecting the clouds.

Kate paused to marvel at the size of the crowd milling about, even on a chill February day.

'We must stop meeting like this.' A voice beside her made Kate jump. She whipped around to see the man from the train walking towards her. His cleft lip distinctive, he was smiling warmly. He was wearing the same overcoat she'd noticed on the train, a glossy brochure rolled up under his arm, his gloved hand on the handle of his walking stick. Kate froze as he continued. 'Daniel Langton, we met—'

'Yes, I remember ... I was just a bit surprised.'

'You and me both, but I supposed the Louvre is a logical place for you to visit. Everyone does. I'm just about to have coffee. Will you join me?' He waved vaguely to his right, and Kate looked over to see stone steps rising to a cloistered area set with tables, heaters glowing bright above them.

'I'm not sure I've time.' She was working hard not to stutter. 'I've got a ticket and I have to get back for the course.' It didn't come out quite as fluently as she would have liked, but he didn't seem to notice, as he smiled at her like the Cheshire cat.

'I'm sure you can spare a few minutes, I'll get them to serve quickly. And I can take you past the line. I'm a friend of the Louvre – a patron, they call it.' He grinned. 'No queuing.' Then, as if realising he needed to explain, he added hastily. 'I've just bought the perfume bottle my great-aunt wanted. The one I was telling you about – It's You, by Elizabeth Arden. It's even got its original stopper. Let me buy you a glass of champagne, to celebrate?'

'I'm not sure—'

He cut her off. 'I can take you straight to the *Mona Lisa*, it's a bit of a maze in there.'

Kate looked at Daniel Langton curiously for a moment, thoughts careering around her head. He looked so chuffed with himself.

Have coffee with him?

She drew in a breath, conscious her hesitation was obvious. But he seemed to be waiting patiently for her to answer, as if he was half thinking of something else and was unaware of her delay.

She only had a short time at the Louvre before she had to go and find Le Studio des Parfums. *Did she really want to have coffee with someone she barely knew?*

Chapter 22

AGATHE STABBED THE lift button in the *Paris Heure* offices, willing the steel doors to slide open and let her in. Stepping back to look at the digital floor indicator, she could see it was still on the fifth floor. Taking a breath, she turned for the stairs. She couldn't wait. She needed to talk to her uncle right now.

It was too much. Too much for the phone.

Hauling the door to the stairs open, she belted up them, the thick soles of her boots ringing out as she pounded upwards. First floor, second floor …

Running across the landing, she punched in the security code and burst through the glass door into the open-plan office. Banks of screens were occupied by intense young journalists who looked up in surprise as Agathe raced across to her uncle's door. In her peripheral vision they all seemed to be male and were all wearing white shirts, as if it was some sort of uniform – open-necked, sleeves rolled up. But she didn't have time to stop and analyse the gender balance or the dress code.

Agathe pushed her uncle's door open without knocking, flinging it back on its vintage hinges.

'Agathe. What on earth?' Gabriel Beaudin looked up from his antique desk in surprise. Squirrelled behind piles of papers and books, he half-rose, his face shocked, a mug of coffee in his hand.

'The redheads.' Agathe caught the door on its return and, closing it behind her, she leaned against it, trying to catch her breath and find her words at the same time. 'I've got loads of cases of missing women, but only a few redheads.' She reached into her backpack and pulled out the sheaf of papers she'd printed off in the university library. They'd come adrift from one another as she'd run through the Métro, their edges uneven and curling. She waved it at him.

'I found most of these yesterday, I was just double-checking this morning. Going back to a student in 2001, here's every one that I could find. There were only five redheads, but they all disappeared in the same way, after a night out. Some of them were looking for a taxi, one went to get a takeaway … Bénédicte Écuyer was one of them. Her head was the first one found in the sewers ...'

Gabriel didn't answer for a moment as she trailed off, his brows knitting. He was older than her mum but his mind was still razor-sharp, and she could see from his face that it was making connections like a child leaping from stone to stone across a raging river.

'A taxi driver?'

She'd wondered the same herself as she'd dived on to the Métro. *Sandrine took taxis all the time.* But why hadn't there been a huge outcry, media attention, police press statements? There had been a controversy over Uber drivers in the United States that had reached the French media, so why hadn't this?

Agathe pushed herself off the door and into the office properly, putting her research papers down on a toppling pile of books. She slapped them as she spoke. 'All in their late teens or twenties, all with red hair. And only one of them had been found. Until now.' She paused for a moment. 'It has to be a serial killer. We've got a serial killer in Paris who has been taking women since at least 2001. The first one I could find disappeared on Valentine's Day – and then Bénédicte Écuyer in 2009, on the same date.'

As if the taxis weren't enough, it had been the month that had sent Agathe running to the office. It had taken her a few moments to draw the threads together. Some of the reports had been vague – hadn't specified a date when the girls had disappeared – and for some reason Agathe had been so absorbed in the details of these girls' lives, their jobs, their ages, she hadn't taken in the individual dates of the articles the previous day – only the years. But as she'd stood at the printer watching the documents churn out, she'd scanned the headlines again and realised the articles she was looking at were all published in February, around Valentine's Day.

Five women with red hair, reported missing in different papers. Only one of them found, until now.

And now Sandrine. The police *had* to take her disappearance seriously. She fitted the profile.

Why had *La Crim* not connected them before? Was it because they weren't important enough? A schoolgirl, a hairdresser, a barista, a waitress, and one who had sounded like a sex worker: Véronique, Bénédicte, Remy, Naomie, Juliette. Agathe felt each name cut through her heart. These were the ones she knew about. *Were there more – girls who hadn't got into the papers, whom nobody had missed?* Agathe shivered.

Getting the police to reopen these cases was vital. Perhaps they had DNA they could check against the remains that had just been found – they had to be doing that already, surely? Agathe didn't know, but she had known that she needed to get to the *Paris Heure* offices as fast as possible to talk to her uncle. She'd only been in the library for about half an hour when she'd noticed the dates, and she'd got here as quickly as she could.

Gabriel sat back down on his chair heavily. 'I was afraid you might find something like this.'

Agathe paced over to the window on the far side of the office. Her body was like a spring, full of nervous energy. She folded one arm across her chest, her elbows tight to her sides, and glanced back at her uncle. He was sifting through the printouts she'd brought with her.

'So what do we do – call the Prefect? I don't understand why these haven't been linked. The police can't keep these quiet. And what about Sandrine? She had her hair done before she disappeared. She had it dyed red. She could be number six.'

Chapter 23

KATE LOOKED DOWN at the ground, at the pale grey stone tiles paving the square, noticing Daniel's impeccably polished shoes. She took a deep breath, could feel her heart beating hard, her palms pricking with nervous sweat. She really wasn't used to this – to men approaching her about anything more than spare chalk, or asking if she could sit with Year 10 during her free period. The longer she was here, Kate was realising how out of practice she was at talking to anyone new. Erik had always wanted an explanation, the full biographical details of anyone she even said hello to.

But she hardly knew the girl in the coffee shop, Agathe, and she'd arranged to meet her later; wasn't this the same?

It wasn't, and Kate knew it.

Anxiety and suspicion nagged at her, old bedfellows that had seemed to colour her every interaction with men since her separation. Chatting on the train was one thing, but what if she made the same mistake again, and got talking to another Erik?

How come this Daniel Langton was here at all? How big was Paris, that he should arrive at the exact moment that she did? But he was right – she couldn't come to Paris and not go to the Louvre. Perhaps it *was* just a coincidence?

Beside them, a woman pushing a child in a buggy appeared out of the entrance arch, a fluffy white poodle trotting along beside them. Pausing, the mother bent down to unstrap her toddler. A red woollen hat was pulled down so far over its ears, Kate couldn't tell from the child's navy coat, leggings and sturdy boots if it was a boy or a girl. The dog jumped excitedly on a pink lead, trying to lick the child's face. Rubbing the dog's ears, the child took off, running in circles with its arms outstretched like a plane, cheeks pink in the chill air.

Distracted by the little family, Kate couldn't hide her smile. She was about to comment when Daniel took the words out of her mouth. 'How incredibly French is that?'

'The navy blue and the poodle.' She grinned, shaking her head.

'Indeed, and *le bonnet rouge*, here, in the royal palace. A true child of the Republic.'

Kate smiled, pleased that the distraction gave her a few more seconds to think. Perhaps she was overreacting? It was an Irish thing to meet people in the strangest places; it happened all the time at home, but it was a small country. She'd heard stories of people from home wandering down the street in New York and bumping into friends from school, distant relatives.

The toddler whooped and started to leap from flagstone to flagstone as if jumping puddles, mother following, the dog yapping exuberantly.

Kate glanced at Daniel, but he was still watching the child and the excited dog, absorbed in their play as the dog strained to get away from the buggy and join the child in its game.

This was ridiculous; how could she not make a decision about something as simple as coffee? She cleared her throat.

'I'm really not sure if I've got time. For coffee, I mean.'

Turning back to her, he nodded sagely, his brows knitting. 'I don't want to delay you. Forgive me. I'm so ridiculously pleased to have secured the perfume bottle. I feel the need to celebrate.'

Kate could feel her mouth twitching into a smile. He was like the child, his delight almost tangible. More importantly, she didn't get a single bad vibe from Daniel Langton.

Her head told her to say no; experience told her to leave the Louvre right away and head for home. But her experience had been honed by years of violence, and this visit was the next step in her breaking away from that, trying to capture the sunny, happy part of herself that she'd lost while living in fear.

Kate felt another shackle drop away. 'If we're quick? Tell me more about this perfume bottle.'

He grinned broadly, his blue eyes lighting up. 'It's quite wonderful, I have a photograph. But first let me show you Café Marly, it's one of the most perfectly located cafés in Paris. Are you OK to sit outside? It's cold, but they have heaters.'

Kate pushed a strand of hair that had blown into her face back behind her ear. 'Yes, that sounds lovely.'

'You get a great view of the square from here. I always think you can almost hear centuries of horses' hooves on the gravel.' He ushered her towards a flight of stone steps. Two hugely long red and white banners, the café name written in cornflower down the middle, hung like ribbons on either side of a cloistered stone arch. 'This way.'

Kate started to follow his lead, glancing around her nervously. But there was no one to see her talking to Daniel. This was such a public space, and if they stayed outside, what could the harm be?

And if Erik was really here, and was watching her, it was time he saw that she was getting her own life back. This was just the start.

Chapter 24

'SO, WHAT'S THE latest from Inspector Travère? I spoke to him briefly last night, but it was late. He wasn't very forthcoming.' Gabriel Beaudin looked at Maxim across the broad desk, his craggy face misleadingly calm. Through the huge window behind his boss, Maxim could just see the ethereal dome of *Sacré-Cœur* glistening in a moment of sunlight, dark clouds advancing threateningly to engulf it. Gabriel had called him last night, too, and then brought him up to date when he'd arrived. Maxim was starting to get a very bad feeling about Agathe's friend.

'Travère confirmed that *La Crim* are linking the two cases – Bénédicte Écuyer was identified through DNA back in 2012. This new one, they're still trying to identify. She had a tattoo, but that's all they've got. And it doesn't match any missing persons reports.'

To Gabriel's left, his niece was sitting forward in a stiff-backed chair, looking hard at Maxim as if he was about to give the million-euro answer on a game show. He wished he could.

Agathe's long hair was pulled up into a messy bun, revealing the row of piercings in her ear. She looked as if she'd found her short black skirt, thick tights and misshapen black cardigan in a charity shop. But as Maxim had noticed on her first day helping in the office back in the summer, she was bright. Laser-sharp, in fact. When she opened her mouth, people listened.

Sighing, Maxim leaned back in the chair and put his hands on his face, trying to rub away the lingering darkness of his conversation with Inspector Raymond Travère. It had got worse when Gabriel Beaudin had called the night before, to share the news about Sandrine Durand's visit to the hair salon.

'He's had Carlier on his back, too.' Maxim's tone was flat as he put his hands on his head, his fingers linking through his thick hair. He still couldn't believe that Carlier could even consider burying this story. 'Worried about the impact on tourism—'

Gabriel interrupted him. 'We can't keep it quiet, whatever Carlier thinks. Does Travère agree with him?

A real policeman?' His voice was like a cannon firing, each sentence hitting home harder than the one before. He shook his head, speaking half to himself. 'I'll have to talk to Carlier myself. How long does he think it will take for those men from the Wastewater Department to tell their wives? Once this leaks, every tabloid in the city will jump on it.'

Maxim knew this wasn't the first time Gabriel Beaudin had been told to keep a story quiet, which, based on his previous experience, was like a storm warning. Maxim could just imagine how his editor's next conversation with the Prefect, Pierre Carlier, would go. The last thing any of them wanted to hear about was another head – with any colour hair – turning up in the complex sewer network below the city.

As Travère had impressed on Maxim, the criminal investigation division were exploring the cases of the heads – plural – but it was slow progress. Maxim mentally corrected himself to use the name of the girl they knew about. Identity was important; Bénédicte wasn't just remains.

And now Agathe had discovered a link with the time of year that they'd disappeared, and the nights out. How had *La Crim* not spotted that? Agathe's research was impressive. She was good, but she was a student – what the hell had *La Crim* been doing?

Gabriel leaned forward in his chair, his face tense.

'All these disappearances Agathe has found, going back almost twenty years ... there's a story there. I want to run it. If we've got a killer in the city, people need to know so they can take precautions. Five redheads have disappeared almost without trace – and now Sandrine. She's the most recent, they have to move fast—'

Maxim interrupted him. 'Precautions? Like what – dyeing their hair a different colour?'

In the corner of the office, Gabriel's niece made a snorting noise. Maxim glanced at her. She had haunting grey eyes, and now he felt like they were boring into him.

Ignoring her, he continued. 'Agreed, we know the girls Agathe has found were all redheads, who were not only around the same age, but who all disappeared in the same month. But we *don't* know if it's the red hair that connects them. It's just the two ...' He hesitated to say 'heads'; it felt almost medieval. 'The two who have been found so far happen to have red hair. There could be others who haven't been found – with different colouring, I mean.'

Gabriel glared at him across the untidy desk. 'I think the red hair is significant. Yes, there may be remains that haven't been found. But who is to know that all five women are not in the sewers, or parts of them flushed out into the Seine? There are more than two and a half thousand kilometres of tunnels under this city. They could be anywhere.' Gabriel's brow creased. 'But the time of year, their age …' He looked at Maxim pointedly. 'This all suggests it might have been the same killer. One who has planned his actions.'

Before Maxim could reply, Agathe stood up abruptly, her arms tightly crossed. She paced over to the window and looked out, over the river. A moment later, she turned around to look at him. He suddenly got the feeling that her arms were crossed because she was trying to stop herself from lashing out.

'I know what you're saying about others, but it's more than just their colouring linking them.' Agathe paused, obviously fighting her emotions. 'This killer could have suddenly got more active. Women need to know.'

Maxim opened his mouth to speak, but Gabriel cut in. 'I want you to work together – two heads … so to speak.' He grimaced as he looked at Maxim pointedly. 'Gather all the evidence and … Maxim, you get it to Travère, find out what else he knows. I want to run this, and as soon as possible.'

Slipping out, closing the driver's door behind him – this time, he'd parked outside the entrance to the underpass – he stuck his hands in his pockets and wandered nonchalantly towards the water.

He'd zipped his windcheater to the neck, had his hood pulled up, just in case. There was no point in taking chances, but, like checking the bathroom in the penthouse, he needed to be sure he'd not left any traces behind, that the body hadn't got caught on the quay wall and was bobbing on the water, waiting to be found.

Behind him, the entrance to the underpass was as dark as it had been the other night. He still couldn't believe how perfect it was for his needs. It was usually quiet here beside the river during the week, the one-way stretch of road ending in a tunnel covered in graffiti. Walkers and joggers used it, families at the weekend, but virtually no one at night.

He'd walked or driven over the bridges that crossed the Seine so often, but had never realised quite how hidden this spot was. The river was wide here, curving around under the road bridge, the trees on the opposite bank dense. When he'd found the spot initially, he'd gone across to the other side to check whether it was as concealed as it appeared. The light beside the underpass had been working then, creating a pool that illuminated the tunnel's dark entrance. But now, with the bulb broken, at night the darkness was complete.

He looked up as if he was thinking, taking in the view of the river: the bridges, the boats moored further down, the bare trees across the water.

He felt anger stirring again. Everything about this one had been different. There was no need for ceremony, no ritual in her disposal, none of the satisfaction. He'd bundled her into the polythene sacks, his hands encased in latex gloves, the thick leather apron, stained with each of them, protecting the white forensics overall he wore over his clothes.

He sauntered over to the edge of the road, crossing the wide flagstones forming a path that continued along the water's edge. Running the events of the other night through his mind, he paused again, as if he was killing time.

She'd been light, easy to manipulate into the sacks. Rigor had left her body by the time he came to move her. He'd driven down into the tunnel, had thought he'd seen a movement as he'd arrived, but he'd waited until he was sure there was no one else there. He'd turned off the van's lights before he'd gone into the underpass, had left the engine idling, waiting to see if the area was clear. All the street lamps had been smashed here; the only light was from some distance further on. He'd felt almost as if he was underground.

He turned to glance over his shoulder. The graffiti was impressive: a black crow filling the whole wall, feathers iridescent, a sharp eye looking over the river, watching him. The other night, he'd thought he'd caught a whiff of the paint, carried away from him on the breeze, but perhaps it had come from somewhere above. Whoever had done it must have felt safe here, too.

The other night, he'd waited in the van for what had felt like an age, just to be sure there was no one around. Then, slipping around to the rear, he had opened the doors and lifted her out.

The grey water sucked and slapped below him as he scanned the length of the river as far as he could see without leaning over obviously. He'd weighted the bags, just to be sure that she'd go down smoothly. He was sure everything was fine, but the need to check everything again was infecting his every thought.

He glanced up and down the river again, making sure – as well as he could from this distance – that there were

no objects lodged beside the boats moored further down.
He was pretty sure he was safe.
He was good at this, after all.
It wasn't as if it was his first time.

Chapter 25

KATE PICKED UP a small purple glass bottle, noting its label. She removed the stopper and sniffed the contents. The scent of oranges burst from the top, making her smile. Years before, her mother had had an orange perfume: Clinique Happy. It made Kate think of Christmas on the farm, of roaring fires and a table full of food. Her mother had tried so hard to make everything perfect. Kate wasn't sure that her mother had ever been happy, except in those moments when it was just her and Kate and Orna, before her father came home.

Kate replaced the stopper and reached for another: *Musc Floral*. Arranged along the marble bench were three circular silver trays crowded with identical damson glass bottles, their silver labels revealing the contents of each one.

At the top of the bench, their teacher, Madame Ducournau, stood leaning slightly forwards, her hands apart on its chill surface, her nails perfectly manicured. She was a mature woman, her fitted black dress belted at the waist, her greying hair swept onto the top of her head.

'Making perfume is an art. The great perfumers learn their craft in Grasse, where they learn the smells of synthetic and natural materials, classifying scents, studying chemistry and botany, how to build a fragrance.' She paused to look around her class.

Kate watched her, mesmerised. Madame Ducournau was impossibly elegant, her nails and lip colour a deep red, matching exactly. She was so confident, so relaxed, explaining the history of perfume, of its links to the city, exuding a passion for her subject that filled the room.

It was a much smaller class than Kate had imagined, conducted in English, although she seemed to be the only native speaker. There was a delicate Japanese couple whom Kate was sure had to be on their honeymoon, and an older German woman who had taken out her pen and started making frantic notes the minute Madame Ducournau began to speak. Another couple, two Italian men, made up the group. Kate glanced at the time on her phone. She'd been here for two hours already, and it felt like five minutes. She'd been enthralled by the history of the huge fashion houses and their battle for supremacy of the market, of the secrecy and skill involved in creating new fragrances.

'The best perfumers understand that scent evokes memory. Our sense of smell is one of the most powerful senses we have.' Madame Ducournau glanced at Kate. 'And scent can smell different on different people. In the same way that a redhead, like you, Kate, needs more anaesthetic than, say, Davide might …' She indicated the younger of the two Italians. 'Because of your colouring, the acid mantle on your skin makes perfume behave differently, too.'

Kate looked at her, surprised. She knew about the anaesthetic issue from when she'd had dental treatment, but she'd never heard about perfume smelling different on redheads. Although it did explain why Orna's perfume smelled terrible on her, not even close to how good it smelled on Orna.

'We can test it as you build your own perfumes.' Madame Ducournau indicated the circular silver trays on the table.

'The most successful fragrance – *le monstre* – is Chanel's No. 5. Launched on the fifth of May, the fifth day of the fifth month in 1921, it revolutionised the industry and is an institution, with sales in the hundreds of millions. It created a sensation before it was even launched, and has become associated with some of the most beautiful women in history.' Madame Ducournau paused. 'Fragrance can transport you, seduce, create an illusion, it can paint a picture. Today is Wednesday, and as I explained, by the time you go home on Friday, you will have created your own scent, one which we will keep the recipe of and which you can order. It will be uniquely yours.'

Kate glanced at the bottles in front of her, all labelled in French. Some of them she could guess from the name, others from the fragrance that escaped as she'd uncorked each bottle at the start of the session.

All thoughts of Erik banished, she was enjoying every second of this afternoon, from the moment she'd walked into Le Studio des Parfums and been guided to the brilliantly lit white lab with its intriguing trays of purple glass bottles, to the moment Madame Ducournau had appeared and begun explaining the role of the perfumer, the training, how a 'nose' could remember perhaps three thousand fragrances.

'And to apply, you must always dab – you spray on the wrist and dab the pulse points at the neck with that wrist. You should never rub. It creates friction and heat, and this will break the molecules in the scent. You apply to the pulse points, or perhaps ...' Madame Ducournau smiled. '... behind the knees, to create a long tail of scent as you walk. In France we call that *suis-moi* – "follow me". It is very seductive.'

Kate realised in that moment how safe she felt here in this space, how energised she felt by learning something new. This whole experience was much more than she'd dared to hope for. Orna had been right that she needed to get away – needed to find herself again, so she could be the mother Hanna needed.

And even her unexpected coffee this morning had been an experience. As she'd chatted to him, she'd felt that Daniel Langton was an old soul; he had an innate confidence and an easy way about him.

She'd long ago got out of the habit of doing anything spontaneous, but Daniel had been charming. The moment they'd sat down, he'd unrolled his catalogue and explained all about Elizabeth Arden and her rise to fame, about his great-aunt working at Bletchley Park, breaking codes during the war, and how the survival of the bottle in the rubble of her home had given her hope that her husband might survive the war. A neighbour had heard his aunt's cat crying and, stumbling over the debris, had found the bottle standing up, completely intact. And then she'd found the cat, saved by a beam.

Sitting on the stone balcony of Café Marly, overlooking the iconic glass pyramid of the Louvre, Kate had become completely absorbed in his story – in the significance of the bottle, shaped like the Statue of Liberty holding her torch. His eyes had shone as he'd shown her the photo in the catalogue. The hand holding the bottle had a blue engagement ring enamelled onto the glass, matching the rich enamel of the flower-shaped stopper.

Kate had to admit, it was the perfect wedding gift: a strong female hand; an engagement ring that apparently matched his aunt's own sapphire. It was something old and something blue, and something that would be new to his niece, just as it had been new to his aunt when she'd married.

Lost in the romance of the gesture, Kate had suddenly realised the time; she'd missed her allocated slot to go into the museum. Daniel had taken full responsibility and whisked her past the queues, showing his pass to the security staff, who immediately ushered him through. He'd taken her straight to the classical statues that she'd glimpsed from above, and then he'd taken her via a route that avoided stairs to see the *Mona Lisa* so she could get to Le Studio des Parfums on time.

Outside the Louvre he'd hailed a taxi, arguing with the driver in rapid French and paying in advance, ignoring her protests, waving her off.

Madame Ducournau's voice rose. 'Now is the time to use your noses. Developing perfume is about using your intellect, but most importantly, your nose. I am going to hand out some forms – you will see three columns. Each column relates to a different layer in the olfactory pyramid. I want you to find your favourite scents from the trays in front of you, make a list, and we will consider how they will combine and how you will create your perfect scent.'

Chapter 26

AGATHE HAD PULLED up a chair beside Maxim's desk in his corner of the open-plan news office and looked across at him. 'Look, I'm just on research, I'm not a journalist.' She paused. 'I don't want to cramp your style.'

She'd seen the look that had passed across Maxim's face at her uncle's suggestion they should work together. It was the emphasis on the 'together' that indicated Gabriel Beaudin wanted her to get more involved. But that was the last thing she wanted right now. She was too worried about Sandrine to think clearly about anything except finding her. Maybe this would bring her a step closer, but maybe it would take up loads of time doing Maxim's grunt work.

Maxim opened his desk drawer and pulled out a lined yellow pad.

'I know, but maybe he's right. You're young and female, and frankly I'm neither of those things ... Well, I'm not that old, but I can't think like a teenage girl.'

Agathe just about stopped herself from rolling her eyes. She reckoned Maxim had to be in his late thirties – pretty soon, his love of leather jackets and motorbikes would be a tiny bit cringe.

He caught her expression. 'OK, don't say it. But you're only as old as you feel, and I'm twenty-three in my head, OK.' He sounded defensive.

'I didn't say anything.'

He threw her a half-hearted warning look and flipped open the pad. 'So, what are we missing? I'm really still not totally sure about this redhead thing ...' He held up his hands as if he was stopping traffic. 'But I know ... Sandrine.'

'The "redhead thing" is the strongest link between them, if you look at it statistically. It's like the rarest common denominator. All the girls I've found came from outside the city, they were all working in service industries, they were all under thirty.'

'It's horrible, but those aren't exactly unusual characteristics for victims, if what we're surmising is true, and these girls are missing because they were targeted.'

Maxim rubbed his face hard, as if it helped him to concentrate. He wrote down what she'd said on the pad and opened his mouth to speak, but Agathe's mind was moving on.

'But these heads ... Killers don't start with dismembering corpses, do they? Or even killing at all. Behaviour escalates.'

'Indeed.'

'So shouldn't the cops be starting with voyeurism or stalking, and then look at assault cases – assaults on women with red hair. I was only searching for missing women, but if they've had other reports, there could be someone who described their attacker. That would bring us a lot closer. We've no idea at the moment whether it could be someone in their sixties or ... I don't know, someone with one leg.' Maxim looked at Agathe sharply and shrugged. 'You know what I mean.'

Maxim spoke half to himself. '*La Crim* will be looking at the CCTV around Sandrine's office and where she had that appointment. But you're right – if they had a description, they might see something.' Lost in his thoughts, Maxim was gazing at the page in front of him.

Agathe felt as if she was about to vomit. She was still struggling to think of Sandrine as a victim at all. She glanced over her shoulder at the door to the newsroom, willing Sandrine to walk in. While no one had found her, there was still a chance that she was absolutely fine. It happened: people went off and, caught up in the moment, didn't think to contact anyone. She just prayed that was the story with Sandrine.

Realising she'd gone quiet, Maxim looked up. Her thoughts must have been written on her face.

'Sorry. But you know we have to …' Agathe stared at him. He was making it worse. He must have realised. 'Look, she's the most recent. Until she turns up, her movements could be crucial in this picture.'

'These girls who have gone missing all had ordinary jobs, though. Sandrine wasn't like them.'

Maxim pursed his lips. 'I agree. And I think that because they were ordinary, that's part of the problem here. It's a fact – and not a good one – that angry middle-class parents make noise. If they report someone missing, things get done. There's more press, the cops need to look like they are doing something. Perhaps these girls didn't have anyone to advocate for them in the same way.'

Agathe ran her fingers into her hair. 'And isn't that another link between them?' This was getting more frightening as they talked about it. 'Were these girls chosen – stalked, maybe – *because* of who they were, *because* there wasn't anyone to speak up for them?' She paused, taking a deep breath. 'Some of them were definitely from out of town. Perhaps they didn't know that many people in Paris. Perhaps they were lonely and someone came and spoke to them ... I don't know, in a bar, maybe? Perhaps that's another link.' She paused. 'But none of those things apply to Sandrine. She has friends, she's been to university, has a really good job. The only thing she has in common with them is the colour of her hair.'

Agathe stood up abruptly and walked to the window, leaning her forehead on the glass. Below her, the river was cold and grey.

Behind her, she heard Maxim's chair creak. 'You're right, but people will remember Sandrine because she's different. The best thing we can do for her is to get this story out there.'

Chapter 27

DANIEL PAUSED HALFWAY across the wooden passerelle Léopold-Sédar-Senghor, and leaned over the bridge's mesh railing, looking down into the swirling waters of the Seine. The sky above him was still heavy, the dark clouds reflected in the river's murky depths. In front of him, the water swung around towards the Eiffel Tower, which rose above the city like a triumphant statement. He'd missed this when he'd been in the desert – missed the sense of continuity a river brought to a city, a witness to the people who had lived here, to history.

Behind him, the Louvre overlooked the Jardin des Tuileries, where the broad sandy paths he could see from his hotel cut through horse chestnut and elm, their naked branches hopeful for a shaft of winter sunlight. The gardens were a haven of calm now, but Paris's history was nothing if not dramatic. Only a short walk from here, in the Place de la Concorde, the guillotine had been raised to cheering crowds. Daniel had skirted the bloodier aspects of the city's history as he'd had coffee with Kate, enjoying her fascination with the buildings, focusing on Paris's association with perfume.

But he'd always loved Paris, and particularly this bridge, its warm wooden boards curving in an elegant fairytale arch towards the Musée d'Orsay. The grilles below the wooden handrail had been replaced with glass panels now, but the brackets that held them in place were peppered with love locks, carved with initials.

He glanced over his shoulder at the pounding of footsteps as a herd of small children scampered across, chaperoned by a teacher whose hoody and beanie hat added to the impression that they were only about fifteen themselves. Daniel rolled his eyes to himself. It was at times like this he felt old, which was ridiculous, as he wasn't even forty. But then, he had managed to pack a lot in since he'd left school. Trauma, stretching yourself emotionally and physically, even simple lack of sleep, all had a deep impact, no matter how much you tried to pretend everything was fine. And he'd had plenty of that.

Daniel felt his phone vibrate deep in his overcoat's inside pocket. He pulled it out to see his aunt's name across the screen: *Lillian Langton*. He answered, turning back to look down the river, the majesty of the city sweeping down the banks on each side.

'Daniel, is that you? I got your text and voice message, I was expecting you to call earlier.'

'I tried you several times but your phone was switched off, I believe.'

Daniel tried to keep the amusement out of his voice. He knew exactly where his aunt had been when he'd called with the good news about his morning at Christie's. She had been trying to seduce the new vicar since his appointment to St John's in Hampstead. Daniel was quite sure that his aunt had taken the poor man out for coffee, ostensibly to go over his niece's wedding plans – again.

'I was telling the Reverend Bartlett about your mission to buy the bottle – he was very interested in my war stories. Did you get it at the right price?'

'I did indeed. They are boxing it at Christie's and will deliver it to my hotel. I can bring it home myself. No point risking a courier.'

'No indeed. And it's in good condition?'

'It's almost mint, and there's even still a trace of scent in the bottle.'

'Oh, how wonderful. Now what else have you been up to? Have you met that friend of yours, Maxim?' She said it deliberately innocently.

'I have indeed, he sends his greetings. And before you ask, I haven't seen Lucien.'

Every time Daniel came to Paris, they had the same conversation about him catching up with his university friends. He'd built a protective wall around his loss now, but every thought of Lucien led him to Meredith, and it still hurt like shrapnel.

His aunt had made it her life's work to get him married off, and she'd adored Meredith, meeting her when she'd come to Paris for the weekend to visit him. Although she hadn't adored her nearly as much as Daniel had.

Recently, thankfully, she'd been distracted by the presence of the Reverend Bartlett and the wedding plans. Daniel really owed him a drink or five for offering him some respite from her matchmaking.

He closed his eyes. Whenever he thought of Meredith's name, it came with a rush of memories: of this city in the autumn sunshine; of Christmas; of sitting out at pavement cafés wrapped up in scarves, or wandering the edges of the Seine hand in hand, watching the winter sun set over the Eiffel Tower; of the promise of spring, and the day they'd gone to the Musée de l'Orangerie. Meredith had been so enchanted with Monet's *Water Lilies* that he'd bought her a silk scarf printed with a reproduction; it had matched her eyes perfectly. It had blown his budget, but it was almost her birthday and her joy had made it worth it.

She'd been studying journalism, like Maxim, had come to Paris for a year as part of Columbia University's French immersion programme. He'd been studying mechanical engineering and French. They'd met in her first week and become inseparable.

Afterwards, he'd wondered if taking her to the rowing club that evening had been the single biggest mistake of his life. It certainly felt like it. Something had happened that night that had made her go off – leave Paris and go ... where? Part of him had always wondered if she'd ended up in some sort of commune, or even a cult.

His silence didn't stop his aunt speaking, and as he fought back the memories, he tried to tune back in to what she was saying, realising he'd missed a bit.

'I don't know why you've fallen out, but I messaged Lucien to tell him you'd be in town.'

Daniel felt as if he'd been hit by an enemy mortar.

'*What?*' A couple walking across the bridge turned to

look at him, surprised by his explosion. He lowered his voice. '*Aunt Lillian ...*' He cleared his throat, trying to keep his voice steady. 'Could you leave my relationships to me? That's all in the past now. You don't have the full picture. It's complicated.'

'But, Daniel ... You need to be happy. It's so important. Friends are important. You need to connect with your friends in Paris more often.'

Maxim's words shot into his head. He'd said Lillian had messaged him ages ago to tell him Daniel would be in Paris. But how had she known? Had she plotted this? He'd assumed that she'd only just found the bottle, but this auction would have been planned for months. Had she intended all along for him to be here, so she could orchestrate some sort of reunion? Daniel could feel his patience slipping, but he could hardly ask her if she'd lied to him. He was a professional liar, after all, and she knew it.

'Thank you for your concern, but—'

She interrupted him. 'Honestly, Daniel, stubbornness might have saved your life in the desert, but it's costing you dearly now.' He could almost hear her drawing herself up. He ran his hand across his forehead. How could someone who was 103 be this much of a handful?

In the background, Daniel could hear the mantel clock in her living room in London striking the quarter hour. Oblivious to his rising temper – or, more likely, to stoke it – she continued. 'I wish you'd talk to him. True connection with other people is a rare thing. You need to hang on to it ...'

Chapter 28

KATE FOCUSED ON the pipette, carefully counting the drops of the fragrance essence into a test tube. At the other end of the table, the Italians were starting to argue about whether their perfume should be woody or floral. Playing with blending the essences in the bottles in front of them, to see how some dominated others, they were working on creating the base notes, the first level of the olfactory pyramid they would have built by Friday.

Kate had had no idea that a scent changed on the skin as you wore it. Or that it might smell different on her because of her colouring. Or that the home of French perfume, Grasse, was on the French Riviera. She was going to show it to Hanna on the huge world map that dominated their living room wall. It sounded impossibly romantic, like somewhere out of a 1950s movie.

Madame Ducournau had explained that most people think in colour – but a perfumer thinks in scent, the very best remembering distinctly over a thousand fragrances and how they blended. Perfumes could be made up of more than two hundred ingredients, each one positioned in a specific way to reveal more as it evaporated on the skin.

'As I explained, the top notes, *notes de tête*, awaken our sense of smell, our memories. They are the lighter notes, they open our emotions, they capture the attention of the nose during the first fifteen minutes of applying the scent. The middle notes are *le notes de cœur* – they are the personality, the most complex level of the pyramid. They are what we remember when we think of a scent/ The heart notes give a perfume its identity. Lastly, *le notes du fond*, the base notes, give the perfume depth. You will begin to recognise them after the perfume has been on the skin for around two hours. The base notes are the layer that lingers, they are the soul of the perfume and may last from twelve to twenty-four hours in the best fragrances. They will determine your loyalty to the fragrance, they are what you remember.'

Listening to Madame Ducournau, Kate concentrated on noting the exact amount of each essence that she was adding to the test tube in front of her, each millilitre marked on the outside. She glanced up as their instructor continued. 'A perfumer is an artist, creating something new and beautiful from their experience, their instinct. They are both scientist and painter, creating something evocative, original, something memorable. Like a conductor in an orchestra, they understand how each layer disperses to reveal more of the scent, and how the fragrances work together to produce a floral bouquet, or a spicy aromatic blend.'

Kate looked for the next bottle, torn between *Jasmin Musqué* and *Jasmin Oriental*. Beside them was *Rhubarbe, Rose Fruitée Cerise, Frésia, Citron Amer*. Behind them, in the centre of the tray, *Ambre Doux, Vanille* and *Cuir*. So many choices.

Madame Ducournau had asked them to write down the scents they associated with happy memories, to try and think with their noses. Kate had had to close her eyes to block out the lab, the other workshop participants. She'd thought of the scent of the sea, of turf fires, of the orange in her lunch box, and her mother's perfume, the scent of the cut hay on the farm in the summer, the coconut of gorse flowers, their seeds popping in the summer sun.

Thoughts of her childhood – of hiding with Orna in the barn, of catching the bus to school – had made her wonder what scents Hanna would treasure. The aroma of the banana bread they'd baked together, or the scent of the cinnamon cookies she loved. Since they'd been on their own, Kate had made sure that she bought a real Christmas tree every year, so their tiny apartment was filled with the scent of pine needles.

Thoughts of Hanna made Kate ache. The first part of the class had flown by, but the scents in front of her had evoked her own memories. She'd put her phone away in her handbag under the table in an effort to stop looking at it compulsively, yearning for a message from Orna or Hanna. She'd checked it as she'd sat down after their break, but had the sound turned off now, not wanting to interrupt the class.

'And how are you getting on?' Kate almost started as Madame Ducournau came to her side of the bench. She'd been totally lost in her thoughts. The perfumer slid Kate's notes towards her, her eyes skimming the quantities of the ingredients Kate was adding.

'I'm loving everything, this is so interesting. I'm so glad I entered that competition.'

Madame Ducournau cocked her finely drawn eyebrow, puzzled. 'Competition?'

'I won this course, in a competition. The Eurostar, an apartment and this course.'

'Oh, I see. I think your place was booked by a PR company. That makes sense.'

'Was it? I don't even know what the competition was about, but it's been wonderful so far. Paris is such a beautiful city.'

Madame Ducournau lifted her eyebrows. 'Perhaps it was Tourism France, or the Eurostar, but if you can't remember, they need to work on their marketing.' She laughed, tapping Kate's list with a red nail. 'This is good, keep going. Find the *Musc Floral* and see if you like it. Perhaps a drop or two. It's very important to follow your instincts. Scent builds memories, it evokes emotion. Follow your heart and your scent will be your own.' She smiled as she continued. 'We will see how each of the scents works for each of us. Let us find the perfect scent for you, our redhead.'

Chapter 29

IN THE OFFICE of *Paris Heure*, Agathe checked the time on her phone. She was due to meet Kate at 6.30 at the café, and she was starting to feel as if she and Maxim were going around in circles. They'd both been searching the newspaper's digital archive for more details on the cases Agathe had found, but also to see if there were any references to peeping Toms, stalking, or assaults on girls with red hair.

Agathe had moved to a spare desk with a computer terminal, and now turned to look back at Maxim. She pulled at her ponytail, tightening it up.

'This guy might have found them on a dating app, you know, or a dating site? You must be able to search by age and location, and colouring would be logical, too. Can we find out if any of them were using them?'

Maxim looked up at her, his mind obviously recalibrating from the article he was going over again, to what she was saying. 'Those searches would leave a digital trail.'

Agathe looked over his shoulder, out of the window. It was getting dark. 'You'd think that would be something that *La Crim* would ask their friends and family when someone went missing – like one of the first things. And if they'd been on the same app, surely it would have set off an alarm of some sort.'

He sighed sharply. 'If they haven't looked at these cases properly, connecting them, they won't have seen any patterns like that. The dating site thing is pretty obvious really, isn't it? I'll chase that with them.' Picking up the cup of coffee beside his keyboard, he sat back and looked at her.

'You should come and work here for a bit, you know. Try it out. You've got the right sort of mind.'

Agathe threw him a withering look.

'I mean it. You can make a difference in the press. More than you can in a museum basement, cataloguing bits of pottery.' He looked back at his screen. 'With a bit of luck, this article will get everyone jumping to reopen these cases and review them for connections. It's only with this second discovery that the red hair is showing as a link, so to give *La Crim* their due, the others could have been lost in a sea of missing persons reports. You'd sort of hope someone would join the dots – but over a long period of time …' He shrugged. 'At least Travère is on the case now. He'll be thorough.'

Agathe pulled a face. 'Sandrine's going to be an outlier, though, again. She hated dating sites.' She cleared her throat. The more she'd read about the girls they knew about, the more unlikely it seemed that Sandrine fitted into any sort of pattern at all. And every difference was like a small win. She shook her head. 'I mean, she can't have been the victim of a serial killer, you know, really, she was too sensible.'

Agathe could feel Maxim looking at her. She knew he didn't want to say it, but being sensible didn't have anything to do with it. The other girls hadn't walked into whatever had happened to them because they weren't sensible. Every woman had an instinctive radar for danger; like a sixth sense, it switched on whenever you walked down a dark street, when you drove into an empty car park at night, or were alone on a train platform. Whatever had happened to Bénédicte and whoever this second girl was, it hadn't been their fault – Agathe was sure of that.

Agathe looked back at the screen and clicked her mouse. She was making a spreadsheet with as many details that she'd discovered about the missing women. It was a bit hit-and-miss, but she'd found a lot of their social media accounts and had been checking back through their feeds to see if she could see any commonalities at all. They all seemed to hang out in similar bars and restaurants; they went clubbing, but so did everyone of that age in the city, so she wasn't even sure that this information was going to be any use.

She glanced over at Maxim. 'I keep thinking the sewers have to be significant.'

Maxim took a sip of his coffee and winced. It had gone cold. 'I was thinking that, too. I mean, a whole body is hard to get rid of, but the dismembering ...' He grimaced. 'That takes dedication. It's not unheard of. There was an American they called "the Last Call Killer", who did the same to two victims in the 1990s, and Jeffrey Dahmer, obviously. And Nilsen in London.' His brow creased. 'The sewers run under the whole city. Remains could have been dropped in anywhere and have been moved around by the effluent, but with the heavy rain we've had ...' He glanced over at Agathe. 'The main problem is that they can't be closed for a forensic search – not all of them, anyway.

But if there were teams down there who knew where to look... Well, who knows what else might be found?'

Agathe shivered. 'It's not something I want to think about, but if you wanted to get rid of something ...'

Starring at her screen, she thought of the street cleaners who washed down the gutters, throwing their red and green pieces of carpet onto the sides of the road to guide the filthy water into the sewers. Washing away the story of the night, so Paris looked clean in the morning.

But the city couldn't clean this away.

'Do you think they're all down there? All the women we've found references to?'

Maxim shrugged. 'I really and truly hope that some of them just got fed up with whatever was happening in their lives and decided to relocate.'

Kate's face flashed into Agathe's mind. Even from the little she'd said about her ex, it was obvious she'd been in an abusive relationship. *Had she had to escape – to reinvent herself somewhere else?*

Maxim interrupted her thoughts as he moved around his desk towards the coffee machine. 'I really hope that's what's happened to Sandrine.'

The Métro was always packed at this time in the evening, everyone concentrating on getting home, on not getting their pockets picked. On avoiding eye contact.

Everyone had somewhere to be, something on their mind as they stared at their phones or at the signal board.

He checked the time. Her class should be finishing up shortly; he should be just in time to catch her leaving.

Watching her made him dizzy with anticipation. It was like a drug. He'd watched them all, but this one was different ... special.

He smiled to himself. What could be more perfect than a perfume course? Analysing the layers of scent, understanding their impact. What sort of fragrance would she make? He knew it wouldn't be as powerful, as addictive as the Belle de Nuit he'd left for her in the bathroom, but he was intrigued to see what it would be.

Had she used it already – the body lotion, the perfume? He hoped so. He couldn't wait to get close to her when she was wearing it, to breathe in the scent of her skin.

There was a jostle on the platform behind him, a movement in the crowd as they heard the next train approaching. He inhaled deeply, catching the scents rising from the travellers crushed around him. Perfume blending with aftershave, the bitter tang of diesel, tobacco on someone's clothes, the warmth of alcohol. Estée Lauder's Azurée, earthy with a dash of citrus, then Pleasures. He drew in white lilies, peonies and jasmine. Gucci's Guilty – spicy, oriental.

And then he caught it: Belle de Nuit.

But not quite the same as he remembered it.

He could see down the blouse of the girl in front of him, see where her shirt strained over her breasts, see the fullness of them, almost feel the weight in his hand. He breathed in again just as the train arrived and pushed up against her, enjoying the feeling of pressure against his body as the crowd surged forwards.

It was the best time to blend in, to be invisible. To watch and savour.

Chapter 30

IT WAS DARK by the time Kate left Le Studio des Parfums, waving her goodbyes to her new friends. The two Italians – artists who owned a gallery in Naples, Kate had discovered – had invited her to join them for some fresh air and a coffee during the afternoon break. She thought they'd suggested that mainly to avoid having to speak to the German woman, who seemed to know a lot about everything – including the Italian art market. But they had been great company.

Standing outside the main door of the elegant art deco building housing the perfume school, Kate checked her phone again. There was a message from Hanna, photos from the zoo, the last one of her clutching a huge fluffy gorilla toy, her smile almost splitting the camera. Kate felt her heart lift.

And there hadn't been any more texts from Erik. *Thank God.*

She still couldn't work out what he had been thinking, sending that photo; it was as if he was taunting her. She shook her head, trying to dislodge the image from her mind. He was playing with her again, but this time she wasn't going to let him win. She'd come so far, Hanna had come so far. She couldn't let him ruin what they'd built.

Kate quickly sent a message to Orna with pictures of her day. By now they would probably be on their way home, exhausted and obviously happy. Hanna was growing up, getting less dependent on her mum, which made Kate feel sad and happy in equal parts. She sighed. She'd known this trip would be emotional, and she'd been right.

She glanced at the clock on her phone. It was just after six; she had plenty of time to stroll to the café to meet Agathe. She glanced backwards quickly, catching a movement in a doorway.

Her mouth suddenly dry, Kate could feel her heart rate increasing. But it had to be a shadow, a trick of the light. And it was only a short walk to the café. She retraced the route she'd taken that morning along the narrow cobbled road, glancing into the shop windows as she passed.

She pulled her coat around her against the evening chill. On almost every corner, restaurants were beginning to come alive, the rich scents of food spilling into the street. As she crossed into the square at the end of le Rue des Corbeaux, it was quieter: a bar on the corner was lit to the night; the coffee shops that had hummed in the morning were dark and shuttered. She hurried on to the top of the lane, and even at this distance could see a figure halfway down, leaning against a shop door, her phone screen lighting her face. Kate glanced behind her again, but she was sure it had been her imagination earlier.

Agathe looked up as she heard Kate's footsteps, levering herself off the door.

'How did the course go?' Agathe put her phone to sleep and put it into the pocket of her oversized tweed coat.

'Fabulous. I hadn't realised the whole process was so secretive, or quite how highly skilled the perfumers are – "noses", they call them.'

'The perfume industry is worth a lot of money, it's massively competitive.'

Kate's eyes widened in agreement. 'It's incredible. So much history, it's fascinating. But have you heard from your friend?'

Agathe shook her head. 'Nothing. I was just at my uncle's office and …' She hesitated. 'I just hope she's OK.'

Kate heard her voice tremble as she spoke, almost as if she already knew something and it wasn't good news. But it wasn't her place to pry. She'd only just met her, and Kate was sure Agathe would tell her when she heard anything.

'Have you eaten?' As if Agathe needed to change the subject, she looked at Kate, smiling brightly.

'Not yet. What do you recommend?'

'Do you like Asian food? Thai, or Korean?'

Kate thought for a moment. 'I like rice and noodles. With Hanna at home I don't get a chance to eat out much.'

'Excellent, so let me take you to my favourite noodle bar. Come this way.'

Kate barely noticed the evening passing. She exchanged texts with Hanna to wish her goodnight as soon as they'd ordered, sending her a photo of the beautiful paper lanterns in the window of the tiny restaurant before turning back to Agathe.

'So, tell me more about your flatmates.'

Agathe took a sip of her wine. 'It's just Sandrine and Roland.' She lowered her voice. 'He's studying economics, but he wants to do art – he's a graffiti artist. He's quite well known, but he has to be really careful nobody finds out who he is.' She was obviously proud of him. 'His pieces make the news, and everyone wants to know what he's going to do next. He's quite political – controversial, I suppose. He says he wants his art to start debates, to get people thinking.'

'Isn't he worried about the police? About getting caught?'

Agathe shrugged. 'Of course. But he's really careful about the spots he chooses to paint. It takes him ages to find places with no cameras or overlooking windows. And he's careful about going to and from each site. The biggest problem is that he hates wearing gloves. The paint is so sticky it gets under your cuticles and you can't get it off, so it would be very hard to pretend he wasn't up to anything, if they did stop him.'

Fascinated, Kate glanced over her shoulder to make sure no one could hear them. 'I thought it was all spray paint?'

'It is, but it's special outdoor paint, it needs to be weatherproof. There can be a lot of competition to get the best spots. The other artists can be as much of a hazard as the police. But right now, Roland's biggest problem is his parents finding out. They have no idea that he wants to drop his course and study design.'

Everything Agathe had been telling her felt like a world completely removed from Kate's own. She opened her mouth to comment when Agathe's phone began to ring – vibrating on the table beside their bowls, the screen flashing.

'Oh, that's my uncle. Do you mind if I take it?'

Kate waved away her apologies and Agathe hopped off her stool, dodging an incoming delivery driver to slip outside onto the pavement. Kate glanced at her own phone; it wasn't even nine o'clock yet, but she was starting to feel tired. There had been a lot of new in one day.

Kate could see Agathe's blonde head bent into her phone as she paced up and down outside the restaurant's narrow window. Suddenly she stopped and put her hand to her face, turning and leaning against the glass for support, as if she'd heard something shocking. Kate glanced down the restaurant, catching the eye of the petite Asian lady behind the reception desk. She indicated that she was popping outside, but leaving her coat on her chair; that she would be back in a moment.

The woman acknowledged her as Kate slipped off her stool.

Outside, Agathe's face was alabaster, her dark make-up making her eyes huge. Frightened eyes. Kate recognised that look. She put her hand out to Agathe's shoulder, and Agathe gripped her wrist with the hand that she'd had tucked tightly under her arm.

'What's happened?' Kate mouthed the words. Agathe looked at her, her face strained as she listened to her uncle. Then the call ended as quickly as it had begun. Agathe didn't look as if she could speak. She closed her eyes tightly, still gripping Kate's hand.

'I have to go, it's about Sandrine.'

Chapter 31

DANIEL PICKED UP the heavy linen napkin and carefully smoothed it over his knee as he absorbed what Maxim had just said. The oldest restaurant in Paris, Le Procope, was busy even this late in the evening. It was in Saint-Germain, a cab ride from his hotel, but one of Daniel's favourite places. Entering the cobbled passageway that formed Cour du Commerce Saint-André was like stepping back in time. Daniel had booked a table at the back, overlooking the famous narrow alley that ran alongside the restaurant. He always sat with his back to the wall, but here it was mirrored. Sitting opposite him, Maxim could see who was coming and going without twisting around.

Daniel looked across at Maxim and frowned, keeping his voice low as he spoke, his tone incredulous.

'A head in the sewers? Two heads?'

In response, Maxim picked up his glass of wine and, swishing it around, looked at the teardrops forming on the sides. He knocked back a large mouthful.

Daniel picked up the menu and realised he wasn't wearing his reading glasses; he reached into his jacket for them. The pleasure of his day was tempered by the frown on Maxim's face. As if this news wasn't shocking enough, there was something else going on: something Maxim wasn't telling him, but he couldn't – yet – work out what.

Maxim had covered all sorts of stories – the bombing of the Bataclan theatre, the attacks on the offices of the satirical magazine *Charlie Hebdo* – but this one seemed to be getting to him.

'Beaudin's niece, Agathe, has done a load of research, found a series of missing women with red hair who could be victims.' Maxim sighed. 'The thing is that Agathe's flatmate's vanished, too.'

'And she's got red hair?' *Perhaps this was what was really bothering him.*

Maxim looked hard into the bottom of his glass. 'She had her hair dyed red right before she went missing.' He looked up at Daniel. 'This is such a big story. The cases Agathe's found are years apart. The trail's so cold with some of them, it's Arctic – except Sandrine, Agathe's flatmate.' He rubbed his face.

'But women need to be warned? That's your job, isn't it?'

Maxim's nod was slow; he looked exhausted. 'Story's running tomorrow about the discovery in the sewers, and linking it to the remains found down there before.' Daniel detected a change in his friend's tone, as if he was trying to keep his emotions under control. He kept quiet as Maxim continued. 'It's just that Agathe's at the Sorbonne, the same age we were when ... Well, when Meredith disappeared. It's taken me back.'

Now Daniel was seeing why Maxim seemed so preoccupied. He was usually buzzing when a new story hit. He'd been the same when Daniel had lived in Paris, although it had been the university paper back then.

But Maxim was usually one step removed from his stories – this one was much more personal. When someone disappeared there was no closure – no closure for any of them. Meredith was probably living somewhere happily married, but it was the not knowing, and the suddenness of her departure, that stayed with you, like a scar.

'So tonight, what's happened?' Daniel indicated

Maxim's phone. 'The call you were taking when I arrived. It was bad news?'

Maxim nodded. 'The police. There was something found in the river this evening.'

Daniel looked across the table at Maxim, and felt his mind shift from personal to professional. He knew it would be reflected in his face – calm, unexcited, impassive. 'Something?'

'A body. Wrapped in black plastic. It had been weighted down, but a dredger was clearing the river ready for the Olympics.'

Daniel regarded Maxim quizzically. Instead of chasing a story, he was here, having dinner with an old friend. An old friend who shared his past. Part of him wanted to reach out and hug Maxim. It was obviously hitting him hard.

'Any idea who it might be?'

'Well, that's the thing.' Maxim sighed and rubbed his hand across his eyes again. 'It was a woman with red hair.'

Daniel put down the menu and looked at Maxim over his glasses, now firmly on his nose.

Maxim shrugged again. 'There's no guarantee there's a connection ... This one is totally different from the two other victims. And the last thing Carlier needs is a scare story that might prevent people coming to Paris, for...'

Daniel took off his glasses and they said it together. '... the Olympics ...'

Maxim trailed off, scowling, and for a moment Daniel wondered who he was working for – *Paris Heure* or the Ministry for Tourism.

'But damn Carlier. If there's any chance this death relates to the other victims, *La Crim* have to act fast. What's different with this one?'

Daniel's mind went back to Kate, and their conversation over coffee that morning. She'd been so charmingly awed by the city, by being away, that she may not be as conscious of her personal security as she would be in London. And she had red hair.

But the last thing he wanted to do was to burst her obvious thrill at being in Paris by telling her to be careful. Surely as a woman living in London – she hadn't mentioned a partner, only her daughter – she'd be fine-tuned to maintaining her own safety? Daniel hoped so.

He'd enjoyed their chat. Even more than he'd expected. She was entertaining, and obviously very intelligent. As they'd talked, he'd felt as if she was coming out of herself, like a delicate flower slowly reaching for the light, poised to bloom. Her lack of confidence in her own capabilities had baffled him a bit, but then she'd picked up her coffee and he'd seen her broken finger again. Perhaps there was a history there.

A rare surge of anxiety made him reach for his own wineglass.

In his limited experience, women who had been abused fell into similar relationships; perhaps it was just that they attracted similar types of men – those who needed to feel they were in control.

Across the table, Maxim looked troubled. 'It's different, trust me. The red hair is the same, but it's rare killers use completely different methods of disposal. The body in the river is intact, there's no sign of an attempt to dismember it.'

'True, it's possible this is a different killer, but if you run the story then a witness might come forward. It has to be a good thing.'

'You are, my dear Daniel, exactly right.' Maxim looked at the time on his phone. 'I need to get back to the office as soon as we're done, to redraft the article. We need to update the front page to lead with this.'

Daniel had sensed there was more. He was right.

'We won't identify her until her next of kin have been informed, but her clothing and jewellery suggest that it's

Sandrine, Agathe's flatmate. Beaudin is doing everything at the moment to avoid Agathe having to identify the body.'

Chapter 32

LEAVING THE RESTAURANT behind her, Kate hurried through the unlit streets towards her apartment building. She'd made sure Agathe had got into a taxi, but she hadn't felt like finishing her meal. She'd settled up and left, retracing their steps, she thought. The restaurant was only about ten minutes from the café, but she was beginning to think she'd taken a wrong turn. *She should have taken a taxi, too.*

Away from the restaurant, the narrow roads were dark and deserted. Her feet rang on the pavement as she walked briskly along. Agathe's news was weighing on her like a cloak; her stomach was churning with worry, tears blurring her vision.

There was no easy way to get bad news, and this sort of news altered your life course, rocked your very being. Kate was never going to forget sobbing with her best friend when Trisha had got back from the hospital that first time, her diagnosis summarised in medical-speak in a letter in her hand. And then hearing the phone ringing in the middle of the night, and her mum coming into her bedroom to tell her that Trisha had gone. It was a long time ago, but it still felt raw, and now Agathe was going through a similar loss.

At least Kate had had time to get used to the idea – had been able to talk to Trisha. Agathe's loss was far worse; it was so sudden.

Kate sniffed and wiped her eyes. She needed to stop somewhere and look at the map on her phone, but she didn't want to pull it out and look lost either. Passing shuttered shops and the heavy closed doors of apartment buildings, she was sure if she kept going up this road that she'd reach a junction and be able to get her bearings. It just seemed to be a longer walk than she'd expected.

She didn't hear the footsteps behind her to begin with; her mind was too busy, her heart loud in her ears.

But as the road swung around and she crossed to the other side, she suddenly became aware that there was someone behind her.

Kate glanced over her shoulder and caught a movement – a shadow slipping into one of the narrow alleys that branched off from this lane. She gasped out loud, her breath catching somewhere in her diaphragm, making it impossible to breathe.

Erik?

There was something familiar about the shadow.

Finally catching her breath, Kate felt fear rip through her like fire. She hurried on, picking up her pace, trying to look confident, but walking much faster.

Behind her, the footsteps quickened.

She glanced over her shoulder again, but there was no one on the pavement. *Was he just behind her around the bend?* With the high buildings on either side of the lane, the wet cobbles, the sound was bouncing, distorted. She couldn't tell how close he was.

She may not be sure of the distance, but she was sure it was a man.

Was it Erik? Was he following her or was her imagination playing with her mind? Was *he* playing with her mind?

He'd been obsessed with true crime documentaries, had forced her to watch so many, the women often finding themselves in this exact scenario.

Terrified, alone on dark streets, footsteps echoing behind them.

Cat and mouse.

He'd always laughed at their fear, enjoying it, and then when the men were caught, laughed at how stupid they were, how he'd never get caught like that. She could see him shaking his head, glancing across the room at her, grinning. He was too clever.

Breaking into a run, Kate reached the end of the lane and suddenly recognised where she was. The supermarket was ahead of her on her left, still open, light spilling on to the road. Hurrying on, she ran past it, turning into le Rue des Corbeaux, relief flooding through her at the sight of her building.

Outside the door, fumbling for her keys, she flashed the key fob on the entry panel and heard the lock click back on the huge front door. Breathing hard, the sound of her heart drowning out the night, she hauled it open and was inside in a moment, pushing it closed and leaning back on it to catch her breath.

She didn't know if he was still following her, whoever it was, but she was home.

Hurrying up the stone stairs to her apartment, her feet echoing on the stone treads like the rapid second hand of a clock, she reached the marble-tiled landing and her own door, and unlocked it as fast as she could.

Inside the hallway she reached for the light switch, breathing in the scent of lavender and beeswax she'd smelled before. Doubling over to catch her breath, she realised there was something different in the air again – a breath of something woody with a hint of spice. Like the smell she'd noticed when the cat had shot out of the door. *Aftershave?*

Leaning back against the door, her hand on her stomach, Kate tried to breathe in calmly, searching for the scent again. Was it her imagination? She'd spent all day breathing in different fragrances, natural and synthetic. Her nose could be playing tricks on her, but she was sure there was something in the air.

Perhaps the cleaner had come back? Somehow Kate doubted it – why would they come again so soon, and when everything was so obviously pristine. Cautiously, she stepped towards the *salon* door. Hadn't she left it open wider? It was now only just ajar. One of the things that had caused friction between her and Erik was her tendency to leave doors open all the time. It was as if she had some deep-rooted compulsion not to close them.

A subconscious need to always have a means of escape.

She pushed the *salon* door open. The soft glow from the street threw shadows on the wooden boards, the swirling ironwork of the balcony like embroidery across the floor. Her hand shaking, Kate took a moment to find the switch, then suddenly the room was filled with light from the twin chandeliers.

Her mouth dry, Kate looked around slowly. The purple file with the details about the perfume course was still on the coffee table where she had left it.

Was she was getting paranoid? Agathe's frightened face leapt into Kate's head, pale in the darkness as she'd glanced at her while climbing into the back seat of the taxi.

But there was no question Kate had heard and seen someone behind her outside.

Had it been Erik? Who else could it be?

Had he started wearing expensive aftershave? Kate shook the idea away. Even if he was here – even if he knew *she* was here – there was no way he could get into her apartment, was there?

Chapter 33

DISORIENTATED, HER MOUTH dry, Agathe started awake as she heard the front door of her apartment click closed. She glanced at the clock beside her bed. It was after four. She knew she'd barely slept. She must have drifted off from sheer exhaustion.

She'd vomited the noodles she'd had with Kate moments after her uncle gave her the news. She'd known, though. The newsroom had been dark and hushed as she'd crossed it, a skeleton staff working at night, their desk lamps creating pools of light like warning beacons on the surface of a stormy sea. Heads had lifted, but she hadn't stopped to say hello. She'd run straight into his office.

Gabriel had been standing, looking out of the window at the river, gleaming in the darkness, the light at the top of the Eiffel Tower rolling over the city like a search beam.

His hands in his pockets, he'd turned slowly at the sound of the door slamming open – for the second time. *Would she ever forget the look on his face?*

He'd crossed the office and reached for his niece before he'd spoken, pulling her into a hug that had almost suffocated her. Agathe had barely been able to hear him, his voice choked with emotion.

'They found her. You were right.'

She'd pulled away, her heart pounding. 'Where? Where is she?'

He'd cleared his throat. 'She was in the river. She's at the morgue now. They are looking after her.'

Her cry of anguish had cut through the silence like glass shattering.

Now, out in the hallway of their apartment, Agathe heard whirring, the sound of tyres sticking to the wooden floor, and then the spring of Roland's bike stand going down.

His bike had been gone when she'd got home; she hadn't been sure if that was a good thing or not. Part of her wanted to sit alone on the sofa in the *salon* and cry her heart out, but part of her needed a hug.

But Roland needed to know. And she had to tell him face to face. This wasn't something you could do by text.

Agathe heard the clunk of paint cans knocking together, dulled by the padding in his bag, then the door to the living room squeaking open. Throwing back her duvet, she reached for her dressing gown, feeling dizzy as she stood up. The room swayed for a moment. She put her hand to her forehead, pushing her hair out of her eyes. She hadn't taken it down before she'd fallen into bed. Her ponytail was loose and lopsided. She hadn't taken her make-up off either, could feel her eyes clogged with mascara.

But she didn't have space in her head to think about that now. On the other side of the wall she heard the kettle go on.

Agathe hesitated as she pushed open the living room door, one hand on the frame stopping her from swaying.

Roland had switched on the side lamps and was sitting in the battered tapestry armchair, one leg flung over the arm, scrolling through his phone, his dark skin as flawless as ebony, earbuds firmly in place.

He'd been out painting. She could smell the faint toxic odour. He'd thrown his black bomber jacket over the back of the sofa, and was wearing a padded red and black tartan shirt with his black jeans.

Sandrine had always loved it when he came home after creating another mural. She had wanted to know everything about how the night had gone, her appreciation of his talent lighting her face. Agathe could almost hear the high notes of her laughter, as if she was in another room.

Roland must have caught her movement out of the corner of his eye; he looked up in surprise. Surprise which turned to puzzlement as she stood in the doorway, unable to speak. One eyebrow went up.

Agathe could feel her chest constricting. She pulled her dressing gown around herself. Had he seen the note she'd left the other day?

When he was painting at night, Roland often slept all day, waking late to work on sketches before he went back out again. Sometimes they didn't see him for a week. It was as if his creativity peaked and he couldn't stop, and then he'd come home and sleep for what felt like days, exhausted by the art as much by the risk, of concentrating on not getting caught. She had no idea how he got any of his essays done, but he hadn't been thrown off his course yet.

Roland looked at her, his head on one side. Agathe opened her mouth, searching for the words.

She didn't know what to say. What could she say? She could feel a tear rolling down her cheek, the chill of the floor creeping around her bare feet.

He pulled out his earbuds and unhooking his leg, sat forward in the chair.

'What? What's happened?'

Agathe drew a shaky breath. 'It's Sandrine.'

Where did she start?

He closed his eyes, the azure silk pressed to his face as he absorbed the layers of scent, old now, but still enough to take him back.

And he could feel the anticipation growing, the fear and the exhilaration.

It wouldn't be long now.

Sitting here in the middle of his perfect space, he smiled to himself, adrenaline flowing, making his heart beat faster.

This one was going to be the best yet. So much planning – such glorious, meticulous detail – for months. But that was all part of it, part of the anticipation. It magnified everything.

When he got a breath of the scent, everything welled up inside him, overwhelming him. The very first time, as she'd lain there, her eyes staring lifelessly at the ceiling, the feeling of release had been magnificent, incredible.

He leaned back into the shadows, the pillows cool against his skin. He knew he was starting to need each one more intensely – that the time between them was getting shorter – but the planning made it more delicious. He'd be able to keep this one, so she would last him much longer.

Keeping them was important. The storage unit had been perfect for so many years, but with cameras everywhere across the city, he knew he needed to be careful. Could he keep coming back to the same spot? The risk excited him, but he couldn't let this place be found.

There was too much evidence: their clothes, shoes – all the things he'd kept. He doubted anyone would understand that he needed them to make the moment last, to stop him going out hunting every night.

He had everything set up inside here: the cameras and the lighting; this bed with its silk sheets; the sheepskin rugs. He'd had it soundproofed when he first bought it, had had it delivered to the very back of the yard. He'd told them he needed the power supply for his tools, his hobbies. He'd layered up the protection – fake IDs, fake accounts, untraceable payments. It looked so real, there was no reason to question it.

Things had fallen so beautifully into place with this next one, he couldn't believe it himself.

He'd always have an alibi, but if everyone was looking in a different direction, he'd be safe. They'd be safe.

Chapter 34

THE SOUND OF the argument rose up the stairwell as Kate pulled her apartment door closed behind her the next morning. Anxiously checking her bag again to make sure she had everything, she tried to ignore the raised voices as she headed downstairs.

She hadn't slept well, her mind turning over everything that had happened last night. Had Erik been following her, or had she got caught up in Agathe's distress and panicked? Perhaps it had been someone completely innocent going home from a bar – someone who had kept their distance, trying not to frighten her?

That didn't explain the trace scents of aftershave she'd picked up in the apartment, but in the bright light of day, it seemed logical that it was a cleaner.

But she couldn't get spooked and thrown off track. Her time in Paris was running out, and she had things to do.

Today was the day she was going to make things right with her past. She had the two tiny locks from her own and Trisha's diaries in her bag, linked together through a larger heart-shaped padlock. In the film, Amélie had brought happiness to the people she met in her pursuit of true love. When Trisha had found the heart-shaped padlock in a market, she'd bought it immediately, explaining to Kate exactly how they would use it to secure their own locks to the bridge in Paris. It was symbolic – a talisman that would help them find true love.

Kate could feel the butterflies printed on the cover of Trisha's diary dancing in her stomach as she stood on the landing outside the apartment. She'd left it so long to do this, but it had been the one thing that had made her decide that she had to go to Paris, no matter how hard it was to leave Hanna. It was as if Trisha were calling her.

Downstairs, a man and a woman were still firing what sounded like insults at each other in rapid French. As she reached the bottom of the steps, she realised that the raised voices were coming from Céline's apartment. She pulled her coat around her, suddenly embarrassed. Céline had seemed so together and in control when she'd shown Kate around the building, and now she was shrieking in pure rage.

Kate could make out occasional words that she recognised from the bit of French she'd done in school. None of them were words you'd use in class.

She could hear a man's voice, also raised, but the vitriol seemed to be coming from his wife.

Kate hurried across the hallway and eased the front door open. If either of them chose this moment to come out, it would look, mortifyingly, as if she was listening. Even if she couldn't understand much of what they were saying, she was definitely getting the gist. And she had a feeling that it involved a younger woman.

Safely outside, she hesitated on the doorstep. *Would Agathe be in the café today?* Kate doubted it. She'd messaged the night before to say that she was thinking of her, and that if Agathe needed to talk, to give her a call. She just hoped beyond everything that Sandrine had turned up safe – perhaps she'd had an accident, or some sort of breakdown. Kate knew she'd been close to that herself in the past, first, losing her best friend, and then getting trapped with Erik. It had taken a long time before she could admit to Orna that anything was wrong. It had only been having Orna as her support system, and knowing that she had to keep going for Hanna, that had saved her.

Kate knew Agathe would need a support system now, and if her own experience could be the tiniest bit useful, Kate wanted to be there for her. It didn't matter that they didn't know each other very well; their bond was instinctive. Deep down, Kate wondered if perhaps the universe had brought them together.

She pulled on her gloves. The ticket for the Eiffel Tower was booked for this morning, and according to Google Maps, she could cross Trisha's bridge on the way.

It was just over an hour's walk to the Eiffel Tower – down along the river and past the Louvre, where she'd been yesterday. Everything she did felt new and fresh – important, as if she was closing the gate on *then*, to focus on *now*. But being away magnified her insecurities. Managing them took focus and planning – her fear of getting lost and not being able to find her way home was uppermost. At least on foot she couldn't go far wrong.

Just after the Louvre, she needed to cross over at Trisha's bridge and then follow the left bank of the river. Going to the Eiffel Tower would be perfect after visiting the bridge.

Thrusting her hands into the pockets of her coat, Kate turned to walk up towards the café to see if she could find Agathe.

It was busy when she got there. Kate couldn't see Agathe, but the man who'd been serving behind the counter on her previous visit was there, laughing with a waiting customer. They were obviously busy. Kate didn't want to interrupt to see if Agathe might be in later. Would she text if she had news?

A woman came out, accompanied by a blast of warm air carrying the mouth-watering blend of coffee and pastries that made Kate's stomach rumble.

Kate caught the door for the woman, who had a newspaper in one hand, her eyes on the headline, her coffee balanced close to her chest. As she passed, Kate caught the heavy bold type under the masthead. Even with her limited French, she could understand it, and the cold hand of shock gripped her.

MORTE! *Le corps d'une jeune femme retrouvée dans la Seine.*

A woman's body had been found in the Seine. Kate felt a chill go through her. Realising she was standing staring after the woman, still holding the door of the café open, she stepped inside, her head whirling.

Could it be Agathe's friend who'd been found? Should she ask the man behind the counter? Or should she text Agathe now?

If it was Sandrine, Kate didn't want to intrude on Agathe's grief. From her own experience, she knew Agathe would need time to adjust and work through her pain. The door opened and closed behind her as another customer left, and Kate finally focused on where she was. The café was warm and cheerful, but a dark feeling of dread was growing in Kate's stomach.

Chapter 35

DANIEL SCANNED THE headline of *Le Monde*, folded neatly next to his eggs Benedict and toast, and sighed. Under it he had *Paris Heure*, Maxim Verdier's name on the byline, the headline slightly more sensational but saying the same thing: a girl's body had been recovered from the Seine. The girl Maxim had mentioned last night.

As he'd said, they weren't identifying her yet, or revealing how she'd been killed, but the fact that she'd been found wrapped in black polythene ruled out suicide or accidental death. Maxim's piece mentioned previous cases and statistics about girls going missing in Paris, about whether the city was safe, about CCTV and the new AI facial recognition systems being used in Nice. He'd covered the discoveries in the sewers, too.

Before this girl's body had turned up, the two heads in

the sewers would have been the headline. Daniel could just imagine the news stations would be going mad.

A waiter appeared at Daniel's elbow, with his coffee in a silver pot. He poured without speaking, putting the pot down on the table beside the *confiture* and disappearing as silently as he had appeared. Daniel always ate his breakfast in the restaurant when he stayed, as much to scope out the other guests as to get a perfectly cooked egg.

He took a sip of his coffee, wondering which way the investigation would go. He knew the criminal branch of the Paris police were usually very efficient, but sometimes information could be lost – particularly if cases hadn't been connected over a long period of time, as Maxim had suggested. Even in army intelligence, things got lost or overlooked. And obviously nobody had spotted the link with these girls' colouring until now.

Daniel flipped over *Le Monde* and continued reading the article. It contained a lot less information than Maxim's piece. Below it was an article about stepping up security for the Olympics; some civil liberties spokesman was criticising the use of extra cameras, of the same facial recognition technology that Maxim had mentioned.

If they were able to use that technology, one of the most important elements of this investigation would be tracking – Daniel checked her name in the column – Sandrine Durand's movements, and finding out who she had been in contact with in the days preceding her disappearance. Daniel pulled out *Paris Heure* and scanned Maxim's piece again.

Perhaps it was knowing her friend that was bothering Maxim so much about this case. Or perhaps he was having some sort of midlife crisis and worrying about his role at the paper. He'd never worked anywhere else, and that could create problems of its own.

Picking up his spoon, Daniel stirred his coffee thoughtfully, remembering his chat with Kate Wilde the previous day. She had been refreshing company. She seemed to have no idea of her own magnetism, of how charming her honesty was. They'd discussed her home on a farm in a distant part of Ireland, his boarding school, living with his aunt. It had been such a natural conversation. And she hadn't asked about his leg, about life in the army. That was usually what people wanted to know all about when it came up at cocktail parties.

Daniel put his spoon down, half smiling to himself at the memory of their encounter. She'd seemed so shy – almost frightened, somehow – when he'd first bumped into her, but then she'd relaxed and they'd talked so much, they'd lost track of time. About the artists and writers who had lived in Paris, imagining what their coffee or dinner party chat must have been like. She'd told him about Oscar Wilde having dinner with Arthur Conan Doyle, about her love of literature.

Would she run scared if he invited her for a drink? It would need to be somewhere nice, somewhere that would make her memories of her trip to Paris a little more special. Considering for a moment, Daniel realised he knew of the perfect place.

But first ... Maxim. He really did seem unduly shaken by this whole case. They went back a long way, and friendship was more important to Daniel than anything else.

In the desert you had to trust; you formed bonds – deep bonds – with your colleagues. It could be a matter of life and death.

Daniel would do anything for his friends, and he had the distinct feeling that Maxim needed him now.

Chapter 36

KATE COULD SEE the arched pedestrian bridge ahead of her as she passed the Louvre. After reading the headline in the paper, she could hardly look at the river. The water was dark, moving rapidly, sloshing and boiling around the barges moored at its edges, a mucky colour as if it was polluted with sewage. And every now and again Kate caught the smell of drains.

Trying to focus on her mission, she could feel the coffee she'd bought in the café sitting like acid in her stomach.

This wasn't how she'd imagined going to Trisha's bridge.

She'd thought the sun would be shining, and it would be a moment to cherish. But perhaps her and Trisha's romantic notions about the city had made her think that it was perfect.

It was certainly beautiful, but even as she'd walked across the market square at the end of le Rue des Corbeaux, she could see that it had a dark side. She'd passed an old woman bundled up in sleeping bags in a doorway just before she'd crossed the road, one of many homeless, if the piles of bedding and tents were anything to go by. London had its own problems, but somehow she hadn't expected to see the same thing in the centre of Paris.

On the other side of the river, she could see a beautiful building rising to her left, a huge clock at either end. Ahead, the hazy shape of the Eiffel Tower stood guard over the city. Trisha had dreamed of Paris through the lens of a film where everything had been brightly coloured, where there were bustling cafés and vegetable stands on the corners of the street, beautiful people and lots of bicycles, and somehow that's what Kate had expected, too. Perhaps she'd watched too much *Emily in Paris*, but she'd thought everyone would be having breakfast in pavement cafés.

There were certainly lots of bicycles, but Kate wasn't sure if it was quite the same as the city Trisha had imagined – the place where she would find her true love, just as Amélie had.

Kate's mood darkened as she came to the bridge. The grilled railings she'd expected had been replaced with glass panels.

Disappointment churned with the coffee in her stomach. *What if she couldn't fix the lock, like Trisha had wanted?* What would she do then? She would really have let Trisha down. She hadn't known how to talk to her about the cancer, had seen her less and less as she'd got weaker, and now she may not be able to fulfil her final wish.

Kate could feel tears pricking at her eyes, her body suddenly heavy with failure. But as she reached the steps and turned onto the bleached wooden boards that curved across the river, she could see that there *were* padlocks attached to the bridge. Fastened in groups at the bottom of each glass section, they were like little bouquets of flowers, some brightly coloured, others with initials scratched into the silver or gold metal. Kate sighed loudly, relief flooding through her.

Her feet ringing on the wooden treads, Kate crossed to the side closest to the Eiffel Tower and counted sixteen glass panels. It brought her almost to the middle. Sixteen panels for Trisha's sixteen years.

Bobbing down, Kate pretended to look at the locks already in place, discreetly unzipping her handbag to slip out her own cluster. She really didn't want to get into trouble for leaving them, so she spent a moment inspecting the locks around the bracket she'd chosen. One was purple, another orange. Bright and cheerful symbols of enduring love.

Glancing around, Kate quickly clipped the heart-shaped padlock, with its two tiny locks attached, into the collection beside her. As she moved them, one of the locks at the bottom of the pile slipped around. It was circular, a gold butterfly stamped on the silver metal. Kate faltered for a moment, her breath catching. *It had to be a sign.*

She wiggled her own lock to make sure it was secure and stood up abruptly, her heart beating hard in her chest. Taking a deep breath, leaning on the weathered wooden banister, she looked down at her feet, making doubly sure that the locks were in place.

She'd finally done it. And, incredibly, there had been a butterfly waiting for her. Like a butterfly, her grief had been cocooned deep inside her, but now she felt as if it had taken off over the river, carried on brightly coloured wings. The pain would never go away, but perhaps now she could revisit the happy memories without a sense of failure, of guilt.

It had taken her so much longer than she'd thought it would – almost twenty years – but she'd finally honoured her promise, and part of Trisha was where she'd always dreamed of being. Kate closed her eyes for a moment, summoning the smiling face of her friend, and felt the tears cascading down her cheeks.

There wasn't anything she could do to stop them, but she tried to rub them away so that she could see properly. She had one more thing to do.

Reaching into her bag, she took the tiny keys out. She'd put them onto the ring with the slightly larger key from the heart-shaped lock to give them a bit of weight. She squeezed her hand around them, feeling them dig sharply into her palm, and then let them go. They hardly made a ripple as they were swallowed by the water.

Her mission was complete.

But as she stared out at the river, Kate suddenly felt the hairs standing up on the back of her neck. She was being watched. Poised on the bridge, she could feel it.

Whipping around, her head was back in the darkness of last night, the sound of footsteps ringing behind her. Her mouth dry, she looked back the way she'd come. At the start of the bridge, the gold-topped gates to the Jardin des Tuileries behind him, she could see the head of the chestnut-roaster she'd passed but barely noticed, the smell of his brazier carrying now to her on the breeze.

But she couldn't see anyone she recognised. There were several couples walking towards her, wrapped up in warm hats and puffer jackets, and a woman with a dog meandering slowly in the opposite direction. A boy on a bike appeared over the rise and shot past her.

Was her imagination working overtime? Or was her sixth sense reacting intuitively to something, like an animal scenting danger?

What if Erik was here? She was sure he'd followed her last night. He'd followed her before, checking that she went directly to work, suddenly appearing if she had to drop into the supermarket on the way home. She'd never been sure how he knew where she was, but he had done, without fail. It'd got to the point where she had to leave a detailed plan of her day on the whiteboard on the fridge. He'd said it was because he was worried about her, that violence in London was increasing and women on their own weren't safe.

But the only person from whom she hadn't been safe had been him.

Chapter 37

SQUASHED IN A corner of one of the Eiffel Tower's glass lifts, Kate held the paper bag containing the snow globe she'd bought for Hanna close to her chest. The lift was full, descending from the third level with what felt like far too many people in a confined space.

The moment she'd arrived, she'd understood why her ticket had a pre-booked time. Like the Louvre, the whole area was packed. She really hadn't enjoyed standing in the security queue after her long walk, but part of her had felt much safer in a crowd. As she'd crossed the bridge and continued following the blue line on her phone, the feeling of being followed hadn't gone away.

The lift came to a juddering stop at level two and Kate grabbed the handrail, making sure she kept hold of the gift bag. She just hoped level two held more coffee options than level three had done. Perhaps it was unfair to judge a historic monument – a masterpiece of construction built in 1889 – on its twenty-first-century coffee facilities, but Kate's need to rest was outweighing her need to see any more. She hadn't had the energy or the patience to queue again to go up to the summit.

Funnelling out of the lift on the second floor, Kate could immediately see that this level was much more what she had imagined the Eiffel Tower to be. As well as the viewing platform, there were kiosks selling coffee and snacks. She looked around, her energy levels already improving.

Could she stretch to lunch? She needed to eat before she started on the walk back to Le Studio des Parfums, and Orna had told her to enjoy her trip. Thoughts of the prices caught in her mind like bunting in the branches of a tree. But what were the chances of her ever being here again?

And if Erik was following her, she'd see him much more easily in a restaurant than here in the open, where he could easily be concealed behind a girder. Kate spotted a sign for a restaurant called Madame Brasserie and made up her mind.

She was early for lunch, but the maître'd showed her to the perfect table right opposite the restaurant's main entrance, beside a window overlooking the river. Unhooking her bag, Kate sank into the soft chair and immediately a menu and a carafe of water appeared in front of her, with a buttoned leather pocket containing two bread rolls.

Kate ordered, and pulled her phone from her bag to check if Agathe had sent her a message. Nothing yet. Anxiety bit at her as she scrolled on. Hanna and Orna had sent her a photo from the London Eye. Kate took a photo of her table, the menu and the view behind it, and sent it to them with a row of kisses.

Just as she hit *send*, her phone vibrated with another message, from a London number she didn't recognise. Opening it, she realised it was from Daniel.

He'd sent her a text, so that she had his number in case she needed anything while she was in Paris, and then she'd texted him to say that she'd arrived at Le Studio des Parfums, thanking him for the taxi. With everything happening since, she'd forgotten to save the number in her contacts.

Hope you enjoyed your first day in Paris. Could I tempt you to join me for cocktails at Bar Hemingway at the Ritz tonight? I can organise a car to pick you up and drop you back.

Kate felt a blast of anxiety hit her almost automatically. She closed her eyes. *Why did this happen every time anyone suggested anything new?* How damaged was she, that she couldn't even contemplate an invitation without panic rising? She could say no. She didn't have to go.

But Daniel was asking her to have *cocktails at the Ritz.* Tonight.

She had nothing planned for the evening, when she got back from Le Studio des Parfums. She'd be tired, but she could get a cab back, which would give her a few more minutes to savour lunch, and save her energy for this evening.

Daniel had been a charming and interesting coffee companion, and hadn't once done or said anything remotely unchivalrous. She could feel Trisha smiling. *The Ritz.* What could be the harm?

Chapter 38

WHEN MAXIM ARRIVED in Gabriel Beaudin's office, Agathe was already there, curled in a leather armchair, her knees pulled up. Her face pale, hair a mess, she had her arms wrapped around herself as if she was cold. She looked at Maxim sideways as he came in, but didn't move.

He knew how she felt. Or, at least, part of what she felt. He pushed the thought from his mind.

The piece had hit the morning's front page, and the whole city was talking about it.

And they didn't even know the half of it.

Maxim pulled out the chair in front of Gabriel's desk and sat down heavily. 'Anything new?'

Gabriel lifted his head from the paperwork on his desk and looked at him. 'Aren't you supposed to tell us that?'

Maxim looked at him patiently. He was upset, too – they all were, but they needed to hold it together.

Gabriel sighed. 'We need to know what the police are thinking.'

Agathe interrupted, her voice raspy. It shook a little as she spoke. 'I really don't think Sandrine can be connected to the other two. Why did she end up in the river? Why not in the sewers like the others?'

Maxim sat down and glanced across the desk at Gabriel. 'Travère said the two found in the sewers had been frozen. That would require access to a large freezer. Perhaps he couldn't get to it any more, or has moved house or something and there wasn't space. So he went for a different method.'

'But it may not be the same person at all.' Agathe shifted in the chair she was curled up in. 'Just because she had red hair and was a similar age, you're assuming it was the same person. What if the police think so, too, and spend ages trying to make that theory work, but it was someone totally different?' Then she stopped, as if what Maxim had said suddenly registered. 'How can they tell? I mean, how can they tell they were frozen?'

Maxim sat forward, his elbows on his knees. 'It's something to do with the blood cells bursting. The ice crystals make them expand when they are frozen, and they burst when they thaw out. I think we're lucky the most recent one was found when she was – she can't have been down there that long. All that bacteria ... I reckon this guy thought she'd be skeletonised really fast and then there would be no blood to test.'

Gabriel looked at him across the desk. 'But there would still be DNA? In the hair and teeth?'

'Yes, but it's harder to extract, and it's only any good if you've got something to compare it to.'

Agathe shook her head, tears beginning to flow. 'Do they know what happened? To Sandrine, I mean, before the river?'

Maxim glanced over at Gabriel again before answering. He didn't want to get yelled at for telling her too much. But his editor had returned to looking glumly at the paperwork on his desk, and didn't offer any support. Maxim cleared his throat. 'It's hard to tell. She wasn't assaulted – I mean, sexually – and the PM suggested she was dead when she went into the water. There was evidence of petechial haemorrhaging, which suggests asphyxiation, but her hyoid bone was intact, so she wasn't strangled. The pathologist found a haematoma – a bruise on the back of her head. Not a huge one that would have knocked her out, but as he said himself, it's a strange place for a bruise. And some bruising under her arms where she may have been lifted.'

'But how …? Were there signs that she tried to fight back?' Agathe had paled even more, her voice little more than a whisper.

Maxim shook his head. 'The pathologist thought she might have been drugged. They are running toxicology tests to see if anything shows up.'

Gabriel's voice was a low rumble when he finally spoke. 'I want you to talk to all your contacts. Show them Agathe's research, find out if these cases should be linked. Dig, Maxim, and keep digging until we get some answers.'

Chapter 39

IT WAS ALREADY dark by the time Kate got back to the apartment.

She'd agreed to meet Daniel at 7.30, which meant she had just under an hour to get ready. Orna had insisted she pack a slinky dark teal dress that draped at the shoulder and tapered to a narrow skirt. The sleeves were tight, long and buttoned. It wasn't in the slightest bit revealing and it complemented Kate's colouring perfectly. Bringing it had seemed utterly ridiculous at the time – she was full sure she'd have nowhere to wear it.

But she did now.

And Orna had insisted that she bring a pair of heels, too. Kate closed her eyes, thanking her sister. 'You always have to travel with a back-up cocktail dress,' Orna had said, 'or something you can wear if you get invited out unexpectedly. You're going to Paris, Kate, not up a mountain. You can't just take your jeans.'

Unexpectedly was right.

Smiling to herself, Kate headed for the living room, pulling Hanna's snow globe in its crumpled tissue paper from her handbag. She didn't bother putting on the lights; the street lamps threw long shadows on the polished floor. Heading for the fireplace, she gave the snow globe a little shake, and put it on the end of the mantelpiece.

She'd taken a photo of it on her table at Madame Brasserie at lunchtime; she'd take another photo in the apartment when it was light in the morning. When she gave it to Hanna, Kate would show her the pictures – mini Eiffel Tower at the Eiffel Tower, and in a real Paris apartment. She stood back, smiling, watching the tiny particles dance inside the glass. It was charming.

Kate opened the door at the end of the *salon* and crossed the dark corridor to the kitchen. She was starting to feel hungry, and she needed something in her stomach if they were going to have cocktails. The glorious-looking cheesecake was calling to her from the fridge.

Flicking on the kitchen lights, Kate lifted the cake box carefully out, and pulled open a drawer to look for a spoon.

Pushing open the bedroom door with her elbow, the box in one hand, the spoon in the other, Kate took a mouthful and savoured it for a moment. Whatever else was happening, right now she was eating an artisan cheesecake in a fabulous Parisian apartment, about to put on an impossibly expensive dress that she could never afford, and go for cocktails at the Ritz. Orna was always telling her that she needed to live in the moment, to collect moments of joy so she could remember them.

Kate put the cake box down on the top of the dressing table and, unhooking her bag, slipped off her coat.

Her biggest problem was that she didn't have time to wash and dry her hair, but a good brush should sort it out, and then she could put it up. Heading for the bathroom, she kicked off her boots and undid her trousers, pulling out her blouse from the waistband and unbuttoning it. She flipped on the shower, water cascading from the huge shower head.

Back in the bedroom, steam began to billow from the bathroom. Shedding her clothes onto the bed, she reached for her hairbrush, about to pull off the hair-tie wrapped around the handle so she could brush and put up her hair.

But the brush wasn't where she'd left it on the dressing table – or where she thought she'd left it, at any rate.

She took a step backwards and looked down both sides, bending to check the floor. Had she knocked it off as she'd left this morning?

Kate knelt down to look under the bed. Nothing. Scrambling up, she checked under the bedclothes, which were pulled up under her pillow. *Had she done that?* She paused. The pillow was freshly plumped. She was pretty sure she hadn't done that. But the bed hadn't been made as it would have been in a hotel; the counterpane was still creased where she'd slept under it.

She lifted the pillow. Still no brush.

Weird.

Unsettled, Kate walked into the bathroom to see if she had another elastic tie in her make-up bag.

But she stopped when she reached the sink. There on the recessed windowsill, beside the bottles of liquid soap and body lotion that had arrived yesterday, was her brush, and next to it, a bottle of perfume.

What on earth was going on in this place? Was Céline popping in and leaving her things?

Puzzled, Kate picked the perfume up. It was a small bottle, the ridged glass topped with a gold cap. She took the lid off. It was flowery – layers of violet, geranium and rose that she recognised from the perfume course.

She read the name neatly printed on the label – Belle de Nuit, like the body lotion. She spritzed her wrist, testing it on her skin. It was warm and fruity with an undertone of musk.

She put the lid back on. She'd need to use it after her shower if she was going to wear it. Conscious that she didn't have much time, Kate reached for her brush, and was slipping the elastic hair tie off when she looked properly at it.

It was clean. There wasn't a single hair caught between the plastic spines.

Weirder. Even if she'd cleaned it and then forgotten, there were always a few stray hairs left tangled.

Straightening up, she looked at it again.

Why would someone have come into the apartment and cleaned her hairbrush?

Chapter 40

IN THE *PARIS HEURE* office, Agathe picked up the mug of coffee her uncle had brought her and warmed her hands on it. His office was dark now, lit only by the desk lamp and the glow from the newsroom coming in through the glass door. Agathe had cleared several piles of books and newspapers, and set up her laptop on a desk under the window. She could see the river from here, the movement of the water reflected in the street lights along its sides, writhing and roiling like a sleeping beast through the city.

It was almost seven, but she couldn't face going home yet. Agathe swivelled around in her chair as Maxim appeared at the office door, then closed it silently behind him. He looked drained; he was wearing the same pale pink shirt with the same white T-shirt under it as the day before, as if he'd pulled them both off the bedroom floor.

'Maxim, sit, update us.' Maxim glanced at Agathe as if he was unsure about whether she should be listening to his report. Her uncle caught his glance.

'She's part of this, Maxim. Let's get on.'

Nodding curtly, Maxim came and sat down in front of the desk, swinging his leather satchel around onto his knee and opening it. He pulled out a sheaf of papers.

'I've just been talking to a contact in *La Crim* – not Travère, someone a bit more flexible. I gave her all our ideas and Agathe's research yesterday, and she said they were looking into it.'

Agathe couldn't help snorting. Maxim glanced at her.

'They are taking it very seriously. She didn't want to be seen with me. I had to meet her on a fire escape. She says everyone is worried. The cases should have been connected, but …' He shrugged. 'Missing persons aren't always murder victims, and they are spaced apart – although I said there may be more, that these were just the ones you found in the press.' Glancing at Agathe, Maxim cleared his throat. 'Anyway, they are all over it now. And Sandrine's parents have been informed. Her father is a big noise in Airbus – like, a *big* noise. He's already been on to Carlier.'

'Well, that's good, isn't it, that they are looking at the other cases?' Agathe leaned forward in her chair.

Maxim nodded. 'Certainly is.' He cleared his throat. 'She's as mad as we are that these cases haven't been connected before. She gave me copies of the post-mortem reports on the remains they have, and Sandrine's.'

'Excellent. So?' Gabriel's voice was like a machine gun.

Part of Agathe dreaded hearing what it said, but another part of her couldn't bear to wait any longer. 'Sandrine? Have they got the toxicology report? What does it say?'

Maxim looked at the papers in his hand, shuffling them until the one he needed was on the top. 'The results indicate that her body was washed in bleach – it had been submerged, obviously, but the plastic was practically watertight. The bleach suggests someone who knew what they were doing, but who also had time on his side.'

Agathe leaned forward to speak, but Maxim stopped her, answering her unspoken question. 'The forensics team are checking the penthouse that she was showing. Given that the building is empty, it would be a logical place for anything like that to be done.'

Agathe sat back, letting him continue. 'The results also show that she was drugged. It says, "chloroform was detected in the blood and tissues by gas chromatographic/ mass spectrometric analysis. Evidence strongly suggests forced inhalation using an impregnated cloth."' Maxim glanced across the desk at Gabriel. 'And he didn't try and cut up her body. If it was the same person who killed either of the girls whose heads were found, the MO is very different.' Shifting in his seat, he continued. 'I mean, you can see why they only linked the heads, and not any of these other cases.'

'Sandrine wasn't even a redhead.' Agathe could feel the tears welling up again. She reached into her jeans pocket for a tissue.

Maxim glanced at her. 'She looked like one, which is what's worrying *La Crim*.'

Gabriel sighed loudly. 'Perhaps the MO is different *because* he realised she wasn't a real redhead.' He put his hand out to look at the reports himself.

Maxim shrugged. 'Perhaps he alternates his methods, and that's part of the problem, too. I mean, the computer doesn't link women with brown eyes does it?' He cleared his throat. 'There could be others who have gone into the river, but weren't categorised as suspicious.'

Like tendrils of fire, the hair gleamed under the light of the lamp. He'd grabbed a few moments for himself, unable to resist looking at it again. Close up, he could see golden threads interwoven with darker strands, blonde, and what looked like deep rust. So many colours, each like a musical note in a refrain that was building to a crescendo.

The notes had been deep and low, like a double bass, as he'd slipped inside the apartment earlier, the sound vibrating through his head as he sought out her scent. He'd needed to savour the moment, standing in the salon, the lights off, breathing her in.

Delaying, he'd gone into the kitchen, seeking out the jar of ground coffee. He couldn't afford to put the machine on, but it was such a familiar smell he could feel it in the fabric of the building, like a voice calling him. The aroma of coffee was like the Seine, winding through the city, always moving. Taking the lid off the jar, he inhaled. He needed the heat – the scalding heat – but this helped; it eased the pressure.

Screwing the lid back on, he'd replaced the jar and paused, listening hard, knowing she wouldn't be back from her course for a while, but now wasn't the time to take risks. There had been too much planning.

It was all in the detail. The research. Thinking through every move.

It wouldn't be long now.

In the bedroom, he'd gone straight to the bed, couldn't resist burying his head in her pillow, breathing her in. He'd plumped it up before he'd gone into the bathroom, taking a moment to enjoy the space. It didn't take much to imagine her in the shower, to see her washing her hair, the water cascading off her pale skin. He'd picked up a still damp towel and, closing his eyes, rubbed it over his face. She'd used the body lotion. The fragrance hit him, spiking his need.

He breathed in the scent of the towel again.

It wouldn't be long now.

Back in the bedroom he'd gone straight to the brush, her thick hair tangled wantonly through the spines, the thrill like a trumpet in the soundtrack in his head.

Soon he'd be able to smell the perfume on her skin. That perfect scent. And he'd feel the thrill, the ecstasy again.

Soon she'd be all his.

Chapter 41

IN THE BACK of the taxi, Kate chewed the side of her nail. She'd barely had time to think about the hairbrush thing before she'd left, had only had time to shower, quickly redo her make-up, and pull on Orna's dress. She'd remembered the perfume then – had hesitated to use it – but she hadn't bought any of her own, and she was going to the Ritz. She'd squirted her wrist, dabbing, as Madame Ducournau had instructed.

It was so odd, finding her brush cleaned – so creepy. She'd quickly checked the bins before she'd left, but there was no sign of the hair. So someone must have taken it.

Which made her feel a bit sick.

As the taxi pulled into an enormous, brightly lit pedestrian square, a statue on a towering verdigris pillar in the middle, Kate could feel her heart rate increase. The huge arched glass doors of the Ritz hotel opened onto a broad pavement. On every side of the square were designer boutiques: Chopard, Louis Vuitton, Cartier, Graff – glittering jewels in brightly lit windows.

Kate pushed open the door of the taxi. *Should she be doing this at all?* Meeting some guy she'd only just bumped into on the train and had a coffee with?

But he wasn't anybody. His name was Daniel Langton, and he was English, and he had a great-aunt who lived in Hampstead and he worked with patents. That wasn't the sort of thing you made up.

Inside the street doors, thickly carpeted steps led up to the main entrance. It felt almost as if they'd carpeted the pavement in a royal blue. There was a central circular swing door, but as she stepped onto the first step, a uniformed porter, wired to an earpiece like a member of the FBI, swung a door open for her.

'*Bonsoir, madame*, welcome to the Ritz.'

Kate couldn't resist a smile at his correct assessment of her nationality, simultaneously thankful for the dress. At the last second, she'd decided against her coat. It really didn't match, and she'd only be outside when she was running from the taxi to the door.

'I'm meeting someone in the Hemingway Bar?' The porter inclined his head and walked her to the start of a wide, richly carpeted corridor before giving her directions to the bar she was looking for.

It was much further than she'd expected. On either side of the corridor, there were restaurants and elegant lounge areas. Further on, she turned right and, heading up marble steps, found herself in a long narrow corridor, glittering with designer boutiques. The doorman had said to go to the end, past the round Ritz bar. But when she got there, there didn't seem to be anywhere to go beyond it. On her left, another set of huge glass doors opened to what looked like a side entrance. A black-suited doorman with an earpiece was hovering at the top of a broad flight of marble stairs. Kate pushed open the door and immediately saw a roped-off area and a sign for Bar Hemingway, the entrance tucked away behind thick red curtains.

Carefully navigating the steps in her heels, she hovered at the curtained doorway to what looked like a tiny, cosy bar – much more like the bar in a pub at home than something she'd expect in Paris. A waiter in a pure white jacket and slim black tie came to meet her, smiling a greeting just as she spotted Daniel sitting against the inside wall opposite the bar.

His reading glasses on the end of his nose, what looked like a newspaper in his hand, he looked up as the waiter welcomed her. Standing, smiling broadly, Daniel took off his glasses and invited Kate to take the low green leather chair on the other side of the table.

There was already a glass of chilled water on the round black glass table, elegantly placed on a cream and gold coaster. Beside it were a silver bowl of crisps and an intricate silver stand holding olives and nuts.

'I'm so glad you could join me. How was your day?'

Kate wasn't sure if it was the warm tone in his voice, or his manners and gallantry, that suddenly made her well up. It was such a simple thing to stand as she arrived, but it wasn't something she was used to. Fighting the surge of emotion, she sat down and tried to compose herself. It took her a moment, during which he must have read her face.

'What's happened? Is everything OK? You look a bit shaken.' Sitting down, he put his glasses down on what Kate suddenly realised wasn't a newspaper at all, but the *Hemingway Star*, a cleverly printed menu. He leaned forward in his seat, his voice full of concern.

'Sorry, I ... Yes.' She drew a breath.

'No need to apologise, whatever it is.'

'Sorry ...' She shook her head, smiling. 'Sorry, I did it again – force of habit.'

'Let's get you a drink and you can tell me.' He held up his hand to the waiter and then, as if he'd realised what he'd said, quickly added, 'But don't feel you have to ... Tell me, I mean ...' He paused, blushing. 'Sorry. My turn. I'm very much out of the habit.' He blushed again as she smiled. He looked so embarrassed, part of her wanted to reach across the table and pat his arm reassuringly.

'I just had a bit of a strange experience back at the apartment and it's knocked me a little. And ...' But she wasn't about to say that she wasn't used to polite men with perfect manners, or that she'd been to the bridge that morning, with the lock from her best friend's diary. She really didn't know Daniel well enough to tell him about Trisha. Not yet, anyway.

A look of concern passed across Daniel's face as the waiter appeared at his shoulder, another folded menu in his hand.

'You look like you could do with a stiff gin and tonic, Kate. Will we look at the cocktail menu in a few minutes?'

Kate could feel her eyes brimming. Cocooned in this beautiful room, she suddenly felt incredibly safe. 'Please, that would be lovely.' She picked up the glass of water, taking a sip to give herself a moment to pull herself together, discovering it was deliciously flavoured with cucumber.

'I've been genning up on the history of this bar to regale you with, but first things first. Bombay Sapphire and Schweppes for my guest, and a Delamain XO for me.' The waiter retreated and Daniel looked at Kate, his eyebrow crooked. His eyes were serious, as if in that moment, she was the most important thing in the world.

'It was just ... I don't know.' Putting the glass down, Kate kept her voice low, conscious of the packed tables close to them as she tried to gather her thoughts. The bar was surprisingly busy. 'Someone was in my apartment. Yesterday they moved a few things and left some bottles in the bathroom. I thought maybe it was a housekeeper or ... Anyway, today they must have been back. I found a bottle of perfume. But ...' She hesitated. 'This time they moved my hairbrush, and ...' She blushed. It felt strange to be saying this to a man she hardly knew. 'They'd cleaned it.'

It sounded such a silly thing to be upset about, but she couldn't shake the feeling she'd had, as if something was crawling across her skin.

Daniel's eyebrows rose as he thought about this. 'From your reaction, I'm guessing you don't think it was a housemaid this time?'

She shook her head, slumping back in the chair. 'No, it was just so ...' She looked for the word. '*Odd*. My make-up was still scattered in the bathroom, so they weren't there to tidy up. They plumped my pillows, but they didn't make the bed. It's ... Well, it's just so weird.'

As she spoke, the waiter arrived with their drinks.

'Boy, I need this. Thank you.'

Daniel raised his own glass. 'Thank you for joining me, *particularly* after that experience.' He said it with feeling. 'Is there any reason to think someone other than a cleaner might have got inside? You haven't seen or felt anything ...' He hesitated. 'Not quite right?' He cleared his throat, shaking his head. 'I'm sorry. I worked with the security services in the army, my mind is set to suspicious.'

She smiled gratefully. 'Thank you for taking me seriously and not saying it's my imagination.'

He looked surprised, as if the thought had never occurred to him. 'You are a very intelligent, sensible woman, Kate Wilde. I think anyone who accused you of overreacting to anything would be very misguided.' He paused. 'But seriously, have you any idea who it could have been?'

Kate felt tears pricking her eyes again. She took a deep breath. She barely knew him, but suddenly she felt as if she needed to explain. 'I have an ex-husband. He was quite … It was an abusive relationship. There's a restraining order. But I think he may be here in Paris. He sent me a photograph of himself under the Arc de Triomphe.' She hesitated. 'I think he might have been following me the other night.'

Daniel took this in. 'Did he follow you home? Does he know where you're staying?'

Kate took a breath. 'I'm not sure if he followed me all the way, but honestly, I don't know how he found me. Paris is a big city, and I've been very careful about saying anything on social media – I always am.' She took a sip of her gin; she didn't think she'd ever needed a G and T more. 'I've sent photos to my sister and my daughter, but they are the only people who know where I'm staying. Well, I thought so, anyway.'

Daniel's eyebrows met. 'But you said you won this trip in a competition you didn't remember entering.' He stopped speaking, as if he was weighing his words. 'Is it possible that he arranged it?'

Kate put her glass down with a crack. 'My God, I never thought of that.'

Chapter 42

AGATHE REACHED FOR the hall light switch and closed her apartment door behind her, leaning on it, listening to the silence.

Well, it wasn't quite silent; Roland's clock ticked on. But she could tell he wasn't here. His bike was gone, for one thing, but she could feel the emptiness, like a physical thing.

It had taken her uncle ages to persuade her to leave the office. Perhaps she should have gone home with him, but she knew she'd just be something extra to think about instead of the story – and an added complication to his bachelor existence. In the end, he'd booked her a taxi and sent her out into the night.

At least the main roads of the city were never truly dark. Agathe shuddered at the thought. She hated the dark. Anything could be hiding.

She had never been able to sleep without a night light, and the emptiness of the house made it all worse. She felt as if they were missing a piece – as if there was a gap, a tear in time that Sandrine had been ripped away through, ripped out of their lives. And she could feel it in the ticking of the clock, in the silence.

Sandrine's parents had called her earlier. Agathe had no idea how they'd got her number – maybe from the police, she didn't know. It didn't matter. They were coming on Saturday to take Sandrine's things home.

Her back pressed to the door, Agathe could feel tears hot on her face. If they took her things, Sandrine would never come back. Agathe knew it was irrational, but …

Heaving a sigh, she rubbed her face and pushed herself off the door and across the corridor to Sandrine's room. Her hand hovered on the door handle. They didn't lock their doors; they didn't need to – they all respected one another's privacy.

Easing the handle down, Agathe pushed open Sandrine's door and quickly reached for the light switch. The room smelled of Sandrine – of her body lotion, of her perfume, as if the scent was caught in the corners of the room.

Agathe leaned on the frame.

Had she known who killed her? Had she met someone – a date, maybe? The police had been already, had looked through her things, not closing her drawers properly, underwear and T-shirts sticking up where they'd been rifled through.

Agathe looked around the room, dominated by the double bed piled with cushions, the headboard covered in a pretty floral fabric Sandrine had found in a sale. The cushions were shades of lilac, soft and cosy. On the right, her bedside table was jumbled with books and papers.

Could Agathe find something the police had missed that might help? There had to be something ... some way this killer had found her – and, if it was the same person, the other women.

Something that connected them.

Agathe closed her eyes for a moment and concentrated on the newspaper reports she'd found. On her spreadsheet was a list of locations, shared characteristics. They all hung around the centre of Paris; they were all young, they all had red hair. But that wasn't enough.

Agathe had spoken to one of the police officers who had come to search Sandrine's room – he'd assured her that they'd check everything. They hadn't found her phone, but they could check to see what calls had been made. They'd check her email to see if she'd registered with any online dating sites, try and find out who she'd been talking to. He'd said that they would be thorough, that they'd look at everything.

But what if it was random? How did you find a killer who had no connection to his victims? The red hair had to be something to do with it, but Sandrine had only had red hair for a day or so, how unlucky could she have been to be spotted by a killer?

Where had she been when it happened?

Perhaps that's where the police needed to look first. They needed to retrace her steps from the moment she'd left the hair salon. Perhaps he was out there, just watching for redheads?

Chapter 43

KATE FELT HER chest constrict, her whole body tightening with fear. Normally she wasn't stuck for something to say, but all her words seemed to have deserted her.

Was Daniel right? Could Erik have organised all of this? Would he have remembered her connection to Paris?

She'd first met Erik soon after she'd moved to London to teach, when she'd hardly known anyone. When he'd mentioned working in Paris, she'd told him about Trisha – about seeing *Amélie* and their schoolgirl dreams, and Trisha's diary. But would he really have remembered?

She shivered, her skin goose bumping. Everything he did was about control – controlling her, controlling Hanna. With the restraining order in place, he wasn't in control any more. And that hadn't ever sat well with him.

Across the small round table, his face only half-lit by the glow of a lamp beside them, Daniel was frowning. He slowly turned his whisky glass around on its paper mat.

'Let's think about this logically.' He cleared his throat, his voice somehow crisper, as if he'd switched into a different mode. It was a good switch. Even as the shock rolled through her like waves, it made Kate feel supported, as if he was taking her seriously.

He pursed his lips. 'So the questions that leap out at me are … why Paris? Why now? What's the end goal? And actually, why a perfume course?' He looked up at her. 'I don't want to pry, but it feels important to consider those points. You're here until Sunday?'

'Yes, the return Eurostar ticket is booked for Sunday afternoon.'

'Please don't take this the wrong way, I don't want to frighten you, but if there *is* an end goal here, some sort of confrontation, then logically it's likely to come in the next forty-eight hours.' He took a sip of his whisky. 'That's something you need to be aware of. Not to change your plans, but just to have on your radar. It feels to me as if the surveillance, contact, interference, whatever you want to call it, is ramping up.'

Kate pushed her glass away, her stomach turning. Daniel was right. *The hairbrush was so personal. Whoever it was had been in her bedroom.* She ran her hands over her face, closing her eyes for a moment. When she opened them again, he was looking at her hard.

'Kate, nothing is going to happen to you, I will do my absolute utmost to ensure that. If we never meet again after this week, you have my word that I will get you home to Hanna.'

He said it so sincerely that tears pricked at Kate's eyes again. She barely knew this man and here he was, going out of his way to look out for her. Before she could finish the thought, he continued. 'I don't want you to feel like you're being cross-examined, but I want to get the full picture here. So why Paris?'

Kate ran her hand into her hair, thinking. 'Erik worked here. He has a cousin here – he used to visit him quite often. They're very close, more like brothers. Erik speaks French fluently ...' She hesitated. 'And I had a friend, my best friend, Trisha. She was very ill. She made me promise to bring the lock from her diary here, if anything happened to her.' She felt a tear slip down her cheek. 'I didn't ... I wasn't ...' She cleared her throat. 'This is the first time I've been able to do it, because of this trip.'

'And he knows this – about the promise?' Kate shrugged. Daniel frowned as he continued. 'When you say "worked" ... give me some background?'

'Erik's part Latvian, part Swedish. They had compulsory military service in Sweden, and he loved it, so he joined their army when he left school. Then he trained as a chef. He was working in a hotel in London when we met, but he'd worked in Paris for a year.'

'So he has access and is familiar with the landscape. And you mentioned a restraining order in the UK, which means he's on the UK police radar, so bringing you to Paris gives him a bit more freedom.' Daniel narrowed his eyes. 'Paris is a place he knows – and more importantly, you don't, which gives him an advantage. Adding in the Eurostar makes it feel more like something promotional.'

'That's what Madame Ducournau thought – she's the tutor at Le Studio des Parfums. She said the course was booked by a PR company, and that it could have been Eurostar or Paris Tourism who organised it.'

Daniel looked over her shoulder, as if he was taking in all the information and piecing it together.

'It feels like there's some sort of significance in the type of course. I mean, he could have waited for you to accept the prize before he booked anything, but there was a risk you might not have taken him up on it. Did perfume make it more attractive?'

'I nearly didn't accept. It's half-term. If Orna hadn't taken Hanna, I wouldn't have been able to come.'

'So the course element of the package meant you had to come on your own. Interesting.' He paused. 'If it had been a different sort of course – I don't know ... cooking or painting, perhaps – you might have been able to bring Hanna?'

Kate nodded. Before she'd spoken to Orna she'd wondered if she could bring Hanna, but three days of perfume would have been too much. In the initial blurb there had been an emphasis on the history and understanding of the perfume industry, as well as the practical side of perfumery. No nine-year-old would sit still for that.

Fear flowed through Kate again. 'Do you think he wants to take Hanna? Is this what this is about – separating us?'

'Has he done that before?'

Kate raised her eyebrows, trying to shut down the memories of the terror she'd felt when Hanna's teacher had said her dad had picked her up from school. 'The police tracked him down, to Southampton – he took her there to see the sea, apparently. I don't know what would have happened if they hadn't found him ...'

Daniel considered this for a moment, then shook his head. 'I don't think he's trying to get to Hanna. Someone ... let's suppose it's Erik, is trying to frighten *you* specifically. He can't be in two places at once, and if he's planning something, he'll want to keep the number of people who know to an absolute minimum.'

'Orna thinks her phone was stolen in the park. That's how I thought he might know where I was. But if he booked the apartment and the course, he knows where I am.'

'Indeed ... The phone theft could be coincidental. Phones get stolen all the time in London.'

Frowning, he turned his glass around on its mat. 'Whoever organised this has access to your apartment. That's significant.'

'I think it's an Airbnb or something. It's definitely set up for holiday rental. Maybe he's stayed there before and had keys cut?'

'Or someone he knew has stayed there previously.'

'It's such a good location. It's only about ten minutes from Le Studio des Parfums, right near Saint-Paul Métro station. There are cafés and a supermarket all within walking distance.' Kate reached for her drink. She didn't feel sick now, but angry – at herself for falling for this, and at Erik, for going to these extremes to get her here.

Daniel contemplated his glass. 'I'm told it's very easy to set up fake accounts on Facebook, and anyone can set up a website, so the competition itself could look very real from the outside.'

It was as if he'd read her mind. 'Orna checked it out. She made sure the train was actually booked, that the apartment was a rental – that it was real.'

Daniel raised his eyebrows. 'Your sister is very sensible. Do you have a photo of him – of Erik? I'll see if any of my contacts here can shed any light on his whereabouts.'

'How can you …?' Kate reached for her bag and pulled out her phone as she spoke. 'Here's the picture he sent from the Arc de Triomphe. You can see his face clearly.' Her eyes met his. 'Perhaps he would have chosen a different seat if he'd known I'd end up sitting opposite you.'

Chapter 44

AS MAXIM PULLED up outside Le Loup Gris, he was still in two minds about whether to tell Lucien that Daniel was in town. He hated that his two oldest friends didn't get along, but after all this time it would need a miracle to repair the damage.

Flicking the stand down on his Suzuki and looping the heavy chain around the wheel, Maxim looked up at the door of the club. It had already been a long day.

But sometimes you just needed to talk a story through with someone you trusted – well, Maxim did, at least. Maybe it was his way to process the darkness, but over the years he'd settled into an easy pattern with Lucien. His office at the club was totally private, right at the top of the building in the attic space, and Lucien always kept a good brandy in his desk drawer. He was also the only other person Maxim knew, apart from cops, who worked in the middle of the night. Very often, as Maxim was on his way home from a scene or a particularly gruelling interview, he felt the need to offload.

Skipping up the steps, Maxim shook his head. The thing about Lucien was that he was so self-obsessed he barely listened anyway, so Maxim was never too worried about revealing details. In Lucien's head, his own successes were far more important than absolutely anything else. It could be deeply annoying, and there were times when Maxim came away feeling like a total failure, which wasn't all that healthy, but Lucien's office was a safe space. Maxim's wasn't the sort of job you could do and keep totally bottled up – they went way back, and that shared experience counted for a lot in Maxim's book.

Normally, the minute Maxim had offloaded – or sometimes even before, if Lucien was itching to tell him something – Lucien would start on what was happening in his life, regaling him with salacious stories about the latest celebrity who had come to the club. He was wonderfully indiscreet, given Maxim's job, but they had an understanding. Once Lucien was in the centre of the conversation, everything was fine.

Lucien was on the phone when Maxim got up to his office, the sloping ceilings and small windows making it feel more like a den than the operational hub of a multimillion-euro business. And Lucien had made it even more den-like, with a huge TV on the gable wall and a massive sofa that was big enough to make a very comfortable bed. His desk was antique, leather-topped, with a marble bust of Ares, the Greek god of war, on one end.

Lucien held up his hand as Maxim stuck his head around the door, finishing up his conversation on the phone.

'Yes, twelve cases. Only the best, you know me. And do drop by next time you're passing, I'll leave members' passes for you at the front door.'

He hung up, and as Maxim came into the room, Lucien jumped up from the desk to give him a hug.

'You look like you've had a long day.'

Maxim flopped into the button-back armchair opposite the desk, putting his helmet down on its insanely tidy surface. He didn't know how Lucien managed it, but perhaps being drilled by Céline helped; she'd always been a tidiness freak. She'd have a breakdown if she ever came to his apartment.

'It's definitely been a challenging day, shall we say—'

Lucien interrupted him, his face alight with curiosity. 'This girl in the river?'

Maxim nodded, scowling as he stared at the toe of his boot, and gave Lucien an overview of what was going on at *Paris Heure*. When he'd finished, he rubbed his hands hard over his face and through his hair, trying to shift the feeling clinging to his skin. He wasn't even sure what it was; it felt like a layer of city dirt or misery, or both.

Lucien sat on the edge of his desk and frowned. 'But I thought serial killers stuck to patterns? Heads in the sewers and women in the Seine – those are totally different. The one in the river can't be connected to the heads, surely?' He looked at Maxim quizzically. 'I mean, if they all had dark hair, would you be connecting them?'

Maxim sighed. 'Perhaps not. And you're right about the different methods of disposal, but Beaudin – and Carlier – don't want to risk it *not* being a coincidence.'

Lucien nodded as if that made sense. 'Anything else in common? All from the same area, maybe? Isn't there a whole science in geo-profiling murders? I saw a documentary about it.'

'There is, and we know they were all based in the city, but from out of town. I say all, but we've only got three bodies. "Only" seems the wrong word … I mean, the other women we've found who could be linked are all missing – no bodies found. But that doesn't mean anything. They could all be in the sewers and just haven't turned up yet.'

'True. Or they could have vanished for a good reason they didn't choose to share. Look at Meredith, and then Daniel hightailing it into the army.' Lucien turned to go behind his desk, bending to open the deep bottom drawer. 'Let me get you a drink.'

Maxim didn't stop Lucien to correct him on Daniel's 'disappearance', but received his glass gratefully. As if he'd already moved on from the murdered women in his head – that was classic Lucien – he continued. 'How is Daniel? Have you heard from him? I often wonder what he's doing – whether he married or has a significant other.'

Taking a sip and savouring the brandy, Maxim shrugged. He did his best to avoid the subject of Daniel when he was talking to Laurance, but on occasion it came up. He'd got drunk one Christmas and had a long chat with Céline about their falling-out, wishing Daniel would come halfway at least to try and mend the past. They'd talked about what Daniel was doing in the army and how he was often in Paris, but had never once tried to get in touch with Lucien. Part of him had hoped Céline would tell Lucien; maybe if he heard it from her, he might reach out to Daniel with an apology. But she hadn't told him

– at least, not as far as Maxim could tell. Maybe she'd forgotten the conversation; she'd been fairly inebriated.

Maxim took another sip of his brandy before answering.

'He's fine, still single.' Maxim hid his grin. 'He's here, actually, came over for an auction.'

Lucien took a sip from his own glass. 'Strange he never settled down.'

Maxim shrugged again. 'Not really – there are bonuses to being single.'

Lucien rolled his eyes. 'Plenty else strange about him, though, you've got to admit. His whole reaction to the Meredith thing. I mean, I only kissed her, it wasn't anything. He totally overreacted.'

Maxim looked at Lucien across the desk. It wasn't as if they hadn't had this conversation before, but this was Lucien all over; he could only ever see the ripples around himself in the pond. No matter how many times Maxim said it, he didn't get it. 'I think it was what happened afterwards that was more of a problem. Meredith went off, and in his mind Daniel's firmly linked that with you having a crack at her.' He shrugged. 'Maybe she had some sort of existential crisis, or realised she was gay or something, and couldn't face telling him. I don't know.

But Daniel blames you for him losing the love of his life …'

Lucien shook his head and threw Maxim an impatient look. 'Mad – I mean, really. Her going off was about him, not me. I reckon it's in his family, though. That aunt of his is completely crazy.'

Chapter 45

AGATHE TURNED AROUND as the café door opened, and almost dropped the frothing mug of hot chocolate that she was holding.

'You *sure* you're doing OK?' Standing beside her, seeing her start, Oumar gently took the mug from her and put it onto the waiting tray he was filling for a customer.

'Yes, yes, sorry.' Looking from the new arrival to Oumar, she smiled weakly. 'I'm fine. Have to keep going.'

Oumar nodded his dark head. They'd had a big chat when she'd turned up for work. He understood, but she knew he couldn't carry a member of staff who wasn't fully functioning, and Fridays were busy.

The problem was that everyone who came in seemed to be talking about the news – Sandrine's name was on everyone's lips. Agathe could see Oumar flinching, too, whenever anyone said it directly to him. Sandrine had often called in for a chat if she was in the area. Oumar had known her as well.

But Agathe had managed to keep it together until now.

'Good God. What are you doing here?' Maxim clearly hadn't been concentrating when he'd walked in. His motorbike helmet looped over his arm, he'd had his eyes on his phone, scrolling for something. Now he'd looked up to order, he'd visibly started, just as Agathe had.

'I work here, actually. I could ask you the same thing.' Agathe thrust her hands into the pockets of her apron, so he couldn't see them shaking, and tried to keep her voice level.

As if Maxim hadn't heard her, he looked back at her for a moment. 'But—'

Agathe cut him off. 'I know. It's horrible. Everyone's talking about it and they don't know I know her. Everyone seems to have a theory.' She screwed up her face for a moment, then blurted out, 'She called in here last week – on Thursday, before work – but I was picking up stuff from the wholesaler.'

Agathe felt her heart break all over again. Oumar had said Sandrine had been thrilled with her new look. *If only she'd been here.* Agathe took a shaky breath as Maxim put his phone down on the counter, and pushed her hair back into her clip.

'My life can't stop. If I want to be useful to her, to help you, I need to be fully functioning, not wallowing in grief. Being stuck in the apartment is driving me mad.'

'How's your other flatmate doing?' Maxim's frown was full of concern.

How did he know about Roland? 'I've barely seen him since it happened. I think he needs to get out, too. Too many memories.'

Maxim nodded slowly as Agathe continued.

'You know her family are coming to Paris today. To collect her things. And …'

Her body.

It hung between them like a spectre.

But they both knew her body couldn't be released until the pathologist was happy with the tests he'd done, and it could take weeks for the results to come in. Until then, they were all in limbo.

Agathe shivered at the thought. Sandrine was in a cupboard in the morgue. A dark cupboard.

Agathe's worst nightmare.

Needing to move the conversation on, she took a

breath. 'I'm meeting her mum and dad at the apartment when I'm finished here.'

'Christ, that won't be easy.' It was as if it had escaped before Maxim could reel it back. He blushed hard. 'Sorry – you know that.'

Agathe took a shaky breath. He was going to say something that would make her cry again in a minute; she could feel it coming. She couldn't deal with him being nice now.

'What can I get you?'

'Large latte. Three sugars, please. I need it this morning. And one of your pains au chocolat.'

Agathe hid her surprise; she hadn't seen Maxim as the frothy coffee type. She'd always sort of expected him to be a hard-edged double-espresso-no-sugar-sort. Working here, she'd learned a lot about people and how they took their coffee, always thought of them in terms of their order.

'Coming right up. Takeaway?'

'Erm …' He looked at his phone again. 'Better be in, I think.' Agathe saw a flash of concern cross his face. *Had he discovered something new?* This wasn't the place to talk about it, that was for sure.

'What brings you to Le Marais?'

As he opened his mouth to reply, the door swung open behind him.

'Good God, Maxim Verdier. What on earth are you doing here? It's been ages.' Céline Arnaud put her Gucci handbag down on the counter and, looking at Maxim in surprise, leaned in to air-kiss him on both cheeks. She had her dark hair pulled back into an elegant ponytail, a jacket slung around her shoulders. She called in every morning for croissants on her way to get the newspaper before she started work, and Agathe loved her clothes. Today she was wearing jeans and black riding boots, a cream silk blouse with a frilled collar under the jacket.

Agathe tore her eyes away from Céline and looked back to Maxim, wondering how they knew each other. Then she registered his expression. She wasn't sure if it was shock or surprise, but he looked as if he'd been caught doing something he shouldn't.

'Coffee.' He waved lamely in Agathe's direction.

'And you weren't going to call in? We're just down the road.'

Maxim looked uncomfortable. 'I was thinking about it, actually. I was in the club the other night, but there's something I wanted to check with Lucien. He's probably not up yet, though, is he?'

Céline smiled knowingly, as if she'd caught Maxim out in a lie but wasn't going to say it. 'He was at the club late, of course, but he'll be emerging soon. He's got a meeting with the designer, they are renovating.'

'Maybe I should wait if he's busy? I just wanted to have a quick chat but he's like a bear in the mornings.'

'He's like a bear most of the time.'

As Agathe watched their exchange, fascinated by whatever the undertone was, a grin flicked across Maxim's face that didn't reach his eyes.

Agathe reached for the tongs to put Céline's croissants into a bag. Part of her suddenly wanted to save Maxim and get Céline out of the shop. It was as if they'd dated years ago and had a bad break-up or something.

'Pop into the club later. The designs for the new look have just arrived, he'd love to show you.'

Céline turned her attention to Agathe, accepting the brown paper bag in her hand with a warm smile.

Agathe rang the pastries through the till and Céline tapped her card.

She turned to Maxim and gave him a hundred-watt smile. 'Call him.'

Chapter 46

O N HER WAY out, Kate pulled the apartment door closed and locked it firmly. Daniel had reassured her so much the night before. He'd asked her to send him the picture of Erik and another one she'd found on her phone. He seemed to think he could find out if Erik was in Paris, although she couldn't imagine how.

As they'd parted outside the Ritz, he'd kissed her on both cheeks and reminded her to be careful, to be vigilant. She'd wanted to hug him, had had to fight the urge. Instead, as she'd leaned in for the kiss she'd put her hand on his shoulder, connecting them for the briefest moment.

Standing on the landing outside the apartment, Kate took a deep breath. She hadn't booked a ticket, but he'd insisted that she go to the Musée d'Orsay this morning. He'd sounded so enthusiastic as he'd told her about the paintings of redheads that took pride of place in the collection, and a statue on the fifth floor that he thought she'd like.

As Kate trotted down the stairs and reached the hall, Céline's door opened. They both started, neither expecting to see the other.

'Goodness, you gave me a fright.' The Frenchwoman put her hand to her chest. She was wearing a beautiful silk blouse, ruffles at the neck and cuffs. It was incredibly simple, but Kate was absolutely sure, incredibly expensive.

'I'm so sorry.' Kate didn't know what else to say, but Céline's face cracked into a smile, her dark eyes lighting.

'Don't worry. I keep forgetting upstairs has been let. How are you enjoying Paris?'

Kate hesitated. *Should she ask about the cleaner?* She didn't want to sound accusatory, or ungrateful.

'It's wonderful. The city is so beautiful.'

Céline crossed her arms and leaned on the door frame, obviously preparing for a chat. Kate relaxed. She could ask about who might have access to upstairs much more easily if she could steer the conversation to the apartment.

'The company who organised the trip thought of everything. There were tickets to the Louvre and the Eiffel Tower in that pack they left.'

'Excellent. And how is the course? Perfume is so interesting.' Céline paused. 'Where are my manners? Come inside for a coffee, we can't chat in the hall.'

She stepped back and opened the door wide. Kate hesitated for a moment. 'But I don't want to interrupt your morning. You must be working?'

'I always take Friday off. Come in, tell me all about it.'

Following Céline into the apartment, Kate was impressed with its size – and the décor. As in the apartment upstairs, pale surfaces were complemented by beautiful drapes, the hall tiled with huge creamy slabs. Céline led her around into the living room, overlooking the courtyard that Kate could see from her kitchen. Huge concertina glass windows opened down one side of the room and, despite being on the ground floor, with buildings rising on all sides around it, it was full of light.

'How do you like your coffee? Cappuccino?'

'That would be lovely.'

As Céline disappeared into the kitchen, Kate unbuttoned her coat and slipped it off. She sat down tentatively on the sofa facing the windows. Outside, a grey cat appeared in the courtyard and slunk across the flagstones. It looked a lot like the cat who had got trapped in her apartment. It sat down and began to wash. The courtyard was beautiful, trees and shrubs arranged around a central area, giving shade and colour even at this time of the year.

Kate looked around the room, at the huge tapestry ottoman that matched the sofa, beside it a leather wing chair. The internal walls of the room were covered in bookshelves, the closely packed spines punctuated by white marble classical busts.

'Here we are.' Céline appeared with their coffees on a silver tray and, moving a bowl of ornamental golden apples from the middle of the low table, slipped it onto the glass top. 'Sugar?'

The sugar was in a tiny silver bowl with matching tongs. Everything about this place was perfect. 'One, please. Your home is beautiful.'

Céline dropped the irregular cube into the coffee and handed Kate her cup, a huge teardrop diamond flashing on her right hand. Kate didn't want to stare, but she was wearing a ring that looked like a complete circle of diamonds on the other hand, like an eternity ring. The combination against her dark jeans was breathtaking.

'Thank you. We like it. It's great to be in the heart of the city. And Lucien's club is quite close, so no commute.'

Kate lifted her eyebrows, not quite understanding what sort of club she meant. 'Club?'

'Nightclub – Le Loup Gris. It's quite well known, one of those places it's cool to be seen in.' She did air quotes as if she was above 'cool' somehow.

It was as if Céline didn't approve. Kate didn't quite know what to make of that. She decided to move on. 'And no commute for you.'

'Exactly ... I have the best of all worlds. But tell me about yourself. How are you finding Paris?'

Kate stirred her coffee with the silver spoon on her saucer. 'Wonderful. It's so beautiful, and the course has been fascinating.' Céline waited, as if she expected Kate to continue. Kate took a sip of her coffee. Where did she start with the last few days? It had been so much more than she expected. 'Scent is everywhere in Paris, isn't it? I don't think I'd realised before.'

Céline inclined her head. 'If you walk around Place Vendôme, you'll find every boutique has a unique signature fragrance – Gucci, Cartier, Louis Vuitton. It spills out into the street.' Céline smiled warmly. 'But tell me about you, your family ... Your husband and daughter don't mind you being away for a week?'

Kate looked at her cup for a moment. 'No. Well, yes

… but it's a bit complicated …' She trailed off, suddenly embarrassed. Her broken life, their tiny flat, were so far from the perfection of this elegant home. As she tried to find the words to continue, her phone pipped with a text.

Chapter 47

AGATHE LOOKED TOWARDS the rear of the café. Maxim was still there, playing with his phone – or maybe he was actually working and researching. Agathe wasn't sure, but he'd been there for ages. She sighed. *Maybe she should take him another coffee?*

Wiping her hands clean on a cloth, she glanced out of the door. There'd been a bit of a rush right after Céline had left, but now there was no one waiting and the pavement outside was clear. Oumar was looking after the table service at the very end of the shop, chatting to one of their regulars. Agathe turned back to the machine and set up another latte for Maxim.

He looked up, startled, as she slipped it onto the table.

'I thought you might like another one. On the house.' He looked surprised as she continued. 'Is there any news?'

His helmet beside him, Maxim leaned back on the bench seat that ran around the perimeter of this section, sitting up a bit straighter. 'Nothing yet.'

Agathe sat down heavily opposite him. She put her elbow on the table. 'I don't even know what I'm hoping for.'

Maxim sighed. 'I know. Whatever happens, it won't change the past – won't bring Sandrine or any of them back.'

Agathe looked at him out of the corner of her eye.

'Whoever it is has to be stopped. They're not going to give this up on their own, are they?'

Maxim picked up the coffee, his jaw taut. 'Most serial killers do, actually. They get too old, or something changes in their life – marriage or illness, or prison. Maybe killing loses its edge.'

Agathe did a double take. 'If these girls are all connected, he seems to have bursts and then goes quiet for ages, but I'm not sure his next victim will be very impressed if hoping he'll stop is the only thing *La Crim* have.'

Maxim pulled a face. 'I'm starting to wonder if they believe me about there being a serial killer, in all honesty. It's a bad look, finding out after this long that a load of cases are connected.' Before Agathe could comment, he said, 'I met her, you know.'

'Who? Sandrine?'

He nodded. 'When you were working at the office in the summer. You met her for lunch once. She was waiting at the door to be let in and I arrived behind her.'

Agathe wasn't sure why this should make a difference to Maxim, but from the look on his face, it definitely did.

Her mind went back to August: to the heat in the city; to sitting beside the river, Sandrine beside her, crêpes in their hands. Two really fit firemen had jogged past, their lean limbs tanned, wearing navy and red shorts and T-shirts fitting exactly where they should, *Sapeurs-Pompiers* emblazoned on the back. A few moments later the two guys had jogged past in the opposite direction, pretending that they weren't checking the two of them out, which had made them both laugh. Men were like bees to a flower around Sandrine, and half the time she didn't even notice.

Maxim continued as if he'd read her mind. 'She was like a bright flame, wasn't she?'

Agathe took a second to gather her emotions. She was going to cry again in a minute. 'She was gorgeous and super clever and a very nice person, and you don't get that together very often.' She sighed. 'Like, everyone I know has some issue, like a dent in their being that they have to navigate round ... They're scared of the dark, like me, or spiders, or they can't sing, or add up, or don't know their left and right, or they drink too much or are just plain mean. I don't even know ... But she didn't have any of that. It's like she was the purest person.'

'Too trusting, maybe?'

'Always. She never saw the bad in anyone. She'd buy coffee for the guy in a doorway, or soup or a sandwich.'

Maxim picked up his coffee again, his face grim.

Agathe needed to get back to work. She stood up, leaning forward with both hands on the table, her voice low.

'We have to find who did this. We just do, Max. She can't have died for nothing. She has to be the last.' She said it with such vehemence that Maxim put down his coffee. He looked at her intensely, as if something important was clicking in his head.

'You're absolutely right.'

Chapter 48

DANIEL HEARD HIS phone ringing from the bedroom. He checked his watch; it was almost eleven. *Surely too soon for news?* But this guy was good – Daniel knew that. And he owed Daniel a favour, one he'd thought he'd never have to call in.

Daniel stood up stiffly from the desk in the living area of his suite and limped through to the next room, cursing his lack of speed. His prosthetic leg hinged at the knee, but the ankle didn't work in the way he'd like it to. He was working with a team in London who were developing a robotic leg, but it felt as if it was taking forever. And he didn't have forever. Losing his team – his closest friends – had proved that to him.

But he didn't want to think about that now. He reached his phone just as it stopped ringing.

It was a French mobile number he didn't recognise. The caller didn't leave a message.

Perhaps this was it.

Daniel hit *call back*. The phone at the other end was answered immediately. He spoke in rapid French. 'I missed a call.'

Daniel immediately recognised the distinctive voice at the other end.

'We picked him up on CCTV, but it looks like he's being careful.'

'In what way?'

'Avoiding the most obvious cameras. We're checking with Interpol to get more background, but we've got him on the Métro at Olympiades. Looks like he's been living around there for a few weeks at least. He gets off at Saint-Paul – he's working there.'

'Around Saint-Paul?' Daniel's voice was sharp. *Kate was staying in Le Marias. Saint-Paul was one of the main Métro stations that connected the area with the centre of the city.*

'Yes. He's travelling very early every morning. Which would make sense if he's a chef in one of the delis or hotels.'

Daniel absorbed this information. 'Lots around there. Can you check when he arrived in Paris?'

As his contact answered, he opened WhatsApp to send Kate a message.

'On it now. This facial recognition software will be linked in with the airports and stations in a few weeks, but the boys are enjoying giving it a live test.'

'I heard it was very effective in Nice ...' Daniel left the sentence trailing as he hit *send* on his WhatsApp message.

'Precisely. It'll be invaluable during the Olympics – we'll be able to monitor the crowds. Avoid trouble.'

They both knew what sort of trouble he meant. Daniel's contact had been involved in the clean-up after the Bataclan bombing.

His contact continued, his voice guarded now. 'There was something else the boys spotted.' Daniel could tell from his tone that it was significant. 'That girl that was found in the Seine, the one with the red hair. She got on the Métro at Saint-Paul, coming into town. Opposite platform to your mark. She went into the station just ahead of him.'

'Recently?'

'Thursday morning. We'll pass it on to *La Crim*, and get her photograph into the system. See what else we can pick up.'

'*La Crim* haven't done that already?'

'They don't have the same access to this technology as we do. This is still a test project. AI is pretty controversial. We have to be careful the news doesn't leak, or the civil liberties crowd will be out on the streets before we've proven its worth.' Daniel's contact paused. 'Although, if we can get something solid on this murder, that could be all the evidence we need that it's a valuable tool.'

'That's for sure.'

Daniel sat down on his bed, his mind darting through a series of scenarios, none of which he liked.

Kate had red hair.

Her abusive ex had been in the vicinity of another woman with red hair, who had been murdered.

As if he was reading his mind, Daniel's contact continued. 'This guy Erik Vanags has a bit of a history. He did three years in the Swedish military and was discharged after an affray. He's got several outstanding warrants for disorderly behaviour, a conviction for assault in the UK against his wife – he did two years for that. There also seems to be a count of GBH, but the case was dropped because a key witness failed to turn up in court. One count of rape, same issue. And it appears the rape victim had red hair.'

Daniel could feel his mind moving rapidly, every other thought and distraction removed; his sole focus was what he'd just heard.

Had Erik followed Sandrine into the station? It was possible it was just one of those coincidences. They happened. But something about this man was very disturbing. Daniel thought of Kate's finger. Of the gaps between the words when she'd told him about the things that had been moved in her apartment.

His job had been to read those spaces between words.

He'd once watched footage of a killer catching sight of a woman in a shopping centre – a total stranger – and turning around to follow her. Had Erik randomly seen something – *someone,* Daniel corrected himself – that he liked, and acted on his base instinct? It brought the phrase 'wrong time, wrong place' to his mind.

And he knew all about that.

Could Kate's ex be involved in the other killings? She'd mentioned he had links to Paris.

Daniel cleared his throat. 'I think we're thinking the same thing. Anything on the internal radar?'

'*La Crim* don't talk to us unless they have to. They're only interested in domestic criminals. International espionage is our problem unless there's a threat. I've only seen what I've read in the paper. Did you see it this morning?'

Daniel grunted an affirmative. He had the Friday editions spread out on his desk.

His contact continued. 'This link they're making with victims ... it makes *La Crim* look incompetent. A serial killer on the loose, and they missed it? They'll be looking for ways to rubbish it.'

Maxim had had the front page of *Paris Heure* to himself this morning. More information linking the new murder with the other redheads had sent the news networks into a spin. Daniel had switched on the TV before breakfast, to see a photo of Sandrine looking back at him. He'd turned it off quickly, unsettled.

He thought for a few moments. 'If the press were to get a still of Sandrine in the Métro, it might help bring witnesses forward, keep the story live.'

At the other end, his contact grunted. 'Someone's got to keep *La Crim* accountable. But it can't come from us.'

'Understood. Can you get me a glossy?'

'With you in an hour.'

'Thanks, I owe you.'

'Not if this bastard turns out to be a killer, you won't. I'll owe you.'

Chapter 49

SITTING OPPOSITE KATE in her light-filled living room, Céline reminded her of a Siamese cat as she delicately rested her porcelain coffee cup and saucer on the arm, and leaned back in the leather armchair. 'Check your phone, it may be urgent.'

The phone pipped again. Kate slid her cup onto the table and quickly looked in her bag.

But it wasn't Hanna – it was Daniel.

His first message made her put her hand to her mouth.

Erik is in Paris. Take a taxi if you're going out, please don't take any unnecessary risks. If you're worried, call me. D.

The second one didn't make her feel any better.

I'll have more information when I see you. Please be careful. D.

'Oh, goodness.' Kate felt herself blush bright red.

'What is it? Your little girl is OK?' Céline's face

creased as she sat forward, putting her coffee down on the table.

'Sorry.' There she was, apologising again. 'It's my ex – ex-husband, I mean. He's here in Paris.' Kate's eyes flicked back to Daniel's text.

'And I can see that's not good.'

Kate shook her head, the feeling of wretchedness that had kept her awake all night overwhelming her.

Céline leaned forward. 'Has he hurt you in the past?'

Kate sighed, closing her eyes for a moment. 'He almost killed me. I was in a refuge for a while, we had to go to court. It's very difficult.'

'I'm so sorry. And you're worried he's here in Paris?'

'I know he is. Someone checked for me. He has family here.'

Kate could barely concentrate on Céline and her questions. As she'd tossed and turned in bed, thinking about the competition, she'd realised that Erik had always bought her perfume for her birthdays and Christmas. At the time, she'd thought it was because of his complete lack of imagination; it was an easy option, and chocolate would just make her fat. He'd always bought the same brand: Yves Saint Laurent's Rive Gauche. She could see the cobalt, silver and black canisters in the bathroom in their old house, on her dressing table ... they were everywhere.

Rive Gauche was what she'd imagine Madame Ducournau would describe as high-pitched – it was supposed to be floral, but it had always smelled bitter and metallic to Kate. She'd hated it on herself – had no idea how Erik could have chosen the most awful perfume available, when there were so many in the shops – but hadn't dared to ask in case it started another fight; in case he thought she was ungrateful.

He'd insisted she wear it every day, picked her up on it if she didn't. Back then, it had felt as if the scent was a way for him to mark her as his.

Rive Gauche. The Left Bank. It was a French perfume. *How had she not seen that before?* Realisation flooded through her like lava, hot and terrifying. Daniel was right – he had to be.

How had she not made the connection? But then, she'd banished a lot of her life before from her mind, her brain blanking out the details where she'd trained it to forget. *If she couldn't remember, it hadn't happened.* Disassociation from trauma was a real thing.

If she ever caught a whiff of Rive Gauche, it made her want to heave.

Kate dragged her mind back to the room and forced herself to sound relaxed. 'Do you know who organised the competition I won? Madame Ducournau at Le Studio des Parfums thought it was a marketing company.'

Céline shrugged. 'We use a letting agent ... I'm not sure. I just need to be here to let guests in, they take care of everything. Cleaning, insurance, everything.'

Cleaning?

Kate cleared her throat. 'I was wondering about cleaning – if there was maybe someone who serviced the apartment. I've noticed a few things have been moved.'

'Have they?' Céline frowned. 'I should have mentioned it. I'm sorry, that must have been a bit strange. I hadn't realised they'd sent anyone, but the letting agent has their own key. That would be part of the agreement with whoever booked the apartment.'

If it was a professional cleaner, they really hadn't done a proper job. But how could Kate suggest someone else had been in, without sounding as if she was complaining?

'Oh, I see. I was a bit worried in case it was Erik, my ex.' It sounded mad when she said it out loud. She laughed to cover her embarrassment. 'I didn't really think it could be, but ... Anyway, that's good to know.'

'You really are worried about him, aren't you?' Céline sounded concerned. Her eyes narrowed, as if she understood.

Kate nodded wordlessly, tears pricking. 'A bit. Very, actually. He's very difficult.'

As Céline spoke, Kate heard a jangling sound. The front door to the apartment was opening. For a moment she felt panic rising, part of her thinking it was Erik.

'That'll be Lucien, I expect he's forgotten something.'

A moment later, the man she'd seen pull up in his sports car outside the café was standing in the doorway to the living room. He'd been wearing sunglasses then, but he had an easy elegance and the sort of looks you didn't forget.

'Oh, hello.' He smiled, looking at Kate for a second too long, and then turned to Céline. 'Have you seen the fabric swatches? I thought they were in the car.'

'This is Kate, she's staying upstairs.' Céline raised her eyebrows. 'They're on the kitchen table – the gold velvet, you mean?'

'That's them. How are you enjoying our humble city?'

Kate started as she realised Lucien was talking to her. 'Oh, it's fabulous, thank you for asking … Paris, and the apartment.'

He smiled enigmatically. 'I'm glad.' He hesitated, obviously unsure if this was the moment to chat. 'Céline mentioned you were here to do a course?'

'Oh, yes – perfume. And I'm getting in lots of sightseeing.'

'Excellent, that's good to hear. I'll leave you to it. I'm meeting with a new designer.' He rolled his eyes. 'He's very … arty.' Kate smiled as he continued. 'I'd better go, although he'll probably be artistically late.' He grinned. 'If you need anything, just ask.'

He vanished from the doorway, and Kate could hear him banging in the kitchen. It was Céline's turn to roll her eyes.

'He always forgets something. But your ex – he'd have to ring on the street door to get inside. You're very safe here. Do you have a picture of him? Just in case.'

Chapter 50

AS THE LIFT doors opened onto the hotel reception area, with its huge chandeliers and Dalí-inspired statue, Daniel spotted Maxim leaning on the reception desk, trying to chat up the receptionist and clearly not getting anywhere.

'Max, thanks for coming over so fast.' Daniel acknowledged the receptionist as he spoke. 'I need to talk to you. I think you'd better come up.'

Maxim raised his eyebrows in surprise. 'I never thought you'd ask.'

Daniel threw him a warning look. 'I need you to be serious.' He turned to the receptionist. 'Can we get coffee upstairs, please.'

'And some of those pastries would be lovely. It's almost lunchtime and I haven't had breakfast.' Maxim looked at Daniel for approval.

Daniel nodded curtly. 'Whatever he wants.'

Maxim grinned. 'In that case, a latte for me – and some of your chef's pancakes, perhaps.' He threw the receptionist a winning smile. Daniel gestured curtly towards the lift with his head.

As the doors closed, Maxim looked at him. 'So what's this all about?'

Daniel cast his eyes around the mirrored interior of the lift. There was a camera in the top corner, which he was sure didn't record sound, but he wasn't going to take any risks.

'We'll talk upstairs. Almost there.'

Daniel's suite was a short walk from the lift, the deep carpet absorbing the sound of their footsteps. He flashed his pass key and the room lock lit up green. He pushed the door open.

'I have something to show you. Sit.' Daniel indicated the armchair as he disappeared into the bedroom, quickly reappearing with a Manila envelope, the top edge torn open.

He tipped out its contents onto the coffee table and sat down on the sofa, leaning forward to sort through a series of large glossy photographs with his fingertips.

'Good God, who's printing photographs these days? I haven't seen anything like these for years.'

Daniel glanced up at his friend. 'No digital trail.' He adjusted the bracelet on his watch. 'Obviously you haven't heard this from me, but it appears that your missing girl, Sandrine Durand, was in Saint-Paul Métro station on Thursday.'

Maxim shrugged off his leather jacket and leaned forward to pick up a photo. It was a long shot of a crowded Métro platform, the date and time stamp clear in the corner.

'I'm not seeing the significance. Agathe said she called into the coffee shop to see her – it's close to Saint-Paul. And we know she had an appointment to show a woman an apartment on Friday. Nobody's been able to get hold of the prospective buyer, though, the number is ringing out. It could be completely innocent, and she could be out of the country or something, but …' Maxim shrugged. 'Where did you get these from?'

'Best not to ask. Let's say I called in a favour.' Daniel paused. 'You'll see the significance when you hear the backstory.' He hesitated. 'This is between us at this stage, off the record.' He waited for Maxim's nod before continuing. 'I was sitting opposite a woman called Kate

Wilde on the Eurostar. We got chatting, and I met her the other day for a drink.'

'You dirty bastard – and you complain about me.'

Daniel sighed. 'Focus, Max. The point is that Kate has red hair. She also has a violent ex-husband – a Swedish Latvian who has done military service. His name is Erik Vanags, and he's here in Paris. In fact, he seems to have been working here for a while. He's a chef, all cash in hand. He's working at a hotel in Le Marais. Has been there for about a month.'

Daniel's contact had done some more digging after they'd spoken, and tracked Kate's ex-husband to a four-star hotel that seemed to employ a lot of migrant labour. But that wasn't their problem right now.

Maxim frowned. 'I'm not following.'

Daniel leaned over and tapped a man's face in one of the crowd photographs. 'This is Erik. I've had him checked out, and he's been backwards and forwards to Paris over the past few years. Usually in the winter. He isn't registered here, works for cash.'

Maxim finally got it.

'You think he could be our redhead killer?'

Daniel shrugged. 'His previous convictions would suggest he's a candidate.'

Maxim nodded slowly, looking at the photos more carefully. Daniel picked up the envelope. 'This is a better shot of Erik.' He handed Maxim another photo. It had been taken from the camera at the entrance to the Métro station.

This time, as Daniel watched him, Maxim narrowed his eyes. His jaw tightened as he looked steadily at the photograph. *What was he seeing?* There was definitely something ... Perhaps he'd seen this Erik Vanags somewhere before.

Standing up, Daniel came to look over his shoulder. 'It was a busy morning – packed. The Métro is almost as bad as the Tube.'

Maxim didn't answer, but his frown had deepened. Daniel looked at the photograph again. 'What are you seeing that I'm not?'

Maxim shrugged. 'Sandrine walking to her death. All she did was go into the Métro, and look what happened. I mean, life can change on the spin of a coin.'

Daniel let out a breath. He was right. 'Tell me about it.'

Chapter 51

KATE PICKED UP the purple glass bottle containing her finished scent and glanced at Madame Ducournau, who was waiting eagerly for her verdict on the perfume she'd made.

Despite her worries about Erik, the past few days had been like a reset – meeting different people, learning something completely new. And leaving the locks at the bridge had been a watershed moment.

Madame Ducournau's enthusiasm was infectious. Kate looked at her shyly as, taking off the stopper, she sniffed her perfume and smiled. It burst with the zest of oranges, with a spicy cinnamon undertone.

At the end of the table, the Italians were testing each other's fragrances. Davide was obviously thrilled with his. 'We should sell these in the gallery – our own brand.'

Madame Ducournau looked even more pleased. 'Get in touch if you'd like to order more—'

His partner interrupted her. 'It would need to be *very* expensive.'

They all laughed.

'Well, I'm very pleased you have enjoyed your few days here with us. I hope you have been able to see some of our beautiful city.'

'It's been wonderful, thank you.' Kate really meant it. If Erik had planned this to lure her to Paris, he'd unwittingly given her something special to cherish. In a few years' time, she might come back with Hanna to take the course again.

Thoughts of Hanna drew her back to her phone. With the constant updates from Orna since she'd arrived, she was starting to wonder if Hanna would want her to go away again so she could be spoiled by her aunt. They'd both be exhausted by the time she got home.

'So ...' Madame Ducournau raised her hands and gave them all a round of applause. 'Enjoy the rest of your time here, and thank you for being a wonderful class.'

Davide stood up. 'Who's joining us for a drink? Kate?'

'I'd love to, thank you.'

Davide turned to the Japanese couple, who looked a little panicked and politely declined, then looked at their German classmate. 'Frieda?'

'No, no, you go and enjoy your evening. I have tickets booked for the Opéra.' Frieda's whole face lit up at the thought.

The two Italians were waiting for her by the door by the time Kate had freshened up and collected her coat. She pulled her gloves on as they opened the front door. It was raining, the cobbles slick, reflecting the street lights in bright pools.

'There's a bar just along the road. I think they do food. I'm starving.' Antonio, Davide's partner, was out of the door before either of them had a chance to reply, disappearing down the narrow lane on the opposite side of the road.

'Oh my God, I need to put a tracking device on him, he always rushes off. You wouldn't believe the number of times I've almost lost him.' Davide pulled on his coat, wrapping a red scarf around his neck.

Kate laughed, preparing to follow him into the damp night. 'My daughter says there's an app you can get to find lost phones. I'm always losing mine. Perhaps that would work?'

Davide rolled his eyes, 'I think he'd turn off his location just to tease me. I'm going to get a full-on spying chip that I can hide in his phone, then he can't disable it.' Davide laughed warmly – it sounded like a debate he'd had with Antonio before. 'He's welded to his phone, never leaves it behind. If I get one that works off a satellite, I'll be able to track him online and I'll always know exactly where he is.' He pretended to cackle, but his humour was lost on Kate.

Frozen in the doorway for a moment as his words sank in, it took her a moment to realise she needed to catch up or she'd lose him as well. Letting the door fall behind her, she ducked to keep her face out of the freezing rain and ran across the road.

The wine bar was starting to fill even though it was early in the evening. Davide was waiting for Kate beside the door, and hauled it open as she caught up. Antonio had secured a high table close to the bar.

'You see why I came ahead. I knew we'd never get a table unless we were quick.' Antonio looked at Davide triumphantly.

'I told Kate I'm getting a tracker for you. One that connects to a satellite so it doesn't need Wi-Fi.'

Antonio obviously found this endearing. 'Only if I

can get one for you.' He turned to Kate. 'What are you drinking, Kate?'

'Oh, thank you. A glass of white wine would be lovely.'

As he bustled off to the bar, Kate turned to Davide. 'He likes the idea of you tracking him.'

'I know, it's hilarious. I really am going to order one. You can get them to go in the back of a phone. They are tiny. Not cheap, but I couldn't bear to lose him.' Davide looked lovingly after Antonio.

It was almost nine by the time Kate left the wine bar. As she'd gathered her coat, Davide had given her his business card, insisting she come and visit them. She'd hugged them both before heading out into the darkness, the bottle of perfume in her bag and a feeling of dread in her stomach.

Kate had never been able to work out how Erik always seemed to know where she was. She knew about tracking on Google Maps, but sometimes her phone had been out of battery and he'd still known. She pulled it out of her pocket as she walked. He'd given her this phone years before – she hadn't been able to afford to replace it. Its battery was a bit iffy, but otherwise it worked fine.

Had he put some sort of device in it? How could she find out?

Crossing the market square at the top of le Rue des Corbeaux, Kate hurried on. If there was something in her phone, it explained how Erik was following her here, too.

She'd definitely had that tingling spine-chilling feeling that she was being watched more than once since she'd arrived in Paris, but a tiny part of her had wondered if it was her imagination. That's what Erik had always said when she'd tried to ask if he was checking up on her: 'Don't be ridiculous, it's all in your head.'

Tense, she glanced behind her, the footsteps of the other night still ringing in her ears. *Had it been him?* And the shadows in the doorway? Was it really all in her head?

Watching her was part of the game. He'd done it before, with the others, but this time he could get so close.

Every now and then her anxiety seemed to flare and he'd thought she'd realised, but he hung back. Feminine intuition was a strange thing – almost animal.

In those moments, she'd look around frantically as if she knew he was there, as if she could feel his eyes undressing her, running his hands over her pale skin, breathing in her scent.

The thought made him dizzy. Could he wait? The timing had to be right. There were things that needed to be done, things that needed to be said, but he was starting to think that he might die waiting.

He'd made sure he blended in: had several hats to pull on; sunglasses, too, in case she caught sight of him. It would all fall apart if she recognised him. Well, not fall apart, but there was a danger she may say something to someone. Sometimes he carried a paper, sometimes he smoked. The trick was to look busy doing something else, as if he was preoccupied with his own business. Then she'd look through him, seeing someone beyond who could be the problem.

Her sister seemed to text constantly. Even from here he could hear her phone ping with a notification. He was going to have to make sure he got hold of it to keep the sister happy, to keep her thinking her messages were being read and answered. He'd probably be able to find some photos she hadn't sent, too.

It would buy him enough time to get everything organised. It worked every time. He just needed to look at some other sent texts and he could pick up tone, repeated typos, so nobody had any idea that the girl hadn't sent the message herself. Like the email to take the penthouse off the market. That had given him the whole weekend to get cleaned up.

Chapter 52

THE HEATING HAD come on while Kate had been out; the apartment was warm as she pushed the door shut and went into the *salon* to close the curtains. She paused for a moment to look out at the empty street, anxiety nipping at her like a flame. She tried to push it away again, to not respond to her fear, but it had been there since Davide had mentioned the tracking device. It seemed a much more likely explanation for Erik knowing where she was, than someone finding her photos on Orna's phone.

Kate pulled the heavy damask drapes tight, telling herself it was to keep the night chill out. Then she slipped off her coat and headed into the kitchen to put the kettle on.

Tomorrow – Saturday – was her last full day in Paris, and the last thing she wanted to be doing was panicking about being followed by Erik. Her plan to go to the

Musée d'Orsay had got sidetracked by Céline, but Daniel had said she couldn't miss it. She'd make sure she booked a ticket this time, so she would definitely go.

The thought of going online brought her back to her phone.

She'd heard of viruses that planted spyware in your phone – viruses that enabled hackers to see what you were seeing, to read your email, as well as to check your location. *Was that what had happened?*

The kettle clicked off, making Kate jump. Pulling a mug out of the cupboard, she dropped a tea bag in and poured the water over it, her mind going over everything she'd done in the last few days.

She had a work laptop at home for her lesson plans, but she kept everything personal on her phone.

She'd seen the Facebook message about the competition on her phone, and had replied to the email address to ask more about the details of the prize *on her phone.*

Picking up her mug, she blew on her tea and went back into the *salon*. Erik wasn't any sort of a software genius, but he could have hired someone to send her an email with spyware in it. Kate thought hard, trying to remember if she'd opened anything vaguely suspicious. She couldn't think of anything, but it could have been years before.

Or he could have physically put something in her phone.

Sitting down heavily on the sofa, Kate put her tea down in front of her and leaned forward to pick the phone up, peering at the edge to see if she could work out where to prise off the back.

She ran her fingernail down the side, looking for a join. There had to be some way to get the back off. But she couldn't afford to damage it. If she broke it while she was fiddling, she'd be lost.

Annoyed with herself, Kate put the phone down again and reached for the folder with all the Paris tourist information in. Part of her didn't want to believe that Erik had organised this trip; it was too frightening. But either way, if he had a tracking device on her phone, he would have seen her moving towards Paris.

One way or another, he knew she was here.

And she was sure he'd got into the apartment to frighten her – to make her doubt herself. It had to be him – it was exactly the type of thing he'd do: moving things and blaming her for losing them.

He knew to keep away from her; he knew if he appeared in person, she'd scream the place down and call the police. She wouldn't have been brave enough to do that a few years before, but she had the law on her side, even if she was in a foreign country.

And if he broke the restraining order, he knew he'd never see Hanna again. The judge had listened to the details of her injuries and the intimidation, and had been very firm. Kate took a deep breath, trying to slow her heart. She could feel sweat pricking at her back as she thought about him. Thank God, tonight it seemed as if everything was where she'd left it.

But that probably meant that he'd follow her tomorrow.

Why couldn't he just leave her alone? He knew there was no way she was ever going to leave Hanna with him. He knew any visits had to be supervised.

Which was one of the reasons he was so angry with her.

Trying to get him out of her mind, she opened the folder on her knee and flicked to the section on the Musée d'Orsay. With a surge of relief, she saw that it was close to the Louvre – it was the building with the clocks on either end that she'd passed on the way to the Eiffel Tower. So she wouldn't get lost. It looked like the perfect place for her last day in the city.

If Erik was watching her internet activity, he'd know what she was doing, but if she was careful to stick to busy places, there wasn't that much he could do.

Apart from frighten her.

She turned the page to see that the gallery housed several of Monet's smaller paintings of water lilies. Just as Daniel had said, it had a whole floor dedicated to the Impressionists. It looked wonderful. Reaching for her phone, Kate hesitated for a moment before opening her browser and finding the website to book herself a ticket. She couldn't let Erik spoil her last day.

As Kate clicked on the confirmation, her phone vibrated with a message.

I just want to talk.

Chapter 53

KATE WALKED UP the broad steps in front of the Musée d'Orsay, the part of her that wanted to hide away in the apartment fighting with the part that wanted to see Paris and didn't want to let Erik win.

His text had said that he wanted to talk, but he never wanted to just talk. There was always more: mind games, snide remarks, gaslighting. She hadn't even known what that was until it had happened to her.

Outside the museum was a magnificent bronze sculpture of a horse, high-stepping up a hill. Below it, rows of vicious-looking spikes stuck up from what appeared to be strips of wood. Kate had a vague idea that it was an upturned harrow, but from here it looked like some sort of torture device.

The statue summed up perfectly how she felt right now.

But she needed to quell the fear and keep moving forward; she'd come so far, she couldn't let that progress go.

She'd been tempted to text Orna to say that she'd be out of touch today, pretend her phone battery was low, and then turn it off completely. But that probably wouldn't make any difference.

If he was here, he'd find her somehow, like he'd found her when he'd followed her the other night.

Kate glanced across the stone plaza that wrapped around the outside of the museum, modern granite slabs meeting the pale Lutetian limestone. Despite the chill in the air, there were groups of tourists queuing to go in, more sitting on the broad steps in front of the main entrance.

Kate took a shaky breath. *Was he watching her right now?* Unsure if it was her imagination or intuition, she could feel the hairs rising on the back of her neck. She thrust her hands into the pockets of her coat, grasping her phone. If Erik was here, she couldn't let him see her shaking.

Right now, not letting him see she was afraid was winning. She pulled out her phone and texted Daniel.

Just arrived at the Musée d'Orsay. Looking forward to seeing those paintings.

Now, at least, if anything did happen, one person knew where she was.

Entering the cavernous glazed entrance hall, Kate took her bag off her shoulder and placed it on the conveyor belt for the scanner at the security checkpoint. *At least this meant people couldn't bring in weapons.* Not that Erik had ever needed to use a weapon against her. His hands were weapons enough.

As she passed through security, the guards regarded everyone with suspicion, which, right now, was comforting.

Picking up her bag on the other side of the conveyor belt, Kate took a deep breath. *She wasn't going to let him frighten her.*

She followed the other visitors into the central section of the museum. Beautiful marble statues reflected the light from the curved glass ceiling, almost glowing as they seemed to watch the crowds milling around them. Kate wandered into a side room, immediately seeing a painting she recognised: *The Angelus* by Millet – two peasants bending their heads to pray as the bells ring out from the church beyond the field they are standing in. Behind her, Kate could hear an American voice explaining why the painting was so radical in its portrayal of working people – peasants, not nobility, taking centre stage – and how Salvador Dalí had become obsessed with it. The couple in the foreground were standing with their heads bowed over a basket of potatoes, but Dalí had been sure, after studying Millet's letters, that in an earlier version the basket had been a child's coffin.

Half-listening to the guide, Kate stood back to look at the painting. Sadness poured from the image. She could almost hear the church bells ringing, just as they did at midday and at six o'clock in the evening, every day in Ireland. The guide continued telling his group that Dalí had been right – when the painting was X-rayed, the angular construction lines of what could have been a coffin were there under the paint.

Kate shivered. Often what the world saw was not what was going on under the surface. She thought of Trisha smiling through the pain of her illness, pretending it was nothing to worry about as the cancer slowly destroyed her from inside. Her marriage had been the same. Everyone who'd met Erik had found him charming; they were the perfect couple. And now, here she was in Paris, in borrowed clothes. *What else was hidden?* What else was going on under the surface? Behind her, she could hear the American explaining more about the painting to a tour group, his passion and knowledge of the subject clear.

Perhaps that's what she needed – someone who could just show her the truth, to get below the paint, under the surface. That was exactly what Agathe needed right now, as well: someone who could tell her what had happened to her friend.

The guide moved on to the next painting, but, suddenly self-conscious that it might appear that she was listening in, Kate drifted through the halls, mesmerised by the skill of the artists. The canvases were huge, and the colours as true as if they had been painted yesterday.

As she emerged at the end of the side gallery, Kate glanced over her shoulder, scanning the arches that led to the galleries on the other side of what she imagined must have been the station concourse, checking for Erik. *She couldn't see him, thank God.* Her anxiety began to settle as she followed the crowds, drifting upstairs. It felt safe here, with lots of people.

Crossing through industrial-looking corridors, Kate passed a gift shop. To her right, she suddenly realised she was looking out of the enormous glass face of one of the giant clocks that she'd seen at either end of the museum. People were milling around it, holding up their phones, but over their heads, through the glass, Kate could just see the outline of the Louvre on the other side of the river. Wanting to go closer, to take her own photo, Kate hesitated. It was so packed that she didn't know if she had the time to wait when there was so much to see.

Moving on, she continued through to another gallery. Daniel had said that the fifth floor was the place to see some of the most famous Impressionist paintings, and a Degas bronze of a ballerina.

The Degas was standing in the centre of the gallery, protected by a Perspex box, a statue of a young girl with her head held high and toe pointed. And Daniel was right: the sculpture hit Kate right in her heart – the girl was so like Hanna when she'd been going to dance classes. Kate stood for a moment, trying to gather herself, her eyes filling with tears. She reached for her phone to take a photograph, laughter erupting behind her.

And suddenly she knew she was being watched. It was as if her sixth sense had suddenly been triggered, as if the air had changed around her, become charged with menace. Freezing for a moment, Kate could feel the pinprick of sweat down her back, fear looming like a dark shadow behind her. The sense that someone was there, looking at her, was like knowing she was hungry or tired – she just knew.

And with that knowledge, her mouth went dry, her heart rate increasing, blood pounding in her ears.

Kate tried to steady her hand as she took a photo of the statue, and then switched the phone's camera to selfie. She held it up, looking over her shoulder around the room. The laughter was coming from a group of Japanese students. The American guide she'd listened to downstairs arrived behind her, leading a small group, his ochre sweater bright against the deep blue walls.

Kate clicked her phone off and casually looked around. She could still feel it. Someone was watching her. She was sure of it.

*

She's here, wandering among the redheads, their likenesses captured forever in paint. He isn't the only one mesmerised by them. He can see in the brushwork, in the way the light gleams off waxen shoulders, that Renoir, Manet and Toulouse-Lautrec had all seen it, too. That coquettish smile, or a knowing look ... les taches de rousseur. Their allure was like the beam of light that shone from the top of the Eiffel Tower at night, focused on him, drawing him closer.

And not just these great masters – so many more. Wandering the lofty halls with the silk scarf balled in his hand, he closes his eyes and breathes in the scent as if it is on their skin. Belle de Nuit.

Seeing her pause by the clock, the light pouring into the dark space from outside illuminating her glorious hair like a halo, he stops for a moment, drinking it in. But the throng closes around her and suddenly she is gone, the moment lost.

He wants to touch her, to brush past, but he needs people for that. She cannot see him. Putting the silk to his nose, he filters into the next gallery, searching for her, for the gleam of her red hair.

And then there she is beside the Degas, but there's no crowd now and he can't afford to get too close. He must merge with the incoming groups and vanish into the melee. She can't see him yet; it's too soon.

But it won't be long now.

Chapter 54

HAD ERIK COME *in behind her? Where was he?* Kate would have bet he was mingling with the gallery visitors so she couldn't see him, holding back to increase her fear.

She had ignored his text last night. She didn't have anything to say to him. After following her in the dark, he was doing his best to freak her out again. The nightmarish memory returned, of the sound of footsteps echoing behind her.

Kate took another look at the Degas statue, silently bidding it goodbye, and searched for the exit.

Filtering through the crowd, out of the gallery, she slowed, realising she was doing exactly what he wanted – showing her fear, running away. Leaving this beautiful museum because of him.

Giving him control.

Nothing was going to happen here. It was too public. That was the reason she'd decided to visit. She drew in a sharp breath.

She wasn't going to run. No. She was going to get coffee and text Daniel to tell him she'd seen the Degas, and then she was going to sit and people-watch and enjoy being here.

But first she was going back to look at the clock properly, and take a photo for Hanna. *Would she walk right past him?* It wasn't like him to hide from her, but frightening her was probably part of his plan. *Perhaps he'd get a surprise if she did the opposite of what he expected now?*

Doubling back through the gallery, she retraced her steps to where she'd come on to this floor. And suddenly the space was filled with light – the clock face took up the whole wall to her left.

There was something arresting about seeing the hands moving from the inside, clicking around the rings of iron circling the glass, like a giant cartwheel. Stark black roman numerals on the dial showed the hours; the minutes were marked on the outermost ring.

Kate watched the hands on the clock move as they clicked on another minute. She turned to look at the view again, absorbing the majesty of the city, lifting her phone to take a picture for Hanna.

Looking out through the clock face, she could see so many beautiful buildings. Agathe had said she was studying architecture and history, and Kate could see why.

Worry nagged at her as she thought about Agathe. She still hadn't replied to Kate's text about the woman found in the river, but perhaps she'd had so many messages, she hadn't seen it.

Agathe was a few years older than Kate had been when she'd lost Trisha, but age didn't make things any easier. Kate pulled her phone out of her pocket.

She tapped out a message to Agathe:

Hope all OK. Last evening here, would love to meet if you're free.

She hit *send*.

Chapter 55

AGATHE CLOSED THE front door and leaned her forehead against it, the tears flowing freely. She'd been out for a long walk this morning, missing Roland emerging from his pit.

Not that she knew what to say to him.

She'd walked down to the Seine, dawdling all the way, had half thought about heading for the café. But she couldn't deal with talking today; she just needed to be on her own, to prepare herself. Oumar had insisted she take the weekend off, and he was right. She needed some time on her own.

She'd left a note for Roland to say Sandrine's parents would be calling in the afternoon, and he'd obviously decided to make himself scarce. There had been no sign of him when she'd got home.

She'd only been back half an hour, anxiously tidying again, wiping down the bathroom, when the street door had buzzed. The next hour had been one of the most painful in her life. While Sandrine's things were here in the apartment, a tiny bit of Agathe thought that she might come home, that she hadn't really gone.

But seeing her parents, pale and silent as they packed her suitcase and put the rest of her belongings into boxes, seeing her room bare, had cut Agathe in two. They'd tried to be friendly when they'd arrived, to make conversation, saying how much Sandrine had loved living here, how much she'd thrived in her new job. But every word was forced.

It had been horrible, every minute of it.

Turning around, levering herself off the front door, Agathe went back to the kitchenette to wash up their mugs. She didn't know what to do with herself. Her grief was like toothache, a constant nagging pain that stayed with her, occasionally receding, only to rise again to stab her hard.

Turning on the tap, Agathe put her hand in the stream, running the water until it was hot. She washed automatically, not concentrating, casting her mind back to their last evening in. Sandrine had cooked; she and Roland had washed up. There had been laughter and teasing and ... Agathe took a ragged sigh and put the last mug on the draining board.

She let the water out of the sink and reached for a tea towel to dry her hands, tears hot on her cheeks now.

What had happened? Sandrine was so clever, so sensible. She must have been tricked into meeting someone, or been followed. Agathe didn't know. But then they didn't know what had happened to half the missing redheads. She just hoped Maxim could get to the bottom of it – that he could persuade his police contact to reopen all those cases and look at them properly.

Agathe looked across the living room. It felt cold and empty, as if a candle had been blown out. Would this feeling of listlessness pass? She felt as if her direction in life had changed, but she'd got left behind, somehow trapped in the middle, like the screw in the hands of a clock. Time was moving on around her, but she was stuck.

Maybe she should go back over the news reports again, see if there was something more that they were missing. Anything that would give some answers about what had happened to Sandrine, and how they were going to nail the bastard.

Anger stirring inside, Agathe went and scooped her phone off the coffee table and sat down in a heap on the sofa. She pulled a cushion in behind her as she opened her messages and she saw a text from Kate. Relief coursed through her.

Kate was exactly who she wanted to see tonight.

Chapter 56

LE LOUP GRIS was more like a private club or a country house than a nightclub – one that had somehow been transported into the bohemian part of the city, but had brought all the grandeur of aristocracy with it. Even the broad granite steps had two perfectly manicured box trees in pots on either side.

Maxim stood back on the pavement and looked at its impressive exterior, steeling himself for what could be the most difficult conversation of his life. It was even going to top talking through Sandrine's post-mortem report with Agathe, whom he was starting to like a lot. She really was like the little sister he'd never had, her sharp mind making him rethink his prejudices. They all had unconscious bias – during the brief moments their paths had crossed the summer before, he'd thought she was some sort of waste of space hippy-dippy art student.

He couldn't have been more wrong.

And Gabriel Beaudin was right – she'd make a great journalist. She had tenacity, and the sort of mind that didn't see obstacles. Maybe if Gabriel could persuade her to work in the newsroom again this summer, Maxim could show her the satisfaction in getting a story out, what it really meant to the people who had no voice.

But Maxim was prevaricating, thinking about Agathe, and he knew it. He was trying to delay going up the steps. When he'd seen Céline in the morning, Maxim had known that she'd tell Lucien he'd been about to call to the house. Which would have been a much easier place to have this conversation, if he hadn't totally bottled it and spent half the day in the café instead, double-checking everything.

He'd got a text just after lunch:

Come to office before we open, see what you think of design plans. ALSO NEW CAR ARRIVED EARLY!! L.

Maxim couldn't avoid it now.

He, Lucien and Daniel been the three musketeers back in the day, and part of him yearned for that easy companionship again. But he knew he had let Daniel, his best friend, down. Maxim cringed at the thought.

The boat club party was scratched into his brain, as if someone had taken a compass to the polished surface of a vintage table.

That term had been the reason why Daniel had been so keen to join the army as soon as he'd graduated.

Which had ended up with him losing half his leg.

Maxim felt as if that was on him, too. His action – or, more to the point, inaction – had led to a series of catastrophic events that had resulted in Daniel almost getting killed.

And maybe worse.

Maxim crossed his arms, the bulk of his jacket keeping out the evening chill. *Christ, he was just going to have to do this.* What was that stupid motto on the bumper of his neighbour's car? Feel the fear and do it anyway.

Yeah, well …

Before he could fully finish the thought, the door opened at the top of the steps. 'Max, I thought that was you, saw you on the CCTV. Come in. What are you doing out there in the cold?' Lucien beamed down at him, then gestured for him to hurry. 'Let's get a bottle of Dom open. Everyone's talking about these heads – that girl in the river. I was going to call to see if you had anything new. Come on up, don't dawdle.'

Maxim grinned weakly. He had a few questions himself. He just wasn't sure how he was going to ask them.

'The designer's just dropped in his new ideas, and they're awesome. I didn't show you what he's already done to the cabaret area.' Lucien paused as they passed a heavy velvet curtain, and pulled it back to reveal an arch into the space. There was a round stage in the corner of the low-ceilinged room, intimate tables scattered over the sunken floor, their white cloths illuminated by a candle in the middle of each one. The walls were plastered in old movie stills, of photos of the American stars who had hung out there when Lucien's mother had been singing. She was in most of them, captured in youth as if she'd never aged.

'We'll go up in a minute, but you've got to see my new car first. I've just had it waxed. Come on, we can cut through the kitchens to the garage.' Lucien was like a child showing off his new toys. He lolloped off down the narrow passage before Maxim could comment. But this was Lucien all over – making everyone want what he had. He'd even had a car in university, had been the centre of attention.

Heading down the passageway, following the delicious smell of bread baking, Maxim could see Lucien had propped open a concealed door. Beyond it, the contrast with the dark period décor of the club was astonishing: gleaming steel surfaces and white walls; huge gas cookers, the rings already alight; huge steel pots bubbling. It was bright in here, too, after the main part of the club. The chef was standing on the opposite side of the counter, a huge knife in his hand. As Lucien spoke to him, he started sharpening it, the sound of metal on metal setting Maxim's teeth on edge. Maxim didn't catch what he said.

Lucien beckoned to Maxim to follow him.

'It's through here.' Another corridor, this one tiled, the walls bright white again, huge doors opening down both sides – walk-in freezers or fridges, Maxim guessed.

Pushing open a door at the very end, Lucien flicked on some lights, bathing a subterranean garage in light. Maxim hadn't even been aware of them going down a storey, but he could see from the raw brick walls and the steep slope of the entrance up to steel roller shutters, that they were underground.

Skirting a black Volvo XC40, its wheels muddy, Lucien stopped and ceremoniously presented a gleaming, low-slung canary yellow sports car.

'California Spyder. Hand-built. Unfortunately not the original 1960 Ferrari, but a perfect limited edition copy.'

Walking around to look at it, Maxim leaned back on the side of the Volvo. Beyond the yellow sports car, a red one was badly parked half in and half out of the bay.

'How many cars have you got now, Lucien?'

'Personally, just these two. We're sorting out branding and decals for a fleet of six like that one,' He inclined his head towards the Volvo. 'They'll move around the city, doing promo. I'm expanding the restaurant and we're going to put in a casino downstairs. The plans are incredible. Completely separate from the members' area, obviously, but a great way to use the space down there.' He wiped a speck of dust off the bonnet of the Spyder and looked back at Maxim. 'So, what do you think?' He grinned. 'And listen … I totally forgot, but Daniel's aunt messaged me on Facebook. She suggested we all meet.' He snorted at the word. 'You said he was here. God, it's been years.'

Maxim opened his mouth to speak. This was the perfect opening. He couldn't have planned it better. But the words weren't coming. He tried again, failed again.

And then the moment was lost.

Totally unaware of Maxim's efforts, Lucien came around the car. 'I'll take you for a spin later, if you've time. Come and get a glass of fizz and see the plans. And tell me what's happening about this girl in the river.'

Chapter 57

AS KATE STEPPED into the street outside her building, the cold bit into her. She pulled her collar up. She couldn't find her scarf, but she needed it now; there was a bitter wind channelling down the street. She started as her eye caught a movement across the street, then she realised it was her own reflection in the semi-darkened windows of the candle shop.

After the morning in the museum, she was jumpy. She needed a glass of wine to calm her nerves.

Kate turned right and hurried to the bar in the little market square that Agathe had suggested. Passing the café, the shock of seeing the newspaper headline jumped back into her mind, her fears that it might be Agathe's friend making her shiver.

Agathe was already waiting for her when she got to the junction, her face lit by her phone screen as she scrolled.

Catching Kate's movement out of the corner of her eye, she looked up.

Kate crossed the road quickly. Close to, Agathe looked even paler than she had the last time Kate had seen her, with dark rings under her eyes, as if she wasn't sleeping. Kate felt a feeling of dread seep into her system. The girl they'd found was Agathe's friend – she was sure of it.

Agathe tried to smile brightly as Kate reached her. 'Last night in Paris?'

'Yes. I can't believe it, it's gone by so fast.' Kate paused. 'You're lovely to meet tonight, but if you'd rather not …'

Agathe sighed. 'It's good to get out, to meet someone new. Everyone—'

Kate interrupted her. 'It was your friend, wasn't it? I saw it in the paper.'

'Sandrine … Yes, yes it was. And everyone I know knew her, so it's good to meet someone who didn't. I need to get my head straight.' Agathe bit her lip.

Kate put her arm around Agathe's shoulder. 'Let me get you a drink. We'll raise a glass to her. Tell me about her – if you want to. If you don't, I can tell you all about the Musée d'Orsay and my sightseeing adventures.' She tried hard to make them sound mysterious and exciting.

Agathe laughed. 'Come inside. This place is usually pretty quiet. Is that OK? I'm not sure I can do noise.'

Inside what turned out to be a snug bar with booths down one side, Kate slipped off her coat, warm at last. Agathe sat opposite her in the booth, the high leatherette back blocking the sound from the neighbouring table.

'Anything more from your ex?' Agathe picked up the drinks menu. She obviously wasn't ready to talk about her friend yet.

'A few texts. I think he followed me the other night, and I keep getting this really creepy feeling that someone's watching me.' Kate paused, trying to make it sound less scary than she felt. She cleared her throat. 'Some stuff's been moved in the apartment.'

Agathe dropped the menu down to look at Kate properly, her face aghast. 'Seriously? You think he knows where you're staying?'

Kate rolled her eyes. 'Someone does. I'm wondering if he organised this whole trip, actually – that he wanted me in Paris for some reason.'

Agathe stared at her. 'To get you away from your daughter? He wouldn't ... He wouldn't try to hurt you, would he?'

Agathe was making the connections that had been staring at Kate all day, but that she hadn't wanted to face up to. 'That's actually what's worrying me.' Kate paused. 'I've been terrified for years that he might do something awful.' She stopped speaking for a second; this sounded so ridiculously dramatic. But it was true. 'If something happened to me, someone would have to look after Hanna and I know he'd fight Orna, my sister.'

'If something happened?' Agathe almost choked on the words.

'I know it sounds crazy, but he *is* crazy. He's made me doubt my own sanity over the years. If he could prove that I was unfit to look after Hanna, by virtue of being mad myself – or, even better for him, if I wasn't around at all – he'd get what he wants.'

'But he couldn't win? A court wouldn't give him custody?'

'I'd hope to God not, but you can never tell these days. Anything could happen.'

Agathe frowned. 'If he did set up that competition, and

the course and the apartment, he must have brought you to Paris for a reason.'

'That's the problem. There's always a reason. It must have cost a lot of money, too. But I'm going home tomorrow. He could just be trying to creep me out.' Kate thought again of the sound of footsteps behind her the other night, and shivered.

'I think women have very strongly attuned intuition. Attuned to survival. It's always men that are the problem, though, isn't it? I just keep wondering if Sandrine knew – if she had a feeling ...'

'So it was her they found in the river? Have they any idea what happened?'

Agathe shook her head. 'Not yet, but ...' She hesitated. 'There could be something bigger going on that Sandrine got caught up in.'

Kate raised her eyebrows as Agathe nodded, her face strained. 'Before we knew what had happened, I was doing some research for my uncle, for his newspaper. There are a whole series of women missing, unsolved cases, that could be linked to Sandrine.'

Kate could see the fear in Agathe's face. 'Linked how?'

Agathe cleared her throat. 'Sandrine had her hair done last week. She had it dyed red. I've found a whole load of women who have disappeared who all have red hair.'

Kate's mouth dropped open. 'Good God. Have any of them been found?'

Agathe looked uncomfortable. 'Not exactly. Not all of them, anyway. A week ago or so – this is so shocking – a girl's head was found, in the sewers. The police didn't want to make it public until they'd positively identified the victim.' She paused. 'They still aren't sure, but my uncle's paper broke the story. She could have disappeared a while ago, though. They think her body was kept in a freezer.'

'My God. Do they have any idea who could have done it?' Kate felt herself pale. Her voice came out as a whisper.

Keeping her voice low, Agathe glanced over to the bar to see if the waiter was on his way. 'They've no idea yet. The worst thing is that there was one before that, twelve years ago. A head, I mean. It's the second head that's been found.' She sighed. 'It's hideous, but that's a huge gap, so perhaps he was in prison, or out of the country or something. They've no idea.'

'In prison ...?' It took Kate a few moments to process the idea that was forming in her head – violence, prison, red hair, Paris ... She knew someone who had a bit of an obsession with red hair. And a violent past.

But the freezer. *How often had Erik joked that he could put her in the chest freezer in their garage and tell everyone she'd gone on holiday and no one would even know that she was missing?*

The possibility bubbled to the surface of her mind like methane in a stagnant pool. *But he'd been joking, hadn't he?*

It couldn't be, could it? *It couldn't?*

Kate kept her voice low, as if saying it too loud made it real. 'What if he's been living away and that's why there are gaps between them?' She paused, trying to find the words. 'I've got red hair. What if it's Erik? It looks like he was here last week when your friend went missing.'

Agathe looked at her, her face shocked. 'Surely not? That's a huge leap.'

Kate let out a sigh and ran her hands over her eyes. 'I know it sounds crazy.' *Was she jumping to conclusions?* But he'd always gone on about her hair. And he knew how to use knives. And the freezer ... It had been on one of the true crime documentaries he'd made her watch – a man in London had murdered his date and ordered a freezer like theirs. There had been two bodies in it when the police had finally raided the flat. Afterwards, every time Hanna had asked for ice cream, Erik's slow smile had made Kate's skin crawl.

Her stomach turned. 'Erik trained in the military and he's dangerous. But he's charming, and good-looking. He convinces everyone.' She felt her breath catch in her chest. 'I know it sounds mad. It is mad. I'm sorry, I'm being hysterical.'

'Don't say that.' Agathe shook her head. 'You're not. Yours is just as important as any other theory. You know this man, you know he's dangerous and you know he's stalking you. Someone must have stalked Sandrine to know where she'd be, to be able to lure her somewhere. It would have had to be someone convincing.'

Agathe's voice had got increasingly desperate as she'd spoken. Kate closed her eyes. She knew Erik was capable of killing; he'd come so close with her. Had there been other women – a life she didn't know about? Had he taken out his frustrations at not being able to talk to Kate about their daughter on Sandrine – another redhead.

'Erik's a chef. He knows how to cut things up, and he'd have access to huge freezers.' Kate put her hand to her face, massaging her temple as the events of the past few days began to come together fully in her head. She looked directly at Agathe. 'I think we need to talk to the police.'

Chapter 58

SITTING OUTSIDE A tiny bar across the road from Le Loup Gris, Maxim sipped his Ricard. He'd found a table right behind a huge potted shrub on the pavement. The bare branches were dense enough to conceal him in the darkness, but he could see the illuminated front of the club through them. The awning was keeping the rain off, and he had pulled up the collar of his jacket.

It was cold, but Maxim had realised as he'd listened to Lucien boasting about his cars and his club, about his plans for his casino, just how much of a narcissistic prick he really was. And how mad Lucien made him. Now that anger was keeping him warm.

While he'd stood there listening, Maxim had felt a full-on need to deck him – for his betrayal of Daniel all those years ago; for never apologising, or even considering that he'd done anything wrong. It had only been much later that Maxim had realised that when he'd seen Meredith leaving the rowing club that night, she had been pushing Lucien away.

She hadn't cheated on Daniel, it had been Lucien, all of it.

If Maxim admitted it to himself, Lucien had always been totally focused on himself, and then today, asking about Sandrine but flicking straight to talking about his cars, he'd got right under Maxim's skin.

Maxim could feel another flush of rage coursing through him. Maybe if he sat here long enough, he'd see something he could feed to another reporter to kick some shit at Lucien Arnaud and his perfect existence. The tabloids all thought he was some sort of god, and, boy, was he milking that for everything it was worth.

Lucien's phone had rung while they were downstairs in the garage, and the moment to challenge him about what had happened with Meredith had passed.

More to the point, Maxim had lost his bottle, which was probably part of the reason he was still here. And why he was feeling so angry. He'd decided tonight would be the night to finally have it out with him, and he'd blown it.

Pretending an urgent text had come in from the office, he had invented an excuse to leave.

Right now, Maxim hated himself as much as he hated Lucien.

He'd let Daniel down. Again.

Lucien had wanted him to stay, but Maxim could no longer keep up the pretence of being interested in anything he had to say. *He was so fucking cross with himself. If he could summon the balls, he'd go back in.* He just needed to get Lucien on his own. And then he was just going to say it. See how Lucien reacted.

As he watched, lights appeared from the slipway that led to the underground garage. A second later, the black Volvo he'd seen in the garage topped the rise. The driver slid down the window and flicked out a cigarette, a gold watch catching the light on his wrist.

Lucien – it had to be. His poxy Rolex was like a flashing sign announcing his success.

The vehicle idled for a moment before pulling into the road.

Standing up quickly, Maxim pulled a twenty-euro note out of his pocket and tucked it under his glass. He dipped down the alleyway beside the bar, where he'd left his bike. Pulling on his helmet, he knocked the Suzuki off its stand.

Throttling up, he was out on the road in seconds. The Volvo had slowed further down the road; a gang of teenagers were wandering across, weaving around it. Taking their time.

Maxim stayed back. His bike was distinctive – bright yellow, the front moulded to protect the rider at high speed.

Then the road cleared, and the dark vehicle slid along the cobbles and turned towards the river. Winding out of the twisty back streets, down beside Le Centre Pompidou with its angular glass walls, it stopped again before turning to follow the river, heading away from the centre of the city. Maxim kept pace with it, staying a few cars back, his curiosity growing.

Hanging back as the Volvo began to pick up speed, Maxim kept his head down. All he needed was for Lucien to clock him a couple of times and he may realise he was being followed.

Maxim didn't even know why he was following him, but sitting on his arse seething to himself seemed to be a total waste of time. Better he was moving. Maybe Lucien was going to meet a girl or something, slipping out when Céline thought he was at the club. Maxim smiled to himself at the thought. If he could discover anything about Lucien that might give him some leverage, then that was a very good thing.

The *périphérique* was quieter than usual as Lucien picked it up, swinging around to the north. Puzzled, Maxim kept his eyes on the vehicle ahead. If he had been heading north from the club, why go down towards the river first? There were quicker ways out of town.

Sitting on the speed limit, the Volvo kept moving until eventually it indicated to pull off. Maxim wasn't familiar with this area, but he kept his head down as they took a side road into an industrial zone, with shuttered units and warehouses off to Maxim's right. Suddenly the Volvo slowed and pulled into another part of the complex.

With the roads empty but well lit, Maxim risked being spotted. He let the vehicle go on ahead of him, keeping as far back as he could.

Then the brake lights went on and it pulled up at a high steel gate. Maxim mounted the pavement, cut his engine and, turning off his lights, coasted along, keeping in the shadows of a fence strangled in weeds.

The driver – Maxim was sure that it was Lucien – got out and punched a code into a keypad. The gates began to rattle open.

What the hell was Lucien doing here? Picking up supplies for the club? Surely he had staff to do that?

Maxim stopped, watching the Volvo inch forwards. He couldn't take the bike in. Jumping off and hooking his helmet over the throttle, he kicked the stand down. Flipping open the seat, he reached under his spare helmet, grabbed his wrench from the tools loose in the bottom, and took off on foot. The place was deserted, but he was going to have to risk leaving the bike unlocked; he didn't have time to wrestle with the heavy chain and padlock.

Sprinting along the pavement, he reached the gates just as they were closing, and slid through, wedging the wrench in place low to the ground to prevent them closing completely.

Inside was some sort of yard, with shipping containers stacked up on either side of a concrete road. In the distance he heard a train passing, and he realised that this must be some sort of goods depot. The lighting was poor, but he could see many of the containers had letters and codes painted on the sides. Ahead of him, he could hear the Volvo's engine. Following the sound, he jogged to a junction. The containers all looked black in the darkness, but as he got closer, he could see some were deep green, some rust red, their sides corrugated.

Slowing, Maxim realised the engine had stopped. Looking around him, he kept walking. Then he heard a door slam off to his right. Keeping behind the containers, he closed in. The ground was rough and uneven; the smells of rust and diesel blended on the breeze.

Turning a corner, Maxim quickly pulled back. The Volvo was parked up, the back door open and the interior light on. As the driver turned, Maxim could see that it *was* Lucien. *What on earth was he doing all the way out here? In a container yard?* Now all Maxim's investigative instincts were kicking in at the same time. There was something weird going on.

Pulling out what looked, from this distance, like a Galeries Lafayette shopping bag, Lucien closed the wide rear door and flicked the central locking, the lights flashing. He was parked beside a container on the end of a block; it had another stacked on top and one to its left. Maxim pulled out his phone and, checking the flash was off, prayed the night sight on the camera would work automatically.

He could hear the jangle of metal as a padlock was unlocked and the steel bar that opened the door was ratcheted back. Maxim peeped around the end of the container as Lucien moved inside. A light flicked just as the door closed.

Dazzled by the bright light, Maxim fired off as many shots as he could.

Who on earth had a container with a power feed? What the hell was Lucien doing?

Chapter 59

AGATHE WALKED INTO the sitting room and almost had a heart attack.

Roland was sitting on the sofa with his head in his hands.

'Oh my God, you gave me a fright.' She put her hand on her chest, her heart pounding. It had been bad enough that the bulb had gone on their corridor and she'd had to dash from the lift in the dark, but now her heart was running like a train.

After everything Kate had said in the bar, she couldn't get this Erik guy out of her head.

Roland looked at her sideways without moving his hands, the whites of his eyes dark in the dim room. He'd put on a side light and pulled the curtains, but the room still felt cold. She let out a breath. 'You were so quiet, I didn't think you were in.'

He rubbed his face. 'I need to talk to you.'

Agathe sighed. She needed to talk to him, too. She'd been sure he was avoiding her, but he was the only other person in her life who'd known the real Sandrine. Agathe was brimming with sorrow, but she knew she needed to talk about her – about the loss, about what Sandrine could have been.

At last Roland was here, but now she didn't know what to say.

'Did the heating come on? It's freezing in here.' *Avoidance.* She could hear Sandrine's voice psychoanalysing her. She had learned to read her clients' body language and behaviour, her sales success down to identifying their pain points. and delivering solutions in the properties they were viewing that they didn't know they needed.

Pain points. Agathe had a few of those right now. And she could see Roland did, too.

He shrugged in response, and Agathe closed her eyes and leaned on the door frame.

'How are you doing? It's so, so awful.'

She heard him sigh. His voice was low as he said, 'The cops were here?'

'They wanted to look in her room. I put all your

paints in the cupboard, under the towels. They didn't see them.'

'Thanks.' His voice was dead, the energy drained from it. 'Did they find anything? Any leads?'

'I don't think so.' Agathe crossed her arms tightly and went to sit in the armchair, perching on the edge. 'Maxim Verdier is covering it all for the paper. He's got contacts in *La Crim* but they haven't told him much yet.'

'He found the link between all those cases in the article?' Roland looked across at her, their eyes meeting.

'I did. My uncle asked me to check some stuff, after the ...' She couldn't say *the head*. 'After the sewers. That was before ... Sandrine was missing, but I didn't know anything had happened.'

'I don't get it, though. In the paper it said she'd just had her hair coloured.'

Agathe sighed. 'Yes, on Wednesday night.'

He shook his head, looking back at the floor. 'Unbelievable. I can't ...' He rubbed his hands over his face and his close-cropped hair, then cleared his throat. He hesitated before continuing. 'Does Maxim know anything about where she could have gone into the river?'

Agathe looked at him. The tone of his voice had changed. It was guarded, but there was a hard edge to it. She shrugged. 'My uncle said they've had some water expert looking at it. All that rain ... The guy thinks she must have gone in close to where she was found. The sacks were weighted down with bricks, but the pathologist thought she wasn't in the water for that long.' She hadn't wanted to ask how he knew that.

Roland was silent for a moment. Then, when he spoke, she could barely hear him. 'I think one of my friends saw something. On Sunday night. Down by the river ...'

Agathe looked at him, shock coursing through her. 'Who saw something? What did they see? Where?'

He rubbed his face again, and she could see that he was crying, the tears falling silently. 'There's this underpass.' Agathe realised she was holding her breath as he went on. 'He can't go to the police because he'll have to say why he was there. He'll get arrested for his street art, and then they'll want to know how I know him. If they find out I'm Shark, and about ...' He let out a sigh of despair. 'All of them, there are so many ...'

Thoughts jumped into Agathe's mind like fighting cats. She bit her lip. She could see his problem. The sort of large-scale graffiti he and his friends did, and tagged with their signatures, was punishable by up to two years in prison and a €30,000 fine. Not getting caught was pretty important, before you even got to what his parents would say. She got it, but it didn't stop her wanting to scream at him. After a moment she replied, her voice low.

'What did this guy see?'

Roland glanced over at her. 'He was filming himself painting a mural, and he heard a vehicle, so he dipped down behind this coffee hut that's down there. But he'd left his phone recording. It was weird. This guy sat in the van for ages before he got out. Then my friend heard something big drop into the water. He'd thought it was drugs at first, but when he watched it back, he thought it was a dog or something.' He hesitated. 'When he saw about Sandrine in the paper, he knew I knew her. He sent me the video.'

'What? You've got it on your phone?' *She couldn't believe this. Why hadn't he said something?*

'It was dark, it's not clear …' It sounded lame. She could see from his face that he knew it.

'But you have to tell someone. Can you see who it was?' The words tumbled out.

Roland shook his head. 'No, but you can sort of see his van – it's an SUV – and a bit of the plate.'

'The number plate?' She was aghast. *How long had he been sitting here? How long had he known?* Now Agathe really wanted to slap him.

'Part of it. But what do I do?' His voice was twisted with pain. 'I can't go to the cops.'

It took Agathe only a moment to decide. 'We need to call Max. He'll know what to do.'

She leaned back and pulled her phone from her pocket. *What if he hadn't told her? What if …?* She knew Roland and his friends spent days seeking out places where they could paint without getting caught. And for all the same reasons he chose his locations, they were the perfect places to dump a body.

She glanced across at Roland as she hit Maxim's number.

Chapter 60

KATE PUSHED THE apartment door closed behind her and, turning, put on the dead bolt. Now no one could come in from outside. She caught her breath, her heart pounding, and leaned back on the door. It was the idea of the freezer that was haunting her. She could still see Erik's face every time it was mentioned.

Agathe had listened to Kate carefully, but then wondered out loud about Erik living in London. These women had gone missing in Paris.

Sitting in the bar, her initial panic beginning to subside, Kate had seen Agathe's point. Surely she would have noticed on the news if any redheads in London had disappeared; it was the sort of thing she would have remembered.

'I'm sure he can't be involved, Kate, but I'll ask Maxim to check what he can, to talk to his friends in the police.'

Agathe had walked her right to the front door of her building and hugged her, but as she'd had walked away, the thoughts had started darting around Kate's head again.

What if he'd been attacking women in the UK, too, and she just hadn't seen it on the news, or they'd been in different police jurisdictions and they hadn't connected the women by the colour of their hair? Loads of women went missing or were killed every year; a proportion of those *had* to be redheads. Kate had felt fear pricking at her.

How many times had she thought Erik might actually do her serious harm?

How many times had he vanished into the night, only coming home when she'd gone to work?

Maybe he'd travelled further away, outside London, on those nights. Kate took a ragged breath, glad of the door firm at her back. She was suddenly feeling very lightheaded, shaky, as if she was having a sugar low moment. Fear was absorbing her energy like a black hole.

She closed her eyes. Deliberately tried to quell the rising panic. She needed to make herself a mug of hot chocolate and sit down.

Flicking on the kitchen lights, Kate poured milk into a mug and put it into the microwave, shivering as she did so. The apartment felt chilly – much cooler than it had before. Setting the microwave, she went to check on the heating. Céline had shown her a panel on the living room wall – the *salon* wall, Kate corrected herself. Perhaps it had gone off by accident.

Kate pushed open the doors across the corridor from the kitchen and stepped inside the *salon*. It was even colder there.

She quicky saw why.

At the far end of the room, one of the tall French doors opening on to the balcony was ajar.

How on earth had that happened? It had stopped raining now, but Kate could hear a stiff breeze rattling the glass, and the door suddenly opened wider. She crossed the wooden floor quickly, glancing outside as she pushed the window closed. She turned the brass handle and heard the lock clicking into place.

Kate looked out again, this time at the balcony itself. It was hard to see anything with the light from the street throwing everything into shadow, but as she moved ... Kate gasped, putting her hand to her mouth. Just inside the ornate ironwork at the edge of the balcony, she could see the impression of a footprint. A muddy boot print, the ridges in the sole clear against the pale tiles. And the toe was facing the window.

Had someone climbed onto her balcony from next door? There were partitions between each apartment, but they were more ornamental than designed to actually stop someone with determination from climbing onto the railing and swinging around from one balcony to the next. And the balcony ran right along the whole building.

Kate put her hand on the thick damask of the curtain, ready to pull it closed, trying to focus. Maybe it was a window cleaner? Perhaps Céline had organised someone to clean and not told her?

But why was the French window *open*?

She whipped around to look back into the room. Was there someone in the apartment?

Kate could feel her heart pounding in her ears, deafening her as she tried to listen to the movement of the building. Frozen with fear, she crossed her arms tightly and tried to think if she'd seen anything out of place. But everything had been fine. She hadn't had the feeling that there was anyone here, anyone hiding. There hadn't been a residue of what could have been aftershave wafting in the air, like the last time.

She was going to have to check to make sure that there was nobody here, though.

Looking towards the fireplace, she spotted a set of brass fire irons on the hearth. Hurrying across the room, she bumped into the end of the sofa in her haste, almost falling on the coffee table.

Grabbing the poker, she straightened up, immediately feeling calmer. She put her hand on the mantelpiece and leaned on it for a second, gathering herself.

She needed to check everywhere.

Taking a step forward, Kate felt her foot crunch on something. She looked down at her boot.

Broken glass.

She took a step backwards. *Something must have ...* It took her a moment to recognise it, but then she saw what looked like a base and a tiny Eiffel Tower. Miniature silver stars glinted from the smooth wooden floor. *Hanna's snow globe?*

The glass was spread across the hearth and around the end of the sofa, as if the globe had been dropped on the marble hearthstone, shattering and spreading across the wooden floor.

Was this Erik? Had he broken in? He'd always scoffed at her buying Hanna the globes, said they were a waste of money.

Kate closed her eyes and tried to slow her heart. Out

of everything in the whole apartment, only he'd know the significance of the snow globe.

She didn't even want to think about what the significance of smashing it may be.

He was leaving her a message – she was sure of it.

Chapter 61

AGATHE JUMPED UP as soon as she heard the street door buzz.

Maxim must have run up the stairs, because a moment later she heard the front doorbell.

He had his back to her when she opened the door, the shoulders of his black leather motorcycle jacket glistening with rain. Hearing the lock click back, he spun around, his eyebrows raised, his brown eyes expectant.

'Come in. It's Roland, my flatmate.'

'The artist?'

Agathe stood back to open the door wide and gave him a side eye. 'I thought only Gabriel and his photographer knew that.'

Maxim paused before he headed down the passage towards the open living room door. 'Your uncle thinks he's a major talent – he's right, too. When Philippe came back with those first photographs Gabriel briefed me to do some digging, get an article ready in case the pictures went viral. Which they did.

'But I explained that we wouldn't be able to run it – that if the cops found out who he was, they'd want to make an example of him.'

Agathe kept her voice low, conscious that Roland might hear her. 'Thank you. Potentially ending up in prison is the reason he hasn't been to the cops with this.'

Maxim let out a breath and glanced at her. 'Let's hear what he has to say.'

In the living room, Maxim put his helmet on the floor and sat on the edge of the armchair. Agathe went around to perch on the arm of the little sofa. It only took Roland a few minutes to bring Maxim up to date.

Maxim took it in, his face clouded. He opened his mouth to say something, but Agathe began to speak at the same time. She stopped abruptly. She needed to tell him about Kate's theory about her ex, but she knew it would sound a bit mad.

'Sorry, go ahead …' He looked at her.

'I don't know how important this is, but I met this lovely girl, Kate Wilde, in the café the other day.'

'Kate Wilde?' Maxim's eyebrows shot up.

'I know – like Oscar, and she's Irish. But the thing is, she won this trip to Paris—'

'In a Facebook competition.'

Agathe looked at Maxim, amazed. 'How do you know that?'

He shrugged. 'Go on.'

Agathe bit her lip. *How* did *he know?* But there wasn't time to get into that now. 'The thing is, she has a really abusive ex-husband. He's stalked her in the past. And he has links to Paris – he's a chef, and he's lived here before. She's sure he's here now and he's been creeping around her apartment. She was followed the other night.'

Maxim took this in. 'And you think he could be something to do with all this? With Sandrine and the redheads?'

'Maybe. Kate really believes it. Given the lack of leads *La Crim* have at the moment, I think it would be good if they checked him out.'

Maxim nodded slowly. 'How did you meet her?'

'In the café. The apartment she's staying in is just a few doors down. I think it's the same building Céline Arnaud lives in, opposite the candle shop. But the thing is, she's got red hair.'

Maxim took this in and turned to Roland. 'Can I see the video?' He glanced across at Agathe. 'You probably don't need to see this.'

She wanted to, but her colleague was right. There would be time enough if it was relevant, and she really wasn't ready now. Roland's description had made her feel sick.

'Or hear it,' she said. 'Call me when you're done.'

Maxim nodded quickly, his eyes locking on hers, full of compassion. Agathe suddenly felt her own eyes welling up. Maxim had only met Sandrine for a few minutes, but here he was behaving like Agathe's big brother, looking as if he belonged in her living room and making her cry because he cared.

She pulled the living room door behind her and leaned on the hall wall, the plaster cool against her shoulder. Further down, Roland's bike was leaning against the wall. Their coats hung on a peg above it, the sleeve of Sandrine's denim jacket poking out from under one of hers. *She hadn't realised it was here – she should have given it to Sandrine's parents.*

Agathe went to the coat hooks and lifted the jacket down, holding it to her face. The police had been through the pockets of all her clothes, through her drawers and wardrobe. This jacket held no secrets, but it smelled of her.

Agathe felt her face crumple, the tears stinging as they fell. What had Kate said about scent evoking memories more strongly than music? It was as if Sandrine was here somewhere – had just popped out for milk or bread.

How was she going to survive this? How were any of them? Agathe let out a shaky breath as she heard Maxim call her name from the living room.

She turned to go back in and realised she was still holding the jacket. She hugged it to herself as she pushed open the living room door.

Maxim was standing up. Seeing her face, he paused for a second, his eyes locking on hers.

'He's got something. I've sent it to my phone and I'll download it and delete the message. I can take this to *La Crim* without revealing my sources. They'll want to know, but it's the content that's important.'

'Is it enough? Will they know who it is?'

'There's a partial licence plate that they can check. It's possible it's fake, but if it's real, and even if it throws up a thousand vehicles, it's more than we had this morning. I'll go straight over to the station.'

He looked down at Roland, who was still sitting in the same place on the sofa. 'You did the right thing, mate. Don't worry about what you and your friend didn't do. I think he's got this bastard on camera, even if we can't see who it is clearly. It's more than anyone else has got.'

As he stepped around Roland, Agathe opened the door wide and Maxim followed her down the hall. He paused as she pulled back the bolt on the front door, as if he wanted to say something but didn't know what.

'Thank you.' Her voice was small.

He looked at his feet; his brown boots were battered and scuffed. Then looked at her, his smile tight. 'I'll call you as soon as I know anything.'

She wanted to hug him, but instead she smiled weakly, her eyes brimming again.

His boots rang on the tiles as he strode across the hall and swung around the stairs, taking them two at a time.

*

He shivered, feeling the grin building. The anticipation and excitement was real now. It felt different when he got this close, as if the gears had changed. He shifted on the bed, pulling the pillow under his head.

He'd hung up his jacket and shirt when he'd arrived, changed into something more comfortable, then made sure the cameras were set up, all the recording equipment was working properly.

The videos kept him going, enabled him to relive every gorgeous moment. When he'd finished getting everything ready, he'd put one on.

The hairdresser tonight.

He'd captured her on his phone in the build-up. Disguised, he'd wandered into the shopping centre where she worked, sat near her as she'd had lunch with a friend. Watched her wide mouth and white teeth as she'd laughed, flicking her glossy red hair over her shoulder.

He relished the planning. Being in control. That was what this was all about. He was finally in control.

He identified them months in advance, followed them for long enough to get their names and then find them on social media.

It was so easy. Searching the hashtags until he found

them: #paris #leloupgris #nightout #party #cocktails #clubbing #girlsnightout.

And then, slowly and carefully, he'd close in.

The snatch had always been exciting – that icy moment of danger before he opened the car door and leaned across. But he was good. He knew where the cameras were. And they trusted him. If he pulled up beside them, they knew his face immediately. They felt flattered, warmed by his concern for their safety.

He'd seen straight away that some of them wouldn't work. They had big families, or they worked in a bank; they were girls someone would notice was missing. But so many had been easy – maybe too easy.

The planning for this one had had to be meticulous. Every single detail had been checked, tested and retested. Nothing came back to him.

That head turning up had been bad timing. But it would end up pointing everyone in a very different direction.

And getting rid of the remains had cleared space for Kate.

The freezer in the corner of the container hummed as he closed his eyes, envisioning the next move.

It was the perfume that drove him crazy – that scent on their skin. There was nothing else like it.

Chapter 62

KATE WAS SITTING in bed by the time she finally looked at her phone.

She'd searched every cupboard, looked behind every door, but she hadn't found anything else amiss. *Thank God.* Then cleaning up the glass had taken ages; the splinters were tiny. She'd closed the curtains and put all the lights on – flooded the room with light – and brushed hard until she'd been sure she'd got as many fragments as she could from between the pale boards. Then she'd gone back to the laundry room for the vacuum cleaner.

Someone had definitely been here tonight – and she was absolutely sure, this time, that it was Erik. Had he been crouching on the balcony and watched her leaving the building to meet Agathe, got in while she'd been in the bar?

When she'd checked the doors at the other end of the room, she'd realised that they weren't actually locked, just secured with an ornate bar. There wasn't a handle on the outside, but it didn't seem very secure. She didn't know how he'd got it open, but she prayed he wasn't planning on coming back during the night. She'd slid the marble-topped semicircular side tables over in front of the long windows, and tucked the curtains tight behind them, just to be sure that they couldn't be opened again. Then she'd shut her bedroom door and manoeuvred the heavy dressing table away from the wall and across it. In the en suite, she locked the external door that opened into the hall, so nobody could get to her bedroom through the bathroom.

Was she safe now? Kate wasn't sure, but she couldn't think of anything else she could do. She had the poker on the bed beside her, just to be sure. But thoughts of the freezer Agathe had told her about kept going around her head. She couldn't bring herself to tell Agathe about Erik's obsession with true crime, about how she'd felt he watched the documentaries as if they were training videos of what not to do, how not to get caught. *The freezer ...*

She pulled the pillow up behind her, her back aching from hauling the furniture around. She was exhausted.

She only had to get through tonight, and she would be going back to Hanna and could put all the things that had happened behind her. Paris had been amazing; meeting Agathe and Daniel had been lovely, but now she'd had enough. She needed to get back. There was only so much she could take of being frightened. And she needed to talk to her solicitor.

Someone had definitely been following her, and it had to be Erik.

Everything about him had always been about control: about making her doubt herself, undermining her confidence until she couldn't think straight, until she thought she'd imagined things.

But that had changed when he'd taken Hanna. She'd felt all the hurt turn into rage. She wasn't going to let him get under her skin again. Yes, she was terrified he'd break in and hurt her; yes, she was terrified he'd organised this whole thing to get her to Paris … but what he hadn't realised was how much she'd changed.

A few years before, she'd never have gone to bed with the poker, fully prepared to use it.

Her phone buzzed. She opened her WhatsApp messages and her heart almost stopped.

Nice apartment.

The message was from an international number – the same one as before.

A second later, as if the sender had been waiting for her to see the message and for the two blue ticks to appear, another message arrived.

I just want to talk. I want to see Hanna.

Another message came through.

You know how much I love you both. We were meant to be together. I can't bear being away from you.

Kate felt as if the phone had come alive in her hand, and was going to explode or burn her. But she couldn't move. She stared at the screen.

It had been Erik all along, watching her, trying to freak her out. He'd been here, and he'd broken the snow globe.

Daniel was right: Erik had organised all this. Kate suddenly felt absolutely sure that he'd intended to be in the apartment when she returned.

What had frightened him off? He didn't often change his mind.

Whatever it was, Kate was fully sure that he'd be back the next day.

Her train was at 2 p.m.

He had until then to reappear.

But this time she was going to be ready for him.

Chapter 63

DANIEL JUMPED AWAKE at the sound of his phone. Rolling over, he picked it up to see Maxim had messaged. And it was well after midnight. He'd been tossing and turning, worried about Kate, felt as if he'd only been asleep for a few minutes.

You awake? I'm downstairs. Need to talk.

What on earth did Maxim want at this time of the night? Daniel's mind was immediately on high alert. He'd spent years living on his nerves, had long ago lost the ability to sleep deeply.

Had Maxim found Erik?

Come up, 411. I'll call reception to give you access.

Daniel reached for the phone on his bedside locker. The lift needed a room key to access this floor, but Gilles the doorman would look after that.

Throwing back the covers, Daniel thrust his good leg out of the bed and reached for his prosthesis, strapping it onto his stump. When he'd told Kate his leg had been injured he hadn't been entirely truthful, suddenly embarrassed that she might be repulsed at the thought of his disability. His aunt called it his bionic leg, but it was a long way from that.

He heard Maxim's knock as he pulled on his silk dressing gown. He must have run down the corridor.

Limping across the room, Daniel opened the door. Maxim was leaning on the door frame, his face pale.

'What's happened?'

Daniel stood back as Maxim came inside and strode to the middle of the room, putting his helmet on the coffee table. His back to Daniel, Maxim ran both hands into the roots of his hair, as if he was cradling his head.

'OK. You know I love you, Daniel. We've been friends for ever. More than friends … brothers.' He still had his back to him.

Puzzled, Daniel looked at Maxim as he closed the door firmly, flicking the lock. *Where was he going here?*

'Spit it out, Maxim. Is it this Erik?' A unexpected surge of fear shot through Daniel, his mind leaping to Kate.

Turning around, Maxim shook his head. 'I understand

if you never want to speak to me again. I don't want that, but I'll understand.'

'Just tell me, Max.' Daniel could hear the testiness in his own voice.

From the look on his face, so could his friend.

Maxim took a deep breath and sat down on the sofa, leaning forward, his hands clasped.

'Remember the night of the rowing club party?'

Daniel frowned. *What was this about? How could he forget?* He'd hated Valentine's Day ever since.

'Obviously. It was the last time I saw Meredith.' He sighed. He'd never understood what he'd said or done that night. She'd said she'd needed to go outside for a smoke, and then she'd vanished.

'That's the thing.' Maxim cleared his throat. 'I don't think she did go off travelling. I think something happened to her.'

Daniel raised an eyebrow. The drink must have finally got to his friend. 'What are you talking about?' He said it patiently, as if he were speaking to a child, and moved to sit down in the armchair.

Maxim sat on the edge of the sofa and ran his hand into his hair again, pulling at his thick fringe.

'We know she went out for a cigarette.'

Daniel nodded in reply.

'And Lucien said he saw her walking back to the Métro – that she said goodbye to him. He thought it was weird. As if it was more than a goodnight, more like a goodbye.'

Daniel nodded again. He could still see Lucien's shrug the next day, as if it didn't matter.

'The thing is ... I saw him. I saw him talking to her that night, after she went outside. I saw him try to kiss her.'

'I know, you told me.' One of his best friends making a pass at his girlfriend, and then her vanishing to God knew where, had been the single most devastating thing that had ever happened to Daniel. Worse, actually, than having his bloody leg blown off.

Your first love was always the deepest. Was that a line from a song? Daniel didn't know, but the memory of that betrayal still hurt all these years later. It was the reason he never needed to see Lucien Arnaud again.

'The thing is, they walked off together – and it didn't really look like she wanted to go with him. He was holding her arm and she was pulling away, but I think I assumed they were messing about. He was laughing.' Maxim drew in a breath. 'I never said anything. It took me too long to figure it out, and then it seemed so ...

well, just so unlikely that he could have been involved in her going …'

Frowning, Daniel didn't say anything. *Figure what out?* Maxim ran his hand over his face and kept talking, his eyes on the thick pile carpet.

Daniel still couldn't see where this was going. He rolled his hand to encourage Maxim to continue.

'It always bothered me. It seemed so out of character for her to just vanish. You were devastated and went back to London.' He shrugged and opened his hands. 'I thought at first maybe she'd taken drugs and something had happened. But then … I only realised later that Lucien must have been holding her really tight, for her to be pulling away from him the way she was.'

Daniel could tell he was working up to something; he didn't want to break his flow.

'The thing is …' Maxim stopped and started the sentence again. 'The thing is, Daniel, that Meredith had red hair.'

Daniel nodded curtly. He was very well aware of that – and of the impact the woman he'd just met was having on him. For the moment he'd sat down opposite her on the train, he'd been aware of her colouring, and how it echoed in his memory like a clock chiming.

Then what Maxim was saying registered.

'What do you mean?' Daniel sat forward in the armchair, his hand on the scrolled wooden arm. 'What's the colour of her hair got to do with it?'

Maxim looked at the floor and then back up at him. 'I found something out tonight. When you showed me those photos from the Métro station, I started thinking. And tonight, more, I think.'

'For God's sake, man, what?' Daniel almost barked it.

'Céline. Lucien's sister was in the background of that photo of Sandrine in the Métro.'

Daniel looked confused. 'But she never uses the Métro – not after …'

'Exactly. That's my point. After their mother was killed by a train. Céline was in the station when it happened – when she jumped.'

Daniel knew all this.

'You're going to have to help me here, Max. I'm not seeing a connection.'

Maxim put his head in his hands. 'I've been trying to get away from this, hoping if I didn't believe it, it wouldn't be true. I know that sounds mad.' He took a breath. 'It's her hair, Daniel. Lucien's mother was famous for her red hair. She was the toast of Paris in her day. She was also an absolute bitch – Céline says it like it's a joke, but ... I didn't make the connection until I saw the photo. Then I just got this feeling in my gut.'

He looked up at Daniel, his face anguished. 'I think Meredith is another one. All these girls who have disappeared are redheads. When I saw Céline in the photo, I suddenly remembered about their mother having red hair. Lucien said Meredith went home, but what if she didn't?'

Daniel looked at him, stunned.

Maxim looked up at him. 'Daniel, did Meredith have any tattoos?' He knew he should have asked the question before, but he hadn't been able to bring himself to say it.

'Christ, that's a strange question. She had one behind her ear, under her hair – stars, I think. She wanted to get it removed. That's why she wore her hair down all the time, so you couldn't see it.'

Chapter 64

DANIEL NARROWED HIS eyes as he looked at Maxim across his hotel room.

'But what's Meredith having a tattoo got to do with anything?'

Maxim looked hard at the floor for a moment, as if he was trying to compose himself. 'I should have asked before. Would you recognise it again?'

'Obviously. But what are you saying? You think Lucien had something to do with Meredith disappearing? That she didn't leave? That he did something to her?'

'Yes, I do.' Leaning forward, his forearms on his thighs, Maxim rubbed his hands together anxiously. 'And now ...' He bit his lip before he continued. 'The thing is, when I figured out about the hair, I went to see him. Earlier tonight. I was going to have it out with him.'

'You were going to ask him?' Daniel's tone was hard.

'I don't know. I just wanted to see if he'd lied to us back then, I think. I wanted him to know I'd seen them – seen him go off with her.' He cleared his throat. 'I just had this feeling. It's always been there with Lucien, just under the surface. He's just so focused on himself.' Maxim sighed. 'You know, I've been in this game a long time, I interview criminals for a living. And I'm not twenty any more. There's something about his vibe …'

He had a point.

Daniel could feel his entire focus lasering in on Maxim as he continued. 'I went to the club, early in the evening. Well, I was going to go to the house, but—'

'Tell me the rest, quickly.'

Maxim looked at him. 'I was heading for their house on Friday to talk to him on his own, but I needed a coffee, and Céline came into the café right behind me. Café Rodolphe, it's just along the street from their place. I think that's where she saw Sandrine Durand. Maybe they chatted. But Céline could be the link between Sandrine and Lucien.' He paused. 'It was a woman who booked for Sandrine to show her that apartment. What if Sandrine mentioned it when she was in the café? What if they are thinking of buying more property and Céline took Lucien with her to view it?'

Daniel crooked an eyebrow. Reading him, Maxim nodded in response. 'I know, it's not evidence. But Paris is a big city and Sandrine's friend works in the café. It's circumstantial, but ...' He opened his hands and shrugged.

Daniel could see his point. And he didn't like it one little bit. The three of them – he, Lucien and Maxim – had been close when he'd lived in Paris as a student, but it had always been Maxim he'd felt a real connection with. They'd kept in touch over the years, and even if they didn't see each other for months, they always picked up right where they left off. To Daniel, that was the sign of true friendship. Lucien had never been quite on the same wavelength as the two of them. And Daniel had never forgiven him for trying to make a move on Meredith.

Daniel trusted Maxim implicitly, but every idea needed to be stress-tested. 'Something must have brought you here now, though. What happened to move this on from a wild theory to something more tangible?'

Maxim's tone suddenly became matter-of-fact. 'Two things, actually.' He closed his eyes for a second, as if he was trying to find the right words. 'The head they found in the sewers ... She had a tattoo behind her ear. Stars, Travère said, but ...'

Daniel sat down heavily, shock radiating through him like a blast wave. He'd read about the tattoo in the paper, but he hadn't consciously connected it with the girl he thought had deserted him twenty years before. But perhaps that was because part of him couldn't process that this thing with the redheads could involve Meredith?

Before he could say anything, Maxim continued. 'Sandrine Durand was found in the Seine close to an underpass. I've information that a graffiti artist was down there that night, working on a mural beside the opening to the tunnel. There are no cameras, and the street lights have been knocked out. The thing is, while this artist dude was there, a vehicle arrived and a man dumped something large, apparently wrapped in black plastic, in the river. The artist has a video on his phone.'

'Of Lucien?'

Maxim shook his head. 'Not exactly. The man has his hood up, but there's a blacked-out SUV in the shot. A Volvo – you can see the bonnet badge in the video. I saw one like it at the club this evening, when Lucien took me to the garage to see his sports car.'

'He's not going to use his own vehicle, Max, that's just idiocy.'

'It's not exactly his. It's leased by the club – he has a plan for a liveried fleet or something.' Daniel sighed, shaking his head again, but Maxim continued, insistent. 'It had been cleaned inside, Daniel. There were covers on the seats, but the wheels were muddy. Why would you clean the interior of a new car and not the outside?'

Daniel shrugged. 'Perhaps it was cleaned and had been used again?' He stood up abruptly, his mind full of the image of Meredith's tattoo. But he needed to concentrate – to do what he was good at, and focus. Much as he wanted to believe it, this information still felt ropey. 'Did your graffiti guy get the plate in the shot?'

'A partial. The last few digits and the *département*. I only glanced at the one in the club garage, but I'm sure it's the same vehicle.'

'Have you told La Crim all this?'

Maxim rubbed his face with his hand. 'Yes, I've just come from there, I called in on the way here from Agathe's. I gave them your photos earlier today. They went to talk to Céline about Sandrine and the Métro this afternoon.'

'I can feel a "but" coming here.'

Maxim sighed and rubbed his hand over his eyes. 'That's it. Céline and Lucien are like celebrity royalty.

Everyone knows them. He's in every society magazine every week. They don't believe me. I mean, why would someone who has everything risk everything? They think I've got a grudge or something.'

'Did Céline have an explanation?'

'She told them that after the accident with her mother, she couldn't use the Métro, but she's realised she can't be held hostage by memories. She's decided it's time to overcome her fear, and she's building her tolerance, apparently. She's a psychologist. I'd say she was convincing.' Maxim let out a breath. 'It's all just such a shit show. I followed Lucien tonight. He left the club just after I did – *in the Volvo*. He went to some container park out on the north side of the *périph*. I reckon he's stashing something out there – drugs or knock-off vintage champagne, or something. I don't know, it was just weird.'

Daniel grimaced; it all sounded crazy to him, too. 'Are they living near the Saint-Paul Métro? Does it make sense that she'd use that station?'

'Yes. They live in Rue des Corbeaux, in Le Marais. They own the whole building. That's the thing ... Café Rodolphe, where Agathe, Sandrine's friend, works, is on the same street. If I'm right, Céline could have seen Sandrine there and followed her to the Métro.'

Daniel felt himself pale. He didn't trust himself to look at Maxim. He glanced at his phone. It was after 1 a.m. And Kate was on her own at 32 Rue des Corbeaux.

Chapter 65

CÉLINE BANGED HARD on the corrugated side of the container with the palm of her hand. The cold metal stung, but she barely noticed. Anger writhed inside her like a serpent uncoiling. It was all going to unravel now unless she acted quickly, and all because of her idiot brother.

She banged again and put her ear to the steel. She knew she wouldn't hear anything; the soundproofing had been expensive, but it was excellent. For a second she wondered if he was pretending he couldn't hear her banging. Standing in the oily mud and the freezing rain. Getting mad enough to kill someone.

Pulling her phone out of her jacket pocket, she checked the screen again to see if he'd replied. They had a code phrase. *I've broken the tall vase. There's glass everywhere.* There were two blue ticks. He'd installed Wi-Fi when they'd had the power hooked up, but he didn't always have it switched on.

The amount of glass related to the level of trouble: *I've found a perfect replacement. / Can you get another one? / It's only a crack, be careful when you come in. / Watch out for shards ...*

She'd added, I'm cleaning up. Let me know where you are

She checked to see when he'd read the message. Only a few minutes ago.

I'm outside, let me in

Céline bit her lip. She could feel her heart pounding, her mouth dry. This was because of him – because of their mother. Her red hair and the distinctive perfume she'd insisted on, Belle de Nuit. If she ran out, or couldn't find her bottle before she went to the club, there was always hell to pay. It was like a cloak their mother had worn to protect herself from the drugs, from the men. It had blended with the applause from the crowd as she came off stage, had been as important a part of her as her red lipstick, her legendary hair. She had been *la belle de nuit*.

Céline had known it was dangerous to indulge her brother, but she'd been so careful. She'd always looked after him, since he was little. He was four years younger than her, and their mother could only focus on herself.

She'd tended his wounds when the cigarette burns had wept, had held him tight in the early hours when they'd heard the front door bang closed and their mother's heels skittering across the tiles in the hall.

After the first time – the first redhead – he'd been so happy, euphoric. That one had been an accident: a random girl wearing *that* perfume, whom he'd met at the club. He'd only been seventeen, a baby. But Céline had never seen him so joyful, so calm; the killing had been like a drug. And his happiness had made her happy.

She'd almost died herself when she'd opened his bedroom door to find the girl lying dead in his bed. But she'd thought fast; she'd taken the girl's bag and some of her clothes and left them in trees down near the river. Close enough that the girl could have walked there, far enough away from home to send the investigators in a different direction. She'd walked the route herself back from the club, then realised that, by some miracle, there were no cameras anywhere that might have caught them together.

But Lucien hadn't wanted to let the body go, and Céline hadn't had the heart to push him.

It had given her time to plan, to work out how to get rid of it. In the end, she'd dismembered it. Meticulously wrapping the parts in all sorts of bags that she'd collected for the purpose, she'd dropped them into waste bins across the city. It wasn't ideal, but it had worked. She'd known, though, that she needed to come up with a better solution.

Because she'd also known, categorically, as she'd watched Lucien in those two weeks, that this was only the first time.

The rain was getting worse, the sound of the drops beating off the steel roof of the container, onto her shoulders. She pulled her hood more tightly around her face. Her impatience growing, she sent another message, careful with her wording. If their phones were seized, it all had to be explainable.

Hurry up! Need to show you. Outside, waiting

This time, she heard the grinding of the bolts being slid back.

Chapter 66

SITTING OPPOSITE MAXIM, Daniel closed his eyes, regulating his breathing as he digested what he'd heard. Maxim could feel the tension across his shoulders, in his neck. Telling Daniel his suspicions, his own failures, felt brutal. A moment later, Daniel opened his eyes and looked at him hard. It was as if a switch had moved in his head.

'Let's assume you're right. Lucien – and, somehow, Céline – are behind a series of murders of women with red hair. These include Meredith, and more recently, Sandrine Durand.' Daniel rattled it off as his mind processed the details. 'And you followed Lucien this evening to a lock-up, a container, on the other side of the city? He didn't go in his own vehicle, but in a leased car that you believe may have been the vehicle used to dump Sandrine's body?'

Maxim looked at him and sighed. 'Yep.'

'And the lad who saw this, or videoed it ... Did he see the driver? Could he identify him?'

Maxim nodded. 'The guy who took it sent the video to Roland – Agathe and Sandrine's flatmate – after he saw the story in the paper. I spoke to Roland tonight, and he said the lad who recorded it said there was something about the way the guy he'd seen walked. You can see it on the video.'

Daniel tapped the arm of the chair, obviously thinking. 'There are people trained to recognise suspects by their gait, it's very personal ...' He hesitated. 'Did you see Lucien leave this container?'

Maxim shook his head. 'I stayed about half an hour, but it didn't look like he was coming out. When I was on the way back to my bike, Agathe called about the video.'

Daniel checked his watch. 'So he could still be there?'

Maxim shrugged. 'It's possible. If he was just collecting something, he'd have left while I was there, surely?'

'Call him at the club, see if he's there. If he's not, get over to the container, but take the artist with you. See if you can get a positive ID on Lucien, or at least on the car.'

'The lad who made the video doesn't want to go near the cops. He's worried they'll realise why he was at the underpass in the middle of the night. But I can take Roland. It'll be better if there are two of us.'

'It sounds like there's enough circumstantial evidence to call in support. The SUV and the container both need to be searched. But you need to be sure your hunch is right.'

Maxim let out a sharp sigh. 'Exactly. The cops won't want to risk upsetting Lucien bloody Arnaud without decent evidence.'

Daniel pursed his lips. 'If you can't get confirmation on either Lucien or the car, then you're going to need to take a look inside the container. You'll need to wait for Lucien to leave and take some bolt cutters. I'm sure there will be a padlock. And latex gloves. Don't leave any prints.'

'So I take Roland with me. If Lucien is still there, I'll see if I can draw him out so Roland can get a look at him. If he takes another video and sends it to his friend, that might be enough. If he's not there or we can't be sure, break in and check the container out?'

Daniel nodded. 'Take photos and have the cops on speed dial the whole way through. Escalate this straight to your friend Carlier. He needs to be seen to be acting on crime, and he could do with a big win. His ratings are plummeting while the papers are speculating about a serial killer.'

'And if I'm wrong?'

'You aren't – you know you aren't. But if Lucien lawyers up, then Carlier can play the "no one is above the law" card. It's always popular here – it was, I believe, the whole point of the Revolution.' Daniel's tone was steely. 'Did you see any cameras in the yard?'

Maxim shook his head in reply. He stood up; he felt like a coiled spring, could feel the tension in his jaw. 'What are you going to do?'

'I'm going to make some calls, and then I'm going to make sure no one lays a finger on Kate.'

Chapter 67

KATE OPENED ONE eye at the sound of her phone vibrating on the bedside locker and, turning her back on it, pulled the duvet over her head. She didn't know exactly what time it was, but it was definitely the middle of the night and she'd been barely able to fall sleep as it was.

This was Erik all over, demanding attention.

She was absolutely going to ignore him. Anger began to rise inside her again. Kate didn't know for sure if he'd planned this whole trip or not – although it was feeling more and more likely. But it had always been mind games with him; one minute he had been generous and caring, the next losing his temper over something tiny and making it all her fault.

As she adjusted the duvet, in her mind she was back there, at the house they'd shared, on the night they'd escaped. She'd held her breath as she crept into Hanna's room to wake her, telling her that they were going on an adventure.

How long had she had their emergency bags packed before she'd dared to take the chance?

Spare clothes, all their documents hidden in old carrier bags in the cupboard where she kept the vacuum cleaner, Christmas decorations spilling out of the top in case he happened to look in. It would have been more than her life was worth for him to find them. Not that he'd ever have reason to go into the cleaning cupboard.

That night he'd come home smelling of alcohol, had slumped in front of another true crime documentary on the TV. Her nerves on edge, Kate had tiptoed around him, making him a sandwich, pouring another beer, praying he'd drink enough to sleep soundly. Then he'd asked for a brandy, and she knew this had to be the night they left.

He'd sleep soundly, but he'd be hell in the morning.

He'd passed out on the sofa and she'd put her plan into action, calling a taxi, waking Hanna. Sneaking down the stairs, avoiding the squeaky treads, she'd prayed with every cell of her being that he wouldn't wake up. Her heart had been pounding, her mouth dry. She didn't think she'd ever been more terrified than at the moment she'd stood in the tiny hallway, her fingers to her lips, easing back the front door latch.

The noises from the TV had masked the sound of the door opening. Ushering Hanna onto the step, she'd reached back into the hall to grab their coats: the good tweed that she'd found in Oxfam; Hanna's purple anorak that she'd get another few months out of. She'd unhooked Hanna's scarf from the peg, her own catching on the Velcro of Erik's combat jacket as she'd pulled it down. Hesitating for a second, wondering if she should leave it, she'd torn it away, wrapping it around her neck as she handed Hanna her coat to pull on.

Hanna had been half asleep, hadn't been able to find the sleeves, so Kate had wrapped her up in her scarf, one eye on the living room window, the lights from the TV dancing on the glass. She'd known she had to keep calm, make it seem as if this was a game.

She'd told the taxi to wait outside the house next door, had used her key to turn the lock in the front door so she could close it quietly, rather than pulling it behind them.

And then Kate had speed-walked with Hanna down the paved drive, glancing back as she'd eased the gate open. She'd been desperate to pick her daughter up, but her arms had been full with their bags and her coat.

She had run through this scenario so many times in her head. *If he woke up, the Christmas decorations were for the charity shop. They were having a clear-out. Hanna couldn't sleep. She was too excited about something happening in school the next day – so excited she'd gone to sleep in her clothes.*

She'd only grab their coats after she'd got the door open. If he'd walked out of the living room to find them putting them on, she'd struggle to explain her way out of it. *They'd heard a fox outside, Hanna wanted to see it.* Every possible story had played out in her head. It had to sound real; she had to act as if it was all normal.

Getting Hanna into the taxi, hushing the confused driver, whose voice had been far too loud in the quiet residential street, she'd thrown their belongings into the boot and jumped in herself.

It was only when he'd driven out of the estate that she'd finally taken a breath. She'd asked him to take them straight to the refuge, praying there would be room for them.

When they'd arrived, she'd barely been able to speak, her throat closed with terror. Erik would have killed her if he'd caught them; she was sure of it.

But they'd got there, and there had been room, and the women who ran it hadn't asked any questions until the next morning. Kate had felt safe for the first time in years. It had been the first step on a long journey.

She'd thought getting away had been the biggest problem, but the next morning she'd realised Hanna couldn't go back to school – that they needed to relocate completely. And she knew the first place Erik would look for them would be Orna's, so she couldn't go there either.

It had felt as if she'd made it to the mountain, but now she had to climb it. With no equipment.

She'd been trying to save money, to siphon off a pound here and there, sometimes taking back some of the items she'd bought in the weekly shop so she could get the cash. But it wasn't enough. She'd called Orna to explain, to say she couldn't risk seeing her yet, and Orna had sent her money, but … Kate didn't want to think about it now – to relive the nightmares.

She'd managed it. She'd got away and started a new life.

And here she was in Paris, having the holiday of a lifetime.

Beside her, the phone started to vibrate again. Erik had stopped texting; he was ringing now.

Kate buried her head in the pillow, burrowing under the duvet. She wasn't even going to look at her phone. She felt like throwing it across the room.

Chapter 68

CÉLINE STEPPED INSIDE the container and the door clanged closed behind her. As the echo died, she could hear the hum of the freezer, loud in the stillness. The only light came from a lamp on the locker beside the bed, the shadows around it bottomless.

'What's happened?' Lucien looked at her, his face angry. 'I was really careful, I told you. The bleach.' Céline knew he hated being disturbed here, but this wouldn't wait.

'They came to question me this afternoon. I've been waiting for you to come home.' She unzipped her jacket but didn't take it off; she only had a few minutes. 'They found a video from Saint-Paul. I was on the Métro with the one I spotted in the café – Sandrine.' The thought made Céline feel sick. She'd been so careful, had gone into the far end of the carriage. It had been packed. How had they even known she was there?

'But you said it was safe. That apartment – the whole building – was empty.'

Céline sighed. 'It was. When I saw her go into the real estate office, I thought it would be perfect. It's still empty. Exactly what we needed.'

'But she wasn't real. She was a fake.' He said it like a petulant child, as if it was Céline's fault.

Her voice hardened. 'I know – you said.'

This wasn't Céline's fault – this was his fault. He'd got too excited about Kate coming, hadn't been able to control himself. After all of her planning, setting up the competition and making sure that they had a backup in case anything went wrong.

Two backups, actually.

She'd been so very thorough.

Standing in the middle of the dimly lit space, Céline could smell the perfume – Belle de Nuit. Their mother's perfume. It set her teeth on edge.

She thrust her hands in her coat pockets. 'It's Max that's the problem. He's covering the story. If he sees that image of me in the Métro, he may put things together. He's been wary ever since Meredith.'

Lucien moved to sit down on the bed, his face taut. 'She was stupid, too close. I'm sorry.' He paused. 'It was just—'

'Her hair. I know.' Céline sat down beside him and put her arm around his shoulders, pulling him towards her, resting her chin on the top of his head. 'It's fine. We've talked about it. These things happen. And look ... You were able to keep her and her things, bring them here and enjoy them. It gave you time.'

Lucien looked around the container desolately.

Céline followed his eye. He'd stripped it now – almost, anyway. They'd taken most of Meredith's belongings – the contents of her university room – to charity shops all over the city. They'd binned the rest, just as Céline had binned the other body parts – in separate bags, in separate bins.

But the head was always a problem. When Meredith's had finally thawed out, Céline had dropped it into the warren of sewers that ran under the city.

She'd tried to mix it up, dumping some of them in the river. That was easier than dismembering them, but she felt safer when there was less to discover. Killers were caught because they kept to the same patterns. And she didn't plan to get caught, ever.

Getting her hands on the key for the manhole cover had been one of those moments of triumph. A bit like the moment she'd bumped into their mother on the Métro platform. She'd been drunk again, her spite red-hot, her tongue bitter. It had been busy; they'd been jostled from behind. And everything had suddenly become clear. With their mother gone, Céline had taken control of all her assets and become Lucien's guardian. She could finally make him happy.

Céline hadn't realised at the time that she'd need it, but the manhole key had just been lying there on the pavement, as if it had fallen out of someone's pocket or tool belt.

When she'd investigated the decomposition rate in an environment seething with bacteria, it had been a gift. And it had proven very useful over the years. They may find bones after time, but the chances of anything forensic surviving, that could lead back to them, was remote.

Or so she'd thought.

Then that torrential rain had come, and the head had somehow been washed into a channel and got caught. And the men had found it.

Céline rubbed her face with her hand. She'd heard some builders talking about it in the café, half disbelieving the story because it hadn't been in the press. It was just gossip, but not the sort she wanted to hear.

They'd been busy getting ready for Kate Wilde; Céline had hoped she would be the last. They'd agreed: she had to be the last.

At least for a while.

When the first head had been found, years before, a sort of backup plan had started to form in Céline's mind, in case something went wrong. Meredith was the key. The trick was getting the timing right.

There had been so much detail to consider this time. Céline hadn't wanted to use their own apartment, but Lucien had insisted, and he had a point. They could clear it, make it look as if Kate had left on her own.

No jury would believe they'd do something on their own doorstep, with the number of properties that were to rent in this city. Sometimes hiding in plain sight was the best option.

And the date Daniel was coming to Paris for the auction had set the time frame.

Céline sighed. She could see Lucien had put Kate's scarf on his pillow, threads of her hair spread across it. Getting ready for this had been so exciting for him, the anticipation as intoxicating as the time spent afterwards.

Lucien had told her about Daniel's aunt wanting them all to meet. When the news had leaked about Meredith's head, Céline had said a silent prayer for meddling elderly aunts.

One thing she'd learned ages before from Maxim had been that Daniel was a creature of habit. He'd once jokingly told her which train and which seat his friend always chose. How he stayed at the same hotel, in the same room. And always selected the same seat on a plane – the aisle seat in the last row on the right.

She hadn't realised then how useful that conversation would become.

It had been easy to make sure that Kate was sitting opposite Daniel on the train. If her first plan didn't work out, and anything came back to her and Lucien, she had the whole Meredith story ready to play out. How Lucien had seen her with Daniel before she disappeared. Everyone knew they were an item.

Narrowing down the women took months, identifying who was vulnerable. Finding the court records of Kate's restraining order had been the deciding factor. It had given them another ready-made suspect in her ex – who, when Céline had begun investigating, had links to Paris. She'd felt so smug that night; everything had come together perfectly.

Erik was a chef. It had been easy to find him work, to bump into him at the hotel where he was working and befriend him. And as Céline had got to know him, he'd been very forthcoming about his problems with seeing his daughter. He'd also been ridiculously suggestible, totally convinced every idea he was prompted to have, was his own.

She'd even shown him the apartment, but, unsurprisingly, it had been too expensive for his needs.

If the police investigated Kate's disappearance, they would quickly find out he'd been there and discover their history.

In the worst possible scenario, she just needed to create reasonable doubt, and these intersecting suspects would do exactly that.

It had always been her job to keep Lucien safe. And she'd managed up until now.

Chapter 69

AS MAXIM HEADED out across the reception area of Le Meurice, his helmet in the crook of his elbow, his phone clamped to his ear, he willed Agathe to pick up. There had been no signal in the lift, but enough time for him to curse himself for not acting on all this sooner.

As soon as he'd heard about the head in the sewer, and then about Sandrine and the possibility there was someone killing redheads, what might have happened to Meredith had started to nag at him. Watching Lucien leave the rowing club with her was etched so deeply into his memory, it still haunted his nightmares.

If Maxim was honest with himself, he'd always felt deep down that her disappearance was a bit strange. She'd been drunk – probably high, too, if Lucien was involved. The kiss he'd seen had been more him than her. She'd pushed him away, laughing it off, but Maxim had known that Lucien had his sights set on her. He couldn't bear for Daniel to have something he didn't – to be happy.

Daniel had been intoxicatingly happy that term. He'd found his soulmate.

And Lucien had taken her away.

As he'd sat in Gabriel Beaudin's office, listening to Agathe's evidence, thinking about Meredith, Agathe had said something about many of the girls disappearing after a night out. Gabriel had thought it could be a taxi driver, and Maxim's mind had gone to the night economy. There was a whole world that only woke up at 10 p.m.

Lucien ran a club; he was part of that.

But how could his friend be involved? It just seemed to be so crazy. Maxim hadn't been able to face that thought.

Or to face his own failure after that night at the rowing club.

If he'd said something before, would the cops have looked at Lucien and found out what had happened to Meredith? Had his hesitation to act caused more deaths?

And then Sandrine … That had cut through him like a blade of ice. He'd only met her for a few minutes, one day in the lift on the way up to the office, but she'd radiated life and intelligence. It was as if she'd had some sort of inner glow.

Maxim suddenly heard Agathe's voice, sleepy, at the other end.

'Agathe? You both still up? I'm coming over. Some stuff's happened. I need Roland to come with me to check something out.'

'Just a minute, I'll get him.' At the other end, Maxim heard rustling and a door opening and closing, then Agathe's voice.

'Roland, wake up, Max needs you. Here – talk to him.'

Maxim heard the phone being passed and then Roland's voice, grainy with sleep. 'Hello?'

He reached the hotel's rotating glass door and barrelled through it, the chill night air taking his breath away after the warmth of the foyer. He'd left his bike chained up down a side street around the corner, and walked as quickly as he could, the phone clamped to his ear.

'Roland, I need you to do something for me, mate. I need some help. I think we've got a lead on the guy your friend saw at the river. I need you to come with me and take a video, so your friend can see if it's him.'

'Woah, but—'

'If we get a video, your friend may recognise that walk.

It won't involve the cops yet, and if it does, I'll make sure that, as my sources, you're both protected, I promise. I'll be with you in about ten minutes. I just need to make a call to check something. Meet me outside your apartment, and wear something warm. I'm on the bike.'

Maxim ended the call, not waiting for Roland to protest more. He didn't have time for a discussion, and he knew he'd need help to capture the footage. He reached his bike and, spinning back the combination on the padlock, he put a call through to Lucien's mobile.

'We cannot connect your call at this time ...'

Maxim looked at his phone. Lucien was out of range somewhere. If there was no reception in a lift, would the steel walls of a container block a phone signal?

To be certain, he dialled Le Loup Gris.

'Hi, I need to speak to Lucien. It's his friend Maxim Verdier – it's urgent.'

He was put on hold, a sexy voice extolling the virtues of the club's private membership programme. Flipping up the seat on his bike, Maxim stowed the chain. After what seemed like an age, the voice that had answered came back to him,

'He was here, but we can't seem to find him right now. Can I take a message?'

'No, don't worry, I'll try his mobile again.'

Maxim ended the call, his brow creased. So Lucien hadn't told anyone he'd left. Was that some sort of an attempt to create an alibi if he needed it? Maxim didn't have the mental capacity to think that one through right now; his head was too busy.

He needed to check out that container.

It was time for him to make things right.

Chapter 70

CÉLINE PULLED THE collar of her coat up against the night as she waited for a second taxi outside the Métro station. She'd taken another one to get here, and arrived to find that the rank was empty. If she waited, she was sure one would arrive. *This wasn't a trip she wanted logged on an app.*

Crossing her arms against the cold, Céline mentally ran through the plan again. This was the part she enjoyed most – the power it gave her to outsmart *La Crim*. She couldn't help the smile that broke out on her face. They'd believed everything she'd said earlier about the Métro station. She'd even summoned a tear when she'd been talking about their bitch of a mother.

Céline and Lucien had so many years of misery and powerlessness at her hands.

Their mother had made them both what they were. All of this was her fault.

And she'd paid for it.

Céline's lip curled as bile rose at the thought of their mother: her red hair; that scent Lucien was obsessed with.

The perfume course had been his idea. It had been the perfect way to lure Kate to Paris: to make it feel like a real competition, with a real prize. Céline had to give it to him – it had worked.

The most important thing now was to be ready in case the head that had been found recently was identified as Meredith's – although Céline rather doubted that would happen very quickly. It hadn't been down there that long, but immersion, combined with the bacterial activity, would make identification difficult. And DNA match was only possible if they had a comparative sample, which would be a long shot after all these years. Céline had been thorough, researching facial reconstruction, too. Some woman called Carla Steele was the European expert, and she wasn't even based in France; she was in Ireland, which presented a further delay.

But if Meredith was identified, they were ready.

Creating multiple layers of misdirection would take any heat firmly away from them. And the timing was perfect. Daniel could so clearly be linked with Meredith, he'd make an even more convincing suspect than Erik.

Anyhow, it was done now. Kate was next. Lucien had been fixated with her since he'd seen her in the online photos taken at that Redhead Convention. Kate had taken her daughter, no doubt to show her that she wasn't alone in the world.

He'd spent months tracking Kate down through social media. He'd promised she'd be the last, but after Sandrine, Céline doubted that.

She should never have told him about Sandrine.

When Céline had spotted the redhead collecting her coffee at the café, she'd been sure the colour was real. But that just showed her how good hairdressers were these days. Céline had followed her all the way to work, weaving through the crowds in the Métro. Arranging to meet Sandrine at that property the next day had been ridiculously easy. They hadn't even checked out the false name Céline had given, had just called her spare phone to confirm. Young women in jobs like that had no idea how vulnerable they were.

Of course, if she hadn't mentioned the name of the estate agent to Lucien and then stupidly left her diary open on the counter, he wouldn't have phoned Sandrine Durand personally and organised to meet her himself. He'd pretended he was Céline's PA, booking a follow-up viewing that same evening, as if she couldn't wait the weekend to see it again. But these things couldn't be helped. He'd used a burner phone; he'd been careful. And he'd thought to use Sandrine's own phone to email her office and ask them to take the property off sale until Monday, so that had bought him some time. But these were all risks, and Céline didn't like risks.

They needed to focus on Kate now, and on executing their plan. Then all lines of enquiry would point to Daniel – or to Erik, depending on which way things went. The press were already connecting the killings. If forensic evidence was discovered – Kate's hairs appearing on a jacket, or perhaps a trophy – one of them would take a fall. One of Céline's patients was a detective with *La Crim*; she'd be able to find out what was happening easily enough.

But she had other things to do first, to get things ready at their apartment. She'd clear Kate's room as soon as she'd dropped off the body, make it look like she'd packed and left.

A cab pulled up in front of her and Céline almost jumped. She'd been so absorbed in her thoughts, she hadn't seen it approach. It was as if the gods were smiling. Everything was coming together.

Chapter 71

THE STREETS WERE almost empty as Maxim sped through the night. He knew where he was going this time; he'd set the satnav on the bike to take the quickest route to the container park. He could feel Roland's arms tighten around him as he swerved around another car, eating up the miles of the *périphérique*.

He'd explained briefly where they were going as Roland was putting on his helmet. Agathe had hovered behind him on the pavement, her hands crammed into the pocket of her jeans, shoulders hunched against the rain. She hadn't said anything, just given him a beseeching look filled with hope and despair as he'd throttled up. Maxim had nodded to her, hoping it conveyed everything he wanted to say. *I'll do my best.*

The two-lane road that wove into the industrial estate looked exactly as it had when he'd left. Street lamps set too far apart threw pools of light onto the wet tarmac, oily after the rain. There was something run-down about this place; litter was blowing across the road and around the warehouses at the entrance, their shutters drawn.

Maxim felt Roland shift behind him. He raised his hand and pointed. They were almost there.

This time pulling up beyond the gate, Maxim jumped off and hauled his helmet off. Roland did the same and Maxim held a finger to his lips. Sound travelled at night, and they needed to approach silently. The rumble of a goods train in the distance reached them, proving his point.

Lifting the seat, Maxim stowed Roland's helmet and pulled out the chain and combination lock to secure the bike. If this went according to plan, he wouldn't need to follow Lucien again.

Beside him, Roland was jumping from foot to foot like a boxer warming up, his nervous energy contagious. Indicating that Roland should follow him, Maxim headed back to the gate. The wrench was still in place, propping the gates open enough for them to squeeze through.

Which confirmed for sure that Lucien was still inside the yard.

Jogging back the way he'd come before, Maxim kept close to the containers, listening hard for the sound of an engine.

As they reached the section at the very back of the yard where he'd seen Lucien, Maxim turned to Roland, beckoning him to come close. He leaned in, to whisper in his ear.

'We're almost there. I need you to look at the SUV and take photos, see if it's the same one as in the video. Send them to your friend. Then we'll make some noise and see if Lucien comes out. I need you to hang back. Video the whole thing.'

Roland nodded sharply. He was breathing hard, his breath visible in the cold air as Maxim continued. 'OK, follow me to the corner. It's close enough for you to see inside when he comes out, but make sure you have the video rolling.'

Roland nodded again.

Maxim took a deep breath, adrenaline coursing through him. *What the hell was Lucien doing inside that container?* It had power, lights. It had to be more than a storage unit.

But he didn't want to think about that now. Deep inside, he had a horrible feeling that this secret place held the answers to what had happened to the missing women.

Keeping his back to the cold, dark sides of the containers, Maxim sidled up to the next path between them. Dipping right, he came to the junction he'd been at before.

'Phone ready?' Maxim's voice was barely a whisper. Roland nodded.

Maxim didn't have a whole plan worked out, but he needed to find a way to get Lucien outside. And as he looked at the Volvo, one came into his head.

Digging in his jacket pocket for his bike keys, Maxim opened up the multipurpose tool on his keyring. It had been a gift from Daniel years before, when he'd first gone to the desert. It was one of those ten-tools-in-one things that morphed between screwdriver, bottle opener and spoon and fork, depending on your needs. Maxim flicked out the knife.

'Ready?' He turned to Roland. Saying it had been more for his own benefit.

'Go for it.'

The sound of another train covered his approach as Maxim crouched down low and ran across the pitted concrete road, avoiding the puddles, diving behind the Volvo. It was a big SUV, the windows blacked out. Sliding down the side of the vehicle, keeping it between himself and the container, Maxim reached the driver's door. Now he had to trust Swedish engineering.

Glancing back towards where Roland was hidden, he inserted the tip of the knife into the lock of the driver's door. The vehicle had remote central locking; he'd seen the lights – and, he hoped, the alarm – flash on when Lucien arrived. But every vehicle had a manual override in the door handle. Not that Maxim was intending to break in.

He jiggled the knife again, trying to work it into the keyhole. And the SUV answered him with an ear-splitting screech, all of its lights flashing on as if someone had set off fireworks.

Maxim ran and dived behind the nearest container, his heart pounding. A moment later he could hear the clang of bolts being shot back, and light fell onto the rough ground as Lucien came out of the container door. The sounds and lights suddenly stopped.

Lucien had turned the alarm off.

Maxim heard the jangle of a bunch of keys, and bent forward to peek around the steel wall of the container he was concealed behind. Lucien was walking slowly around the vehicle, trying to see what had caused the alarm to trigger. He'd changed into a sweatshirt and jeans, his hair mussed as if he'd been lying down.

As Maxim watched, Lucien shook his head to himself and hit the central locking, opening the vehicle and locking it again. He hadn't even got as far as the driver's door.

A few seconds later, clearly puzzled, he shrugged and headed back inside. The steel door clanged shut and the bolts were shot across.

Maxim just had to pray Roland had caught everything on film.

Chapter 72

J**OGGING AROUND TO** where he'd left Roland, Maxim could see him leaning against the container, his face illuminated by the phone screen.

Maxim indicated for him to follow. The last thing he needed was for Lucien to hear them talking.

The ground was rough, uneven, and pooled with brackish water, the puddles slick with oil. Maxim stayed close to the line of the containers, Roland right behind him, his feet in step.

Close to the main gate, Maxim stopped to catch his breath. They were far enough away, and there was no sign that Lucien had heard them, or followed them. Car alarms went off randomly all the time. He must have thought it was an accident. At least, that was what Maxim was hoping he thought. Realistically, there was no one else here. The yard was empty, and as far as Lucien was concerned, he was on his own.

Leaning on the cold steel of a container, Maxim turned to look to Roland. 'Did you get it?'

Roland glanced at him, his face hard. 'Yep.'

'Is it the same guy?'

Roland's dark eyes filled with hate. 'Looks a lot like him to me. Same height, same build. He sort of swings his hips when he walks. I'm sure it's him, but I've sent it on to ...' He hesitated, almost saying his fellow artist's name. 'For my friend to check.' He paused. 'And that's the same vehicle.'

'Sure?'

Roland nodded. 'It's the same make and model as in the video.' He flicked to a different screen on his phone. 'See? And the last two letters of the plate are the same – ET – and the *département* number is 60. That's *Oise*, not Paris. It must be him.' He held up his phone again, showing Maxim a still from the original video. 'It's not the whole plate, so I'm sure there's a margin of error here, but realistically, what are the chances?'

Maxim looked at him, nodding slowly. This was the evidence he'd been looking for. It was still circumstantial, but with everything else—

Roland interrupted his thoughts. He was switching screens again, replaying the video he'd taken. 'And you know that container?'

'Lucien's?' Maxim's thoughts were already elsewhere, the enormity of the situation blending with a good dose of shock. He'd been right. *Could he have stopped this if he'd said something back in the day?* He was starting to feel sick. But Roland hadn't noticed his preoccupation; he was still talking.

'He left the door open when he went to switch off the car alarm. I got a shot of the inside.'

Suddenly Maxim was back with him, his eyebrows shot up. 'What's in there?'

Roland glanced at him as he passed Maxim his phone. 'See for yourself.'

As Maxim watched, the door swung open. It took a moment for the camera to adjust to the change in lighting conditions. Then the lens focused on the container, the time stamp showing 2.10 a.m.

'What the fuck …? Is that a bed?'

'I think so. And to the side of it there's the hood of a studio light. It's like he's got a porn movie set in there.' Roland handed Maxim his phone, still warm from his hand.

Maxim's stomach turned as he played the video again. *What the hell had gone on in that container?*

'I think it's time we made some calls.'

Chapter 73

THE SUDDEN POUNDING on the door made Kate throw back the covers and sit upright, as if she'd had an electric shock. Every muscle tense, she listened trying to work out what the noise was, where it was coming from. *What on earth?*

She'd been tossing and turning since Erik had tried to call, was sure she'd heard the clock in the living room chiming two. She must have finally fallen asleep afterwards.

It took her a moment to realise that the noise was coming from the front door.

'Kate, Kate, are you OK?'

What? The woman's voice sounded like Céline: the concern in her tone was clear even through the walls. What on earth had happened? And why was she yelling? She had Kate's number, why hadn't she called?

For a moment, Kate wondered if that had been her trying to call earlier, and not Erik at all. Perhaps she'd been ignoring the wrong person. Kate tried to shake herself properly awake. She had fallen into such a deep sleep that coming out of it was like rising too fast from the depths of the ocean.

The banging came again.

Why was she making so much noise? She'd wake the whole building. But now Kate thought about it, she wasn't sure there was anyone in the rest of the property. She hadn't heard anyone in the apartment above at all, and the pigeonholes downstairs were empty.

Céline banged on the door again. 'Kate, please answer. Are you all right?'

Perhaps someone had seen Erik on the balcony and had told Céline? A voice inside Kate asked her why this was happening in the middle of the night, why not earlier – but maybe Céline had been out and had only just picked up a message.

The pounding on the door came again. Confused, her head still heavy, Kate fought to wake up properly. All of her fears had coalesced in one sickening moment.

Céline knew about Erik. Perhaps he was out in the street right now? Or on the balcony again?

Could he be in the apartment now? Had her efforts to block the French windows been a waste of time?

Kate's heart picked up speed as she threw back the duvet. Pulling her jeans on over her nightshirt, she hauled open a drawer and grabbed a sweatshirt.

She was halfway across the room when she remembered her phone.

Reaching for it, she shoved it in the back pocket of her jeans. She still didn't want to look at it in case it had been Erik, not Céline, calling earlier. His messages always got more and more toxic, as if he was spiralling into a dark tunnel with violence at the end of it. She needed to be really strong about not reading them, and just delete them all.

Kate turned to go out of the bedroom door, realising she'd blockaded it earlier. She didn't have the energy to move the chest of drawers. Instead, turning, she headed into the bathroom. Unlocking the door to the corridor, Kate ran down to the front door, her bare feet silent on the wooden boards.

As Kate reached the front door, Céline thumped on it again.

'Kate, please, open up and show me you're OK.'

Kate opened her mouth to answer, but stopped herself. What if Erik was in the apartment – in the *salon* right now, waiting to jump out on her?

Kate cursed. She'd left the poker on the bed. Should she go back for it? She looked anxiously at the double doors that opened into the *salon*. They were closed, but they were directly opposite the front door. If he was inside, he'd hear Kate undoing the locks. Could she get the door open before he pounced? She'd put on the deadlocks, ensuring that they were all engaged before she went to bed.

Her hand on the door, Kate looked back at the *salon* doors. They were closed tightly, just as she'd left them. Was he in there, or was her imagination running away?

Her attention on the front door, Kate made her decision. She flicked the locks open as fast as she could and pulled the door open.

Chapter 74

AS SOON THEY'D seen the blue lights approaching in convoy, the sirens off, Maxim had sent Roland out of the gate to wait beside the bike. It was cold, but Maxim had a feeling adrenaline would keep him warm. It certainly had him fired up.

The first jeep pulled up beside him. Travère killed the blues as he looked out of the passenger window, his face a potent blend of pissed off and the smallest dash of admiration. 'Jump in, brief me on the way.' His tone was curt, but Maxim didn't care. He'd already taken too long to act. *Thank God they'd got here so fast.*

As Maxim pulled the rear door closed, he indicated where the driver needed to go. He put the jeep into drive and accelerated gently down the main arterial road into the depot, the headlights bouncing off the wet road as they hit the potholes.

Travère turned back to look at him. 'So who is it? Do we know him?'

Maxim leaned forward, his eyes fixed on the windscreen. He wasn't about to derail this by revealing the suspect's identity. 'Someone who has killed, conservatively, at least five women. Did you bring forensics?'

'They're on call. We need to assess the situation.'

Maxim lifted his hand to indicate that the driver needed to take the next turn. 'Right here. Left at the end. It's the dark red one on the end of the next bay. Black Volvo SUV parked outside.'

As the jeep they were in pulled over, the two vehicles behind them did the same. Their doors opened and officers in black body armour spilled out, carrying machine guns. Maxim watched them through the rear window. Raymond Travère was with *La Crim*, the Criminal Investigation Bureau, but these guys were GIGN – *Groupe d'intervention de la Gendarmerie nationale* – the highly trained crisis management division. Carlier wasn't taking any risks.

Daniel had been right. Carlier would be on the front page of every newspaper when this came together, and he'd made sure they had high-profile firepower to get the first part of the job done.

Maxim didn't reckon Lucien had an army hidden behind that steel door, but whatever happened next, these guys were going to scare the shit out of him. Maxim was going to relish every moment of that.

For Meredith and Daniel, and for Sandrine and Agathe, and for all the others.

Travère glanced at the time on the dash as he looked back at Maxim and unclipped his safety belt.

'Stay here.'

Maxim nodded, his face serious, thinking exactly the opposite.

It was 2.30 a.m., and they were finally going to get some answers.

The GIGN commandos were already in position as Maxim reached a good lookout point, at the side of a container almost opposite Lucien's. He'd circled around the back of the next block – he had no idea what you called a pile of containers – so he'd get the best chance of a clear video, but still be concealed. It was prohibited to photograph these guys, but he needed to get something for the paper. Once he had pictures, they could be edited for publication. Maxim had never seen something like this unfold so quickly, but he knew Gabriel Beaudin wouldn't ever forgive him if he missed the opportunity.

Maxim could see three officers in a triangular formation in front of Lucien's container, their weapons at their shoulders. Dressed in black combat gear, balaclavas under their visored helmets, their flak vests bulky in the darkness, they were like panthers waiting to spring.

As Maxim watched, another officer got into position, facing outwards, his back to the steel wall of the container, something in his hand. A limpet bomb, Maxim reckoned. He'd been to see these guys in training. Blowing open doors was something they were very good at.

The guy facing him hit the side of the container, the sound ringing out sharply across the yard like a rifle crack. Even Maxim jumped, and he knew it was coming.

'Armed police. Come out with your hands in the air.'

The hairs stood up on the back of Maxim's neck. *What would Lucien do now? Try and talk his way out of it?*

Chapter 75

A BLACK POLICE RANGE Rover was waiting for Daniel when he got to the front door of his hotel. The officer driving was friendly, but cagey. Daniel could understand that. He wasn't operational, which in some ways made things simpler – there wasn't time for masses of red tape – but nobody wanted a spare part on an armed mission in a residential area. Especially one with an obvious disability.

Daniel wasn't surprised at the officer's reticence. His security services contact had sounded smug when Daniel had called to explain what was happening, and to request clearance to be looped in.

'If Lucien Arnaud is on his own at the container park, Céline is likely to be at home, in the same building as Kate Wilde,' Daniel had explained. 'I'm positive that Kate's their next target. It's imperative we secure her safety, and arrest Céline before she becomes aware that Lucien has been compromised.'

'I'll see what I can do,' his contact had replied. 'It's hitting the fan on the other side. *La Crim*'s not looking good.'

Daniel had been tempted to roll his eyes; it was the same in every country he'd worked in. The services always loved it when they got one over on the police. It was a fraternal rivalry that went both ways, and his contact was enjoying every minute of it. They'd been the ones to find the video of Céline Arnaud following Sandrine Durand, proving just how useful their technology was.

'I'll talk to them,' Daniel's contact had assured him. 'Leave it with me.'

The police inspector who had called him shortly afterwards had been blunt: 'This isn't your war and it's not your soil.'

He was right about the soil, but Daniel wasn't so sure about it not being his war. Not after what Maxim had told him about Meredith. It sounded very much as if it was his war. But he hadn't needed to get into that.

Daniel knew his contact would have made it clear he would be able to adapt to the brief. Their friendship dated back to a field operation in Afghanistan when they'd both been much younger, but they'd kept in touch, had been very useful to each other over the years. Daniel had been equally curt in his response to the inspector.

'Kate knows me, as does Céline Arnaud. I can provide the distraction your team need to get in cleanly. We may not have much time.'

He was right, and they both knew it.

As they pulled into le Rue des Corbeaux, stopping outside the café and killing the lights, Daniel looked up. He could see the snipers already in situ on the roofs of the buildings opposite number 32. Lying flat, they were only visible because he knew what to look for. There would be teams on the balconies of the apartments on either side as well. Obviously whatever they'd found in the container park had set off alarm bells up the chain, and they weren't taking any risks.

There was a movement in a doorway further down the street, and Daniel recognised the glint of a visor. They had the whole road covered.

The driver turned to him. 'The situation is escalating across the city. We have communications jammed in the immediate area, but we need to move quickly. We'll wire you for comms. We need you to distract Céline Arnaud while we establish the safety of the other female. Our guys are ready to move in via the balcony – textbook stuff.'

Daniel put his hand on the door release. Behind him, the rear of the vehicle had been opened and a full communication point was rolling into action. He could already hear the officers checking in from their assigned positions.

'The building seems to be unoccupied apart from the rental, and the Arnauds' apartment on the ground floor.' The driver – Daniel thought he was also the scene co-ordinator – sounded sceptical. He was right: in this area, property was at a premium; empty space just didn't exist.

'Do you have any information on firearms?'

The driver shook his head. 'Nothing registered. No licences issued.'

It wasn't a guarantee, but that was good news, Daniel hoped. He had no idea how deeply Céline might be involved in all of this, but she was the link with Sandrine. She'd known Meredith. And she'd been beside her mother when she'd fallen to her death. He didn't want Kate to be alone in the same building with her any longer than was absolutely necessary.

Chapter 76

AS KATE SWUNG the door open, she realised she should have checked the spyhole, but she'd been right. It was Céline.

'Oh, thank God, I was so worried.' Standing on the threshold, Céline put her hand to her chest. She looked impossibly elegant for ridiculous o'clock in the morning, her dark hair sleek in a ponytail, her navy sweater unmistakably cashmere, her make-up perfect.

Kate didn't understand how anyone could look that poised in the middle of the night. Her heart rate calming, she pulled the door open and ruffled her hand through her own hair, suddenly self-conscious.

Céline glanced anxiously back at the stairs. 'Can I come in?'

'Of course. I'm sorry, I was asleep.' Kate stood back to let Céline into the hall and, closing the door behind her, hesitated for a split second before she pushed open the door into the *salon*.

In the light from the hall, she could see that the room was just as she'd left it.

Thank God.

Kate followed Céline inside, flicking on the lights.

'Oh, goodness, what happened?' Céline indicated the heavy curtains tucked in tightly behind the marble-topped half-moon tables.

Kate crossed her arms, suddenly feeling tense. 'I'm sorry to move them. When I got home one of the French windows was open. I thought perhaps Erik had—'

Céline interrupted her. 'Broken in?'

Kate nodded slowly. The anger she'd felt when she'd got home had gone, replaced by a sick feeling of worry.

Céline strode over to the windows. 'I think he was outside. That's why I'm here. I thought I saw someone lurking across the street as I arrived back from the club.' She paused. 'Do you mind if I check? He may still be there.'

Feeling suddenly chilled, Kate shook her head. She watched as Céline moved the first table away from the window and started to open the furthest curtain. It was heavy, the rings jamming on the rail.

Kate felt her phone vibrate again in her pocket. It had to be Erik sending her messages. Céline was peering out through the window.

Kate got out her phone and punched in the code to open it.

'It's too dark. I'll just open the door and see if I can see anything.' Céline turned the handle and pulled. A blast of cold air whistled in as she stepped out onto the balcony, looking up and down the street. 'The thing is, I think I might have spoken to him outside, when you first arrived. I didn't realise…'

With her head outside the French window, Kate could only half hear Céline, but she felt her heart clench. *Erik had been here?* The shock turned her stomach and made her feel dizzy. *He must be tracking her phone.* He'd been following her all along.

Suddenly Kate registered the missed calls on her screen. They were from Daniel, not Erik. Out of the corner of her eye, she could see Céline pulling a plastic bag out of her back pocket, something white inside it. But she was concentrating on the screen.

Why on earth was Daniel texting and trying to call so late?

Puzzled, Kate opened WhatsApp to see he'd her messaged about six times.

The last message made her freeze.

ON MY WAY. DO NOT LET ANYONE IN. AT ALL. NOBODY.

What on earth?

As Céline stepped back into the room and pushed the door to, Kate shoved the phone into her jeans.

What did Daniel mean? Did he know Céline had seen something – someone outside?

'Did you see anything?' Kate tried to make her voice sound steady, but it came out much more shakily than she'd intended. She cleared her throat. As if Céline understood Kate's fear, she shook her head. She crossed her arms; whatever she was holding in her hand was tucked into the crook of her arm.

'I thought I'd be able to see from up here, but he's vanished.'

'Thank you for checking on me. I think he was in here earlier today. I came home and found that door open. That's why I moved the tables.' Kate paused, running her hand over her eyes. 'I probably should have told you … I didn't think.'

'Were you here? Did he hurt you?' Céline took a step forward, looking searchingly at Kate. Behind her, the door hadn't closed properly, but Céline didn't seem to notice.

'No, I wasn't here. But someone broke the snow globe I bought for Hanna. It was the only thing disturbed. I'm sure it was him.'

'And he texted?' Céline's face creased with concern. 'Today also?'

'Yes ...' Kate shrugged. She couldn't explain what was going on in Erik's head, but she knew it was because he couldn't get what he wanted. In *his* head he'd done nothing wrong; he had been even angrier when the judge had convicted him and issued the restraining order. Suddenly she felt exhausted.

'Should we call the police?' Kate's voice shook as she spoke. 'I'm sure he broke in earlier, and if you've seen him hanging about, that's really not good.'

Céline's arms were still folded tightly. A smile of acknowledgment flicked across her face as she looked at the floor, apparently thinking. She seemed a bit irritated, for some reason Kate couldn't figure out.

'Why don't we have a coffee, and you can tell me what happened? Then we can decide what to do.'

Kate looked at her, confused. *Coffee, now?* Kate still wasn't quite awake, but this was Céline's city. Perhaps she hadn't been sure that it was Erik outside, or perhaps there hadn't been anyone at all. Kate tried to unravel her thoughts. She really didn't want coffee, but tea would calm down her racing heart and help her feel less groggy.

Chapter 77

STANDING OUTSIDE THE front door of number 32, Daniel said a silent prayer of thanks to the small child in the red hat whom they'd seen playing in the Louvre. Over their coffee, Daniel had explained the significance of *le bonnet rouge*, and Kate had laughingly realised the door code to her apartment was the date of the French Revolution – 1789.

She'd been charmed, thinking that perhaps it was some sort of gimmick to help tourists remember it, so they didn't keep bothering her hosts.

As the lock clicked gently back, Daniel glanced at the two commandos with him. They all knew where Lucien Arnaud was, but they didn't know for sure where Céline was. The GIGN had blocked the phone signals as they closed in on the container, so Céline should have no idea what was happening to her brother. But with Kate's time in Paris getting shorter – if they were right, and Céline was acting as her brother's accomplice – the level of danger was increasing.

Pushing open the huge oak door, Daniel stepped inside the stone hallway and looked quickly around, assessing the ground floor. Behind him, the two black-clad commandos slipped silently in.

While Daniel was being wired up and having his earpiece tested, an officer had shown him the architect plans of the building. According to their records, the upper floors were let to businesses, all of which were apparently registered outside the country. Therefore, they were likely to be empty, which simplified things enormously. Trying to covertly evacuate a building like this, spread over several floors, was a real challenge. Daniel had had to do it before, and it hadn't gone as well as he would have liked.

The plans had shown a central staircase, the ground floor apartment wrapping around it to take up almost all the entire floor, the rear opening onto a central garden courtyard.

As Daniel stood inside the front door, he could visualise the plans in three dimensions. In the far corner of the hallway, the door to the basement was located beside a bank of pigeonholes. It was shut tight – locked, he hoped. One of the two men with him headed over to it. They didn't need any surprises.

The lights were on in the hall. Normally in apartment blocks like these they were on a motion sensor, only coming on when someone entered, and timed to go off shortly after. Perhaps someone had come through the hall just ahead of him.

Was Céline at home? The team had scoped out her apartment, but the drapes had been pulled in the kitchen at the front. Although there was a lamp on in the sitting room, they hadn't seen any movement inside. Most people would be asleep at this time of night.

Waiting for his cue, Daniel looked up the sweeping polished granite staircase. Beside it, a concertina door was pulled across an antique cage-like lift which, from its gleaming paint, looked as if it had been recently restored.

Daniel heard a voice in his ear and glanced at the commando with him.

'Everyone in position, we've got eyes on the apartment. Curtains open. Two females in the *salon*.'

Two females? That wasn't what Daniel wanted to hear.

'The two women – looks like the redhead, Kate Wilde, and Céline Arnaud.'

Daniel felt his anger begin to rise, blending with the adrenaline already in his system. It was a dangerous combination. Whatever Céline was doing in Kate's apartment at this time in the morning, it wasn't good; he was sure of it.

Hadn't Kate seen his text?

He should have been more specific. It was logical that she would consider another woman to be safe. And Céline knew it.

Was that what had happened with the others? Had Céline somehow made them trust her, and reeled them in? Daniel knew it wasn't common, but there had been cases of couples working together to kill.

A *folie à deux*.

Madness shared by two.

Names immediately sprang to Daniel's mind: Myra Hindley and Ian Brady; Fred and Rosemary West. In those type of cases, the dominant partner had had a psychotic disorder, and induced or influenced the other to follow their delusions.

He'd couldn't think of a brother and sister who had killed together, but that didn't matter now. It was time to get moving.

He pointed upwards and the officer nodded curtly, taking up position at the bottom of the stairs.

Walking across the hall, his walking stick tapping loudly on the flagstones, Daniel headed for the lift. It was his job to create a diversion, but he hoped his role would extend beyond that.

He had questions for Céline Arnaud.

Chapter 78

LEAVING CÉLINE IN the *salon*, Kate headed towards the kitchen and looked at her phone again, puzzled. *What did Daniel mean, don't let anybody in?*

Had he found out something out about Erik?

Kate flicked on the kitchen light switch and shivered. If Erik was behind these murders ... If he'd hurt Agathe's friend ... She could feel her stomach heaving at the thought. She pushed her hair back behind her ear and rubbed her face with both hands, trying to work it out.

Now she'd got out of the habit of having her sleep constantly broken by Erik – of sleeping with half her senses on full alert – she struggled to function when she was woken suddenly. It was as if her body was making up for lost time.

She needed some ginger tea, for sure.

Filling the kettle and flicking on the switch, she texted Daniel quickly.

Something happened with Erik, he broke in earlier. I'm fine. Céline here now.

The kettle boiled, and it only took Kate a few moments to pour the water over her tea bag and reach for the cafetière to make Céline's coffee. She really wasn't up to fiddling with the machine at this time in the morning.

Putting everything onto a tray, she padded back to the living room. Céline looked as if she'd been pacing like a caged animal between the window and the sofa.

Which didn't feel right at all. Every time Kate had met her, Céline had been totally composed, as if nothing could ever rattle her. But now there was definitely something wrong. Very wrong. Kate could feel tension rolling off her like a cloud.

Kate put the tray down on the coffee table beside the bowl of hydrangeas. They were fading now, she realised, the petals browning at the edges as if they were decaying. But Céline didn't sit down. Kate glanced over to the French window. It still wasn't quite closed.

Kate's anxiety spiked. If Céline had seen Erik outside, he could be waiting for his chance to get back in.

This was definitely not the way she wanted her stay in Paris to end.

'Help yourself. I'm just going to close—' Kate was halfway to the window when she felt Céline's hand grip her arm. Half turning in surprise, she felt something cold pressed to her face. She caught a whiff of a sweet, clinical odour, but ducked. Her instincts took over; the lessons she'd learned over the months she'd spent in self-defence classes after she'd left Erik, kicking in. Memories flashed through her head. *Erik catching her in a chokehold, throttling her until she'd almost passed out.*

Twisting away and bending, catching Céline's leg with her own foot, Kate tried to pull her off balance. Whatever Céline had been holding to her face slipped. Kate tried to turn to face her. She wasn't going to let anyone overpower her again. She was a different person now.

But Céline's grip on her arm was pincer-like. And she was fighting to get the cloth she was holding in her other hand over Kate's face again. Writhing, trying to kick out, Kate managed to push her hand up between the crook of Céline's arm and her own face, pushing her arm through the gap. The pressure dropped for a moment, and Kate gasped in a breath of fresh air. She didn't have time to think about what might be on the cloth. She could feel her head starting to swim.

She had to get away – had to keep struggling, to make this as difficult as possible, whatever this was. For Hanna, for herself.

Kate felt Céline adjust her stance, her grip on Kate's arm like a vice as she struggled to cover her nose again. Somehow they'd turned around so Kate was facing the fireplace and the huge mirror. She could see Céline's face, flushed and angry, rigid with determination.

As she breathed in the chemical soaked into the cotton pad over her mouth, Kate could feel her limbs getting heavy. Then, in the mirror glass, she caught the movement of the balcony door behind them.

'What the hell? You'll bruise her, you stupid bitch. It won't look like she jumped. You said we needed to be careful, so it looked like she jumped …' Erik's voice cut through Kate like a sliver of broken glass. Despite her sluggishness, she could feel fear flooding through her like electricity. She knew that tone – the anger, the outrage.

Jumped? Jumped where? Into the river? Behind her, she could see him looming in the mirror, a black hood pulled up over his blond hair. But he couldn't disguise himself from her.

The room was starting to blur at the edges. Kate's whole body felt heavy. *What was happening?*

Céline screamed, and Kate felt her jerk as if she'd been grabbed from behind. Suddenly Kate found herself released and falling sideways onto the floor, hard. Her brain was processing everything in slow motion, trying to catch up with what was happening.

'*Que fais-tu? Dégage conard.*' Céline's screech was white-hot. Lifting her head, Kate tried to see what was happening. Erik had grabbed Céline. Grunting and hissing, she was using his weight against him, trying to throw him to the floor. As they grappled, the sound was suddenly drowned by glass shattering and an animal roar of pain.

Erik fell, his body sending a vibration through the floor that reached Kate at the same time as his cry. Fighting the heaviness that seemed to be descending over her, she tried to crawl away from them.

Céline was standing with her back to Kate, frozen rigid, looking down at Erik lying on the wooden floor. Beyond them, the balcony door was wide open. Erik was lying on his front, groaning, shards of glass glittering in the pool of blood growing around him. His face was turned towards Kate, blanched white, his eyes wide open with shock.

She hadn't imagined his voice – it *was* Erik.

Whatever had happened, he wasn't used to anyone fighting back.

As he tried to move, Kate could see a knife lying on the floor close to him, its blade bright with blood. *Had Céline stabbed him? Or had he stabbed her? And what had broken the window?*

Confused, Kate couldn't piece together what had happened, but she knew she had to get away. A gust of icy air whistled into the room from the open door, making her head feel a little less woozy. Crabbing her way backwards, shaking her head, trying to clear her vision, Kate fumbled for her phone. Céline still had her back to her, looking from Erik to the window as the pool of blood spread across the pale boards.

Kate saw Céline glance out of the balcony doors, then at Erik again. She leaned forward, roughly pushing his body across the floor, reaching for the knife.

Her attention back on her phone, Kate found Daniel's last message and, focusing all her energy on it, pushed the call button.

Chapter 79

IN THE CONTAINER park, the officer shouted again, repeating his instruction.

'Armed police. Come out with your hands in the air.'

A few moments later there was a clattering sound, and the door of the container opened a crack.

'Come out with your hands up.'

Backlit from inside, even in shadow, Maxim could see Lucien was rubbing his head, acting puzzled, as he pushed the door wide.

'Hands where we can see them.'

Lucien lifted both his hands, managing to shrug at the same time as if he couldn't understand what was going on.

'What is this?' Maxim could hear Lucien's voice clearly carrying in the night air.

Maxim had set the phone to take photos on rapid repeat. He held it up as Lucien stumbled out of the container.

The officer whom Maxim thought had been about to blow the door stepped forward. He pulled Lucien's hands behind his back and cuffed him, manoeuvring him out of the doorway.

'What the hell's going on?' Lucien's voice was full of indignation, bluster and bravado.

Maxim lowered the phone. He really wanted to get a look inside that container. As if the officers outside it had heard him, they pushed the door open wider and entered, their guns still drawn.

From his hidden position across from the action, Maxim quickly adjusted the settings on his camera and zoomed in on the doorway as the men reappeared, giving the all-clear. He'd only know what he'd managed to capture when he got back to base. He just hoped it was something they could use.

His phone suddenly vibrated.

Travère.

We've got him. On his own. Says he's making porn. Come and take a look. I hope you're right on this, or Carlier is going to string you up.

Maxim turned around, quickly retracing his steps so that when he appeared, it would look as if he'd just got out of the jeep.

The team were relaxed now, standing around in groups far enough away from the container to have lit cigarettes, the tips glowing in the darkness.

Travère raised his hand and Maxim ambled over to him. 'That was easy.'

Travère shrugged. 'Sometimes.' He cocked his head. 'It looks like a film set inside.' He said it as if Maxim had the whole situation wrong.

'I bet.' Maxim felt his stomach turn. *Had Lucien been filming the killings?* The recordings had to be stored somewhere, and he didn't envy whoever got to watch those. 'Can I?'

Travère raised his hand, inviting him to take a step forward. 'Don't touch the sides and don't go in, just in case this *is* a crime scene.'

Maxim glanced at him 'It is, trust me.'

Taking a step towards the door, he leaned in. The inside of the container had been clad with plasterboard – and no doubt insulated – to make it look like a room. The floor was covered in laminate boards, sheepskin rugs scattered over them. Studio lights had been set up to illuminate the bed, and as Maxim glanced up he could see cameras on tracks suspended from the ceiling.

Maxim heard Travère beside him. 'You can't see it from here, but there's a massive screen on the inside wall.'

Maxim took it in, scanning the 'set'. The duvet was rumpled on the bed, as if Lucien had been lying on it. Cupboards and shelves lined the far wall. At the far end was a dark curtain, partially pulled back. Beyond it was the unmistakable shape of a white chest freezer.

And tied to the end of the bed was a powder-blue silk scarf printed with the distinctive images of Monet's *Water Lilies*.

Maxim thought for a minute he was going to vomit.

'When your forensics people get here, get them to look at that scarf. I think you'll find it belonged to an American student called Meredith McCarthy.' His voice cracked. He indicated the freezer, but couldn't say it. He'd read the post-mortem report.

Once the forensics team got in here, he was sure they'd find everything.

Chapter 80

LYING ON THE floor in the *salon*, Kate shook her head, trying to dislodge the thick layer of fog that had descended on her. She felt as if everything had slowed down, as if the room wasn't quite real.

But she could feel the draught from the open French window. She gasped involuntarily, and tried to scramble backwards as the balcony door was suddenly flung open. A stream of men, clad from head to toe in black, swarmed into the room like insects. Groggy, her vision blurring, part of Kate felt that she must be hallucinating. But their shouts were real, and their heavy boots were loud on the floor as they swept through the room like something out of a movie.

Dressed in combat gear, his visor down, one of them stood beside the window, covering the room with a heavy-duty machine gun, as the others poured in.

Kate closed her eyes, feelings of wooziness and dislocation growing as the men moved around her. *Were they police, or some sort of private army brought in by Céline or Erik?* She really wasn't sure. They were shouting instructions to one another that she couldn't understand, and moved in an effortless, co-ordinated motion. Kate's head began to pound.

Kate could hear one of the police – they *must* be police, even if they looked more like soldiers – kicking the doors in the apartment. She jumped as each one banged open, someone shouting the all-clear before moving on to the next. Retreating inside herself, Kate wished she could curl up into a ball and disappear.

The room swam into focus for a second, and she realised two of the commandos were crouching over Erik; another was standing beside Céline. Céline was shaking her head, one hand on her forehead as if she was shocked, perhaps about to faint.

Before Kate could take in more, one of the commandos came over to her. He was wearing a balaclava under his helmet, a padded bulletproof vest over black combats, a gun slung over his shoulder. As he bobbed down to squat beside her, she caught a flash of warm brown eyes.

He said something that Kate didn't fully understand,

but before she could reply, another wave of dizziness enveloped her. She must have paled because he reacted immediately, supporting her with his arm as she put her hand to her brow, trying to massage away the pain gripping her forehead.

Then she heard footsteps on the other side of the room, and a voice she recognised.

'Good evening, Céline. Long time.'

Daniel, thank God.

Relief swept through Kate as she reached out to push herself up, the young commando helping her.

Jumping physically at the sound of Daniel's voice, Céline whipped around to look at him, her eyes wide with shock.

'Why so surprised? Did Max not mention that I was in Paris?' Daniel's eyes were fixed on her. 'Max is over with Lucien and the GIGN at the container park right now. Interesting set-up you have there.'

Kate saw a flash of fear cross Céline 's face. She hesitated for a fraction of a second and then, in a sudden burst, ran for the hall.

But Daniel was quicker.

Flicking out his walking stick, he tripped her, sending her sprawling forward on the wooden floor with her hands out to save herself. The momentum of her fall carried her forward, and Kate winced as she struck her face on the open *salon* door. As she struggled up, a black-clad commando calmly materialised from the hallway, blocking her way. Dazed, she ran towards him. He grabbed her wrist, unhooking a pair of handcuffs from his belt.

As Kate watched, Céline turned to look at Daniel, her face set in a snarl. Her forehead was bleeding, her nose already starting to swell.

Kate hoped it was broken. She didn't know what the hell was going on, but she was pretty sure Céline had tried to knock her out, and if Erik was involved, Kate didn't think they had a cruise down the Seine planned for her. What had he said? *Don't bruise her, it needed to look like she'd jumped?*

Kate could feel shock starting to grip her.

Chapter 81

SITTING UP ON the *salon* floor, Kate lifted her knees and rested her head on them as she tried to breathe deeply, taking in the cool night air. Her heart was beating too fast and she was starting to shiver, her head pounding.

'Kate, can you hear me?'

Forcing open her eyes, fighting the layers of confusion, Kate could just see Daniel through her lashes. She felt him grasp her hand.

'Erik ...' It came out as a croak.

'One of the snipers got him. He came in over the balcony from next door.' Daniel paused as Kate tried to speak. *Snipers? Where had they come from?*

'Céline attacked me, put something over my face ...'

The commando said something in French to Daniel, who frowned and turned back to her. 'It was chloroform.

Céline was trying to knock you out. We'll have a paramedic here in a second. You'll feel better very soon.' He squeezed her hand. 'Come on, let's get you up onto the sofa.'

Daniel leaned forward and Kate felt hands lifting her gently, propelling her towards the cream couch. Then she was sitting, and a paramedic had materialised in front of her and was rolling back her sleeve.

'He's going to give you an injection. Your head will start to clear then.' Kate felt Daniel sit down beside her at the same time as the pinprick of the needle. Turning to him, she put her head on his shoulder.

The one thing she needed more than anything else was a hug. She felt his arm encircle her and the dizziness began to fade.

'You're all right now. I've got you.' His voice was so low, she could barely hear him, but she could feel the strength in his arms, his chin resting on the top of her head.

Then there was another voice she recognised – a girl's voice. Lifting her head, Kate turned towards it and opened her eyes more fully.

'I'm Agathe Delevingne, I'm a friend of Kate's …' Kate didn't understand the next bit, but she could see Agathe was squaring up to a commando standing at the door. *Why wasn't he letting her in?*

Agathe's voice rose, and Kate could tell she was remonstrating with the man, even if she couldn't understand what she was saying. Daniel said something in rapid French and the officer glanced at him. Agathe took a step around him and ran to Kate, falling onto the cushions beside her.

'Are you OK? My God, there are police everywhere. Max had to call someone to let me in. Roland and Max said they think Lucien Arnaud killed Sandrine.' It tumbled out so fast, Kate could barely keep up. She became aware of Daniel again, holding his hand up to try and calm Agathe. But Agathe didn't seem to notice. 'They think he's murdered the girls I found out about, the ones with red hair. I came over straight away.'

Even in Kate's muddled state, she was beginning to join the dots and realise that Céline must have attacked her for a reason. Icy fear flooded through her, and she could feel tears pricking at her eyes.

None of this made sense. *Was Céline jealous of her husband's interest in redheads? Had he been interested in her?* It all felt so muddled.

Daniel interrupted Agathe before she could say more.

'You don't need to worry about any of that now. We'll find out what's been happening very soon. Céline and her brother have a lot of explaining to do.'

'Her brother?' Kate leaned back to look at him. 'Lucien is her brother? I thought they were married.'

Agathe rubbed her hand. 'Céline's divorced. I can't understand why anyone in their right mind would marry either of them.'

'But—' Kate started to speak but Daniel interrupted.

'We can talk about it all later. We need you to recover first.'

'You're OK, Kate. Thank God, you're OK.' Agathe sounded as if she was trying to reassure herself as much as Kate. 'I didn't realise until Roland texted to say about Lucien's sister, and then I came as fast as I could.'

Across the room, the medics were loading Erik onto a stretcher. Another crisp gust filled the room with cool air, making Kate shiver, but Daniel was right; she was beginning to feel better already, her head starting to clear. She turned to Agathe.

'Tell me about Lucien. What's been happening?'

Before Agathe could answer, Daniel cut in. 'Let's get you a cup of tea, and we can find out what's happening from Max.'

Chapter 82

AS DANIEL REACHED the bottom of the stairs, the ground floor apartment door was standing wide open. Several white-suited forensics officers were filing in, one carrying a camera, another a steel toolbox. They had their hoods up, masks on, their shoes covered.

The incident lead was leaning back on the banister, talking to the driver who had collected Daniel from his hotel. Daniel nodded a greeting to them both as he spoke. 'How's Céline Arnaud?'

The incident lead responded with a stoic look. 'She's under guard, but we can't talk to her until the doctors give her the all-clear. Then *La Crim* will have a few questions for her. That knife wound is pretty bad. Forensics will tell us if she was holding the blade, but I doubt the guy stabbed himself.

'From what our colleagues tell us, it sounds like she was involved in all of this.' He inclined his head towards her apartment. 'There's heavy-duty plastic spread out on the kitchen floor, as well as in the elevator, and a hire car parked in the basement beside the elevator doors. It looks like she was going to disable Kate Wilde and bring her down here before taking her over to the container.'

Daniel glanced at the open apartment door. Céline had obviously thought this through. *How many of the others had she been involved with?*

He'd been devastated when Meredith had vanished without a word; it had scarred him. He'd been self-conscious of his cleft lip until he'd met her, hadn't had much confidence with women, but she'd seen past it, to love him. And then she'd vanished. Part of him had been sure it had been his fault – that she'd changed her mind about him, but couldn't face him to say it. That he was too ugly for someone as beautiful as her.

He'd focused on his studies, joined the military as soon as he'd left university, and gone into a job where it was even harder to form close bonds, where you couldn't talk about what you did, where being single was positively encouraged.

Discovering that Lucien and Céline could have been involved in Meredith's disappearance, and now had targeted the first woman he'd felt relaxed with in the many years since, was reopening all his wounds and liberally sprinkling them with salt.

Losing his leg was nothing compared to this.

But Daniel was sure they'd know soon enough what had been going on. If Céline didn't start talking, he was pretty sure Lucien would tell them everything. He loved the limelight, and he was about to become front page news.

But part of Daniel didn't want to know what the forensics team would find in that container. He leaned on his stick as he spoke. 'I believe you'll find the intruder you shot is a man named Erik Vanags. He's Kate Wilde's ex-husband, he served with the Swedish armed services.'

The incident lead looked interested. 'We were wondering what the hell was happening with him. We've checked the apartment he appeared from next door, and he has all sorts of surveillance equipment in there. The team had a quick look, and he's been watching Kate Wilde and recording the activity in the apartment. The techs will review it fully back at base.' He shook his head.

The officer who had driven Daniel to the scene shifted against the banister. 'It's another rental, the apartment next door. It was taken last week, we couldn't get hold of anyone to give us access. Our guys were on the balcony above, ready to rappel down. The minute Céline grabbed Kate, the guy was straight out.'

It sounded to Daniel as if Erik had taken the team by surprise, but they'd been focusing on Kate and Céline. Someone swinging into the middle of things from the neighbouring property must have been somewhat unexpected, even though they were trained to anticipate precisely that.

Kate had said she'd felt as if she was being followed, but whether it had been by Erik or Lucien remained to be seen. It sounded to Daniel as if there was a good chance that it had been both of them.

It all fitted with Kate discovering that things had been moved in her apartment, too.

The incident lead straightened up. 'It would be good if we could prove that this Erik Vanags was stalking Kate. That stab wound's bad, but the bullet in his shoulder hasn't helped. It's looking a bit touch-and-go, he's lost a lot of blood. The guy who fired is very young, first outing. He's a crack shot, though. I don't think anyone else could have got him cleanly when he was so close to Céline Arnaud.' He paused. 'I don't want to lose him from the team over some do-gooder civilian jumping in.'

Daniel had wondered at the wisdom of taking the shot – he hadn't heard the order to fire. But it had done what it was meant to do, and broken up the fight. He didn't think too many people would be upset when the full story came out.

'I don't think you need to worry about Vanags being considered an injured party. Kate has a restraining order against him in the UK.' Daniel glanced back up the stairs. 'Can you take a statement from Kate now? I'm going to book her into Le Meurice. She won't want to stay the night here, and it'll give your team more space to work.'

Chapter 83

AFTER EVERYTHING THAT had happened the night before, Kate hadn't expected to sleep at all, but as soon as she'd pulled the counterpane over herself at Daniel's hotel, she'd closed her eyes. Sunshine had been flooding into the room when she'd woken up.

As she lay in this gorgeous room with its oil paintings and beautiful decor, she realised that for the first time since things had gone wrong with Erik, she finally felt really and truly safe.

All it had taken was a near miss with a serial killer.

Daniel had been cagey about what had been going on, but Agathe had let slip enough about Lucien and Céline for Kate to get the picture.

Kate rubbed her face, suddenly needing to hear Hanna's voice. She turned to look for her phone, finding it right next to her on the bedside table. Beside it was a note from Daniel, saying to call him when she woke up, and one from Agathe, saying that she hoped she'd slept well.

Agathe had been amazing, collecting all Kate's clothes and make-up and repacking them to move to Le Meurice. She'd even helped Kate to bed, assuring her she'd see her in the morning and that Daniel would sort out her train ticket.

Kate dreaded to think what this room was costing, or how Daniel could change her Eurostar ticket at such short notice, but he'd been calmly insistent and she hadn't had the energy to argue.

Picking up her phone, Kate called Orna. Her sister answered after one ring, sounding annoyed.

'Kate, I've been trying to get hold of you.'

Kate sat up, pulling up the pillows behind her. 'Sorry, things went a bit crazy last night—'

Orna cut in before she could finish the sentence. 'Are you OK? It's not Erik?' Kate could hear the concern in her voice.

'It was. But it's all OK. He got shot and he's been arrested, I think.'

'What?' Orna's shriek hit Kate like a missile.

'It's fine, really. I've moved, though. I'm in a lovely hotel. Sorry I can't remember the name of it, but it's right beside the Louvre. And I'm going to have to get a later train. I'll let you know what time. Are you OK with Hanna for a bit longer?'

'Of course I am, don't be silly. But when ...? What ...?' Orna had so many questions, they were obviously tripping over themselves to be asked.

'It's a long story. I'll tell you when I get back. It may be tomorrow, though. Hanna's school uniform's in the hot press at the flat. She'll be able to show you where her bag is. Is she there?'

'She is. She's right next to me. We're having pancakes and maple syrup for lunch.'

For lunch. Kate looked at the time on her phone. She hadn't realised how late it was.

'Hi, Mummy, are you coming home today? I've got loads of new clothes, and Auntie Orna's bought me *The Sims.*'

Kate smiled at the happiness in Hanna's voice. 'I'm coming home very soon, I promise. Have you had a lovely time?'

'Yes, brilliant, and Auntie Orna says I can come again next time you go to Paris. Did you make the perfume?'

'I did, sweet pea. I'm bringing it back with me so you can smell it.'

'Did you go up the Eiffel Tower?'

It took Kate a few moments to answer. 'Paris has been quite an experience, and yes, I've been up the Eiffel Tower. I'll tell you all about it.'

She suddenly felt overwhelmed, emotion flaring inside her, tears threatening.

'Can you put me back to Auntie Orna and I'll chat to you later?'

''Course, Mummy. I'll save you a pancake.'

Kate heard the phone being passed back to her sister. 'Kate? Are you sure you're OK?'

'I am, I'm going to have to talk to you later, but I'm very OK. For the first time in a very long time.'

Kate hung up just as a text came through from Daniel.

If you're awake, we're in Restaurant Le Dali.

Who were 'we' …? Agathe and Daniel? Kate hoped so; she wanted to thank Agathe. She needed to see her before she left Paris.

Chapter 84

AGATHE LOOKED UP just as Kate appeared at the door of the restaurant, her red hair piled up, the overhead lights catching the strands and making them glow. She opened her mouth to tell the others, but as she turned to Daniel she could see he'd already spotted her. His reading glasses were perched on the end of his nose, his eyes locked on Kate as if she was the most beautiful thing he'd ever seen.

Agathe smiled to herself. One day she wanted to find a man who looked at her like that. She turned to her other side, to speak to Maxim, but he was looking at Daniel, too, a smirk on his face.

When she'd got back to the apartment the previous night, Roland had told Agathe exactly what had happened: how Maxim had got Lucien out of the container so Roland could identify him. Rather ridiculously, she thought, she'd suddenly felt immensely proud of Maxim Verdier and his quick thinking.

In their living room, Roland had had the sidelights on. His sketch books had been spread across the coffee table, photographs of Sandrine printed beside them. He'd already marked several up with a grid so he could enlarge the images to wall-sized. Roland had looked up at Agathe as she'd collapsed into the armchair, exhausted, rubbing her eyes. His face had been intense.

'I'm going to go to the underpass and do a huge mural of Sandrine.' The tears had come then, for both of them.

In the restaurant, Agathe stood up from their table, raising her hand to Kate to show her where they were.

The dining room was huge, already busy, waiters gliding around the tables covered in white linen and sparkling with glass, silverware and graphic Dalí-inspired china. Agathe had never been here before, and had been stunned by the entrance hall, and then by this ochre and gold room designed by Philippe Starck. When they'd sat down, Daniel had said something about Starck's daughter Ara, who had painted the fabric draped across the ceiling.

Spotting them, Kate began to weave her way across the room, looking around in surprise at the décor. The delicate chink of china and crystal and the low burble of conversation filled the air. Daniel put down the menu he'd been looking at and, taking off his glasses, rose out of his chair as Kate approached. He was wearing a tweed jacket and a tie. He looked so English, Agathe had had to hide her smile when she'd arrived.

Daniel and Maxim were such unlikely friends, but she'd been able to tell from the minute Maxim had arrived, shrugging off his motorcycle leathers, that they were like brothers, almost finishing each other's sentences.

'Hello, everyone, sorry I'm so late.'

Daniel pulled out the chair beside him. 'You aren't late at all. I trust you slept a little?'

As Agathe stood up and reached out to hug her, Kate caught sight of the tattoo on her wrist. Releasing her, Kate tapped it. 'I've a story to tell you about butterflies. Not now, though.' Puzzled, Agathe put her head on one side, but she could see now wasn't the moment for whatever Kate had to say.

Kate tucked her bag under her chair and sat down. 'Honestly, I slept like a stone. I think I needed it.'

Sitting down herself, Agathe grinned across the table at Kate, relieved that she looked so happy and relaxed. The past twenty-four hours had been intense.

Agathe turned to introduce Maxim, and Kate reached across the table to shake his hand, although it was obvious she had no idea who he was. Daniel supplied the missing pieces as a waiter appeared and filled a glass in front of her with water.

'Max is an old friend of mine from university. I was on Erasmus in Paris many moons ago. He's a journalist now, the crime editor for *Paris Heure*.' Daniel played with his glasses for a moment, obviously uncomfortable. 'Max and Lucien Arnaud and I used to hang out at the rowing club.' Kate's eyebrows shot up as he continued. 'We've got history, as they say, and not all of it good.'

Agathe looked curiously at Maxim. He'd never mentioned knowing the soon-to-be infamous Lucien Arnaud, but that would explain how he knew Céline. Her uncle was always saying Maxim Verdier knew everyone in Paris, and he was right.

Kate nodded slowly. 'I only met Lucien once, when Céline invited me in for coffee.'

Daniel cleared his throat. 'Perhaps that's as well. He was arrested last night. I hear that he's quite enjoying being the centre of attention. He appears to have a lot to say.'

Beside Agathe, Maxim reached for a bread roll from the brightly coloured plate in front of him. 'It's as bad as we thought – if not worse. He had a container out on the north side of the city. Anyway, it's being examined.'

Kate picked up her napkin, looking at Daniel. 'Did he organise the competition – him and Céline?'

Daniel straightened his cutlery. 'It's looking that way. The police are examining his computers. They may need to speak to you again, but we'll worry about that later.'

'They asked loads of questions last night, but I didn't feel like I was being very helpful.'

Daniel frowned. 'You'd had a bit of a traumatic evening, I think they understand.'

'Will I be able to do it by Zoom?' There was a hint of anxiety in Kate's tone.

'I'm sure you can.' Daniel smiled. 'But perhaps we can tempt you back to Paris at some stage.'

Before Kate could answer, Maxim jumped in. 'We'd look after your expenses. I'm sure I can swing that with my editor. I'd love to do an exclusive interview with you.'

Agathe could see from the confusion on her face that Kate didn't quite know how to answer. She cut in. 'Maxim works for my uncle. He was the one who found Lucien's container and took the police there last night.'

Kate took this in. 'It sounds like I have a lot to thank you for.' She paused. 'And I do need to get my daughter a snow globe with the Eiffel Tower in it. I promised I'd bring one home to her, and the other one got broken.'

'I've taken the liberty of rebooking your train for the morning. I hope that's OK. We could go to the Eiffel Tower this afternoon, if you feel up to it.' Daniel sounded tentative, but Kate's eyes immediately brightened.

'Are you sure you don't mind? I'd love to go with someone who can tell me what I'm looking at. I'm sure I took the wrong lift the last time. After last night, a complete change of scene would be wonderful. I'd rather my last memory of Paris wasn't of almost getting killed.'

Agathe couldn't help but smile at the look on Daniel's face. 'It would be my pleasure.'

Kate turned to Agathe, suddenly frowning. 'And your friend, Sandrine ... Do you know any more?'

'That was Lucien Arnaud. For sure. I hope he rots in Hell.'

Epilogue

'WELCOME, MY DEAR, I've heard so much about you.'

Standing on the doorstep of the huge double-fronted house in Hampstead, Kate glanced at Daniel nervously.

He frowned. 'My Aunt Lillian is teasing you, Kate. I haven't had a chance to update her fully.'

'Come in, come in. He did mention that you had incredible colouring, though. A redhead ... My goodness.'

Catching a glint in Lillian's eye, Kate stifled a smile. She was teasing – but teasing Daniel. He'd said that she was always meddling in his private life – actually, in everyone's private life – and that she had her sights on the new vicar. Kate just hoped he was able to manage this grey-haired woman in tweed trousers and pearls. She was tiny, almost bird-like, but Kate could see the family resemblance. Daniel had her sharp blue eyes and obviously quick mind.

Inside, the house was just as grand as it looked from the road. Lillian ushered them into a huge Victorian drawing room, tall windows opening onto the garden.

'Now you must have tea, and I have some delicious florentines. Sit, please. Just push Archie over, he thinks he's in charge.'

Archie, Kate could see, was an enormous long-haired white cat stretched across the middle cushion of the brocade sofa, regarding them coolly with amber eyes.

Lillian sat down and a moment later, a thin woman dressed in black appeared at the door and put a laden tray down on the coffee table. The china was beautiful, gilt-edged and patterned with delicately coloured butterflies.

'Thank you, Helga. I think we have everything. Now, Kate, you pour.' Lillian handed her an elegant milk jug as the woman disappeared back to the kitchen. 'I saw the papers. I'm very sorry about your ex-husband.'

Kate leaned forward and, pouring milk into each of the beautiful porcelain teacups on the tray, smiled. 'Trust me, I'm not. The police have discovered that Céline Arnaud was in touch with him long before she set up the competition. She realised that he wanted custody of my daughter, and would do pretty much anything to get it.'

Replacing the milk, Kate picked up the teapot, keeping her face open and relaxed. Even thinking about it terrified and enraged her, but this wasn't the moment to show her emotions. 'It seems that Céline was planning to implicate him in my disappearance. She'd let him into my apartment and made sure his fingerprints were all over the place. But I don't think she'd anticipated him renting the apartment next door and spying on me.' Kate shivered again at the thought. 'As it turned out, she stabbed him with his own knife.' She paused. 'I think he found his match.'

'Indeed. My goodness … ' Kate felt Lillian's eyes on her. She'd sat in the armchair opposite Daniel. Kate put the pot down, and passed her a cup on its delicate fluted saucer as she continued. 'I have a feeling there is more of that story to come. Now, let me see this perfume bottle.' Lillian's face brightened. 'Have you seen it, Kate?'

Daniel reached for the box and, lifting it onto his knee, opened the lid. Polystyrene pieces drifted onto the chair beside him as he lifted out the perfume bottle wrapped in generous layers of tissue paper. Carefully, he unwrapped it.

It was beautiful, the gilt finish on the glass catching the lights from the many lamps that lit the room, the blue like lapis lazuli, one of Kate's favourite colours.

Half standing, Daniel leaned across the coffee table to hand the bottle to his aunt. Her smile lit her face. Taking it carefully, she lifted the stopper, closing her eyes and breathing in the scent.

'Gosh, that takes me back.' Opening her eyes, she inspected it as if it were treasure. 'The power of scent is quite incredible, isn't it. When I breathe that in, suddenly I'm in my wedding dress again, at the dressing table in my bedroom at my parents' house.'

Kate smiled, her mind going back to Le Studio des Parfums – to the scent she'd made for Hanna.

'There is one small problem, though.'

Kate looked quickly at Daniel. His eyebrows had shot up. 'It's the right bottle – It's You, by Elizabeth Arden?'

'It is, Daniel, and everything about it is perfect. But …' Lillian paused dramatically. 'You've been too busy for me to tell you, but your niece has broken off her engagement. She's running off to Australia instead, apparently, and *not* with her fiancé.'

Daniel rolled his eyes and shook his head. 'I wouldn't worry. I'm sure you can think of something to do with it. It took me to Paris when I needed to be there.' He met Kate's eye and blushed slightly.

Kate could feel Lillian's eyes on her again, and turned to look at her. She was smiling benevolently at them both.

'I thought ...' She hesitated. 'Given its significance ...' She glanced at Kate. 'My own bottle of It's You was a lucky charm. It survived the Blitz, you know. I wondered if you may like to give this one to Kate?'

Daniel snorted. 'To remind her of Paris?'

'No, Daniel, not just of Paris. To remind her of you.'

Lillian said it as if he was about ten years old. He blushed hard.

Desperate to save his embarrassment, Kate looked back at Lillian. 'It's so special, though. That would be absolutely lovely, but it's so valuable.'

'And so are you, my dear.'

Kate's own blushes were saved by her phone making a chirping noise in her bag – the sign of an incoming message. Daniel cut in, obviously relieved by the interruption.

'That'll be Hanna, looking for you.'

Kate glanced at him. 'I think so.' She pulled her phone out of her bag and checked the screen. 'Oh goodness, I'm sorry, she's been let out of school early. I ...'

'Aunt Lillian, we need to go, but we'll come back.' As Daniel stood up, his tea untouched, his aunt stood, too, and reached for the tissue paper to wrap the bottle again.

Lillian raised her hand. 'No need to explain, my dear, I understand.' Fitting the bottle back into the box, she looked pointedly at Daniel. 'Women are like the finest scent, Daniel – they evaporate unless cared for *very* carefully. I don't think you should let this one go.'

Kate could feel herself blushing. 'I'm so sorry about the tea.'

Lillian waved her arm dismissively. 'Don't be. Do bring Hanna next time, will you? I'm hoping to see a lot more of you. And this bottle will be waiting.'

Dearest Katie

This is the last entry I'm going to be able to write. I'm weak now, but my head doesn't hurt any more.

Before we saw *Amélie* we swapped keys, so if anything ever happened to one of us, the other would be able to keep their diary safe.

It's going to happen to me in the next few days, and I wanted you to read my list of thank-yous, because you're such a big part of them. I didn't have any friends really when we first sat next to each other in geography, and then I had you.

You made the years that we were friends amazing. We laughed and we cried, we made promises and we shared our dreams. That was so special.

I need you to take my lock to Paris like we planned, and put it with yours on the bridge. I know you are going to find your true love in Paris. I don't know when, but I know you're going to have a wonderful life and Paris is part of that. Something will happen there that will change you, and it'll be wonderful. I won't be able to go, but it's our city, Katie, and I'll be with you on the bridge.

I'm always going to be sixteen, Katie, but I'll love you always. Whenever you see a butterfly, that'll be me.

Trisha xxxxx

Author's Note & Acknowledgements

It's finally happened! Despite my obsessive need to check details, and three trips to Paris to research this book, there was one fact that I slipped on! Rather than upsetting the fictional timeline to put it right, in this instance I'm asking you to suspend disbelief and go with the flow. Did you spot it as you were reading?

For those who didn't, it relates to the Pont des Arts and the love locks that sprang up on it following a 2006 Italian movie. In *Ho Voglio di Te*, two lovers write their names on a lock and attach it to the Ponte Milvo bridge in Rome, before throwing the key into the river below. This piece of movie magic was copied in Paris, and I think has become more French than Italian at this stage. In this story, however, Trisha falls in love with *Amélie* and Paris when the film is released in 2001, and makes her pact with her best friend Kate in what is actually a wonderful moment of psychic prediction.

It's the first real-time error in twelve books, and was, of course, picked up immediately by my incredible copy editor Steve O'Gorman, but this is fiction, and in fiction, anything can happen, so please forgive me. I've also taken a small liberty with the underpass mentioned and the traffic flow. If you recognise it, you'll know. In real life it *is* covered in incredible street art, and it's well worth a wander through.

This story originated in an image that popped into my head of a woman with red hair travelling to Paris on the Eurostar. Embarrassingly, I hadn't read *Perfume* then, but I had discovered that perfume reacts differently on the skin of redheads, and like many other crime writers, I love an interesting fact.

I also have the great good fortune to know Professor Jim Fraser, one of the UK's leading forensic scientists, and his words below became very significant:

'The murders of serial killers are not identical, they are similar. There is rarely a "signature" as crime fiction would have you believe, more a text to be read and interpreted.'

Jim has worked on many cases involving serial killers, and this statement stuck with me. Steven King talks about original story coming from the collision of unrelated ideas, and when Jim's thoughts on serial killers collided with redheads and perfume in my head, and then the persistent image of two people on a train, *The Killing Sense* began to gestate.

Huge thanks to Jim for always being so generous with his time, as well as being a brilliantly entertaining lunch companion – he's the man I call when I need to know about decomposition, blood spatter, fibre evidence ... The list goes on.

Thanks, too, to Ambre Morvan and Hugh Roberts for their invaluable input on French phrases – any mistakes are definitely my own.

I always say in acknowledgements that a book is the culmination of the work of many people, not just me, and that is so very true. There is amazing support within our crime writing community, and I have the most wonderful and supportive friends-in-ink. I think we all play a role in keeping each other sane! Thank you, ladies, you know who you are.

From my amazing agent Simon Trewin, to the editorial and publicity team at Corvus Atlantic, the PR team at Gill Hess, and every blogger, reviewer and journalist who has helped bring the news of a new Sam Blake story to readers, there are so many individuals to whom I am truly grateful. Without them, you would not be holding this book in your hand.

But my biggest thanks is to you, my reader, for picking up this book and sticking with it to this point. I work alone at my desk, conjuring words that unfold in your head as you sit alone, reading them. I don't know you, or where you will read them, but they connect us like a psychic thread, and I hope you have enjoyed them.

You enable me to do the job I love. Thank you for reading.

Sam Blake